The Fall of Night

The Fall of Night

Christopher G. Nuttall

The characters and events portrayed in this book are fictitious. Any similarity to real persons, living or dead, is coincidental and not intended by the author.

ISBN-13: 9781530967438
ISBN-10: 1530967430

Chapter One

Raging at Infinity

The problem with the British Army is that there is a British Army.
Unnamed Progressive, 2007

London, England

It was turning into a very bad day.

"They're about to begin the march," Sergeant Harold Page said. "The Superintendent wants to ensure that everything is ready for them."

Inspector David Briggs said nothing, merely looked down at the images from countless CCTV cameras scattered around the centre of London, from the park where the marchers were gathering to the entire region of Hyde Park, which had been designated as the endpoint for the march, where the leader of the Front for Peace, Freedom and Progress would address the crowd. There were thousands of people there, some of them dedicated marchers, some of them students or tourists drawn into the excitement, some of them there merely to pick up girls...and a hardcore of real troublemakers.

"We have over a thousand police officers on duty," he said. The Metropolitan Police had drawn in officers from all over the country, as well as calling up all of the reserves. The remainder of London would be shorthanded for the duration of the march, something that worried the Superintendent enough for him to pass local control over to Briggs. The Superintendent was a political animal; he knew that little good would come out of the march, and it would be a career-wreaker for any officer if something went wrong. "We have medics, riot control squads and even armed anti-terrorist units on alert. What could go wrong?"

Page shrugged. The Metropolitan Police dreaded a repeat of the protest marches that had occurred in America, where a handful of local terrorists had used car bombs to slaughter the protesters and incite anger. The American War on Terror had been going on for twenty-three years and the British public – along with the remainder of the European Governments – feared that it would one day spread back to Britain and Europe. It would only take a handful of hardcore troublemakers – and the Home Office had warned that several dozen known troublemakers were planning to attend the march – to kill thousands and further stain the reputation of the Police.

Briggs was, for a moment, lost in thought. If it had been up to him, he would have banned the protest from taking place, no matter what the law said. It was a disaster waiting to happen…but the Prime Minister would never allow the Metropolitan Police to prevent protesters from marching. The protesters had played a major role in the fall of the British Government after the RAF Mildenhall Incident…or perhaps it had been after the Sudan Disaster. They would never dare prevent the people asserting their right to protest, no matter the dangers, or the extremists who would use it as political leverage. Peace was important, the Government said, peace at any price…

The Sergeant coughed. "Yes, I know," Briggs said, more in private irritation than anger. The Metropolitan Police had what seemed like a permanent manpower shortage and they couldn't afford to lose anyone. "Tell the Superintendent that everything is ready and we hope that it can be concluded quickly."

He leaned back in his chair and muttered a curse under his breath. It was just like the Metropolitan Police of 2024; they could build a mobile command centre that was capable, in theory, of commanding a police operation over the entire United Kingdom…while at the same time, they could neither provide the manpower to police Britain effectively, or even comfortable chairs for the officers on duty. He would have preferred to have handled matters from New Scotland Yard, but procedure called for the officer commanding – at least until politics decreed his replacement – to be on the scene. At one point, that had meant something; now, all it meant was chaos.

The protesters hadn't waited for the police go-ahead; that would have been dreadfully conformist of them. The stewards provided by the Front for Peace, Freedom and Progress hadn't attempted to stop them; three of them were already cooling their heels in a police van, handcuffed to the seats, until they could be transported to the nearest police station to be charged with assault and attempted rape. The Front for Peace, Freedom and Progress was a genuinely transnational organisation; Briggs had been disgusted with some of the stewards who had been

http://www.chrishanger.net
http://chrishanger.wordpress.com/
http://www.facebook.com/ChristopherGNuttall

All Comments Welcome!

Author's Note

All details given as to the size, composition and technology of the British, Russian, American and European Forces involved in the story were derived from reasonable speculation as to the future of those armed forces. Likewise, the details of the updated British emergency protocols are purely fictional, although based on protocols known to be in existence for the Cold War period. I apologise for any confusion that might have been caused.

Please let me know if you would like a sequel.

CGN

Prologue

From: *The Guardian. 1st June 2007*

Following questions in Parliament, Scotland Yard confirmed that the prime suspect in the rape and murder of Judy Lewisham near RAF Mildenhall was Corporal Michael Collins, an American serviceman stationed at RAF Mildenhall, a base operated by American forces in Britain. Collins, one of thousands of Americans stationed in Britain, was apparently confined to the base following the rape and murder; the Police investigation conducted by Inspector David Briggs was taken over by the Home Office, following the use of DNA remains to trace the murderer. The attempt by the Home Office to hush the entire affair up has caused great distress to the people of Judy's community.

Unconfirmed reports have further reached this reporter that Collins was flown out of the country as soon as the Home Office contacted American authorities regarding the possible extradition of Collins for trial and sentencing in Britain. Protesters, led by Judy's family, have surrounded RAF Mildenhall and have refused to be dispersed by either police or American guards; a number of violent incidents have already been reported near American bases in other locations, with Americans attacked and in some cases banned from pubs and shops.

Condolences, many directly addressed to Judy's family, have been flowing in from all over the world. President Nekrasov of Russia has offered his sympathies and support, if necessary, to ensure that Collins is brought to justice. General Henri Guichy, who is in line for a seat on the European Defence Commission, called for the incident to be treated as a symbol of American arrogance in the world and for Europe to insist on revisions to the various Status of Forces agreements, particularly the ABM bases established in Poland against the expressed resolution of Brussels.

Although neither Ten Downing Street nor the White House have commented, it strikes this reporter that relations between Britain – and to some extent the European Union – and America have reached an all-time low. Between inflammatory comments made by Senator David Howery and Congressman Reaper, and calls for American bases to be placed firmly under British jurisdiction by a multi-party group of Members of Parliament in London, it seems that relations between Europe and America are about to go through a very rapid series of changes, perhaps even a total break. This reporter says; not a moment too soon.

brought in to provide crowd control. The Superintendent hadn't allowed him to use that as a cause to have the march cancelled; politics, once again…

The bastards would probably get away with it as well.

"Two pickpockets caught by the crowd," Page said, interrupting his thoughts. The dumber of London's petty criminals had gravitated to the crowd, seeing an opportunity for quick profit; the crowd might allow them to get away with it, or they might turn on the crooks. Socialists, in Briggs' experience, tended to get very irate when it was *their* pocket being picked. "The local officers have them in custody."

"Good," Briggs said. There had been several marches where the crowd had fought police officers to free criminals, for whatever reasons made sense to the vast human body; this march, so far, hadn't turned nasty. "Get them to the vans and transported to the police station."

He flicked through the images from different CCTV cameras. The march organisers had predicted that over ten thousand interested people would come; it looked to Briggs as if they had been out by an order of magnitude. The elaborate programs scanning the images faster than the human eye could begin to grasp were reporting well over a hundred thousand people in the vicinity, including identifying thousands of people known to the police though Facial Recognition Software. Some of them were people who had had a brief run-in with the police, some of them were famous figures; he spotted two MPs, one MSP and five candidates for the local elections, coming soon. The Mayor of London was there, glad-handing with his constituents, including some that Briggs would never have expected to see together…

Before the world had gone crazy.

One large body of marchers were very openly homosexual; they wore garish clothes and marched with exaggerated movements, designed to shock as much as attract. A second body – several bodies – of marchers was composed of Muslims, marching in a bizarre combination of groups, united temporarily by their dislike for the Americans and suppressing their dislike for the homosexuals. Iran had put a dozen gaysexuals to death the week before the Iran War had begun; the homosexual marchers could expect nothing but death under Islamic rule. Briggs knew, even if the government ensured that the general public knew little about it, about the young Muslim men killed by their peers…merely for being gaysexual. To Briggs, a practical man, it made no sense; why were two groups with so much reason to hate each other allied?

The answer made itself clear as the first American flag burst into flame. Everyone knew that North Korea had been rattling the sabre – again – in Korea and the South Korean Government had screamed for help. Despite America's overstretched position in the Middle East, the American Government had organised the hasty dispatch of an American force...ignoring the protests from Europe and Russia alike. American spokesmen had pointed to the ongoing Chinese Civil War; Kang Seung Jae, the Dictator of North Korea, had to know that North Korea was finally coming to the end of its existence...and appeared to be preparing one final gamble.

Everyone also knew that North Korea had nukes.

Page was tapping instructions into one of the consoles. "Sir," he said, "is that her?"

Briggs peered past the 'BUSH; WAR CRIMES,' 'RAPE KIRKPATRICK NOW' and 'NO MORE BLOOD FOR OIL' signs, and nodded. "That's her," he said, shortly. "Daphne Hammond, otherwise known as the Leader of the Front for Peace, Freedom and Progress, cast-iron stone-cold bitch. Those stunning looks, Harry, conceal a mind that is cold and very calculating."

Page cocked an eyebrow. Daphne Hammond was around thirty and looked twenty, with long blonde hair, a balcony that someone could perform Shakespeare from, and stunning blue eyes. She was also a trained lawyer, a woman who had outlasted at least two husbands, and privately considered to be the most dangerous woman in the world. He had been on the receiving end of her tongue more than once; as the leader of the Front for Peace, Freedom and Progress, she was formidable...and perhaps destined to be Britain's second female Prime Minister. Certainly, her name had been put forward as a possible candidate...

Briggs shook his head and wondered; what was Daphne playing at? She might have been blonde, but she was no dummy; she had brought together a coalition that included factions that wouldn't be impressed by her good looks, or would regard a woman in power as an abomination. The Front had smaller sections all over Europe; as a mainly European Party, it might even have more clout than the figures suggested.

"That's definitely one of the troublemakers," another operator injected. Briggs pushed the issue of Daphne's actions to the back of his mind – it wasn't as if anyone had any proof that she was involved in anything other than political actions, even if her two husbands had met early graves – and turned to the console. The Facial Recognition Software was certain; the CCTV cameras had locked onto a known troublemaker, someone who had caused more than a few riots…and somehow was never jailed. "That's Baz Falkland, all right. I'm not sure if he is chatting up that girl or if he's up to something."

Briggs scowled. "Have supporting units moved up," he said. If it did turn nasty, a lot of people were about to be hurt. "I want…"

Page interrupted him. "Sir, the stewards just muscled him off," he said. Briggs blinked; he hadn't known that the stewards had either the knowledge or the determination to move the troublemaker along. Baz Falkland was trouble, everyone knew it; a reputation that had started in Manchester and moved through many of England's cities. Only sheer luck had saved him from a jail term. "It looks as if they were pretty rough."

Briggs nodded. "I want additional constables in the area," he said. He would shed no tears for Baz Falkland, but if the stewards started muscling innocent people around, the police would have to intervene quickly, even if it meant his career. "And someone reassure the Superintendent; everything is under control."

It said something about the general opinion of the Superintendent that no one even blinked at the scorn in his voice.

"I would have thought," Caroline Morgan remarked, as her shoulder-mounted camera sensor tracked a set of marchers carrying 'BUSH MUST FACE THE ICC' signs, "that beating the President Bush horse is just a little outdated by now. It is 2024, after all."

"But it was President Bush who started the American grab for the Middle East," Daphne Hammond said, her voice almost girlishly innocent. Caroline would have been fooled, perhaps, were it not for her instincts; Daphne Hammond was bad news. She seemed young, and sincere…except for her eyes. They were cold and hard, as if she had seen everything a thousand times over, and hadn't been impressed the first time. "Even now, the Americans are fighting to hold down the Middle East and extract the last drop of oil from its soil."

Caroline almost tuned the speech out of her mind, knowing that it was all carefully prepared to impress people who were already inclined to distrust America. According to Daphne Hammond, after CIA operatives had carried out the terrible atrocity of 9/11, the Americans had used it as an excuse to first invade Afghanistan, and then Iraq, before luring the Europeans into first Iraq, and then Sudan...before cutting off their supply lines and leaving General Éclair to take the blame and kill himself, incidentally weakening EUROFOR to the point where it could not provide the counterbalance to America...and then luring Iran into a war. The Americans had bombed Israel, for some reason that had only made sense to them, and then allowed their own soldiers to endure two nuclear attacks...and a long and bloody occupation of the Middle East.

As history, it was utterly grotesque.

"Thank you," Caroline said, as soon as Daphne had finished. "But tell me, what do you really think?"

Daphne's eyes flickered with rage, just for a second, and then the mask was back in place. "I think that the European compliance with the Americans has gone on long enough," she said. "It wasn't anything like enough to evict almost all of the American forces from Europe after that *terrible* incident in Mildenhall. We have to create a United Europe which can provide a strong and positive voice in the United Nations towards creating a strong and dignified Earth."

Caroline took a moment to sort it all out in her mind. "You must be aware that the European Union has become much more unpopular in both Britain and France, to cite, but only two cases," she said. It was true; the British believed that Europe had been ruining British industries, while French opinion blamed the endless influx of Algerian and Palestinian refugees on the EU. "Why do you feel that your...transnational group would win elections to the European Parliament?"

"We have already won seats in several elections across Europe," Daphne reminded her dryly. "I have also been offered the chance to compete in the Liberal Democrat internal elections for leadership as the party approaches the coming election." She smiled. "I don't know if I will be running as an independent MP, or if I will leave that to others within the

Front and take up the nomination, but it should give you some idea of my…electoral chances."

Caroline considered. There had been a time when it had been almost unthinkable for politicians to switch parties; now, it happened almost as often as footballers changing football clubs. What did it mean to the country? Had the Liberal Democrats decided that Daphne was a vote-winner, or had their own Far Left insisted on her challenging the current leader, or…?

There were too many possibilities. There were people who would detest her; they wouldn't vote for the Liberal Democrats if it meant that Daphne got to plant her arse in Number Ten. The march today wouldn't help matters; for everyone who saw the marchers and felt admiration, there would be ten who would be disgusted. The Far Right was also making a comeback; the fallout from the American War, everyone was certain, would eventually fall on the United Kingdom. They allowed themselves to forget London, Glasgow, Blackburn…

Daphne shrugged "I would love to continue chatting to you, my dear, but I fear that I have to walk all the way to Speaker's Corner and give a speech," she said. She grinned suddenly. "Of course, it is only five minutes from here, and the stewards have kept the passage clear; would you like to come with me?"

Caroline shook her head. She had been lucky to be granted the quick interview, but there was already too high a price; the price for the scoop of walking beside Daphne was too much for her to pay. There would be dozens of audio and visual sensors trained on her as she mounted the soapbox – literally; the Front had found one specially for her – and she would gain nothing from being close to her.

"Be seeing you, then," Daphne said.

"Break a leg," Caroline replied.

It would not have surprised Zachary Lynn – or the man who refused to think of himself as anyone other than Zachary Lynn – that the Police had a command post near Hyde Park. It was common sense…and, if the government of the day had little in the way of common sense, or even self-preservation instincts, the Metropolitan Police had plenty of experience in real police work. Besides, Lynn himself had a command post, far too close to the heart of the action for anyone's comfort.

Lynn smiled as the marchers flooded into Hyde Park. There were more than he had predicted, even with his own opinions of the degree of foolishness of the British public set very low indeed. It was impossible, among other things, to give every citizen an 'above average' income, let alone provide a counterbalance to America and cut the military at the same time. France's attempt at 'assisting' Algeria should have proven that…that, and the reappearance of the Argentinean claim to the Falklands.

There was a buzz in his earpiece. "Sir, we have apprehended Baz Falkland," his aide said. The aide knew everything, the only person in Britain apart from Lynn who knew the entire scope of the plan. If the Police stumbled onto them, he would have to carry on while Lynn killed himself to prevent interrogation. "Do you have any specific instructions?"

Lynn nodded. "The same as usual, assuming that the Police haven't noticed," he said. They had a link into the heart of the Metropolitan Police, a mole who provided information that they had used for their own reasons; they would know pretty quickly if the Police had realised that Baz Falkland had been more than just muscled away. "Tell him that he can work for us at good rates of pay, or he can enter the Thames with concrete overshoes."

On the display, broadcast by half a dozen news channels, some of them old and trusted, some of them new and inexperienced, Daphne Hammond was beginning her speech. It was a good speech, one of her speechwriter's best; she would condemn the Americans, praise the European Union, and promise a new Heaven and a new Earth if her party was elected. He was proud of Daphne Hammond, in his own way; it was a shame that her talents could not be used openly for the cause.

He smiled. American flags were burning, London was almost at a standstill, and the plan was moving ahead.

It was turning into a very good day.

Chapter Two

Armageddon Rising

A great wind is blowing, and that gives you either imagination or a headache.
Catherine the Great

Moscow, Russia

The line of cars appeared out of nowhere, seemingly entering the city at the same time and angling into a single line that advanced mercilessly towards the Kremlin. They were all black, all with tinted windows; the police herded the population of the city out of the way as the cars flashed onwards. There were few protests; the citizens of Moscow knew that their lords and masters were in the cars, many of whom deserved actual respect. A handful of criminals, convicted and sentenced to work as brute labour, made obscene gestures as the cars passed; their supervisors, themselves brutes, laid around them with their whips. Order would be maintained.

General Aleksandr Borisovich Shalenko sat in his car as the vehicle entered the Special Security Zone at the heart of Moscow, the heart of Russia. Decades of war with the Chechen rebels and the re-absorption of the former SSR states in Central Asia had made Russia a target for every international *Jihadist* group; even the extreme control practiced over the citizens by the new government found it hard to prevent all attacks. No one was allowed to enter the Special Security Zone without being searched, not even a General and one of the President's closest friends and confidents; Shalenko would have had the guards executed if they failed to search him with as much care as they would devote to a lowly civil servant.

"Papers, please," a guard said, his AK-2015 pointed just away from Shalenko's chest. He wouldn't hesitate to fire if there was something seriously wrong, or even if his suspicions became aroused; no one would forget the truck bomb that had devastated Stalingrad, or the LNG tanker that had devastated

Oakland in America. Shalenko passed over his papers without comment; the days when Russian Generals could barge though security were long over. "You may pass, sir."

The driver took the car into the car park, where it would be searched, while Shalenko himself walked into the guardhouse. The search process was through; the guards removed his service weapon even as they checked his identity, his possessions, and the contents of his security briefcase. They weren't cleared for any of the information in the briefcase; they had to wait for one of the President's aides to inspect it for them, just in case there was a bomb inside. It wouldn't be the first time that an unsuspecting officer was turned into an unknowing suicide bomber. Finally, however, Shalenko was permitted access to the inner heart of Russia.

"Welcome back, General," Colonel Marina Konstantinovna Savelyeva said. Her official rank was Colonel; her position as chief aide to the President gave her status and power well above her station. In Russia, power, responsibility and rank sometimes existed in inverse proportion to one another; Shalenko himself had once been a mere Captain with Colonels and even Generals reporting to him. "The President is keen to begin the meeting."

They walked the remainder of the way into the Kremlin in silence, their only escorts a handful of security troops, intent on ensuring that there was absolutely no threat to the President and the bureaucracy that made up the core of Russia. Shalenko had once considered it overkill, before the series of attacks in America had begun; the Russian state might have suffered some attacks, but nowhere near the number of brutal attacks that the Americans had weathered. The price for that was a police state that would have had the old KGB reeling in astonishment and a disregard for any notion of civilised warfare. They paused for a second in front of the new statue of Stalin – Russia had been caught for years in a wave of Communist nostalgia – and then entered the Kremlin, passing through still more checkpoints and finally entering the main room. It had been renovated in the years since the new government had taken power; it was now both a testament to Russian military glories in the past, and the advanced technology that Russia had adapted from the West. The old and the new merged seamlessly, all embodied in the face of the man who accepted Shalenko's salute as they entered.

He was old, but with youthful eyes; his short-cropped white hair seeming too white to be real. He was shorter than Shalenko, with a stocky body and hints of a greater strength than seemed possible, but he dominated the room by the sheer force of his presence. No one doubted that the man facing them was the undisputed lord and master of Russia; Shalenko knew that if the President gave the order, his own troops would shoot Shalenko down within seconds. He was respected and feared; a hard man to love, but not a hard man to follow.

President Aleksandr Sergeyevich Nekrasov.

"General," Nekrasov said, without preamble. His power sat easily around him; the only times he had ordered one of his inner circle executed had been when the member in question had concealed information from him. Failure wasn't an automatic death sentence, not like it had been in Stalin's day, but lying to him was never tolerated. The Russian disease could not be allowed to spread. "I trust that your inspections were successful?"

Shalenko nodded. "The vast majority of units are ready," he said, truthfully. He had kicked arse and taken names all over European Russia and Belarus to ensure that the units were at their optimum condition. "The commando units need to have their specific targets assigned, but in most cases they would be capable of carrying out their missions without further preparation."

"We have time," Nekrasov assured him. They had been old friends for years, long enough to ensure that they understood one another. Shalenko's private fear had been that he would be asked to take up the post of Minister of Defence, but Nekrasov had spared him that; the role Shalenko held was the one he wanted. "We will review the operation as soon as the entire Cabinet is assembled."

They trickled in, one by one, as they were cleared by the security forces. Nekrasov waited patiently as they came in, taking the time to exchange comments with a handful of people, asking after the health of wives and children with one breath and discussing the career of promising officers with another. The new Russia needed promising officers; Shalenko himself had ensured that dozens of officers who had talent received training to go with it. The reform of the Russian military since the end of the Soviet Union had been a painful process, but it had been worthwhile; Nekrasov controlled what was perhaps the most powerful land force on the continent.

As the doors closed, Nekrasov tapped the table. "My Friends, it has been over thirty years since the power of Mother Russia was broken by the Americans and their European lapdogs," he said. "We were cast down and forced to be humble; our power and prestige was stripped from us and we were outcasts, always the target of jibes, always prevented from gaining the help we needed to develop ourselves. Our people starved as America abandoned us and Europe lectured; military bases moved ever closer to our powers and America deployed ABM systems intended to ensure that our nuclear arsenal was no longer dangerous. I remember the final withdrawal from Poland...

"I swore then that we would return.

"For the past ten years, we have been pulling ourselves up by our bootstraps," Nekrasov said. The room was very quiet. "We have developed our energy sources and have been using them to earn hard cash, that we have in turn used to develop and reform our military, and finally give Russia something to be proud of. Now, we have a window of opportunity...and a deadly threat to our very well-being."

Shalenko listened as Nekrasov listed, one by one, the insults and indignities piled on Russia by Europe. Nekrasov had nothing but contempt for Europe; Europe wasn't the Americans, who had the military strength and geographic luck to back up their words. Brussels hectored and hounded, persecuting Russian immigrants, while meddling in the endless state of Ukraine unrest and assisting the Baltic States to break their agreements with Russia. Ever since he had come to power, Nekrasov had used the advantages of Russia ruthlessly, from ensuring that the fuel that Russia supplied came at a high enough cost to impede Polish economic development, to using the positions in Belarus to build a support base for the greatest military attack the world had ever known.

"We have been preparing for this for years," Nekrasov finished. "We have been waiting for the window of opportunity...and now we are ready. In a month, Operation Stalin will commence...and a continent will be brought to its knees."

The reactions ran around the room. Some of them had known from the start that the operation would be launched unless something very significant occurred to prevent it. Some of them had thought that the entire operation was a pipe dream, or a desperately impossible gamble; they had never expected that anyone would actually try it. They all burned to avenge the multiple insults that Russia had suffered over the years, but Operation Stalin…

Nekrasov smiled at them. "General?"

"I have completed my review of the units that have been assigned to Operation Stalin," Shalenko said shortly. "The security requirements were quite high – most of the units have little idea that they will be going to war within a month – but training and supplies are excellent. The logistics chain has been carefully prepared and the logistics units will be able to supply the advance forces with everything they will need to maintain the offensive. It would be nice to be able to capture European supplies, at least of fuel and rations, but we are not dependent upon it. We just completed RED STORM, a major exercise, and I am pleased to report that the battlespace management system worked fairly well. Striking the balance between control from the rear and local awareness of conditions was tricky, but we believe that we have successfully mastered the art.

"The Special Forces units have been largely prepared for their own missions, although we have been unwilling to assign them any specific intelligence on their targets," he continued. "Their role in the operation is absolutely crucial, but until we are ready to inform them of their targets, further training is likely to be counter-productive; we will begin practical training once all units have returned to their barracks and entered lockdown. Security will be maintained."

He paused. "The operation has been extensively wargamed," he concluded. "Assuming that everything goes in our favour, we will win within a month; assuming that the enemy is aware of our intentions and takes steps to thwart us, we should still be able to win, but within six months. It is therefore important that the long-range strike plan is launched; if we can destroy the European logistics chain, our victory is certain."

The Minister of Industry, Ostap Tarasovich Onyshenko, coughed. "That assumes, of course, that we neutralise both the European nuclear deterrent and the prospect of American intervention," he said. "Can you guarantee that we can accomplish both?"

Nekrasov smiled thinly. "All warfare is based on risk," he said. "We can knock out most of the nuclear deterrent in the first round. Olga?"

Olga Dmitriyevna Sedykh, the Foreign Minister, spoke from her part of the table. "The Americans are fully committed in the Middle East and Korea, where the North Koreans are preparing to launch an attack against the south. We have said nothing about this, of course; Kang is unlikely to need encouragement from us to attack either the Americans or his southern brothers. The rift between Europe and America is a deep and apparently permanent one; the Americans no longer have an obligation to come to Europe's rescue. We expect that they will protest and secure Iceland, somewhere we are not even preparing to threaten; even if they intend to interfere, they have very limited forces at hand."

She paused. "The main danger is the American ABM units in Poland," she concluded. "They have to be neutralised...carefully. We cannot afford to give the President a bloody flag to wave."

"I have a specialised unit prepared for that mission," Shalenko assured her. "If nothing else, avenging the insult offered to us in Iran will seem like an excuse for the American public, as unreasonable as the Americans are on such matters."

"In any case, they would hesitate, I think, before becoming embroiled with us," Nekrasov said. "They will be confused, at first, as to what is actually going on. Maksim; what about our security?"

Maksim Nikolayevich Zaripov, FSB Director of External Intelligence, smiled. "There have been no signs that anyone within the American or European intelligence services suspects the existence of Operation Stalin," he said. "We have very good penetration of the establishment in Brussels and Poland and while the Poles are worried about the presence of so many Russian soldiers in Belarus, to say nothing of the influx of refugees, they do not have any actual proof that we mean them ill. The greatest proof, I think, is the ROE that Brussels gave the three EUROFOR deployments; Poland, Ukraine and Bosnia. All of the units have no authority to so much as blow their noses without permission from Brussels."

"Requested in triplicate, of course," Admiral Petr Yegorovich Volkov said. "Fifty-page forms, no mistakes, in three different languages."

There were some chuckles. "I believe that our security remains intact," Zaripov said. "Our deployment of submarines and weapons to the Algerians and Serbs has excited some comment, but nothing major; the main complaint is that we have been muscling out their weapon manufactures when it comes to sales to the Far East. For some reason, not many people trust European weapons."

Shalenko smiled. The French had supplied weapons to Iran, weapons that they could turn off at will…and they had been caught at it. The Americans had forced the French to hand over the shutdown codes; the final radio broadcasts from Tehran had warned the world of the danger. The integrated European defence industry had taken a major drop in sales.

Nekrasov tapped the table. "Margarita?"

Shalenko found his eyes turning to Margarita Sergeyevna Pushkina, the FSB Director of External Operations, with interest. She was pretty, but dangerous; she was known as the 'Black Widow' behind her back. There were rumours that Nekrasov and Margarita were lovers, but informed opinion tended to disregard the possibility; the idea of the Black Widow having anything to do with anything as soft as love…

"We have established penetration of all countries within Europe, some of them through the use of long-term FSB sleeper agents, others with the assistance of the Algerians," Margarita said. Her voice was soft and very musical, but there was a hard edge that undercut her dark-haired appearance and soft skin. "This has the added advantage that if the Europeans stumble onto some parts of our network, the Algerians and radical Islam will get the blame. The Algerian plan for a major uprising can, with our help, succeed to a certain extent."

She smiled. There was no humour in the smile. "The Islamic Government of Algeria has been plotting its war for a long time," she said. "Their problem was that they would get their arse kicked if they tried it alone; with our help, they have a fair chance at pulling it off long enough for us to make our gains permanent. Afterwards…well, it's not as if we owe them anything. They have been smuggling in weapons and preparing terror cells for years; we took advantage of the opportunity to move some of our own people into the region."

She paused. "I should stress that this part of the plan could fail," she admitted. "I have every confidence that our own people will carry out their missions or die trying, but I don't trust the fanatics the Algerians have been sending in, or the Palestinians who took up residence in France. Some of them probably suspect that we intend to stab them in the back as soon as we secure all of the vital targets, others will intend personal revenge, rather than anything that might help us. As long as they keep the French and Spanish busy..."

It went on and on; Shalenko found his head getting heavy as every last part of the plan was reviewed, examined, hacked apart and rebuilt and finally approved. The planners had built friction into the plan; Shalenko was too old a dog to expect that everything would go perfectly, even if the first steps of the plan were played to perfection. Over a million soldiers, sailors and airmen, some of them *Kontraktniki* officers, had been prepared for their mission; thousands of tanks, aircraft, missiles and warships had been produced for the greatest military attack that the world had ever seen. Nothing would ever be the same again...

"I think that we have taken care of every detail that we can control," Nekrasov said finally, after the details of the diplomatic offensive had been examined. "Are there any final issues we must cover?"

There was a pause. Stalin would never have said anything like that, or at least he would never have meant it.

"There is a point," Shalenko said. "We must avoid causing atrocities, at least until we are firmly in control, that involve the general population. If they believe that they have a future under our rule, sir, they will be less inclined to fight to the death."

Nekrasov looked briefly at him, and then at FSB General Vasiliy Alekseyevich Rybak. Rybak was known, not without reason, as the 'Butcher of Chechnya;' he had brought peace to the region, the peace of the grave. He had also been mocked mercilessly because of his name. The International Criminal Court had tried to indict him; the Russian Government had told them to go to hell.

"We will have to establish control as quickly as possible," Rybak protested. He met Nekrasov's eyes. "We cannot tolerate defiance, but we can try to ensure that there are no...incidents."

"Good," Nekrasov said firmly. "Revenge can wait until we have won the war; we cannot take the risk of doing the Europeans a small injury, after all." He looked once around the room. "In a month, Operation Stalin will begin... and the global balance of power will shift towards us. Good luck to us all."

Chapter Three

They Also Serve...

War is an ugly thing, but not the ugliest of things. The decayed and degraded state of moral and patriotic feeling which thinks that nothing is worth war is much worse.
John Stuart Mill

Edinburgh, United Kingdom

The girl was waiting for him in the darkness...

He could see her, her haunting dark eyes in her dark skin, wrapped in a purple cloth that had covered her young body. He had seen her in the refugee camp, her dark eyes pleading for the safety that the Europeans had promised her...and then withdrawn. He remembered her, dreaming – had the dream become reality or had reality become the dream? – her body charred and burnt by the fires that had consumed the camp, her body dying even as it moved sinuously towards him. He could make out her curves, slowly being washed away by the fire; her breasts and thighs consumed, leaving only her eyes to glare accusingly at him. She blamed him...

Captain Stuart Robinson woke up screaming. His body was coated in sweat; there was a body by his side. It took him long terrifying moments to remember that the body was that of his wife; he checked her pulse with one practiced hand, only to sigh in relief when he realised that she was alive. The remains of the nightmare still floated around his mind; they were not in Sudan, but in Edinburgh.

His wife looked up at him. "The nightmare?"

Robinson would have lied to Hazel if he could, but they had lived together long enough to know that lying would be futile. Hazel had been there for him when the remains of the Sudan Deployment had returned to Europe, some of them to face charges of disobeying orders, others to quit the various armed forces in disgust, others to soldier on as best as they could. Hazel's father, a powerful local businessman, had offered to take his son-in-law on, but Robinson had refused the offer. The military was his life.

"Yes," he said. The nightmare always returned the day before a deployment. The long period of leave for his infantry company had come to an end. "I saw her again."

Hazel placed her hand in his and they held each other. It wasn't fair on her, Robinson thought, but there was nothing he could do about it. The girl – he had never learned her name – had been one of the teenage girls at risk of losing honour, dignity and lives to the insurgents in Sudan, the type of people that the deployment had been intended to protect. Instead, they had merely made a bigger target for the insurgents, the bastards who killed, raped and looted across the entire region. The Rules of Engagement had made engaging them difficult… how else were they meant to prevent a massacre? General Éclair's decision to tell the politicians in Brussels to go fuck themselves and order the enemy engaged had come too late; thousands had died in the 'safe' refugee camps. And then…

They had been ordered home, of course, some of the British soldiers to face charges of disobeying orders. Robinson had been a young private at the time, newly married; he had been spared any formal prosecution, but morale in the armed forces had plummeted. General Éclair had killed himself, taking the blame on himself. Some said that European military tradition had died with him. There had been a time when 'damnation to the French' had been a British toast; now, soldiers drank to the last of the European commanding officers worth a damn. All Robinson had to worry about had been the nightmares.

Hazel's blonde hair spilled down as she straddled him. "Do you have to go back?"

He knew what she meant; *why don't you leave the army and take the job offer from my father?* It wasn't as if he hated George Alban; the man had been quite accommodating to the squaddie who had courted, and then married, his daughter. They might not have managed to provide him with any grandchildren yet, but Robinson was sure that they would have time for that one day; it was the thought of becoming dependent upon his father-in-law that bothered him. He loved the junior ranks of the army.

And besides, even in these times, it was far better than life as a civilian.

"I don't have a choice," he said, as his hands explored her breasts. Nearly a decade of living together, since they were both in their teens, had given them unmatched knowledge of one another's body. She could draw anything from him and he could make her come for hours; nothing he had experienced before matched it. She pushed down on him, pulling him into her, and he forgot himself for nearly an hour. "Hazel..."

"Don't you dare fall asleep," Hazel said, afterwards. "You have to have a shower and then I think I'll make you change your sheets."

"That's your job," Robinson said

He ducked the pillow she hurled at him, running into the shower before she could find something harder to throw. He took a moment to use one of the new vibrating shavers to quickly remove all of his stubble, before running through a quick exercise routine and showering to remove the sweat. The nightmare always made him wake up screaming; he wasn't the only one who had been to Sudan to have nightmares, but the Government had refused counselling to the soldiers. They had just wanted to forget about it. It had brought down a government, after all; they would have been happier to dance across a minefield.

Shaking his head, he dressed quickly and neatly and headed into the living room. They kept such a large house because of the lodgers – something that George Alban had organised to ensure that his daughter was kept in the manner to which she was accustomed – but none of them worked in the mornings. They had only two lodgers at the moment, something that Robinson was privately relieved about; the last thing he wanted was to run into them after a nightmare.

"I'll have your breakfast out in a moment," Hazel called, through the doorway to the kitchen. She was a pretty good cook; she had been surprised to learn that Robinson could cook, something the army had bashed into his head. "Why don't you watch telly and find out what's going on?"

Robinson laughed and sat down, finding the remote and clicking the interactive television on. It had been a gift from his father-in-law on their wedding day, a new system that could present news to them based on their requirements, or give them an entire series of programs, if they had time to download them. He had once downloaded all twenty seasons of *Doctor Who* and watched them, end to end; now, he put the temptation aside and turned to the BBC news. The system knew his preferences.

"American spokesmen today informed the world that American soldiers had been dispatched to South Korea in conjunction with a division from Australia and a smaller unit from New Zealand," the newsreader said. She was a computer-generated program with impressive vital statistics; she was also the most popular pornographic character in the world, all computer-generated. It had sparked off an entire series of studies into the human character. "Despite protest marches in a dozen European and Latin American capitals, the administration of President Joan Kirkpatrick is determined to avoid any appearance of weakness in the run-up to the forthcoming American elections. The marchers..."

"Leftist morons," Robinson muttered, knowing that it had been the marchers who had gotten Europe into Sudan and then out of the damned country. George Alban had been really scathing about them. "Next!"

Another computer-generated face, this time vaguely French in appearance. "The leader of the French National Front yesterday called for Arab and Palestinian immigrants to be forcibly sterilized," she said. Images of protest marches and riots spread across the scene. "Jean-Luc Barras claimed that the rising tide of immigration was permanently changing France's demographics and insisted that the French Government take firm steps to prevent further immigration. The pronouncement was greeted by riots and protests; the European Court of Justice will meet today to decide if they should prosecute him for hate speech. Both *Radio Jihad* and *Islamic Law*, broadcasting from Algeria, have called for his head. The Islamic Government of Algeria has demanded that the French Government hand Barras over to them for trial."

Robinson rolled his eyes. The French would probably give in too.

"The Canadian Government today refused to hand over a suspected terrorist to American authorities without some proof that he was a terrorist," a different face said. "This comes in the wake of American draft-dodgers fleeing to Canada and being turned back by the Canadian authorities, despite an underground movement intended to help the young Americans. Congressman Dave Howery, of Michigan, demanded that President Kirkpatrick show resolve and compel the Canadian authorities to surrender the man. The White House has not commented."

"Cheerful news," Hazel commented, as she placed his breakfast in front of him. Robinson grinned; bacon, eggs, fried potatoes and hash browns. What more could anyone want? All of it was cooked by his wife, not by a mess officer; the British Army had a recurring joke about men taking one look at the meals and deserting to the enemy. "Is there any good news?"

Robinson passed her the remote, allowing her to skim through the hundreds of different news articles that were available to them. It wasn't like it had been when he'd been a child, when it had taken hours to download one episode of *Doctor Who*. Now, it only took minutes to have an hour-long episode streamed over to them, and seconds for a short and chunky news piece. He'd read articles that claimed that it was bad for people to have such access, but personally he loved it; the service was available everywhere in the UK and America. They could even access news reports from Poland, or watch Polish television…and the world became a little smaller.

"Ah, a kitty caught up a tree," Hazel said, after a moment. "Shall we watch that?"

Robinson realised that he was being teased. "No," he said. "Anything of more interest to me?"

"Alfred Ashford, the convicted killer of a child molester, was today remanded to the custody of a medium-security jail," the newsreader said. Robinson felt his jaw clench; there had been protest marches against that, the only protest march he had ever attended. Ashford had caught a convicted paedophile molesting his daughter and killed the bastard, only to be charged with murder; the streets of Britain were no longer safe. "Ashford is expected to spend at least ten years behind bars…"

"Assuming he survives his first year in prison," Robinson snarled. He glanced down at his watch. It was almost time to leave. "What are you doing for the next hour?"

"We have another lodger coming to look at the third room," Hazel said. "I want to give it a clean-up before they look at it and make their choice. I need to check that Rashid and Sergey have left the bathroom in good condition, just to impress the newcomer. The conditions here are so much better than the hostels and the rent isn't much higher."

Robinson shrugged. Rashid Ustinov and Sergey Ossetia were both refugees from Russia, people who had fled the police state that the new government had created, somehow finding their way to Britain and temporary workers permits. They both had jobs in the city and paid taxes; they were quiet and soft-spoken. He had worried, at first, about leaving Hazel with them, but they had behaved themselves. Sergey was homosexual, something that Robinson knew was taboo in Russia, while Rashid had brought home a girlfriend from time to time. It was hard to see what they actually had in common.

"So, no time to get back into bed?" Robinson teased. He wanted her so badly at that moment. "I'm going to miss you."

"Randy animal," Hazel said, teasing him. He reached out for her and their lips met in a long kiss. "I'm going to miss you too...and if you get killed, I'm going to kill you, understand?"

"Yes," Robinson said. He gave his wife a second kiss, then a third, and then a fourth. He would come back to her or die trying; what they had was too important to lose. "I do have some sense of self-preservation, after all."

He kissed his wife goodbye and started the long walk towards Redford Barracks, pausing only to throw a quick salute to the portrait of General Éclair that he had attached to the wall. It was – officially – frowned upon, but hundreds of soldiers had decided to ignore official warnings and keep the pictures of those who had died or been betrayed by their own governments after Sudan. The Netherlands and Denmark had been particularly vile to their soldiers; if a far-right group did manage to get into power there, Robinson privately predicted blood on the streets.

Redford Barracks was a set of massive buildings, set within Colinton, home to The Rifles as well as several smaller units and a Territorial Army base, right next door. Robinson showed his security pass to the guards at the gate, armed and ready for trouble; they searched him and allowed him to enter the base. He paused to salute the flag flapping in the wind, and then headed into the briefing room. Other soldiers would be trickling in over the coming two days; as a Captain, Robinson had the pleasure of being called back into service early. It wasn't an easy time to be a junior officer in His Majesty's Army.

He stood and saluted, along with a handful of other officers, when Major General John McLachlan entered the room. McLachlan was fairly well-known; unlike Robinson himself, he had seen service in the ill-fated Iraq campaign, as well as Afghanistan and several other places where the general public would be astonished to learn that British troops had served. His dark hair was fading to grey now, but he still gave the impression of strength and, more importantly, competence. Rumour had it that he wanted to retire, but the person who was likely to get his job was an incompetent paper warrior.

"At ease," McLachlan said, as he returned their salutes. "You will be pleased to know that we are being deployed, along with several RAF and SAS units, to Poland. You may have heard rumours about the repeated Argie claim to the Falklands, and the Government has authorised the deployment of a major force of Royal Marines and Royal Navy ships, but we are going to Poland. So far, the fact that a major force is going to the Falklands, in the hopes of preventing a repeat of the 1982 war, has been kept a secret; the requirement for a deployment to Poland has not. I assume that all of you know the background, seeing that you did a tour two years ago during the first crisis; there are few changes of importance in the background.

"Almost the entire regiment is going, along with several other regiments, under my national command and the European command of General Konrad Trautman, who has experience in the Balkans and the Ukraine. No one expects serious trouble on this deployment, but we have been able to gain permission from Brussels to deploy some units to expand our control of the area and hopefully increase our ability to react to any real emergency. It should be noted that there have been several incidents recently in Ukraine that Intelligence fears will trigger a full-scale civil war; if that happens, we may find ourselves working with the Poles to seal the border. We are supposed to have reinforcements in that case, but with the Falklands becoming a trouble spot again, we may have reinforcements from France or Germany, rather than Britain."

He paused. "Forward deployment will be at Rheindahlen Military Complex, North Rhine, Westphalia, Germany," he said. "You have all been there before, so you know the area; kindly ensure that your soldiers always use their contraceptives if they intend to sample the local nightlife before we get permission to move into Poland. We will have a long and enhanced period of training; the good news is that we will be getting some of the new equipment that they promised us five years ago. The 7th Panzer might have the new Eurotanks, but we will have several smaller vehicles, including some Close-Air Denial Systems with the latest antiaircraft missiles. I expect heavy training from all of you."

Robinson nodded. McLachlan could be a martinet from time to time, but he knew his business, even if he was known for insisting on perfect grooming in the field. Everyone hated training until they had actually been under fire, in which case they loved it; they could never get enough training. The newly enlisted soldiers, who had been surprised by the intensity of their early days in the army, would be astonished to discover that they would be expected to train until they reached the end of their careers. Far too many of them had come to the army unprepared.

"We will be deploying one week from today to Rheindahlen," McLachlan finished, after briefly detailing the other units that had been assigned to EUROFOR, including several French, German and Spanish units. "I expect that all of you will have your battalions and companies ready before we move to Catterick Garrison, where we will be transported to Germany. It may not be the Falklands, but I expect each and every one of you to carry out his or her duty to the best of your ability. Besides, we have to show up the French at something other than football."

There were some chuckles. "Dismissed!"

Chapter Four

Storm Warning

A form of government that is not the result of a long sequence of shared experiences, efforts, and endeavours can never take root.
Napoleon Bonaparte

Brussels, Belgium

"You know," Captain Saundra Keshena remarked, as the two American officers made their way towards the centre of Brussels, "I'm fairly sure that it is impossible for one man to have so many muscles."

Colonel Seth Fanaroff smiled as he studied the statue of General Éclair. It said something about how highly General Éclair was regarded that the Pentagon had flown its flag at half-mast the day his death had been confirmed – although, incidentally, not the manner of it. Even the most data-constipated bureaucrat in Brussels had hesitated before admitting that their finest commanding officer – a Frenchman who had had the political skills of Eisenhower matched with the military skills of Sherman – had killed himself because of the impossible task he had faced and the disaster that had occurred. The Americans had learnt something about accomplishing the impossible after the Pakistani Incursion and the Second Afghanistan War; the European Union hadn't learned anything until too late.

Fanaroff wasn't that surprised. His role as the United States Military Intelligence liaison to the European Defence Force – EUROFOR – gave him a unique insight into how the institution worked. It had been the result of so many political compromises that it was surprising that the attempt to send troops to Sudan had ever gotten off the ground; EUROFOR was all chiefs and very few Indians. The day that NATO had dissolved in a shower of acrimony had been proclaimed as the 'hour of Europe' – years later, the

Europeans were still waiting for their military to actually do something useful. Billions of Euros had been spent...on what?

"They idealise him," Fanaroff said, without any real anger in his voice. America and Europe were decoupled these days; even his message wouldn't change anything. There had been a time when V Corps had been stationed in Germany; a powerful force of tanks, infantry, mobile rocket launchers... even tactical nuclear weapons. Now, there were only a handful of American officers in Europe, mainly liaison officers like Fanaroff himself, even though there was little actual cooperation, at least in the public eye. There were people in the Pentagon who believed that the real reason for Turkey's rejection from the EU had been because of the possibility of having to work with American forces in the Middle East. "The one man who could have built EUROFOR into a real army."

The entire system was bizarre, something that proved, more than anything else, that Europe considered itself unthreatened. EUROFOR had only four multinational regiments; the remainder of the force consisted of units that were assigned to EUROFOR by the national governments that owned them. It was worse in the European Air Force; all that was owned was a handful of helicopters and the former NATO force of Sentry AWACS. As for the navy...

His lips twitched. The European Standing Force in the Mediterranean consisted of units from five different countries, trying to work together in the face of mounting political infighting over just what they could do to the immigrants that swarmed across the water every night. For some reason, the people in Algeria thought that France would provide a better home for them than Algeria...and, with the show trials and executions for everyone who showed even the slightest urge to question the government, it was easy to see their point. Nothing short of machine gunning every last boat would have stopped it...and the European Governments refused to take that step.

Captain Saundra Keshena looked up at him. "Sir?"

Fanaroff smiled to himself. "Yes?"

"Sir," Saundra asked, "why are we here?"

"I assume you don't mean in the cosmic sense," Fanaroff teased her. She was a conscript, one of the unlucky third of the American female population who had been drafted into the armed forces. There was some evidence that the five years service that each conscript had to do in the Army was improving America, but Fanaroff himself wanted more information before passing judgement; Saundra seemed only suited to be a paper-pusher, something the army already had too many of. "We're here to talk to the European Defence Commission and see if they'll listen to us."

He felt his eyes narrow as they passed a series of protesters. Brussels saw more protests than any other European city, ever since it had become the capital of the European Union, in name as well as fact. Some protesters were demanding restrictions on immigration, others were opposing the desperate attempts to limit immigration, some were demanding military intervention in one struggling country or another...and all of them were opposed to America. One protester was even against the American determination to maintain embassies in every European country; never mind the fact that that had been a European balls-up from start to finish. The European Parliament had tried to set itself up as the only voice for Europe and national governments had stamped down hard. America hadn't been involved.

It was the first time that Saundra had visited the headquarters of the European Defence Commission, the home of EUROFOR. Judging from her stare, she wasn't impressed; the Europeans had spent enough money to create and outfit two armoured divisions on a building that could only be described as an eyesore. The security around it was a joke; Fanaroff had seriously considered taking a bomb in one day and rubbing the collective nose of EUROFOR in its own weakness. Everyone knew, one day, that the Terror War would spread to Europe...apart from those responsible for Europe's defence.

"It's a giant dick," Saundra protested. "What were they thinking?"

"You should hear what the grunts call it," Fanaroff said, for once serious. "That, my dear, is what happens when you let Joe Shit have free reign."

The security hadn't improved since the last time he had visited; the guards swung sensors over their bodies and checked the mobile phones, terminals and briefcases they both carried. Fanaroff, who knew that sensors could be spoofed quite easily by someone with the right equipment, was nervous; there was a reason why the Pentagon insisted on a strip search before allowing anyone into the building. In Europe, after a couple of occasions where guards had strip-searched a veiled woman, even female guards had been forbidden to search anyone. It was a disaster waiting to happen.

The interior of the building looked like a palace; the interior decorations alone had cost more than the richest man in America brought home in one year. A giant portrait of Napoleon I took up most of one wall, other portraits of famous military leaders dominated the remainder of the ground floor. Someone unfamiliar with the military might have been impressed; Fanaroff, who had volunteered for the army, could see the weaknesses…and knew enough to know who had been left out. Bomber Harris, Rommel, Petain, Bismarck…

"I could take a suitcase bomb in here, blow it up, and do EUROFOR a vast favour," he muttered, as their escort finally appeared. Leaving two strangers alone in a military complex - even a worthless complex - for any time at all was just plain stupid. "Remember, be nice to the poor gentleman."

"Welcome to EUROFOR HQ," the young man said. His uniform was so spotless that Fanaroff immediately deduced that he had never seen active service. "I have been ordered to escort you before the Commission."

"Thank you," Fanaroff said. "Lead on."

He amused himself with making notes about how dangerous the building was for anyone unlucky enough to get caught in a bomb attack; the Europeans hadn't even created a clear air space around Brussels. The only countries that had done anything like that were the French and the British, both of whom had faced terrorist attempts to use airliners as weapons. The guards weren't armed…and while he was sure that there was a security force nearby that could stand off a major attack, the real danger was a quick strike, not a major attack. A single airliner could wipe out much of the European Union's high command.

"I am afraid that your aide will have to remain outside," the escort said, as they reached the doors. "Please would you come this way?"

The office was large enough to play football in, Fanaroff considered; it was only a slight exaggeration. It was more luxurious than the Oval Office and considerably less practical; the five men in the office turned to face him as he entered. One of them wore a European Service Uniform – the equivalent of American BDUs – the others wore the more flamboyant dress uniforms of

REMFs. Fanaroff knew General Konrad Trautman by reputation; the others he had met from time to time in an official capacity.

"Welcome to EUROFOR HQ," General Henri Guichy said. He carried the additional title of Commissioner, as France's official representative to the European Defence Committee, the closest thing that Europe had to the Joint Chiefs of Staff. Fanaroff had long ago ceased wondering which tail wagged which dog. The EDC had vast power and influence in Europe…and its structure was such that it promoted paper-pushers, rather than fighters, to high rank. "I was quite surprised when you requested this meeting."

I bet you were, Fanaroff thought. He took a moment to study Trautman with care; the German, at least, was a real combat soldier. There were some who wondered if he was the real heir to General Éclair, not a thought that would please Guichy and his kind. The brown-haired General looked competent enough; his posting to Poland had been proclaimed as Europe's reaction to Poland's unjustified fears about the Russians. Fanaroff suspected, along with several others in the American defence establishment, that those fears were not so unjustified after all.

"I have been asked to convoy some information from Langley," he said, referring to the catch-all term for American Intelligence, in particular the CIA. The information had been gathered from a dozen different sources, but it had been an overworked analyst in the CIA who put it all together. "The White House was keen that you heard the information as quickly as possible."

Guichy shrugged and waved them all to chairs. "One hopes that this information is more accurate than the vaunted American search for weapons of mass destruction," he said. "You must understand that Brussels is hardly going to jump into action at the command of the American President, no matter how important she is."

"Of course," Fanaroff said, unwilling to argue politics with either Guichy or one of his people. He opened his briefcase and pulled out a small secure datachip. "I assume that you have a reader here with biometric sensors?"

Guichy nodded and passed him the reader. Fanaroff inserted the chip and placed his hand on the sensor, allowing the reader to confirm that he, Colonel Fanaroff, was permitted to access the information on the chip and share it with others on the cleared list. The CIA and the other intelligence services collected thousands of gigabytes worth of information on everything under the sun; the problem was using the information before it was too late.

"You will know, of course, that the first Russian surge of troops into Belarus occurred in 2018, following a request by the Dictator to protect himself and his cronies from their own people," Fanaroff said. It had been one of the few things that Europe and America had actually been in agreement upon; it was a bad thing. Both nations had protested, to no avail. "Four years later, the Russians surged more troops into the country and sealed the borders; those units included armoured divisions, attack helicopters, and other units that seemed useless for a counter-insurgency operation."

"And the Poles panicked," Guichy snapped. "I remember."

"You didn't have other problems at the time," Fanaroff said. "The Russians have been fuming about the actions of the Baltic States against the Russians living within the states…and you have been backing the Baltic States. But…the Russians have been shipping weapons, including Scud missiles, to Algeria…and other weapons to Argentina. The British have already had to dispatch a major force to the South Atlantic; what about the danger of Algeria?"

Guichy looked up at him. "The Algerians do not have the capability to launch an attack on Europe," he said. "They might fire missiles at us, but they will all be downed by the Patriot missiles that we purchased from you at vast expense."

Fanaroff took a breath. "There is also the fact that the Russians have been backing the pro-Russian factions in the Ukraine," he said. "You have two regiments, one Swedish, one Irish, providing peacekeeping forces in the region; you're overstretched and the Russians are pouring on the pressure."

"The Poles have been worried about the safety of their borders since the first cross-border raid," Trautman said slowly. Guichy shot him a 'shut up' look that he ignored. "Still, I would hardly call that pouring on the pressure."

Fanaroff frowned. "What is EUROFOR's position when it comes to Ukraine?"

Guichy matched his frown. "Our orders from the European Parliament are to maintain the peace of the region, safe in the knowledge that the long-term interests of Europe will be satisfied by Ukraine becoming prosperous, and then joining the European Union as a full and equal member."

"Interesting concept," Fanaroff said. He paused, just long enough to make them nervous. "What about the Russian attitude to all of this?"

Guichy blinked. "I do beg your pardon?"

"A while back, you offered to buy Kaliningrad off them, following the independence demonstrations that took place in the Oblast," Fanaroff said, as calmly as he could. "The Russians reacted with speed and fury; they sent in thousands of airborne soldiers and muscled the Lithuanian forces into allowing them passage through Lithuanian territory. Thousands of refugees fled west...while hundreds of others were shipped into Russia and sent to the gulags."

"There are no such things these days," Guichy protested.

"I can show you the satellite photographs, if you would like," Fanaroff said. "It hardly matters; the point is that Kaliningrad is now a loyal component of the Russian Federation, which has also reabsorbed Belarus, most of the Central Asian states and, for the first time since 1960, no longer has a threat in the east to worry about. The Chinese Civil War has seen to that.

"So tell me, how are the Russians going to react?"

"They are not going to start a war with us," Trautman said. "If the people of the Ukraine decide that they want to vote to join us, what right have they to interfere?"

"It is no use passing resolutions on vegetarianism when the wolves are of a different opinion," Fanaroff said. He had had a girlfriend who had been a vegetarian once; she had been so self-righteous that he had dumped her right after one argument too many. There was a point when even great sex didn't make up for the fact that you really didn't like each other. "The Russians have launched a major military build up" – he pointed to several locations on the display – "here, here and here, perfectly positioned for a rapid advance into the Ukraine. They could brush the Ukrainian Government forces, such as they are, aside within a week...while you're arguing over what to do about it. The American Government..."

"Is worried about the security of the ABM stations in Poland," Guichy snapped. "I would like to remind you that they're there are the sufferance of the European Union..."

"The Polish Government, which for some reason wanted to keep the military agreement that Poland signed with us," Fanaroff snapped back. "The Poles agreed to keep them, because they wanted the radars to provide additional coverage for their own air force. EUROFOR is not involved and doesn't even get a feed from the stations!"

He took a long breath. "It is the recommendation of the American Government that you reinforce Poland so that you actually have something in position to react when the Russians decide that the Ukrainian elections are tilted against them and come over the border," he said, as calmly as he could. "For what it is worth, the American Government has also agreed to offer EUROFOR access to the direct feeds from the stations, if EUROFOR would like to take them up on the offer!"

There was a moment's pause. "That would be quite welcome," Trautman said. "In fact..."

"There is no intelligence to suggest that the Russians intend to do anything other than abide by the election results," Guichy said. He nodded to a young carrot-topped man. "Major?"

Major Nekropher O'Mans, of EUROFOR Intelligence, shook his head. "There have been no reports that the Russians have dire intentions towards the Ukraine," he said. "They actually played quite an important role in getting the Swedes into position, providing some help with transport and intelligence to prevent some of the factions from starting a civil war. A civil war is hardly in their interests."

"I hope you're right," Fanaroff said. He unlocked the chip and passed it over to O'Mans. It puzzled him that an Irishman had been appointed to EUROFOR Intelligence; the French or British had much more capable intelligence agencies and far more contacts to draw on. "That is the information we have been able to gather, Major; I hope that you are able to disprove the conclusion, but...I have a nasty feeling that you're wrong."

He saluted them and left the room; Saundra was waiting outside, skilfully deflecting the escort's attempts to chat her up. The escort passed her his email and telephone number before escorting them back outside the building, into the warm sun. Brussels was lovely in spring, apart from the new buildings; they had been built to a standard where taste didn't apply.

She tossed the note away as soon as she was outside. "Sir, how was it?"

Fanaroff looked back at EUROFOR HQ. "They're all doomed," he said. He ignored her astonished questions. "Come on, we have to get back to the Embassy; I need a stiff drink."

Chapter Five

Sleepers

A fifth column is a group of people which clandestinely undermines a larger group to which it is expected to be loyal, such as a nation.
Emilio Mola

Edinburgh, United Kingdom

"Welcome to Edinburgh," Hazel said, as the new prospective lodgers arrived. "I understand that you are living together?"

She took a moment to check out their appearance; one man, his eyes hidden behind sunglasses, and one woman, her eyes faintly desperate. The Scottish Parliament might have issued grandiose proclamations on how it intended to create new housing in the city, but in a fit of typical brilliance, they had managed to build houses that were too expensive for most buyers.

"Yes, thank you," the man said, his voice clearly from the Highlands. He held out a hand. It felt limp and sweaty to her touch. "We were recently offered a transfer to Edinburgh and...well, it was the sort of transfer that you take or you leave permanently."

Hazel nodded in sympathy, reappraising them. She had assumed that they were lovers, at least, not merely colleagues; they had to be desperate to be sharing a flat. She had no objections to them sharing a room, but they would definitely be sharing a double bed, unless one of them had a sleeping bag. Her husband had a spare one if it were needed; she would go the extra mile for them if she could.

"The rent is seven hundred pounds a month," she said. In theory, she could accept Euros instead, but she had no real trust in European money. It just didn't look real. "If you are sharing a room, I assume that you will be sharing the cost?"

"Yes," the woman said. "I'm Shelia and this is Grant Murdock."

"Pleased to meet you both," Hazel said, leading them up the stairs. "There are two floors to the building; the flats are all on the second floor. There are no real restrictions on what you can do here, except smoking; smoking is firmly banned in this building. If you bring anyone home, you are responsible for any damage they might do, and if you do break one of the rules, your possessions will be seized until you pay up. How long do you think you'll be staying?"

Shelia seemed to be doing most of the talking. "We honestly don't know," she admitted. "The way things are these days, we just don't know what to expect; the damned boss gets the golden handshake, we get the door and a kick in the arse if we don't move fast enough to suit them. We hope to be here for at least a year, but..."

Hazel nodded. She understood; her husband shared her concerns about the job market these days. They all had debts to pay off, debts and endless taxes and red tape complicating their lives; there were times when she wanted to just go up to the HRMC and detonate a really large car bomb right in front of the building.

"This is the main living room," she said. She noticed Rashid Ustinov sitting on the sofa, probably waiting for his friend to come out of his room; the Russian wore simple labourer's clothes. He worked on a building site somewhere; it was probably how the pair had met. He waved absently at the three of them and turned his attention back to the book in his hand. "You'll notice a fridge, for cold and frozen items, and a microwave, along with a computer port and a television. There's a internet port in the room itself; the shower is just at the end of the building. It's shared, I'm afraid."

She showed them the room itself and knew instantly that they weren't intending to rent it. It was smaller than they had expected, even if it did have a large bed; she had hoped that there would be more married couples moving into the house. She went through the entire explanation anyway, pointing out how the designer had hidden drawers and other units in the room, including a larger wardrobe than seemed possible. There was a sink for their basic needs; she even pointed out the washing machine that the two Russians used for their own washing. It wasn't as if they had many clothes, after all; she'd only seen them in their basic labourer's outfits.

"I think that it is a little small for the pair of us," Shelia said finally. Hazel nodded in grim understanding; it wasn't as if Stuart and her were short of money, but she knew better than to assume anything. The Government might just decide that her husband was no longer needed in the army. "We *will* keep it in mind, but..."

"I quite understand," Hazel said, keeping her face blank through determined effort. "You do know that if someone else comes with an offer, I am going to have to accept it...?"

"Yes, thank you," Shelia said. "We do understand."

Hazel showed them both out, sighed, and headed back upstairs to the living room. "You can count them out," she informed Ustinov, who shrugged. The Russian was a man of few words; he'd only unbent far enough to tell her that he had committed a political indiscretion that had resulted in him being chased out of the country. Her husband had once commented that Ustinov was as fit as a soldier, something he explained was due to the Russian program of conscription. "You won't get them as flatmates unless they change their minds."

"That's bad, I guess," Ustinov said. He glanced back down the corridor. "We'd pay more if we could."

"It's not the money," Hazel assured him. "It's the fact that this place is meant to be full of life and it...isn't. If Stuart and I ever have children, then perhaps there will be little feet running around, but..."

Ustinov grinned. "Perhaps," he agreed, as the sound of a door opening echoed down the corridor. "Ah, here he is."

Hazel smiled at Sergey Ossetia as he entered the living room. She had never gotten a gay vibe from him, not in the sense that some gaysexuals dressed in a feminine fashion, often comically exaggerated for effect, but she presumed that that was because Russia had a dim attitude to homosexuals. She had been looked at by enough men to know the difference between lust and dispassion...and Ossetia had shown no interest in her body whatsoever.

"Sorry about the delay," Ossetia said. He spoke perfect English; neither of them had much in the way of an accent. "I was just emailing home and lost track of time."

Ustinov glowered at him. "We're late," he said. "Come on; we'll see you later, Mrs Robinson."

"I assume that you don't want your rooms cleared?" Hazel asked, teasing them. "I can do it for a small charge..."

"No, thank you," Ustinov said, with great dignity. "You have a break while we go to work to earn the money to keep you in house and home."

Hazel laughed and waved at them as they headed down the stairs and out onto the streets, and then got back to work. The house didn't clean itself, after all.

Ustinov, who was a Captain in the FSB Commando detachments, checked around them out of habit as the two men strolled through the Meadows, heading towards the other side of the city. The Meadows made a good place for them to have a private chat; it was somewhere where the British security services would have real problems spying on them, even though there was no sign that the British had even noticed them as more than the simple labourers they appeared to be.

Ossetia, who was a Lieutenant and technically Ustinov's subordinate, frowned as he carefully hunted for signs of pursuit. "Are you sure that the items are safe?"

Ustinov nodded. "She hasn't gone into our rooms since we took them," he said. He had taken the precaution of scattering a handful of portable sensors around since the first week they had spent in the building; Hazel hadn't even poked her head in, let alone anything else. "In any case, we have them all secure, don't we?"

"More or less," Ossetia agreed. They had moved beyond the ordinary relationship between a Captain and a Lieutenant; there was little point in maintaining the formalities when it was just the two of them. They knew that there was at least one other officer in Edinburgh, their superior, but they knew nothing about him…or about the others they assumed would exist within the city. Neither of them had been assigned to specific targets; both of them knew enough to know that some targets in the city would not have been left alone. "The boxes should remain secure, short of someone actually managing to burn through the casing, triggering the self-destruct system."

"One hopes that that won't happen," Ustinov said shortly. They were almost at the university. "The blast would vaporise the entire house and hopefully be blamed on Islamic terrorists."

They kept their mouths closed as they passed the university library, noticing the protesters protesting the American deployment to Korea without showing their disdain, and headed towards the Mosque. It was a little piece of Arabia in Edinburgh, built by money supplied by Saudi Arabia before it collapsed into chaos; the two Russians kept their faces blank as they passed it. Once they had completed their first mission, perhaps the Mosque would make a good second target for chaos. The streets were packed with cars, despite the limited supplies of oil from the Middle East; it was easy to get into the crowds, lose themselves within the swarm of humanity, and finally reach a nondescript building near Arthur's Seat. Every base had been covered; if anyone had asked, they had been called to the building and paid minimum wage to perform some basic repairs.

Control was waiting for them in a shabby room.

Neither of them knew his real name, nor did they know anything useful about him that the security services could use to track him down. They assumed that he was a deep-cover agent, working somewhere within Edinburgh, perhaps within the entire United Kingdom, to touch base with all of the Russian operatives within the country. They had been given some specific instructions concerning him; they were to tell him *nothing* about their positions, or where they stayed or…

The planners had tried to plan for everything.

"Boris and Boris, pleased to meet you," Control said. The name Boris was a private joke; anything else would have kicked off alarms in their heads. If Control had called them Ivan, he had been captured and turned and they would have to run for their lives. "Take a seat; events are moving faster than we had anticipated."

Ustinov nodded. They had privately expected to be called back to Moscow; they had run plenty of dry-runs before and nothing had ever come of it. When they had been inserted into Britain this time, they had expected nothing else; they would be just a pawn in Moscow's endless power games with Europe. The acts they had planned and prepared, ever since they had come out of Chechnya with a burning hatred of all things European, Islamic or both, had seemed meaningless on their own. In the context of some much larger operation, however…

They seated themselves on the floor. "This building has been checked carefully," Control said. "You have some work to do afterwards, but for the moment, the agency has ensured that we had some time together. I assume that you have a secure base and have placed your weapons somewhere where you can lay claim to them?"

Ustinov nodded again. "Yes, sir," he said. That was as far as he was prepared to go when it came to sharing details. If something happened and they lost Control, there were contingency plans for himself and Ossetia to either launch attacks on their own, or flee the country. "Everything is as safe as it could reasonably be."

Control smiled. "Good," he said. "The start day of the operation has been set; the 1st of June, local morning. You have been assigned to target set A; I assume that you have scouted out possible locations?"

"Yes, sir," Ustinov said. Again, he couldn't share details; men who shared information knew that sooner or later, accidentally or otherwise, they would be betrayed. They had, as it happened, found the perfect place for their actions. The only real danger was running into another team with similar ideas. "We also have the equipment we need."

"Good," Control said. He leaned forwards. "Are you sure that you can carry out the mission without problems?"

Ustinov nodded. "Yes, sir," he said. There were questions he wanted to ask and didn't dare. "Once we carry out the mission, we should be able to escape without serious problems."

"We need you to continue attacks," Control said. Ustinov nodded slowly; he had expected that much. "There is a mighty storm coming and we will need all the help that you can muster to make certain that we win. I won't give you a list of secondary targets, some of which may be hit by other teams" – both men drew in their breath at the vague confirmation that there *were* other teams – "but you are ordered to hit as many targets as you can with the aim of causing disruption and chaos in the streets. Keep watching your email; we'll send you a message if we want you to end the attacks and come out."

Ustinov scowled. He would have been much happier only using email, but the Americans had refined their techniques for tracking and decrypting emails, and while the Americans and the Europeans seemed to be permanently divorced these days, it was folly to assume that the Americans wouldn't tip off the Europeans if they knew that there was something big going down. Pre-planned messages had their uses, but there were only a limited number of possible messages that they could agree upon…and one certainty of the universe, as far as Ustinov knew, was that anything they planned for wouldn't happen as they planned it. Friction was worked into every good plan, but the smaller the plan, the more chance for friction to terminate operations with extreme prejudice.

On the plus side, at least they'd be choosing their own targets.

Control stood up. "There will be no further contact," he said, tapping a small case in the centre of the room with his shoe. "You have some details in there of other arms caches, but there were obvious limits as to what we could emplace in the city; the British are rather paranoid after Glasgow and Blackburn. You both know where to find some specific stocks that you can use for terror if you need them, so…all I can really say is good luck, and I'll see you again in Moscow."

Ossetia looked up at him. There was almost a nervous tone in his voice; anticipation mixed with concern about how he would perform when it all went into action. Ustinov knew the feeling; he had had it himself on his first mission in Chechnya.

"Something really big is about to happen, isn't it?"

Ustinov smiled inwardly. "Yes," Control said flatly. Ustinov wondered just how much Control knew about what was coming; it didn't seem likely that he would know everything, but at the same time, he wouldn't be completely in the dark. "Your task is to sow random terror."

Until we are either killed or run out of weapons, Ustinov thought. He knew better than to assume that the British police would just let them get on with it. The British SAS were almost as good as the Spetsnaz…and Ustinov knew that neither of them were trained to the peak of Spetsnaz perfection. Their skills lay in infiltration, not commando shootouts in the middle of schools and government buildings. He would have been delighted to have had some Spetsnaz helping out, but few of them could pass for harmless foreign slaves or stupid British people. It was up to them, he reflected; *this could get very interesting; nasty, brutish and short.*

"Good luck," Control said shortly, assuming the face of the capitalist exploiter again. The Russian immigrants *were* exploited, Ustinov had found; both of them had been worked to the bone more than once, just because their position was so precarious. He had studied British politics enough to be certain that the ruling party was going to lose the next general election, putting in a Conservative Government with a mandate to, among other things, evict all immigrants. Or, perhaps, they would just move right to the British National Front; the European laws against hate speech hadn't managed to put the BNP out of business...and they had even some MPs in Parliament. "I'll see you again in Moscow."

He strode out of the building, looking to all the world as if he had just given two downtrodden lackeys their orders. Ustinov checked the building quickly, then transferred the contents of the case into their own bags; money and some documents. The documents would be memorised at night, and then shredded; both men had near-perfect memories. There was a great deal of work to do in the building, mainly the plumbing; neither of them complained as they got to work. They needed to work to prove they'd earned their money legitimately.

Ossetia coughed. "Lunch at Euro-Burger?"

Ustinov smiled. Euro-Burger had been set up in direct competition to McDonalds and had been winning the struggle for dominance. He didn't really understand it; both of them tasted like crap. They had moved some of their operations into Russia, where they were ruining the taste buds of countless Russian youngsters; Ustinov would have quite happily bombed either of them if he had thought that it would have managed to achieve something. It wouldn't; they would need a bigger target to really shock the British public.

An aircraft flew high overhead.

He shuddered. He knew what it portended.

Chapter Six

The Lords and Masters

The State, in choosing men to serve it, takes no notice of their opinions. If they be willing faithfully to serve it, that satisfies.
Oliver Cromwell

London, United Kingdom

"Your papers, please, General," the guard said. His weapon wasn't – quite – pointed at Langford's chest. "I must insist."

Major-General Charles Langford passed over his identification and waited patiently for the guard to complete a biometric scan of his body, comparing it to the details stored in both the ID card and the PJHQ computers. The tiny microchip in the card was supposed to be impossible to fake or alter, but Langford knew better than to assume that anything was impossible. It was why there were armed guards emplaced around the PJHQ – the Permanent Joint Headquarters – and why there was an entire company of armed soldiers stationed within the surrounding buildings. The last terrorist attack on the United Kingdom had been years ago, but it was only a matter of time.

"You may pass, sir," the guard said. His partner saluted; the guard himself didn't. Saluting on duty was a punishable offence; it could distract a guard from his duties. Langford would have understood the guard's nervousness about not showing a superior officer respect – he had been written up for once saluting a superior in a combat zone – but there was no helping it. Security came first.

"Thank you," Langford said, as the gate opened. It had been designed to prevent a truck bomber or something similar from entering the parking lot, but it all seemed absurdly flimsy compared to the Green Zone in Baghdad, even though the Americans there had known that they were likely to be attacked at any moment. The government of Britain hadn't wanted to invest in much in the way of security, let alone the forced buy-outs of the property surrounding the PJHQ, but almost every security officer had threatened to resign and go public unless the government agreed. Security came first and, despite the Liberal Government, there were still people who wanted to keep the country safe.

He passed through the gate and entered the main building, receiving a second security check as he entered, before heading down into the bunker. It had been designed years ago, during the threat of Russian nuclear attack – in typical MOD fashion, it had been finished after the Cold War had been won – and seemed far too flimsy these days. Both the Americans and the Russians had deployed heavy bunker-busting bombs, ruining the reputation of the French and British engineers who had built the bunkers where third world despots had hidden from American aircraft. Many of them had died with defiance on their lips.

"Sir," Captain Christopher Drury said, standing to attention and saluting. The bespectacled officer didn't look much like a combat soldier, nothing like the guards in battle dress on the outside of the building, but as one of the operators of the PJHQ, he was one of Langford's most trusted officers. He might have given off the impression of a blonde Jeff Goldblum, but there was little eccentric about him. "Welcome back to the PJHQ. I must remind you that you have the weekly situation meeting at 1300 hours and there are still protesters blocking the roads; the Metropolitan Police suggest that you use one of the helicopters."

Langford scowled. He had never married and had been an army brat; he had never understood why protesters picketed military bases, such as the handful of barracks scattered around London and the PJHQ, rather than government buildings. The military didn't decide when to go to war; that was the choice of the politicians. Every European general had advised against the Sudan deployment, and then against withdrawing half of the force…and had been ignored. They had also gotten the blame afterwards.

"Wonderful," he said, crossly.

It was annoying. The weekly situation meeting and security brief was supposed to be a simple task, but it wasn't anything of the sort when some security matters were handled by EUROFOR and others by PJHQ, while Brussels kept attempting to expand their authority. It didn't help that a united front of French, German and British officers had pointed out that there was no need to spend billions of Euros on a new headquarters in Brussels; the PJHQ alone could have provided all of the coordination that EUROFOR could have required. The French headquarters – the public one, that everyone knew about, and the secret one that no one was supposed to know about – could have accomplished the same tasks; the European Defence Commission had insisted on its own headquarters and the various governments had given in. It was empire-building at its worst; that money could have mended a few defects in EUROFOR's actual line of battle.

He shrugged. It wasn't something he could do anything about. "Is there anything I should know about?"

"There's a torrent of *Jihadist* invective coming from Algeria and to some extent from Libya, thanks to some frog who wanted to cut the balls of every Algerian or something like that," Drury said. Langford felt a flicker of sympathy for the unnamed Frenchman. "It's all the usual stuff; the Frenchman must die before the Eiffel Tower comes crashing down and exterminates the French when it hits the ground."

"Pretty big explosion," Langford observed dryly. The image made him smile; the French had tougher laws on terrorism than the British, although they were mild compared to either the American or Russian laws. "Anything else?"

Drury shook his head. "The French Air Force has requested that we provide an AWACS and a couple of fighters for a drill in a week," he said. "The French think they have a new way of detecting aircraft at very low level and want us to be the aggressors in a raid on France. The Chief of the Air Staff was very interested and wants us to agree."

"That is within my purview," Langford said. Unless something went very wrong, the government wouldn't have to know about it...and the RAF's training standards had been slipping badly, recently, due to the torrent of complaints about the noise of low-flying aircraft. "Anything on the Threat Board?"

"Only some suggestion that the Russians are considering a move into Ukraine," Drury said. "EUROFOR HQ is handling the matter, but they don't anticipate trouble; in any case, it's out of our hands. Major-General McLachlan says that the Poles are worried, but EUROFOR HQ is convinced that the Russians are going to wait until after the elections before they move, if they move."

"Then I see no reason why we should not go along with the French request," Langford said. The French commander skirted the edge of what could be done without EUROFOR's knowledge; it was fitting to show that not everything needed EUROFOR to go along with it. "Coordinate it with CAS, but unless something new appears, then we should try to beat the French at their own game."

He smiled at Drury's expression and headed into his office, taking the time to pick up a cup of coffee before reading through his secure emails. There was little of importance, but seventy percent of his work was never important; hurry up and wait applied even more to the PJHQ than it did to soldiers in the field. They, at least, got to shoot at the enemy - sometimes. The entire Falklands situation seemed to be calming down now that a major task force, including the *Prince of Wales*, was on its way to the area. That was nearly a third of the Royal Navy…and the politicians would probably claim that it was all a wasted deployment.

"Damned Argies," Langford muttered. Every so often, Argentina would shake its fist and make threatening moves in the direction of the Falklands, and British forces would be forced to react. Even the Liberals who were in power knew better than to simply give up the islands, no matter their anti-colonial sentiments; their government would fall quicker than an apple from the tree, or an American bunker-busting bomb. "I wonder…"

"Sir, your helicopter is ready to depart," Drury said, hours later. Langford nodded tiredly; he had been studying deployments, wondering where he could draw a company or battalion from to make up some of the overstretch. It wasn't like 1914, where Britain had had worldwide interests, or even 2003, but it was still tricky…and the endless cuts in the deployable forces hadn't helped. "The Police are still reporting that the streets are blocked."

"I should go in a Challenger tank," Langford said. He smiled at the thought; the British Army had intended to switch to Eurotanks, of which there were nearly a thousand units on order, two years ago. Naturally, the project had overrun and only one European unit had Eurotanks. "That might show them something about the world."

Drury said nothing.

The Metropolitan Police hadn't exaggerated, Langford realised, as the helicopter came down towards Whitehall and the MOD Main Building.

Protesters swarmed as close as they could to the centre of British Government, the organised protests disintegrating into peaceful anarchy. The protesters seemed to just want to protest; Langford had heard that the police wanted to disperse them, but the government had forbidden it for political reasons. The weather forecast had promised heavy rain in a day or so; it had been hoped that the rain would put most of the protesters off their game. Some of them shouted towards the helicopter as it came in to land on the roof; they were too far away to know what they were shouting. He doubted that it was anything important.

"Welcome to the Main Building, sir," Captain Scott Hammock said. "They're all waiting for you in the briefing room."

"Thank you," Langford said. He wasn't surprised that the others had arrived first; they could use the series of tunnels linking Whitehall together without having to face the protesters. They walked down the corridors, the monotony broken only by a faded VOTE SAXON poster that no one had had the heart to take down, and into the main hall. A small set of aides and assistants were waiting outside; they were wallflowers as far as the weekly security briefing was concerned.

The interior of the briefing room had been renovated several times, currently designed to resemble a corporate office, rather than the dignified centre of government that Whitehall aspired to be. The Prime Minister stood to greet Langford as he came to a halt and saluted; his bulk made it seem as if he was a beached whale. Prime Minister Nicholas Donavan actually believed half of the statements he made in public and in private; Langford gave him that much credit. Like John Major, no one really questioned his integrity; his grasp of political affairs was another matter. If Labour and the Conservatives, to say nothing of the Scottish Nationalists, hadn't so thoroughly discredited themselves…

"Thank you for coming," Donavan said. Everyone else in the room, with the exception of a dour-faced Police officer, was a political appointee or politician; Langford was uncomfortably aware that he was outnumbered. The ongoing budget crisis, seemingly impossible to solve, had left Donavan with a desperate need to cut costs, anywhere. The MOD's budget got smaller every year. "I believe that we can begin now."

Langford took his seat, noting the presence of the Chief of the Defence Staff, Jack Redding, and the Secretary of State for the Home Department,

Neddy Young. The Deputy Prime Minister was off pressing the flesh for a by-election in Scotland; his place had been taken by one of his trusted aides. The Chancellor of the Exchequer, Bruce McClain, looked grim; he was the third person to hold that role since Donavan had become Prime Minister.

"You may have heard that there was an...unfortunate incident in France last week," the Policeman said. His nametag read BRIGGS. "There have actually been some protests in several southern cities in Britain relating to it, all coordinated through the network of mosques that we have identified as being hotbeds of Islamic fundamentalism. The protests have been carried out without violence, but there were some incidents of genuinely worrying behaviour and, I believe, signs that there is a real network coordinating their actions. This cannot be coincidence, Prime Minister; I believe that this represents a disturbing trend in Islamic behaviour."

He tapped the display. "You will remember that the Americans killed seven British Muslims in what remains of Saudi Arabia last month," Briggs continued. "All of them came from these four mosques" – the display changed again – "and all of those mosques held protest marches demanding that the Americans turn over the bodies for proper disposal. This was impossible, of course; the Americans simply destroyed the bodies once they had been identified. Less well known is the fact that the Americans took an eighth British Muslim alive...and forced him to talk. He was talking about an entire recruiting ring that gave him training before shipping him into Saudi."

Donavan shuddered. "The Americans tortured him," he said. There had been any number of articles on the practice when it had begun, before Oakland; afterwards, the American public would have been quite happy to bathe the entire Middle East in radioactive fire. Hundreds of thousands had died in Oakland. "He would say anything under torture."

"The Americans gave us some of the information and we checked it out," Briggs said. Langford felt a moment of sympathy for him; his superiors should have handled such matters, not dropped them in the lap of a relatively junior officer. "Sir, there *is* a network there and it represents a clear and present danger; we need to take it apart, quickly!"

He paused. "The growth of right-wing extremism is also becoming worrying, with reports of illegal arms and training flooding the inner cities," he continued. "Incidents of racial hatred and even outright violence have been on the increase, some of it in response to the actions of the Islamic network. Something has to be done."

"If we arrest the people behind the network, we'll have a riot on our hands," Neddy Young said. "We cannot afford that, not when we are making progress at last."

"You mean when you are appeasing them," Briggs snapped, too tired to continue. Langford silently applauded him. "This situation is too unstable to continue..."

"We will take it and think about it," Donavan said. Briggs heard the note in his voice and sat down bitterly. "Major-General?"

Langford exchanged a long look with Briggs before taking control of the display. "The main item on the agenda is the deployment to the Falklands," he said. "The fleet is currently one week away from the islands and the number of incidents has fallen sharply. ASW frigates reported some contacts with submarines – we know that the Argentineans have purchased several newer submarines from the Russians, including three nuke boats – and there have been some long-range aircraft flying out to take a look at us, but nothing of great importance. The Americans..."

"I told you so," Bruce McClain snapped. "This little operation cost us billions of pounds, money we can ill afford to lose; I knew they were bluffing."

"It had to be done," Donavan said reluctantly. "We could not afford a repeat of the Falklands War. General?"

Langford could almost read his thoughts; to a man like him, the wishes of the islanders were paramount...and he assumed the same was true of the archetypical reasonable man. The problem was that nationalists were not given to being reasonable over some issues. The Argentinean Government, back in the economic dumps after the fallout from the American War on Terror had spread into Latin and South America, had been beating the nationalist drum again...and what better cause than the Falklands?

Langford smiled. "The other matter of importance is the deployment to Poland," he said. "Under the auspices of EUROFOR POLAND, we have dispatched several regiments to join the defence force, assuming that it is actually needed. There are some reasons to be concerned that the Russians might attempt to take over the Ukraine if the elections there don't go their way. Sir,

I must request that we force the European Defence Commission to revise the ROE, at least for units that might have to go into Ukraine and support the EUROFOR units already there."

"Out of the question," McClain snapped. The fury in his voice was almost a tangible thing. "The last thing we need is to get embroiled in a war with Russia."

Donavan tapped the table. "Major-General, do you have any reason to be suspicious?"

Back to Major-General, I see, Langford thought dryly. "The Russians have been moving forces into positions that they could use to jump into Ukraine and they have said, several times, that they would not tolerate an anti-Russian policy on the part of the Ukraine," he said. "It was hard enough to convince them to accept the deployment of two European battalions into the Ukraine, and they have prevented us from any serious joint operations. The Irish and the Swedes might be tough, but they're not ready to act if the Russians try something and don't have the firepower to act in any case. We would have to react instantly if something happened…and we don't even have a political line to fall back on."

Donavan tented his fingers. "It has been discussed in the European Parliament," he said. "The general consensus is that eventually Ukraine will apply to join the European Union, and so patience is all that is required."

Langford shook his head. "And what happens if the Russians refuse to go along with it?"

Afterwards, he took the helicopter back to PJHQ. He had some leave coming up, but he hated to go on leave when he had the sense that something bad was about to happen. Not for the first time, he thought about accepting the offer of American citizenship to any European soldier and his or her family who was prepared to spend a few years in the American Army. At least the Americans were doing something…while Europe fiddled merrily away.

Chapter Seven

To Be in Poland, In the Summertime

"...In general the bravery and heroism of the Polish Army merits great respect"
Generalfeldmarschall Gerd von Rundstedt

Near Warsaw, Poland

The Polish countryside scrolled past as the line of jeeps, trucks, and three CADS moved along the country road, heading well away from civilisation. They passed a handful of farmers and traders on the way to their deployment zone, using the SATNAV system to ensure that they found the correct location within Poland. For the common soldiers there was little to do but wait in the trucks; some talking, some catching up on their sleep...a handful playing with electronic toys.

"It's only a couple of kilometres further," Captain Jacob Anastazy said. The Polish liaison officer, there to help the British soldiers find their way around the country and smooth out any difficulties that they might encounter with Polish citizens, looked confident. There hadn't been any real difficulties; the only problem they had encountered had been an impromptu victory parade when they had passed through a small town. "This area is pretty much deserted."

"Good," Captain Stuart Robinson said. He was one of the lucky handful who got to ride in a jeep; the other soldiers mainly had to sit in the trucks. It was better, he supposed, than marching all the way from Germany to Poland, but not by much. The trucks had been designed for dozens of different purposes, including both heavy transport and prisoner transfer and it showed. Comfort had never been on the agenda. "We can do without a friendly fire incident."

It was easy to believe that they were at war, looking around them; the area was almost deserted and there was no sign of any other military force, hostile or friendly. EUROFOR had deployed the equivalent of two divisions to Poland, but they were spread out to provide hasty reactions to any Russian cross-border raid into the refugee camps in eastern Poland. From what Anastazy had said, some of the Poles would be quite happy to allow the Russians to destroy the camps; the refugees were either competing for Polish jobs or merely a drain on Polish resources. The Polish army was deployed near the border, at least, some of it was; European pressure and economic constraints had prevented the Poles from a full mobilisation.

They passed a handful of Polish tourists, who gaped at the military convoy as it passed, before being left alone again. Anastazy had admitted that there were fewer cars in Poland these days; Poland was already too dependent on the Russians for energy supplies and had been rationing fuel for nearly a decade. Warsaw and the other major cities had a new system of electric trams that used power from the European-designed nuclear power plant ten kilometres from the city…and closer to Robinson's position than he could have liked. He had grown up near Torness Nuclear Power Plant, but the thought of being near a nuclear plant in a weapons-free zone chilled him.

His mind slipped back to the base at Rheindahlen Military Complex, Germany. The EUROFOR briefer had made them work for their supper, both ensuring that his company had the required number of German, French, Polish and Spanish-speaking soldiers, and that he understood the ROE. The ROE were basically simple; he was not to engage any targets unless his command was either under attack, or had orders to engage targets. He was grimly aware that his unit would be out on a limb if there were serious problems; the sixty men of his company would be isolated from the remainder of the regiment.

"Bastards," he muttered.

He checked his terminal. The Americans had designed the system and EUROFOR command had fallen in love with it, even though every soldier worthy of the name would have preferred more tanks and guns. It was communicator, computer and GPS system all in one, allowing him to accept orders from Brussels without having to go through the British command system. The other soldiers had shared his disdain; one French Captain had rudely remarked that it meant that they couldn't do anything without asking permission first. He had been a paratrooper, much to Robinson's amusement; were they going to be parachuting EUROFOR into its positions? A French armoured or infantry division would be much more useful.

"Russian bastards," Anastazy agreed. His voice was disdainful; the Poles both hated and feared the Russians, not entirely without reason. The Polish Government had been horrified at the restrictive rules of engagement, which would almost

certainly allow the Russians the first shot if they were plotting something, but the European Defence Commission had stuck to their guns. "Nearly there…"

They came around a corner and reached a small hill. Someone had been busy; there were signs everywhere informing the Polish public and tourists that the entire area was off-limits. He inspected it quickly as the jeep drove around the hill; they could set up the radar on the hill, and then deploy the other soldiers around the hill, providing protection for the CADS units.

He glanced over at Anastazy. "How large an area have you cleared?"

"Around a kilometre, centred on the hill," Anastazy said. "We didn't want to risk an accident where one of your men shoots a farmer."

Robinson nodded. Accidents happened and some of them had nightmarish consequences. He tapped a command into his terminal and then shouted at the driver to halt the jeep, bringing them to a halt just outside a fallow field. It would make an ideal place for the tents, he decided; it would spare them the horrors of Russian-built barracks. The trucks came to a halt behind him and the soldiers spilled out, helped along by shouts from the Sergeants and Corporals. Robinson was proud of them; some of them might have been bastards, but they were good men to have behind you in a firefight. Most of them had seen combat before.

"All present and correct, sir," Sergeant Ronald Inglehart reported. Despite his name, he was as black as the night, a Jamaican who had enlisted in the British Army and served for several years as an NCO. He was the toughest son of a bitch that Robinson had ever met, always ready for a fight – and yet he was also one of the kindest men imaginable to his old mother. "No desertions to the fleshpots at all!"

Robinson had to smile. "Secure the area, and then set up the tents and field kitchen in that field," he said. The orders, he was sure, were unnecessary; Inglehart would have done everything without a young Captain teaching his grandmother to suck eggs, but they had to be given. "I'll deal with the CADS."

The CADS themselves looked like something out of Captain Scarlet; *a short squat set of lorries, carrying four missiles on their roofs. He'd seen the videos; the CADS could engage four different targets simultaneously, reload, and engage four more, until they ran out of missiles. Each truck carried twenty-four missiles; one of the supply lorries carried a complete set of replacements for all three of the units. He had heard that the RAF, upon attempting to penetrate an area defended by a single CADS unit, had lost five Tornados to their fire. It had all been simulated, of course, but it suggested that the company would have some protection from aerial attack.*

Lieutenant Benjamin Matthews saluted as Robinson came up. He hadn't been idle while Robinson had been deploying the company; his crew had all dismounted and were running basic systems checks. There were twelve of them, four of them women, something that might cause problems later. The Company had seven women, but all of them were very definitely off-limits; the CADS crewers might be courted by bored and horny soldiers. Robinson made a mental note to consult with Anastazy about nearby brothels; the mental state of the company had to be treated with care.

"We are ready to deploy on your command," Matthews informed him. Technically, Matthews wasn't in the same chain of command, but Major-General McLachlan had been very clear on the subject. Matthews would serve under Robinson as long as they were guarding the godforsaken hill. "One of the missiles developed a fault, but the others all read out as working fine."

Robinson eyed the missile that two of Matthews' crew were carrying away from the trucks. "Is that thing safe?"

"We removed the warhead and the propellant," Matthews said. "The problem is in the computer chips that are supposed to guide it to its target; they weren't working right."

Robinson scowled. It seemed that the more advanced equipment became, the more things that could go wrong…and were impossible to fix on the spot. The missile would be sent back to Germany, where the technicians would try to find a replacement for the computer chips and send it back to them. Missiles were expensive; no one would just junk it.

"Good," Robinson said absently. "You have to deploy now, then we can report back and hopefully spend a couple of weeks getting bored out here."

The camp slowly took shape. The entire area was searched twice, finding nothing, but a handful of birds and wild animals, and then the real work began. Sergeant Inglehart organised it all, from sensors designed to detect anyone approaching to organising regular patrols around the outskirts of the camp. Robinson would have been happier with a fence or something that would keep ramblers out, but EUROFOR Command had refused to allow permission; they would just have to be careful. The first mobile radar was deployed on the hill, an insulated cable leading down from the hill towards the CADS systems, limiting the amount of electronic emissions that an enemy could pick up. Robinson wasn't impressed; the radar itself would attract attention, a perfect case of penny wise, pound foolish.

"I wouldn't be so sure," Matthews assured him, when he said that out loud. "The radar itself is a target, sure, but only when the radar is activated. In an ideal world, we would be taking readings from ground-based radars further to the west and merely shooting at the targets using their readings. If we do use the radar, and we are going to have to use it, any missile launched at it will not take out the actual missile launchers we have here, while we can move them to prevent the enemy from locking on to their positions."

He tapped a command into the mobile command system. "Now…let's see."

The display lit up, seemingly reporting hundreds of unknown targets. The computer went to work, tracking IFF signals and microburst transmissions, identifying nearly a hundred targets as civilian airliners from Russia, Germany and Sweden. Other aircraft proved to be Polish helicopters or Eurofighters; the Russians themselves were flying a Combat Air Patrol of MIG-41s – Flatpacks, according to the western designation – a hundred kilometres to the east.

"There's more traffic than I would have expected," Matthews commented. "Of course, with all the instability in Ukraine, a lot of traffic has been routed over Russia and then Belarus, rather than risk flying directly over Ukraine and panicking someone. It doesn't make sense, but what do you expect?"

Robinson shrugged. "Do we have a direct link into the EURONET?"

Matthews nodded. "Yep," he said cheerfully. His face twisted into a smile. "We're getting data from them and they're getting data from us."

"Good," Robinson said. "I want you to maintain a permanent watch on events, with at least three people on duty at any one time, understand?"

Matthews's face twisted slightly, Robinson could almost read the thought in his mind. Asshole. *It didn't matter; they were deployed to maintain the safety of Poland and even though neither of them really expected trouble, he was determined to ensure that it wouldn't manage to surprise him, should trouble actually come knocking.*

"I understand, sir," Matthews said. More Russian aircraft blinked into existence on the display, low-level anti-insurgency aircraft, deployed in Belarus. "We will treat this as a military situation."

Robinson quickly inspected the camp, finding it excellent; Sergeant Inglehart had outdone himself. The conditions would be Spartan, but they would be tolerable until they had to move to Warsaw, or took leave when some new detachment was spared. He had been informed that EUROFOR intended to rotate them pretty regularly, but he would believe that when he saw it; EUROFOR POLAND had too many tasks and nowhere like enough men to handle them all. He shrugged and made plans to engage in more training and exploration of the surrounding area tomorrow, then started to compose an electronic message to Hazel in his head.

He missed her already.

The Polish guards at the main gate to the military camp were brisk, but firm; a female guard inspected every last inch of Caroline Morgan's body before allowing her access to the camp. She had had boyfriends, even one who had an ass fetish, who hadn't explored her body with such thoroughness. The privacy hadn't made it any easier to take; she had been all-to-aware that there were armed guards outside who would burst in if she made any noise at all.

It was odd, she reflected, as she dressed again under the watchful eye of the Polish guard. The Poles provided most of the security for EUROFOR…and they were utterly paranoid when it came to maintaining security, even to the point of making themselves unpopular with the press by sending back any reporter who gave away something that enemies could use against EUROFOR. They were desperate to keep their country safe, even if it meant annoying the reporters; Caroline wasn't sure if that was admirable, or just irritating.

"Right this way," her escort said, and led her though a maze of Soviet-era buildings. The camp had been built back when the Red Army had occupied the country…and the Poles hadn't improved it much, even if some enterprising Polish officer had planted some apple trees in the middle of the camp. Soldiers, some of them in full battle dress, were everywhere, all of them trying to organise EUROFOR into something that could actually put out more than one regional fire at once. She'd heard enough to know that rapid reaction forces had been flown all over Poland at the drop of a hat, only to get there too late, or be called back before anything could actually happen. "Major-General McLachlan is in this building here."

There was a Union Jack in front of the building, marking it out as a British building, even though it was something that the European Defence Commission hated. They had an uphill fight to prevent it from happening; she could see French and Dutch flags just in the camp alone, and there were detachments from nearly a dozen nations in Poland. The bureaucrats would probably win in the end, she was sure, but it was surprisingly good to see all of the flags. She wasn't sure why.

"You must be Caroline Morgan," Major-General McLachlan said. "Welcome to Camp Three."

Caroline smiled. "Camp Three?"

"All the proposals for names were shot down," McLachlan said. "Some places have names that they couldn't get rid of easily - Rheindahlen Military Complex, for example – but this place was soulless even back in the days of the Red Army. I understand that you wanted to be attached to this unit?" Caroline nodded. "Who did you piss off to get that job?"

Caroline laughed. "My supervisor wanted some background impressions on how EUROFOR was shaping up as a military machine," she said. It was truthful, as far as it went; the BBC needed to prepare itself for the coming elections. The people of Britain were hungry for news and the BBC had to provide or lose even more of its market. "I got the short straw."

McLachlan laughed. He had a surprisingly deep laugh. She found herself liking him on sight. "He wasn't just trying to get into your panties?"

"The first woman who gets him interested will be the first," Caroline admitted, remembering the resolutely gaysexual activities of Fell Nelson. There was a moral in that somewhere, perhaps young men and women should be made to cover their faces when they were interviewed. Many of his staff complained of sexual harassment, something that wasn't new in the recording business, but mostly it was male on female. "No, I just drew the short straw."

"Lucky you," McLachlan said. He met her eyes. She was almost lost within soft brown eyes that seemed to harden, then soften, at will. "I assume you read the background material?"

Caroline nodded. "I read everything they gave us," she said. She had too; it was long on glossy photographs and elaborate statements of principle, but short on actually useful details. "Most of it was quite bland and uninformative."

"Don't breach security here," McLachlan advised. His voice had become very serious. "The Poles will arrest you, send you to an uncomfortable jail and charge you with malicious accidental espionage. Don't rely on the Court of Human Rights getting you out, either; after it was proven that that young reporter fool from Portugal caused the deaths of three soldiers…"

He smiled thinly. "Apart from that, we will be showing you everything within the camp," he said. Caroline gulped. Was there any way for her to be certain that she was not breaking any security laws? "Do you have any specific questions?"

"A few," Caroline said. She forced her smile up a few watts. "Do you feel that EUROFOR is a viable military force?"

McLachlan's smile vanished. "A truthful answer?" Caroline nodded. "The truth is that if we had all the units we were promised, we would be the most powerful force in the region. We were promised ten divisions; what we have is around two divisions, many of whom have never worked together before, trained together, done anything together...does that answer your question?"

Chapter Eight

Special Purpose Units

If any foreign minister begins to defend to the death a "peace conference," you can be sure his government has already placed its orders for new battleships and aeroplanes.
Joseph Vissarionovich Stalin

Near Moscow, Russia

"Go!"

Colonel Boris Akhmedovich Aliyev was first out of the aircraft as it stabilised its course for a matter of moments, falling towards the ground in free fall. The shape of buildings became clearer and clearer as the paratroopers fell towards the ground, the black bursts of ground fire dancing in the air towards the planes as they pulled away, tossing the final paratroopers all over the landing zone. They had targeted the runways of the airport…and, as the seconds ticked away, Aliyev became very calm.

At precisely the right moment, he pulled his parachute, coming to a far more controlled descent as he steered himself and the remainder of his team towards the runways. The black bursts of ground fire were coming closer; Aliyev dismissed them as irrelevant. There was nothing that he could do about them, but endure; if one of those puffs of smoke caught him, he was as good as dead. His fall was still slowing rapidly, but the ground was coming up, and up and…

His legs bent as he hit the ground, an impact that had knocked the wind from him in his first jump, something that he was used to after practicing combat jumps for most of his career. He didn't hesitate; he barked orders and drew his weapon as the defenders moved to protect their airport, bringing up rifles and heavy machine guns. His team fired back, sending flickers of laser light dancing across the airport; one by one, the defenders fell to the ground and didn't move as the commandos fanned out and searched the airport quickly and efficiency. They knew the airport almost as well as they knew their own home bases; it was a matter of minutes to search and snatch every last security guard and enemy soldier defending the terminals and the control tower. Some fought, killed and were killed; others held up their hands in surrender. They were searched roughly, cuffed, and dumped in one of the terminals under armed guard. Resistance would be punished with a bullet to the head.

Aliyev himself led the team that seized the control tower. Intelligence had been impressive as to the degree of alertness on the part of the tower staff, something that he was used to and had planned for, even to the degree of risking the destruction of part of the tower to secure it before the controllers could raise support from the outside. Aliyev had every confidence in his men, but they were basically light infantry; a single armoured enemy detachment would make short work of them, or at least shut down the airport and prevent the exploitation of their victory. The control tower had been sealed; a shaped charge made short work of it and the team charged upwards.

"This is Airport One, we need help," a female voice was pleading, high above them. There was no point in being stealthy now; the team advanced as quickly as they could, finding a second locked door, but one light enough to be kicked aside with a single kick. The paratroopers swarmed into the room, seeing a set of flight controllers, their eyes wide with terror and shock. One of them was screaming into a radio; Aliyev shot her, just on general principles. The others raised their hands and were rapidly secured, searched, and placed out of the way.

"Delta-lead, we have secured objective two," a voice buzzed in his ears. Aliyev had had years of training to come to grips with the local secured communications network that the Americans had invented and the Russians had copied. "There are seven aircraft and plenty of fuel; five down and seventeen prisoners."

"Move them to the terminal," Aliyev ordered, as the flight controllers were herded out of the room, pushed and shoved by Russian commandos. The body of the dead flight controller was moved out of the way as Aliyev took the main terminal, shouting for two of his specially trained commandos to come in and take over the flight terminal. The airport had to be cleared of traffic so that their reinforcements could come in and help them secure it. "Have the pilots check the aircraft and let me know if they can be used for our own transport."

"I have locked the airport out of the general network," a commando reported. "We have full control over the terminals and there are no signs that anyone intends to come take it off us."

Aliyev smiled once; had it really been ten minutes since they had begun the operation? It felt as if it had been hours. "Get the radioman to work," he snapped. They had been lucky; one of the other random variables would have been a destroyed or damaged civilian airliner on the runway, something that would prevent them flying in reinforcements until it could be moved out of the way. "I want them to know that they can send in their reinforcements as quickly as possible."

He took a breath. There were hundreds of aircraft holding position well behind the front lines; they would have their chance to move in and reinforce the new position, with thousands of additional commandos, some heavy weapons, and even a few light armoured vehicles. By the time the enemy got themselves organised, Aliyev would have an entire brigade sitting on the airport and expanding his zone of control as rapidly as he could. Unless they reacted quickly, the enemy would discover that their rear area was disintegrating under his pressure…and that of the main body of the Russian forces.

"This is Control," a new voice said. Aliyev lifted an eyebrow. He hadn't expected *that* so quickly. "Stand down; I say again, stand down. This exercise is terminated."

The 'shot' flight controller stood up, rubbing the side of her body. She had been lucky; it wasn't unknown for participants in Spetsnaz exercises to come away with broken bones, if not worse. The soldiers were trained to be ruthless, even with the units who were playing the role of the defender; the only concession to humanity had been the use of laser weapons instead of real assault rifles. It was enough to know that if it had been a real assault, the unit would have taken the airport very quickly, without a real fight.

"I trust I was convincing," she said, as they headed down the stairs. "I thought I might actually have managed to raise someone on the outside that time."

Aliyev shrugged. They came into the main terminal, where commandos were untying the hands of the defenders, while the 'dead' defenders were abandoning the pretence and assisting the commandos in freeing their allies. Like soldiers everywhere, there was plenty of bullshitting going on, but the lieutenants in command of the smaller detachments were trying to gather the early results. The referees would tell them just how well they had done, but damn it; Aliyev knew that they had done well! He was proud of his people; it was the ninth time they had played the exercise and they'd won almost all of them.

He glanced at Captain Alexander Vatutin, his second-in-command. "Causalities?"

"We lost twelve men in simulation and four serious injuries in reality," Vatutin said. He sounded pleased with himself and he had reason to be; the expected loss rate for attacking a defended target with paratroopers was very high. In some of the more aggressive simulations, where the enemy had an entire armoured unit nearby, the loss rate had been total and the game had been lost. "Sergeant Ulya Kozlina is the worst; he broke both legs and several ribs."

"Have a medic see to him and the others," Aliyev ordered shortly. "Any news on why the exercise was discontinued so rapidly?"

"That would be me," a voice said, from behind him. Aliyev almost jumped; he was a trained Spetsnaz commando, with an almost supernatural awareness of the area around him, and the voice's owner had slipped up behind him. He turned sharply, taking in the uniform and the badges that marked a former Spetsnaz officer, and saluted sharply; it wouldn't do to irritate the President's most trusted officer.

"General Shalenko," he said. The General returned his salute. Shalenko had been an officer in the Spetsnaz himself for a while, before transferring to the combined arms sections following an injury while taking part in a dangerous antiterrorist mission. "Welcome to Airport One."

"Your men did well," Shalenko said. "The referees are still counting beans, but I think that you will be declared the undisputed winner of the contest."

Aliyev laughed at the dry tone in his voice. The Russians knew, better than the Americans, that it wasn't body counts that were important, but victory. If Aliyev had lost half of his force and taken the airport, he would have won; if he had saved his force, but been driven away from the airport, he would have lost.

"Still, there are other matters at hand," Shalenko continued. "If you would care to pass over command to your second and come with me…?"

Aliyev followed him outside, into the cold morning air. Airport One was a giant simulation of an airport, built to allow the interior to be continuously revised and allow the defending force considerable advantages. Aliyev was certain that *he* could have held the airport with his paratrooper force alone, assuming that he had had a few days to prepare the defences; a handful of mines alone would have made the attack much harder. The Spetsnaz used it to prepare antiterrorist operations, or at least that was the official explanation; their recent operations suggested something else.

They were going to war.

"This room has been secured," Shalenko informed him, as they passed a set of guards outside the door. Paranoia didn't just run in the FSB, it galloped; there was hardly anything in the room that could conceal an electronic surveillance device. It was almost like a prison; no television, no computers, no radios…nothing. The cold hard benches reminded Aliyev of his early days in the Russian Army. "We can talk freely."

"I see," Aliyev said carefully. If he were in trouble for something, Shalenko wouldn't bother coming out from Moscow to scream at him in person; one of his minions could do that. The odds were vastly in favour of this being good news.

Shalenko seemed to read his thoughts. "How would you rate the performance of your brigade just now?"

Aliyev didn't hesitate. "We are ready for anything," he said, and meant it. The unit was oversized for a reason; they could soak up training accidents and move on. It was the sort of attitude that had kept them in business even though the dark years of Yeltsin. "Do I assume that you have a mission for us?"

Shalenko clasped his arm. "This is ultra-classified information," he warned. "If you breath more than you are permitted to breath, you will be shot in the head; understand?" Aliyev nodded. "On the 1st of June, we will go to war with Europe."

Aliyev stared at him. "Yes," Shalenko said, understanding his concern. It wouldn't be the first time that a Spetsnaz unit had been put through hell, or deliberately misinformed for political reasons, but Shalenko seemed deadly serious. "All of the training that your unit and almost every other unit stationed in European Russia and Belarus has been angled towards this moment."

"I see," Aliyev said finally. It made a lot of sense; they had attacked Airport One so many times now, so many different scenarios, so much that he had wondered if there was a motive behind it besides simple sadism. "Our mission, then, is to seize an airport?"

"Szczecin-Goleniów Airport, otherwise known as 'Solidarność,'" Shalenko said. He pulled a small flash drive out of his pocket and passed it over to Aliyev. "That is *all* the information we can gather about it, reviewed by me personally, and the overall details of the plan that we have spent five years putting together, reviewing, updating, and finally implementing. We slipped as much as we could of Szczecin-Goleniów into Airport One; taking the airport is important to allowing us to establish a presence in western Poland as quickly as possible and deter the Germans from trying anything clever. There are details in the CD, but one possibility is that the European forces in Poland will attempt to retreat into Germany; it might be a good idea not to let that happen."

"Of course, sir," Aliyev said. He paused. "What about the other airports in Poland?"

"All of them will be targeted," Shalenko assured him. "If everything goes to plan, you should only have to hold out for a couple of days at most before we manage to place an armoured force in the area from the sea, or a little longer from the east. The enemy should be heavily confused – we have a number of operations going to give the Germans and Poles other problems to worry about – and you may not be attacked for hours or at all."

Aliyev studied the map for a long moment. "That's quite close to Berlin," he observed. "Will we be advancing on the city?"

"Perhaps," Shalenko said. He met Aliyev's eyes. "I have been in your shoes, Colonel; your main concern here is to secure the airport for us to fly in supplies and equipment to you. Unless you get very lucky and capture a lot of Polish tanks, we don't expect you to do more than hold the airport until relieved."

He held up a hand. "It's not an insult, Colonel," he said. "Russia needs your young men too much to simply throw them away."

"I know, sir," Aliyev said. He felt real excitement spinning through him…and a desire to even the score a little. Some of Russia's worst enemies would never have taken up arms against them, were it not for Europe; some of the Chechen leaders whose forces he had fought and defeated had taken up residence in Paris, well out of Russia's reach…or were they? "I won't let you down."

"I know you won't," Shalenko said. He tapped the map thoughtfully. "I don't expect you to secure the city either, but I do expect you to behave yourselves; we don't need to make either the Poles or the Germans think that they're doomed under our rule, understand?"

Aliyev smiled. "Sir, my men are not…Kazakhs," he protested, referring to the soldiers from Kazakhstan who had taken up service with Russia after Kazakhstan had hastily rejoined the Russian Federation. The Kazakhs had a reputation for being mad, bad, and dangerous to be anywhere near, although Aliyev also considered them vastly overrated as soldiers. "They can behave themselves."

"See to it," Shalenko said. He tapped the flash drive. "Get them all briefed and confined to barracks; I want you to have all bases covered before the attack is launched. Friendly forces, known hostile forces, the reinforcement plans, best case, worst case…you know the drill. If there are problems, I expect to hear about them before we launch the operation; *Glasnost*, remember?"

Aliyev nodded. President Nekrasov's policy of 'openness' was different from the original; in the new Russia, the bearer of bad news didn't get the blame. He knew enough to know that he could rely on it, if there was something wrong with his force, but he knew that there would be nothing wrong with his men. There was only one slight problem, but he was sure that it could be handled…

"We may need to do a handful more combat jumps," he said. "I want everyone right at the peak of fitness when we launch the operation."

Shalenko looked at him for a second, and then nodded. "Requisition whatever you need from stores," he said. "Failure is not an option."

Aliyev saluted. "We won't fail the President, sir," he said. "We will take the airport or die trying."

Shalenko returned the salute and left the room, leaving Aliyev alone with the CD-ROM. For a long moment, he just stared at it, feeling his thoughts whirling around his mind; he had wanted to be part of a massive combat operation…and now, it seemed that he would have his chance. The last major war the Russian Army had engaged in had been Afghanistan; Chechnya had been a miserable task, butcher's work…and Aliyev had hated it. The FSB security battalions, mainly the dregs of Russian jails and barbaric recruits from Central Asia, had loved every last minute of it. Fighting in Europe would be different…

He remembered his younger brother. Pavel had wanted to be in the Spetsnaz too; he had had to spend a year in the infantry first, and had been blown up in an ambush by rebels in Belarus. They had to have known that Russia was prepared to be merciful, instead they had fought…and taken Aliyev's younger brother from him. His mother's heart had broken because of it; she had died blaming Aliyev, who blamed Europe. Hadn't they known what they were doing?

He pocketed the flash drive and left the room. The commandos were finishing the clean-up, ensuring that nothing was left behind for the cleaners to remove. There was no such thing as a spare moment in the Spetsnaz; a handful of commandos who had nothing to do were running laps around the runway, just to keep fit.

"I want our lorries back here as soon as possible," he said, to Captain Alexander Vatutin. They had known that they would be returning to the barracks, but again, they hadn't expected to be doing it for hours; some drills were known to last for weeks. He had expected to spend a week defending the airport against whatever forces had been assigned to the defending force. "It seems that they have finally found something for us to do."

He allowed a smile to break through his cold face. "We're going west…"

Chapter Nine

While Europe Slept

I wonder whether any other generation has seen such astounding revolutions of data and values as those through which we have lived. Scarcely anything material or established which I was brought up to believe was permanent and vital, has lasted. Everything I was sure or taught to be sure was impossible, has happened.
Winston Churchill

Moscow, Russia

It was the 30th of May.

"This is the point of no return," Margarita Sergeyevna Pushkina said. The FSB officer sipped her drink carefully. She was never one to get drunk, something that was wise for a woman in Russia. "Everything is in place; the chaos will begin in two days and…well, we will be committed."

President Nekrasov smiled to himself. "How certain are you of success?"

Margarita flushed slightly. "The people we emplaced will carry out their missions or die trying," she said. "Some of them may be detected by the local authorities – too late. There is nothing perfect in any of these plans; we could lose half of the operations and still win, particularly the random terror part of the operations. We built so much redundancy into the plan just in case we lost half of our people; frankly, I expected to lose more than we have."

Shalenko leaned forwards angrily. "We have lost people?"

"Four of our people were picked up by the German police within Berlin, following a major riot against Turkish immigrant workers," Margarita said. "None of them knew much; even in the worst case, they couldn't have told the Germans anything about the overall plan. A handful of Algerian illegal immigrants were picked up in France, but the French Government contented itself with dropping them into the refugee camps, rather than shooting them in the head or a rigorous interrogation."

She grinned. "Frankly, I expected that the Algerians would have lost control over their own people well before we reached the point of no return," she said. "We didn't plan for that nincompoop in France calling for them all to be sterilised; idiot should have just waited a couple of months and he would have gotten much more than his wish. There were a handful of other nasty incidents, but the main body of the cells remained underground...and in any case, we can handle the important part of the mission without their help."

"But I would be happy to have it," Shalenko said, thinking cold thoughts about the dangers of an alert Europe facing his forces. He had expected to see sudden bursts of activity, expected to see the Germans, French and British suddenly realising their danger and dispatching their forces to the Polish border, as well as wiping out the sleeper agents and revising their rules of engagement to make survival a much more likely prospect for EUROFOR. "You know that we cannot rely on the enemy simply folding at the first blow."

He closed his eyes for a moment. Russian military doctrine called for making the first blow of any offensive as hard as possible, to try to make the first blow the last blow...but it wouldn't work in Europe. The enemy would have time to withdraw to more defensible lines if they had time to realise what was happening and the authority to order a general retreat. If they had a war going on in their own backyard, their commanding generals would have too many problems to handle and EUROFOR would disintegrate.

He hoped.

"I know," Nekrasov said. "What are we facing?"

"In theory, we're facing two divisions of European soldiers and the Polish Army," Margarita said. "In practice, the Europeans are not working as an integrated group and two-thirds of the Polish forces remain un-mobilised. Even if they give the order now, they would have real problems getting them into position to actually oppose us before it was too late. The targeting plan will knock out most of their reserve forces and hopefully make it impossible for them to muster any of their home forces before it's too late. The French and Spanish will be looking in the wrong direction, rather than towards us."

Nekrasov nodded slowly. "The time is so slow," he said, wryly. Shalenko recognised it as nerves and said nothing. "General, what about our own forces?"

Shalenko glanced down at his notes. "We have over forty divisions in the region or ready to move in as soon as we kick the offensive off," he said. "Furthermore, we have five thousand dedicated Special Forces units operating behind the lines, all slipped into Poland and Germany and lying low for the offensive. Several other units will knock out the EUROFOR units in Ukraine, while one division apiece has been dedicated to each of the Baltic States. None of them are particularly strong and have placed their faith in EUROFOR to defend them; we do not expect much trouble in overwhelming their defences.

"On the naval front, Admiral Volkov and Admiral Sulkin have their forces prepared for action," he continued. "The Turks have turned a blind eye to our submarines as they move though the choke point there; officially, of course, they're being moved to the bases in the north. The Northern and Baltic fleets are ready for operations in support of the army; we will move the Black Sea fleet through the choke point as soon as war is declared, unless the Turks decide to get involved. They shouldn't – they're not keen on the Europeans since they were told they couldn't play in the European club – but it doesn't matter. Our main priority in the Mediterranean is clearing the European Standing Force out of the way and assisting the Algerians, until the day that we knife them in the back. Again, there is no sign that the Europeans have any idea that anything is untoward; the only point of concern for them is the *Gazprom* strike."

Nekrasov laughed shortly. The *Gazprom* Company handled almost all of Russia's exports of energy supplies, including LNG; it wasn't likely that its workers would want to strike. Now, however, there were over a dozen fully-loaded *Gazprom* tankers in a variety of harbours across Europe, all apparently held there by a strike. The Europeans had laughed and believed the claim that they were striking in Europe because strikers in Russia would be shot; the Russian Government had paid for the docking slips and negotiations were dragging on.

Or, at least, that was the official story.

"Finally, we will have over three thousand aircraft dedicated to the operation, from bombers and fighters to heavy transports that will support the paratroopers and the other forces behind enemy lines," Shalenko concluded. "The doctrine has been revised countless times and prepared; we should be able to destroy most of the opposing air forces within the first week or force them to expend their supplies faster than they can replace them. At the worst case, the Americans will ship missiles and spare parts from America to the British, but they cannot replace pilots or airframes."

Nekrasov smiled. "It was nice of the North Koreans to finally launch their offensive," he agreed. "That should give the Americans something to worry about."

Shalenko nodded. The North Koreans had pushed back the South Koreans and the Americans through sheer weight of firepower…and through some advanced weapons they had purchased from China before China had made its desperate grab for Taiwan, lost, and plunged into civil war. The Americans were rushing in more air power and soldiers from all over the world; insurgents in the Middle East were not slow to take advantage of it. The Americans would have their hands full.

Nekrasov looked up at him. "Alex, how good would you say our chances actually are?"

Shalenko had thought about it, time and time again, attempting to cut as many variables out of the equation as possible. The plan had been years in the making, but he knew, as well as anyone, that anything could go wrong. Friction had been built into the plan, but the urgent need to knock as much of EUROFOR out of the fighting within the first few hours had meant that there had been compromises made…some of them truly nerve-wracking. What would happen if…?

He owed Nekrasov a honest answer. "If everything goes to plan," he said, "we should win the main body of the fighting within a month at most. We will then have to consolidate, ensure that the Algerians don't get a chance to make their own gains permanent, and secure most of what we need from Europe. Consolidation could take months, but our victory would be certain.

"If everything does not go to plan, we still have a good chance of winning, but at a much higher cost," he continued. "We might also have to concede some gains to the Algerians, something that we don't want and they will be working to force us to accept. If they trust us, I would be very surprised; they have to know that we intend to take most of the gains from Operation Stalin."

"If worst comes to worst, we can block their shipping lanes and ship their people off to Siberia," Nekrasov said. Shalenko nodded; the fate of the thousands of people in Europe who were considered either dangerous or worthless had already been decided. The FSB would handle that part and do so with gusto. "There's no need to permit their dangerous cancer to spread into our new lands."

"The most dangerous prospect is that of a nuclear release," Shalenko said. "The ABM system is good, but if there is one failure…disaster. Whatever it takes, we have to ensure that there is no permission for nuclear release."

"That has been taken care of," Margarita said coldly. "Whatever happens, no politician in a position of power will survive the opening rounds of the war."

Shalenko nodded. "I have been speaking to the commanding officers and the soldiers," he said. "Most of them are certain that they can handle the missions, many of them are looking forward to it, seeing that Europe was behind many of their woes in Belarus. The important thing is to keep moving; cities can be reduced later, but mobile forces must be destroyed as rapidly as possible. A pause could prove fatal."

"I know," Nekrasov said. He looked up towards the portrait of Stalin on the wall. Russians had both feared and loved Stalin; Shalenko knew that no one, apart from Nekrasov himself, had come close to the ideal of the Russian leader. "Are you going to be taking up your command in Belarus?"

Shalenko nodded. "I have a flight back tonight," he said. "Time enough to ensure that everything goes to plan and that the Poles remain quiet long enough for us to take over quickly. Civilian resistance could put an unexpected spanner in the works."

"If that happens," Nekrasov said, "deal with it. No scruples."

Shalenko bowed his head. "No scruples," he agreed.

Near Warsaw, Poland

The fire was a tiny concession to the campfire atmosphere of the location, Robinson had decided, when Captain Jacob Anastazy had lit it. Nothing had happened in the week that they had remained in position, nothing of importance anyway; the only excitement had been a flight of aircraft leaving Russia that had turned out to be civilian aircraft that had been routed away from the Ukraine. He missed Hazel, more than he could admit, even to himself; her sheer presence was missing from his mind. Emails…just didn't come up to it.

> *Dear Hazel,* he wrote, and concentrated on several passages designed to remind her of just what he was missing in Poland. *I hope that you are enjoying yourself in Edinburgh and that you did get to see the McCalmans like you intended; I wish that I could have gone with you and the old man. How is he, by the way? Is he still nagging you about grandchildren?*

The thought almost brought a tear to his eye. It was possible, of course, that they could have had children. He had just felt as if it wasn't the time, even though they had been having more unprotected sex lately. Some of the soldiers were in their teens; they had never even thought of getting married, even if there were advantages in the army to having a wife. A couple of them were openly homosexual; Robinson didn't care, as long as they remained within the rules of fraternisation. The British Army might never have quite adapted to the concept of homosexual behaviour, but as long as there was a manpower shortage…

He was wracking his brains for something else to say when Sergeant Ronald Inglehart appeared in the command tent. "Captain," he said, "the journalists have arrived."

Robinson had to smile at his tone. He couldn't have announced the arrival of child molesters and rapists with more disdain. "Thank you," he said, as he put the laptop aside and came out of the tent. Two women stood there, one of them clearly British, the other Polish; he remembered Captain Jacob Anastazy telling him about the Polish reporter. She was some relative of his, he recalled; a heart-stopping young woman with honey-blonde hair. Robinson found himself surprisingly tongue-tied as he faced her. "Welcome to the camp."

"Thank you," the Englishwoman said. She was dark-haired and surprisingly attractive in her own right. "We won't be staying long, Colonel; we merely need to get some background interviews."

"Of course," Robinson said, watching as two of the soldiers played court to Marya Jadwiga. Anastazy was looking more and more grim as they chatted about nothing in particular. Robinson had read, once, that American soldiers had often brought home a Polish bride; looking at Marya, it was easy to see why. "What do you need to know?"

"I'm Caroline, by the way," the woman said. Robinson blushed at the amusement in her voice and reminded himself that he was a married man. "How are you enjoying your time out here?"

Robinson laughed at the question. "It could be better," he said, "but so far it has been more like an adventure holiday than anything else." He had gone on an adventure holiday with Hazel once; he had found it trite and easy after actually soldiering with people trying to kill him. The instructor hadn't known half as much as he had; he shuddered to think what an SAS trooper would have made of it. Mincemeat, probably. "We're just sitting here waiting for something to happen and monitoring this particular section of Polish airspace."

Caroline seemed to understand. "Do you get bored out here?"

"It beats Sudan," Robinson admitted. He had to smile when he looked over at Marya; if the poor girl wasn't careful, she was likely to end up with a very different kind of background interview. He had had to discipline a soldier once for sending a request to a female correspondent for a more revealing photograph and had been laughing too hard to make a proper job of the chewing out. "In a week, we'll be somewhere else, perhaps guarding somewhere even more important, but until then..."

Caroline nodded in understanding. "And don't you want a real barracks?"

"Most of us would sooner sleep naked than sleep in a soviet-built barracks," Robinson said. "Have you ever slept in one?" She eyed him carefully, and then shook her head. "It explains why many Red Army soldiers were nasty bastards; they just couldn't sleep properly."

"Ah," Caroline said. "What about the Poles? Do you have any contact with the locals?"

Robinson opened his mouth to answer, and stopped. There was something wrong; he could feel it, right on the edge of his instincts. He couldn't have explained it to her; it was just a sense that something wasn't quite right, somewhere. He had had it in Sudan, just before some refugees had brought out swords – swords, for the love of God – and started to hack apart their fellows.

"No," he said slowly. "It's very tranquil out here."

London, United Kingdom

Major-General Charles Langford stepped out of the Convent Garden Royal Opera House with the sense that, finally, something was going his way. He had always loved the opera – not the depressing and seemingly endless Wagner operas, but the light-hearted Gilbert and Sullivan operas – and going to see a properly produced version of one was delightful. *The Mikado* might have run afoul of the Race Relations Board, but the sheer torrent of protest had brought the Board to heel for once; only a handful of people could be bothered to picket the first production since the edict was repealed.

The sun was fading in the sky as he climbed into the underground train, waving his ID card at the young Pakistani manning the barrier, who glanced around and then gave Langford the finger. The temptation to report the young man was overwhelming, but Langford forced it down; it wasn't easy getting a job these days. There were times when Langford wondered if it wasn't just worth taking early retirement, or even leaving the country altogether. England was no longer what it once was...

He got off the underground– technically, over half of the network was actually above ground – and walked up the hill towards his flat. His mother had left him her house in Croydon when she died, but it was large enough for a family and Langford lived alone in Redhill, near London, but not quite part of the city. He passed a group of grieving Indians on the way, the weeping women dressed in brightly-coloured clothes, and headed out onto the hill. He was on leave, technically, even though he didn't really want to go anywhere. There was plenty of reading he wanted to catch up on, but for the moment, all he wanted to do was pace. The hill was empty; most of the young men and women who used it would have gone to the community centre, even though it was turning into a haven for crime. It was starting to look as if Britain was already dead, and men like him were only struggling against the inevitable.

Trying to banish such thoughts, he sat on the bench and looked towards the sunset. It all seemed so safe and tranquil.

Interlude One

Tick...tick...tick...

Tick...tick...tick...

They waited.

In Belarus, in Serbia, in Algeria, in Russia itself, they waited. Soldiers checked their weapons obsessively as they waited for the dawn; their commanders checked their intelligence and battle plans, some of them wondering if they would be worthy commanding officers, others, more relaxed, tried to sleep. Missile crews checked their missiles carefully, ensuring that all of them had their guidance systems locked onto their targets, hoping that nothing would go wrong at the worst possible moment. Under the waves, Russian submarines made the final GPS checks to ensure that their targeting data was up to date, while aircraft revved their engines on hundreds of runways across Russia.

Tick...tick...tick...

In the darkness of the European night, commandos moved closer to their targets, preparing their weapons for action. In every major European city, other commandos prepared their strikes, to unleash terror and destruction right across Europe. In hidden bases, human voices spoke hatred unheard since Cain murdered Abel, inciting a hatred that would soon burst out into the streets. In nondescript rooms, cyber-warriors prepared to hack into and disrupt countless computers right across Europe; the population would wake to find themselves trapped in a nightmare, from which they would never escape.

Tick...tick...tick...

Warships moved silently under the waves, closing in on their targets; Naval Infantry prepared themselves for the desperate dash across the water. Hunter-killer submarines moved closer, their targets long identified and selected; their captains waited impatiently for the countdown to reach zero. Others kept their ships well back from any risk of detection, waiting for the final moments before they moved in for the kill. They would not miss their targets; surprise would be absolute.

Tick...tick...tick...

Thousands of targets had been designated; thousands of separate acts of sabotage planned. High overhead, cold mechanical eyes peered down, refining the information now that it was too late, while other objects moved into firing position in the dark of space. The intelligence had been better than any Russian had dared to expect; the Europeans had taken almost no precautions for the first total war of the 21st Century. Europe was asleep...and by the time it awoke, it would be too late.

Tick...tick...tick...

Zero...

Chapter Ten

Cry Havoc, and Let Slip the Dogs of War, Take One

The war was bound to be merciless. Wars that begin with sneak attacks always are.
Robert A. Heinlein

London/Near London, England

"Five minutes, Captain," the young enlisted seaman said.

Captain Ilya Ivanovich Mikhalkov nodded. The *Akula-II*-class submarine *Vladimir Putin* had been lurking near England for nearly a week, waiting for the firing command, and that worried him. The *Putin* might have been one of Russia's latest submarines, designed to serve as both a hunter-killer and shore-assault ship, but he had no illusions as to its fate if a European ship stumbled across them. Technically, they were lurking in international waters, but so close to Europe, they might encounter more than just the Royal Navy. The Dutch might be military lightweights, but they had a navy, while the French were known to patrol these waters too.

He mentally reviewed the sealed orders he had been given before the nuclear-powered submarine had been sent out from its base in the north. They had been simple; head to a predetermined location, or as near as practical, and then wait. At a certain time, they were to listen for instructions; if they received the command, they were to fire their cruise missiles at the targets and return to base, sinking any European shipping they encountered along the way. If they received no command, they were to maintain radio silence and wait until they ran short of supplies; the mission would only be cancelled by shortages. There had been no provision for a recall command; it was too easy to fake.

They'd taken up position, far enough from most shipping to be fairly certain of avoiding detection, and waited. The *Putin* was a new ship, built to new specifications, and tested, but there was always something for the crew to do. The design had been vastly improved, ever since several of the class had been built for India and China; the Russians had quietly built a new one for themselves for every one they had exported to foreign buyers. Iran had bought several before the Americans had closed them down permanently; Algeria and Libya had expressed interest in purchasing some for their ambitions in the Mediterranean. He had every confidence in his ship.

Two days ago, they had received the order; a simple 'go' command and a time. They'd had their targets selected already; it had surprised him to discover that the targets were all within the English capital, London. He had assumed, at first, that they would be making a point to the British – like the new government had done from time to time by sending a Backfire or Blackjack into British airspace to remind them that they had the capability – instead…they had real orders to fire. It made him proud; a long career in the Russian Navy had finally given him a chance to fight for his country.

"Confirm our location," he ordered. The seas around them were surprisingly empty; the antenna was almost impossible to detect under normal circumstances, but he knew from the ballistic missile submarine captains that they had to be very careful. The GPS position check had to be perfect, or they might miss their targets; the die had been cast and the *Putin* would not be found wanting. "Make sure that the targets are perfectly locked."

"Targets confirmed," the weapons officer said. If anything, he was more nervous than Mikhalkov himself; the cruise missiles had been tested time and time again before they left harbour, but it was too late for them to replace a malfunctioning missile. The *Putin* carried thirty missiles in its bays, but a delay could be fatal; the British ships would come boiling out of their harbours with blood on their minds, the minute they launched the first missile. "All missiles report ready."

Mikhalkov's hand shook slightly as he pulled the key from around his neck. "I confirm that all of the targets have been locked," he said, glancing down at the display. Thirty targets glowed red in the dim light of the submarine. "Mr Exec?"

His first officer nodded. "Targets' locked, Captain," he said. There was a minute left to go. The first officer inserted his key and twisted it once. "Armed and ready."

It was not as elaborate a procedure as launching nuclear missiles from a ballistic missile submarine, but Mikhalkov knew that it was important; an accidental launch from the *Putin* could have disastrous consequences. The Russian Navy was full of stories about missiles that had accidentally been fired, or storage dumps during the bad old days following the end of the Cold War, where a single spark had triggered an explosion that set off nuclear warning sensors around the world. The Putin Government had started a long-term program for reforming and repairing the worst of the damage; the new President had completed the program. The Russian Navy was again one of the most dangerous in the world.

Mikhalkov watched as the weapons officer inserted his key and twisted it. He wanted to say something dramatic, but words failed him; he inserted his own key and turned it, activating the firing sequence. Thirty missiles, packed into tubes, ready to launch in a rapid-fire sequence. His breath was coming short as the display changed again; one single tap and the missiles would be launched.

The countdown reached zero.

"Firing," he said. He pressed the firing key and held it down for the precise number of seconds. "May God have mercy on us all."

Moments later, the first of the missiles was launched…and the war began.

There was one station in PJHQ that was manned at all times; the ballistic missile warning system. The British Government might have shared the general opinion that the threat of all-out nuclear war had ended with the Cold War, but the threat of a rogue state remained in existence. The possibility that North Korea might launch a missile towards America if the war went badly – as it might well – was ever-present, and the British government needed the most up to date information. Besides, it was at least theoretically possible for terrorists to produce homemade cruise missiles.

Captain Katy Harland was on duty when, one by one, the links to the orbiting European satellites began to go down. She instantly activated the emergency procedure, linking several other radars into the main warning network, before trying to establish what had gone wrong. The European military satellites, boosted into orbit by the ESA, had been problematic right from the start; she, like many of the other staff in PJHQ, regarded them with some suspicion, even if the ESA kept claiming that all the bugs were being worked out of the system. Moments later, alarms started to sound…

For a long moment, Katy just stared at the display; hundreds of red icons were flickering into existence. Out of habit, she glanced at the console to ensure that someone wasn't playing a training tape; it wouldn't be the first time that someone had accidentally started a training program that had been mistaken for the real thing. The new icons were appearing from the sea and being picked up by conventional radar systems, heading towards London. Entire sections of the command network were starting to fail; Katy realised that it was not a drill.

"Trigger the alert, now," she snapped.

It was a simple task, but one difficult to actually accept doing, except in drills; she hit the command and hoped that she wasn't too late. The alert command should have warned the handful of TMD batteries around London that they would be needed, but she saw now that it was too late. One of the missiles – two of the missiles – was heading right for the PJHQ. The air raid alarm was sounding and staff were beating feet towards the bomb shelter, but it was too late. There were only moments left as the supersonic missiles raced closer towards their targets.

Katy closed her eyes.

Nicholas Donavan had never quite gotten used to his position as Prime Minister. He had never seriously expected that the Liberal Democrats would become the party in power, and indeed, some of its power was only maintained through an alliance with the Greens and the Socialists. Labour might have been pretty much discredited by the failures of both Blair and Brown – the disaster in Sudan had put an end to that particular government – but the Conservatives had been going from strength to strength recently, as had the BNP. Donavan knew that the economic crisis was growing worse; people were starting to look towards the more extreme parties for government…

It didn't seem fair. Donavan had once had ideals, but government work had drained most of them out of his soul. He had had hopes of turning Britain into a truly progressive society, but Britain had proved very resistant to change; his hand had been forced or held back on dozens of occasions. He had wanted to create a land with social justice for everyone, only to discover that people wanted social justice for themselves, but not necessarily for everyone else. There were times when it seemed like the news was a constant funeral dirge for Britain; racism, sexism and worse stalked Britain's streets…

Europe didn't make matters any easier. Didn't they see, he asked himself, that Europe was the only way forward? America couldn't be depended on any more; Pakistan had learned that lesson, even after an American serviceman had raped a British girl. The world needed a counterbalance to American power, and Europe was the only real contender, but…didn't they see? It seemed as if even the Euro-Socialists didn't realise the dangers, while the other local governments were proving resistant to greater integration. A United States of Europe still seemed like a dream…

An alarm rang. He started, and then flinched as two armed men raced into his room. He opened his mouth to protest, but they grabbed him and pulled him to his feet, half-carrying him down the stairs to the stares of astonished civil servants. Donavan had been due at a meeting with the Home Secretary in an hour; the Home Secretary and the Deputy Prime Minister were in Parliament, addressing a packed house on the measures that the government intended to take to resolve the Falklands Island Crisis peacefully. Surely, if Britain gave up something…

He forced his mind back to the present. "What are you doing?"

"There's an incoming attack," one of the men said. He was one of Ten Downing Street's security staff. "We have to get you into the shelter!"

The alarm was making it hard to think. "An attack?" Donavan asked. "Who's attacking us?"

"I don't fucking know," the man snapped. Donavan didn't know who he was; in all the years of government, he had never bothered to talk to any of the security staff, viewing them as holdovers from the days when a British Prime Minister was among the top ten targets for assassination. "We got a warning that there was a cruise missile incoming and we have to get you into the bunker…"

They reached the top of the second set of stairs, leading down into the basement and the bunker below. "I can't just..." Donavan protested. His legs seemed to refuse to move; he cursed his lack of exercise even as the two guards picked him up and carried him down. "I can't...I need to talk to my family!"

"You must," the man snapped. "There's no time and we're being jammed and all hell is breaking loose..."

The first missile struck Ten Downing Street. It had been designed as a bunker-busting warhead; it punched through the façade of the normal, civilian, house and buried itself in the masonry before exploding. The blast tore through the complex, sending shockwaves down into the tunnel system and collapsing many of the tunnels; for those in the bunker, the roof caved in and crushed them before they even had a moment to know that they were dead. The second missile struck moments later; its warhead was different, a compressed fuel-air explosive mixture that detonated just before hitting the ground, sending a wave of super-hot flame blasting out across Whitehall. It was almost like being at ground zero of a nuclear detonation.

No one ever found a trace of Nicholas Donavan.

The skyscraper apartment was luxurious; Zachary Lynn loved it and so did the girls he brought back to the apartment on a fairly regular basis. He had a habit of relaxing by picking up girls in the nearby nightclubs; one of them, Faye Martin, lay on the double-bed, quite naked. Lynn would have liked to have spent more time with her, but duty called; only the cold awareness that tomorrow might be his last day on Earth had prompted him to pick up Faye. She had been a good lay, but there had been an understanding; there would be no permanent relationship.

He stared down over London and saw them coming; the first of the missiles. His hackers had gone to work already, attacking the computers that made up the most important and vulnerable part of the defence network; it looked as if they had succeeded, although the fact that the British hadn't been on war alert had certainly played a role in the success. He knew very little about the overall plan, but he did know that thirty missiles had been targeted on London...and they were coming down like rain.

The skyscraper shook as the first explosion echoed over the city. The first missiles had been targeted on government buildings; it was vitally important to kill as many government ministers as they could. The British politician was a strange beast; some of them even had the iron determination that had characterised Britain, years ago. The Houses of Parliament had been meeting to discuss the Falklands – Lynn knew that the Government would have been happy to give away the islands, if the MPs would have allowed it – and he doubted that many of them would survive the explosion and fires spreading through Whitehall. Other missiles were coming down now; the PJHQ, the various barracks scattered throughout the city, even New Scotland Yard…all of them had been targeted.

He smiled and lifted his mobile phone. It had been produced by the Americans; the British mobile phone networks were either down or about to fail, while the BBC and the independent television and radio channels had also been targeted. As London started to burn under his gaze, he sent a simple text message; *go*.

The building shook again. A sleepy voice came from the bed. "What's happening?"

"London town is falling down," Lynn said, and laughed. The chaos had only just begun. "Why don't you and me celebrate?"

The alarm had shocked Inspector David Briggs out of a doze in the rear of the mobile command post. They had deployed to set up security for a protest march later in the week, one that would have gone back to Hyde Park and the Mall; he had been tasked, again, with overseeing the procedures. He was starting to think that it was a punishment; certainly, some of his subordinates had had to help the overworked park workers clear up after the last protest. There were parts of Hyde Park that looked as if they were a rubbish dump.

He glared down at the console, wondering what the hell was going on; that code meant military emergency, but what military emergency? A terrorist attack? He knew the procedure for an attack; all units had to report in to the nearest command post, and then await orders. He hit the key transmitting their location to New Scotland Yard…and then looked up. Something had registered in his mind…and then he saw it, a streak of light crossing the sky, heading towards Westminster and Buckingham Palace. He stared, unable to quite believe his eyes, as the streak of light vanished…and moments later, an explosion shook the ground.

The door burst open. "Sir," Sergeant Harold Page snapped, "that was a fucking missile."

Briggs was already jumping out of the vehicle, service pistol in hand. "Get the engine started," he snapped, as he looked towards Westminster. He could see it now, towers of smoke reaching into the sky…and then a second string of explosions echoed out over the city. Everywhere he looked, every direction of the compass, he could see smoke and flames billowing up into the sky. The missiles…

His mind refused to grasp it. Were they at war? The last time London had been attacked by missiles had been during the Second World War; that had been nearly eighty years ago. There had been no mistaking it; there had been a missile…and there were flames coming from the direction of Ten Downing Street.

"Get us moving," he snapped. Scotland Yard hadn't responded to his signals, nor had the Disaster Recovery Centre; the implications of that didn't bear thinking about. Briggs had never considered himself a military man, but he knew something about how terrorists thought; one of their prime objectives was to cause casualties among emergency workers. If they had knocked out…

A squeal of static blasted out of one of the speakers. "I can't make any contact at all with the dispatcher," Page said. His face was very pale; his hands clutched his pistol as if it was a life-saver. Briggs remembered that Page had been courting Christine in Dispatches and silently prayed that she was all right. They had made such a cute couple. "What do we do?"

"Drive us to Whitehall," Briggs snapped. "Now!"

The streets were coming alive with panicking people; the driver hit the siren to help move them out the way. Cars had been barred from the centre of London – except emergency vehicles – for years, but it hadn't helped the remainder of the congestion problem. Buckingham Palace was all right, he realised, but Whitehall itself was burning brightly. People – policemen, guards and soldiers from the barracks, which looked to have been hit as well – were milling around; no one seemed to be in charge.

Ten Downing Street was gone…and, somehow, he had to gain control of the situation.

It all seemed so futile.

Chapter Eleven

Cry Havoc, and Let Slip the Dogs of War, Take Two

It takes two sides to make war. It only takes one side to make a massacre.
2nd *ACR, 1991, Al Samawah (attributed)*

Edinburgh, Scotland

"There's definitely no sign of pursuit," Lieutenant Sergey Ossetia said, as the white van drove off the bypass and into Sighthill. It wasn't Edinburgh's most attractive area; drab oppressive housing blocks, unimaginative smaller houses and industrial estates dominated the landscape. There were few shops in the area; the owners had discovered the joys of being regularly looted and, in some cases, physically assaulted. The economic downturn had had its effects right in the heart of Scotland's capital city; half of the buildings were boarded up and apparently closed for good. "I think we're clear."

Captain Rashid Ustinov nodded once. They had hired the white van from one of the companies that tended to the needs of immigrant workers, such as themselves. It was an old van, outdated; it said something about the state of the economy that there were plenty more like it, all utterly anonymous, on the streets. As far as the tracking device was concerned – it appeared that immigrants and the others who hired such vehicles were not trusted by the owners – they were somewhere on the other side of the city, Portobello. It made him smile; if *he* had been designing a car or a van that was intended to be impossible to *steal*, he would have made sure that the tracker was impossible to remove. A blind child could have removed the tracker that he had carefully removed and left the day before in a dustbin. It might well be found, or destroyed by the refuse department, but by then it would be too late.

"Good," he said. "Time to move on."

He had also taken the precaution of replacing the number plates and adding a design to the side of the van, but there was always the danger that the Police would notice something suspicious and pull them over. Both men were armed, of course, but a shootout with the local police wouldn't serve the interests of Russia. If the Police saw the weapon they were transporting in the rear of the van, there was no way that they would believe that they were innocent immigrants.

They had scouted the entire city, looking for the ideal spot; it was amazing just how much information was on the Internet, waiting for them to access it and confirm it over the years. Moscow would have had a fit and sent anyone who committed such vast breaches of security to the Gulags, assuming that they weren't just shot in the head to improve the breeding stock of the human race. It was harder to mount a serious terrorist operation than most people understood, but Ustinov was confident that Ossetia and himself could carry out the task. If they were lucky, they would even be able to escape before anyone realised what was happening.

An aircraft thundered overhead as they pulled into the small warehouse's parking lot. They had checked it out carefully before ever setting foot near the place; it helped that the person who had designed the area had had no imagination. People were always getting lost, even with the most up-to-date SATNAV units; naturally, the van they had hired didn't have one. They had prepared a cover story, but no one had questioned them; the warehouse had been abandoned, left open, and looted. No one had cared.

"Check out the area," he muttered.

Ossetia nodded and slipped off into the darkness of the warehouse; he had half-expected to see squatters within the warehouse, desperately hunting for a roof over their heads. He glanced back at the rear of the van, and then slipped out himself, stretching to indicate that it had been a long drive. They were both in the peak of heath, exercising regularly, but he was uncomfortably aware that they hadn't been able to do anything more than limited practice runs. Another aircraft thundered overhead, heading further over the city, as Ossetia returned; judging from its flight path, it was in a holding pattern before coming in to land.

"It's clear," Ossetia said. His voice was starting to become a little excited. "Shall we proceed?"

Ustinov climbed back into the driver's seat and drove the van closer to the main entrance. It was locked and barricaded, but some looters had damaged the locks enough to allow them to enter, carrying the weapon under a white cloth. They were committed now; they had no choice but to proceed with their mission. The warehouse was drab and empty inside; the only decoration was some graffiti of the anarchy symbol on the ground and a calendar from 2017. The images in it were banned in Russia; hardcore porn. Ustinov shrugged; the decadence of Europe had played midwife to radical Islam, the religion that had caused his mother such woe. They would pay for that.

The ladder to the roof was half-broken, but he had been through worse in Spetsnaz training, some of which had involved building a ladder in sub-zero temperatures. That had been...well, he wouldn't have called it fun, but it had certainly made life exciting. It was easy to scramble up the ladder onto the roof; Ossetia passed him the weapon quickly and followed him up, remaining low on the roof. They would probably be seen, but it would be too late by now. Something streaked across the sky from the east and headed into the centre of the city. He knew what that was.

Ossetia put it into words. "That was a missile," he said. "Sir..."

"Move," Ustinov snapped.

The weapon in his hands had a long, complicated designation, but terrorists everywhere called it the Yank, because it was the bane of American existence. The weapon had been designed by the Russians, sold to the Iranians, reverse-engineered, duplicated, and sent everywhere; it was one of the most dangerous antiaircraft missiles in existence. The Americans had countermeasures, of course, but they were almost useless on helicopters, particularly if the missile was fired at very short range. For a civilian aircraft...

He heard one approaching now. The controllers at Edinburgh Airport might not have figured out – yet – that the city was under attack. Once they did, all aircraft would be ordered away from the city, searching for non-existent safety. The sound of the missile explosion drifted across his ears; he lifted the Yank to his shoulder and peered through the sensor towards the massive 747. The latest variant on the design could hold around five hundred people – all of whom were dead. They just didn't know it yet.

The targeting sensor locked on. "Firing," he said. Ossetia had already stepped well away from the back-blast of the rocket. The missile launcher grew warm in his hands as the rocket fired, heading up towards the passenger jet. By his rough calculations, it would come down somewhere in the heart of the city, perfectly placed to spread a little terror. "Time to run!"

Both of them had worn gloves, but he took a moment to set a charge by the side of the launcher anyway, just in case. The British Police were experts at tracking down people from the slightest clue, and even though they would have some other problems to keep them busy, he knew better than to take chances. If he and Ossetia had been detected earlier, without them knowing that they had been seen, they would lead the police right back to their base.

"There," Ossetia said. Ustinov paused to look, just for a moment, as another explosion shattered the peace of the city. Even the birds had stopped singing. The aircraft was slowly spinning and falling, falling, towards the ground. "I think we succeeded."

Ustinov nodded. The best pilot in the world wouldn't have been able to save the passenger jet now. "Time to leave," he snapped. They fled to their van, leaving the charge behind on a short timer as the aircraft crashed into the city with a thunderous roar. As he put the van in gear and fled the area, he smiled; whatever happened, life in the city would never be the same again.

Silence fell.

Hazel had been walking through Princes Street Gardens, contemplating the news she had received from the doctor's office. It was the best news she could have hoped for; only the fact that her husband had the right to know first had prevented her calling her father. She was happy, and content...and then an explosion had shattered the tranquillity of the city. She had spent long enough around the army to know that it was a bomb that had detonated; as she turned to look, she could see smoke and flames rising from Holyrood, where the Scottish Parliament was in session.

A second noise split the air…and then she saw it. There had been an aircraft flying over the city, one of dozens that passed overhead every day, despite the chorus of complaints from the citizens. It took her a moment to understand as smoke and flame began to billow from the rear of the aircraft, and then it started to plummet. She watched, her mouth a wide 'O' of shock, as the aircraft came down, lower and lower until it smashed into New Town. On instinct, Hazel threw herself to the ground, covering her head as the shockwave blasted over her head, thanking God that she had some shelter in the Gardens. Others wouldn't be so lucky; she could see chunks of buildings flying past overhead.

It was the screams that brought her back to herself; she realised that she had been in a mild state of shock. The entire face of Princes Street was on fire, flames licking up and consuming the people who were trying to escape the carnage. There were thousands of people in the city for the shopping; what would happen to them in the fire? Hazel was sure that it wouldn't be anything good. She placed one hand over her chest as a line of cars, illegally parked in defiance of the local government, detonated one after the other as the flames reached their fuel tanks; the wave of heat reached out towards her, almost hypnotising her as she stared.

"Get the hell out of the way, you stupid bitch," a policeman shouted, as he pushed her back. "The entire city is going to burn down!"

The Police seemed to be just as disorganised as anyone else; the regular patrols of Princes Street, in the vain hope of cutting down street crime against the tourists, were utterly unsuited to the task of trying to put out the fires. She could hear fire engines in the distance, but the power seemed to be failing; the lights in Old Town had failed.

Hazel got the message and practically ran up the Mound, into Old Town. The panic was everywhere, with teenagers and older people screaming as they poured onto the streets, trying to get away from the terribly hungry monster that had appeared in the middle of Edinburgh. A handful of soldiers – Royal Highland Fusiliers, she recalled from her husband's grumbling about overpaid fancy dress soldiers – were coming down from the Castle, trying to help maintain order, but only adding to the chaos. No one seemed to be in control; she fled further away, towards the Meadows.

"Fucking Muslims," someone was shouting, perhaps jumping to a conclusion that Hazel found impossible to dispute. Who else, but Islamic fanatics, would have done something like that to their beloved city? "Burn the Mosque!"

The younger elements of the crowd surged towards the Mosque; Hazel pushed and shoved and broke free of the mob, trying to escape towards Tollcross. She could hear the noise of fire engines now; she had never been so pleased to see the red fire engines as they made their way onto the bridge, trying to reach the site of the airplane crash. Water hissed as the firemen tried to use their hoses to disperse the crowd, the crowd blocking their passage to the fire. Hazel fled into the Meadows and tried, hard, to catch her breath.

A hand caught at her bra strap. "It's the end of the world," a voice said, drunkenly. He was a typical down-and-out; his breath almost made Hazel gag. "Wanna party?"

The drunkard's hand was reaching into her bosom. The feeling brought her back to full awareness. "No," she said, and brought her knee up hard. The drunkard bent over, gasping in pain, and she kicked him as hard as she could in the side, sending him crashing to the ground. He was a pathetic sight; the thought of him trying to force her legs open sent a wave of fury through her and she kicked him in the head. "Go fuck yourself!"

She fled towards her home. The flames didn't look as if they were going out quickly; the streets were packed with people trying to escape. She reached for her phone, to call her father, and…nothing. There was no signal at all. She had one of the Thande Phones, which had access to several different networks, but none of them seemed to be working. The shock almost brought her to her knees; it was all she could do to keep walking, step by step, until she was back home. As soon as she was home, she went into the shower to wash; she could still feel his touch.

Halfway through the shower, the water failed; moments later, so did the power.

Although the drivers of the two vans didn't know it, their timing had been based on the timing of the first missile to enter visual range of Edinburgh. They wouldn't have cared if they had known; they had planned the operation on the basis of sacrificing their own lives for the cause. Survival was not an issue; the drivers had been through years of training in the most brutal region of Russia to ensure that when the time came, they died for a reason. The vans made their way from where they had been waiting, in a Tesco car park, and headed into Colinton, towards the barracks. There were several minutes between the two vans; that, too, had been planned.

Corporal Max Weinberg was feeling exposed in the guardhouse. He knew, of course, that there was a reaction team in the barracks themselves, but the threat of a terrorist attack against the barracks had been judged to be minimal. Despite public belief, many of Britain's high value targets, such as nuclear power plants, were very well guarded; several would-be terrorists had been caught and arrested trying to break into them under the impression that a fake ID was enough. The barracks, full of armed and very dangerous men, could normally look after themselves.

The base CO had triggered the alarms as soon as the first missile had appeared over the city; Weinberg had thought it was a drill at first until the CO had warned everyone that someone had fired at least one missile into Edinburgh...and then the airliner had come down. Weinberg himself had been born in Glasgow and felt more than a little disdain for Edinburgh, particularly during football season, but he wanted to find the people who had shot down an airliner and do horrible things to them. His stepfather had beaten social responsibility into him, turning him from a teenaged tearaway to a young soldier with a promising career ahead of him; he would do anything rather than let the old man down. He had fought in the Gulf; Weinberg himself had never seen action.

It was strange; he could see soldiers being lined up for emergency dispatch to help the handful of soldiers based at Edinburgh Castle on the inside, and outside everything was proceeding as normal. Weapons and emergency kits were being issued on the inside; the cars and buses were running as normal on the outside. It was almost eerie, unreal; had anyone really expected to be attacked in Edinburgh? The city hadn't had a terrorist attack since the Scottish Liberation Army had managed to blow themselves up while trying to build a bomb. There was even a delivery van coming to make its regular delivery of supplies to the barracks.

Weinberg stepped forward as the van turned into the gate. The driver seemed different, more intent, but he put that down to nerves. It was a different man from normal, but the company kept rotating their staff to avoid having to pay any benefits; Weinberg sympathised with them. The British Army did the same thing; the Generals and other senior officers got fat bonuses, the common infantryman got peanuts. It just didn't seem right.

"You can't stop here today," he called, as the driver looked at him. There was something in his expression that Weinberg really didn't like. His senses were warning him that there was trouble here; carefully, he prepared his rifle so that he could bring it up within seconds. "There's been an accident."

"*Allah Ackbar*," the driver said. Weinberg felt his blood run cold. This wasn't just trouble, it was a suicide attack! He hit the emergency button on his radio as the driver leered at him. "Long live the *Jihad*!"

Weinberg was still bringing up his rifle when the bomb detonated. He was atomised instantly and the blast tossed hundreds of infantrymen into the air, killing or seriously wounding those unlucky enough to be caught in the open. The second van drove into the barracks and headed directly for the main building; this time, soldiers managed to open fire and kill the driver, unaware that there was a dead man's switch on the bomb. Moments after the driver died, the bomb detonated and shattered the remains of the main building, killing and disorientating hundreds more young soldiers.

It was only the beginning.

Chapter Twelve

Cry Havoc, and Let Slip the Dogs of War, Take Three

[The Race Relations Bill] is the means of showing that the immigrant communities can organise to consolidate their members, to agitate and campaign against their fellow citizens, and to overawe and dominate the rest with the legal weapons which the ignorant and the ill-informed have provided. As I look ahead, I am filled with foreboding. Like the Roman, I seem to see 'the River Tiber foaming with much blood.'
Enoch Powell

Manchester, United Kingdom

Darren Cooper *hated* Pakistanis.

It was all the more curious that Cooper had never spent much time with any Pakistani – or Indian, or Bangladesh, or indeed any Asian at all – before developing this hatred. Like many British, he had rarely socialised with any outside school, but his history with them had already been set in stone. Darren Cooper had lost his father to one.

He remembered it as he drove though the streets, looking for their target. His father had been a policeman, back when that had been a respected profession; the young Darren had idealised his father. He had only vague memories of him now; a tall man who had had a beard and a smile and loved his only son. When Cooper had been seven years old, and preparing to go to school, his father had gone into an Asian household with his partner. It hadn't been anything, but routine; no one had expected trouble.

There had been different accounts of what had actually happened, but Cooper knew which one he believed. As Cooper Senior asked questions, his partner had stumbled over something, evidence of terrorist or small-scale criminal activity. Even then, a drug smuggler would be very unlucky to get more than a few years in prison; terrorists had been sucking money in from the Social Services while plotting the downfall of British civilisation. One of the inhabitants of the house had leapt at him and stabbed him; Cooper Senior had tried to restrain him, sending the attacker reeling to the floor, where he bashed his head against the ground. It had killed him.

Cooper had been too young to understand just what had happened then. The incident had shocked the area; Cooper Senior had become the scapegoat for the charge of police brutality, cut loose from all of the backing he had had a right to expect from his superiors. They had wanted to appease the Asian vote and so Cooper Senior had been stripped of rank, hauled before a kangaroo court and convicted of manslaughter. He hadn't lasted a month in jail before one of the other inmates had cut his throat in a gruesome revenge killing; Cooper Senior had taken his job seriously.

"Yes, this is the place," he muttered, as the seven of them reached their target. He glanced at his watch; like all of the members of 'rent-a-mob,' insofar as it had members, he had synchronised it with the other watches. "Get ready."

Cooper had grown up a marked man. Already predisposed to hate Asians – although his first girlfriend had been as black as the night – he had swiftly converted that hatred into an all-encompassing hatred of Islam. It was easy for him to see how Islam was devoted to taking over the world; it never occurred to him that young Muslim men had similarly deluded views about the western world. With poor grades in school, only the determination of the Labour Government that every child had a university education had ensured him a place in Manchester University; there, he had seen more signs of infiltration and the subversion of British values, as defined by his father, who had done his duty, by Muslims. He was literally incapable of seeing the world though a clear lens.

He remembered, as they checked their weapons, his stepfather. The man had been all glitz and nonsense at first sight, but he had learned quickly; his mother's husband – it was impossible to think of him as 'dad' – was one of the leading lights of the National Front. Cooper had gravitated towards the National Front with glee; he had few prospects and fewer skills, apart from cracking heads. He might have a university degree that was almost worthless – degrees had become more and more worthless every year – but his taste for violence was almost insatiable. Only the belief that the Army, too, had been perverted by Islam had prevented him signing up; as it was, by twenty years of age, he had a string of assault charges to his name, mainly racist attacks.

His stepfather had beaten him, then; the first time in his life that anyone had dared to raise a hand to him. The ease of his defeat when he had tried to fight had shocked him, as had the cold precise lecture; random violence helped no one and only gave the police, who were no longer the shining paragons they had been when his father was alive, an excuse to clamp down on the National Front. Instead, Cooper had been assured that he would have a chance to shine; once he had been introduced to Baz Falkland, he had seen that day coming soon.

He glanced down at his watch again. No one was quite sure who had come up with the idea of 'rent-a-mob,' but the idea was simple and almost impossible to prevent. At a given time, people who wanted to earn some easy cash – and with unemployment running higher than ever, there were plenty of them – would riot in a given area. The organisers would send them along to their targets, be it a protest march, a football match, or even a police station holding a prisoner who needed sprung…and any fines would be paid afterwards. The police hated it, of course, but between the Internet and mobile phones, it had been almost impossible to shut down. Falkland had told him that it was quite possible that the originators of the idea were already behind bars, but as a network, someone else had merely taken over the reins. Some of the non-BNP members would have fairly simple jobs; rioting in front of every police station in Manchester. By the time the police clamped down, it would be too late.

"The thing about the system, any system, is that it relies upon the consent or the silence of the majority," Falkland had said. "We are merely going to make the majority aware of just what has been happening under their noses."

"Now," he said. The seven young men got out of the van. They all looked violent, even though the most dangerous person Cooper had met looked soft and harmless; they would be counting on their appearance deterring interference until it was too late. The building that rose up in front of them was the rear of a Mosque, but a special Mosque; it had been built from donations from Manchester Muslims alone. They were proud of it; as far as Cooper was concerned, it was something alien in the fabric of British civilisation. The handful of people sitting outside saw them and drew away; three young Muslims stepped forward, carrying staves as if they had watched too many ninja movies in their youths.

"You can't come in here," the leader said. Cooper could hear the nervousness in his voice, confronted with serious opposition for the first time; he knew what those young men did to people who they caught alone. A girl had been beaten to death for daring to sleep with a man outside marriage. He would have liked nothing better than to take the young man on and kick his arse, but there was no time. "The Police are being called..."

Cooper had been told that the telephone networks would go down, but he had also been told to move as quickly as possible. He lifted the small pistol out of his pocket, remembering how his stepfather had hammered weapons care and safety into his mind, and shot the young man through the head. Red blood stained a spotless white robe as Muslim women started to howl; the other two were shot down before they could react. It was the work of a moment to smash one of the Mosque's windows and toss in the fuel; a second moment and the detonator was in as well, triggering the fuel into a fire that would be unstoppable unless it was extinguished quickly...and one of the 'rent-a-mob' groups was blocking the nearest fire station. Flames started to roar upwards as Cooper fired a shot into the leg of a Muslim woman, and then jumped back in the van, charging away from the Mosque and back into the streets of Manchester.

He laughed aloud. For the first time since...well, ever, he felt in control of his life.

One of his friends leered at him. "Fancy a bite to eat?"

Cooper chuckled. "Yes, but none of that foreign muck," he said. He was coming down off the high now; he wanted nothing more than to wisecrack until he felt more himself again, then go out and do it all over again. "Give me a pizza or a curry any day."

They laughed again.

Her name was Khadijah, named for the first wife of the Prophet Muhammad, Khadijah bint Khuwailid. Like many other young Muslim girls, she walked the line between religion and society, even though it was harder to walk the line these days. Khadijah, like many others, knew the terrifying stories of womenfolk killed by men for being insufficiently Islamic; secretly, she knew that there would come a time when she would have to choose between her family and her planned career. She wanted to be an air hostess, something that would be sure to excite disapproval in the community. It just wasn't fair.

Khadijah was a believer, in her own way, although nothing short of perfect submission would have pleased some of the men in her family. She was also intelligent and knowledgeable; whenever they protested at her spending time learning as much as she could about Islam, she was able to ensure that she had a piece of learning on her lips that would justify her search for knowledge. Her father's support was important, but she had that; he had been hoping that one of her brothers would become an imam, but they were all wastrels as far as Khadijah was concerned. They seemed to spend their time lounging around at home doing nothing; if they had been asked to do something, they would have agreed and then simply not bothered to do it. Her father had had to come to terms with the possibility that Khadijah might be the only one in the next generation with any Islamic knowledge at all.

And she loved the library in the Mosque. She could read nine different languages, mainly Asian ones, but she had taught herself some of the variants of Arabic just so that she could read some of the books and documents from Africa. The Mosque librarian, a man old enough to be her great-grandfather – and who looked old enough to be her great-great-grandfather – had been puzzled by the girl who came every day after noon prayers to read, but as no true Muslim would ever seek to put barriers in the way of anyone learning about Islam, he said nothing. If he disapproved, he kept it to himself; the handful of young men who tried to chat with her soon fell afoul of his cold stare and disapproving eyes.

It was almost as good as having a proper chaperone. The librarian didn't make eyes at her and couldn't have done anything even if she had acted shamelessly in front of him...not that she would have done such a thing, of course. She was a virgin and proud of it.

The noise of the van didn't bother Khadijah, but the first shot had her jumping up in shock, her headscarf almost becoming tangled in the chair before she wrapped it back around her hair. There was an art to wearing a headscarf and Khadijah had never quite managed to master it. The windows were set high in the room, but she was able to see one of the bodies falling backwards, one of the young men who were appointed to guard the Mosque from criminals. She opened her mouth to scream, staring helplessly as a skinhead white youth smashed one of the windows and poured some clear liquid inside, and then dropped something in the liquid. The smell of fuel made her dizzy…and then she realised what was about to happen. The smell was petrol and it was about to catch fire; she had seen enough movies to know what would happen then…

"Get back," the librarian snapped. A strong arm yanked her back as something sparked and the rear of the library burst into flame. Khadijah watched in horror as the fires spread throughout the library, burning books and pamphlets alike; microfilms, cassette tapes, videos and DVDs added their smells to the air as the fire consumed them faster than seemed possible. "You have to get out of here."

Khadijah couldn't face it. "Help me move the books," she screamed at him. There were copies of the Qur'an there; cheap ones, but still the holy words of Allah. They could not be destroyed. They must not be destroyed. Her rage gave her strength; she pulled at a bookcase and felt it shift, moving backwards and bringing the fire with it. She screamed again, in rage and hatred, as the fires danced towards her; the smell was making her faint and confused. She was trying to take books off the shelves, tearing off her scarf to carry them in; she expected to wake up any moment and discover that she had been studying too hard. Her eyes were starting to tear up as the heat rose still higher; she was finding it harder and harder to think…

A hand pulled at her and she went down. "Stay down," the librarian hissed. She realised with a shock, almost with a giggle, that his beard was on fire. She reached out, greatly daring, and swatted at it; he snorted and pulled her forward on her hands and knees towards the door, forcing it open through sheer force of will. "Khadijah; you're burning!"

She felt it then, just at the same time; a wave of burning pain on her thighs. Her eyes were still stinging, but she could see it now; her dress had caught on fire. She had once wanted to wear tight jeans; for the first time in her life, she thanked Allah for the Mosque's strict dress code. Jeans would have had her own body ablaze instead of her dress; she tore at it, forgetting modesty, only to be surprised when the librarian grabbed her and forced her to roll on the ground, putting out the fires. The remainder of the fire was still blazing; it struck her suddenly that she couldn't hear the fire alarm. She should have been able to hear it.

No one had come to help them, she realised; the librarian was puffing and gasping for air. It wouldn't be long before the fire brought down the Mosque and they were still trapped inside the Mosque; they had to get out and the side doors were bound to be blocked. She pulled the librarian to his feet – she realised, for the first time, that he was an old man – and they staggered off towards the men's section of the Mosque. It was the only way out…and it was locked. She banged at it, too tired and weak to scream again…and it opened, a worried dark face peering at her. Strong arms took her and the librarian and carefully carried her out of the Mosque; she wanted, desperately, to save the rest of the books. A pair of hands passed her a cup of water and she sipped it gratefully; she felt like collapsing as she stared at the Mosque.

It had been built by the resources of the community, trying to escape the flow of poison money from the Middle East. More and more people were boiling out of the houses…men only, she noticed; some of them were carrying makeshift weapons. They were all staring at the Mosque as the flames grew higher…and then the dome caved in, crashing down on the prayer rooms, crashing down on the washing rooms…and crashing down on the library, where she had enjoyed so many days.

A young man came over to her. She saw his eyes and his beard and just knew that he was going to be trouble. She almost mouthed his words along with him. It would be something insanely ridiculous in the face of the disaster that had just overtaken the community, something so banal as to almost be foolish.

She was right. "Where's your headscarf?"

The librarian cut loose with a hideous torrent of Arabic, mixed with coughs and gasps for breath, including several words that her father would have beaten her brother for using. The young man, clearly an Arab himself, paled, muttered apologies too softly for her to hear most of the words, and fled to one of the groups of young men who had gathered with weapons. She could hear some of their conversation, calling for *Jihad*, calling for war…and reminding everyone that neither the Police nor the Fire Brigade had come to help them. Everyone knew some of the attackers, people known for hating them...and they had to pay.

"Khadijah," a voice called. It was her father, coming running from their house, sweat running down his face. It was almost worth the pain in her chest to see the fear on his face at what had nearly happened to his daughter. The young man protested to him and he quelled him with a glare, all of his attention on Khadijah. "Are you all right?"

The young men were marching off now, heading towards one of the poorer parts of Manchester, carrying their weapons in hand. They would attack the whites themselves, or perhaps they would just attack a church or a Hindu Temple or something that would only make the violence worse. Khadijah had read enough extremist propaganda, even the fearsome *Turner Diaries*-like *Aisha of Arabia*, to know what would happen and what would result. People would die...

Lots of people would die.

Khadijah put her head in her hands and wept.

Chapter Thirteen

Cry Havoc, and Let Slip the Dogs of War, Take Four

The curious fact about British preparations for total war is that the British Government has never seen fit to share any such information with the people who voted it into power. Such attempts as there have been in informing the public have always been of the 'there, there, it won't be that bad' category, rather than the facts. The blunt truth is that the problem was insolvable.
Unnamed Commenter

London, United Kingdom

Major-General Charles Langford tossed aside a Police report on the spread of illegal copies of *Aisha of Arabia* and threw himself to the ground, away from the windows, before his thinking mind quite caught up with what was going on. He hit the ground hard enough to hurt, cursing himself before the noise of the first explosion echoed out over the area. More explosions, fainter, followed; he realised dimly that he had heard the noise of a cruise missile passing overhead. It was absurd…and it had happened; instincts that had kept him alive in Iraq were warning him that something was very badly wrong.

"It's not bloody likely that I personally am the target," he growled, as the lights failed. There was a major transformer station nearby, something to do with the power supplies for the city; it was quite possible that it had been the target nearby, or one of the barracks, or the TA base, or…his mind caught up with his thoughts and realised, with horror, that London was under attack. The building shook violently as another explosion, far too close for comfort, echoed out in the distance. "What the hell is going on?"

Soldiers were trained to seize the initiative; it had been the goal of NATO, before NATO had passed away into the ashcan of history, to overcome Warsaw Pact's numerical superiority with better trained and better equipped soldiers.

Langford knew that his leave had just been cancelled; even if he was wrong and it was just – *just* – an unusually dangerous terrorist attack, he would have duties. He snatched at his military-issue mobile phone as he came up to the window, looking south towards the London skyline. It was like something out of a nightmare; he could see flames and smoke rising up into the distance, some of them alarmingly large. He did a quick mental comparison; unless he was very much mistaken, some of the missiles had come down in Whitehall, where the…

The Prime Minister! He realised. The thought was almost impossible to grasp; only one major world leader had been assassinated since 2009, when the leader of the French National Front had been shot down in the streets by a rogue Algerian. A single cruise missile might have been a terrorist attack, but so many meant only one thing; they were at war.

Britain was at war.

Training asserted itself and he tapped a command into the mobile phone. It took him a second to realise that there was no signal; the phone had power, but there seemed to be no signal at all. Sheer disbelief held him for a heartbeat – he had overseen the improvements to the military communications network himself and knew how robust it was – and then training swept it away. He switched to a civilian network, and then another, and then another. Nothing.

"This is impossible," he muttered, too stunned to focus properly. The British Army taught skills like adapting quickly, but most of the time, soldiers had some idea of what was going on. Britain had been plunged into war…and he didn't even know who they were fighting! Was there any resistance at all? A billowing explosion rose up from the rough direction of Regent's Park and he cursed; were they in the grip of a mass insurgency? "I don't know…"

He dived into the kitchen and opened a cabinet, carefully opening a second, secure cabinet inside the first one, removing a pistol, an assault rifle and several rounds of ammunition. The military insisted on soldiers having some weapons with them, or at least within easy reach; it was one of those precautions that never made the news under most circumstances. He chambered a round, and placed the pistol carefully in his holster; the assault rifle he slung across his back, before picking up the radio and activating it. The battery, much to his private relief, was full; it was a court-martial offence to allow it to slip below one-third power.

"Home One, this is Hercules Grytpype-Thynne," he said, using the radio call sign that had been assigned to him when he took on the role of Chief of the Joint Staff. "Are you receiving me? Over."

A screech of static answered his words. *Jammed,* he realised, feeling cold. The Americans might have developed powerful jamming equipment, but it had only a limited range; that meant that the unknown attackers had to have a base somewhere on English soil. Even if it was in France or the Netherlands, the range wouldn't be enough to be effective…who the hell was it? He was sure, now, that his country was at war…and he didn't know…

"No point in staying here," he snapped, and headed out of the flat, locking it behind him. Some of the other residents saw his weapons and turned very pale, others demanded advice, or instructions. They knew who he was, or at least that he worked for the Army, but Langford didn't even know what to tell himself, let alone them.

"Stay in your flats, lock the doors, and listen for broadcasts," he snapped finally. He heard, in the distance, a rattle of gunfire; he didn't recognise the precise weapon. "For God's sake, stay off the streets!"

He ran up the stairs, trying to reach the top; the landlord had locked the door permanently after one of the resident's daughters had been caught sunbathing in the nude. Langford hadn't understood it, until he had seen the landlord's wife; she would never have allowed her husband to spend his time ogling a teenage girl, even if she did look lovely in the nearly-altogether. A swift kick brought the door down and he burst through…to see a scene from hell.

London was burning. There were at least seven columns of smoke rising into the air, one of them clearly coming from the Docklands, where – if he recalled correctly – there had been a Russian LNG tanker stuck while strikers fought over their rates of pay or something. He hadn't been paying attention at the time…and he remembered, suddenly, what a bunch of Saudi terrorists had done to Oakland. An aircraft zoomed into view suddenly, one jet fighter, heading towards the south. There seemed to be no other aircraft in sight.

"That can't be right," he said, grimly. The scene was one of unimaginable horror. Whichever way he looked, he saw fires. There were normally at least a dozen aircraft stacked up over Heathrow and Gatwick; PJHQ had been becoming increasingly worried about the chances of an accident for years. The lone jet fighter up there might have a link into MILNET…or he or she might be trapped in the sky, unable to communicate with the ground. It looked as if there was nothing to do, but walk to the PJHQ, or at least the local police station and try to find out what was going on. "I wonder…"

He looked down at his mobile phone again, flicking through the different options. There should be an option…*wait*; had he seen a signal? Heart pounding, he flicked back…and saw it, a signal on the military network, very faint, but there. He lifted the phone and selected the emergency option; the call should be routed at once to the emergency control centre at PJHQ.

There was a long delay…and then a voice answered. Young, female, and terrified. "State your name, rank and identity number," she said. The fear underlying her voice made her sound on edge. "I repeat…"

"Major-General Charles Langford, Chief of Joint Operations," Langford said, and recited his serial number. "I request a situation brief."

"One moment," the girl said. He heard, very briefly, another voice in the background. Langford had good ears, but it was hard to pick out voices in the faint signals. "I need a voiceprint check; recite the standard rhyme."

Something had to be really wrong, Langford realised. He forced himself to remember the normal choice of words. "Peter Piper picked a peck of pickled peppers; a peck of pickled peppers Peter Piper picked. If Peter Piper picked a peck of pickled peppers, where's the peck of pickled peppers Peter Piper picked?"

He paused. The routine had always struck him as silly. "Now; identify yourself."

"This is Captain Erica Yuppie," a new voice said. She sounded a lot more assured than the first voice, and clearly was much more in control of the situation. "Sir, we need to arrange a pick-up for you; please can you give me your location?"

"Of course," Langford said, and gave his address. There was another hail of gunfire, mercifully brief, over the city. It sounded as if there was a war going on out there. "What the hell is going on?"

"I have dispatched a helicopter to pick you up," Erica said, without answering his question. "It should be there in five minutes."

Langford scowled as the connection broke. Erica had sounded as if she had known what she was doing, but it was hard, looking out over the city, to feel any confidence at all in the future. A helicopter that close suggested that it would be coming from one of the barracks, or perhaps the emergency vehicles at Buckingham Palace; just for a moment, he wished for a pair of binoculars he could use to check if the Palace was still standing. He would have given his right arm to know if it was still standing, a reminder of happier times, or even…

In just under five minutes, a small helicopter – a generic civilian model used by rich kids mainly - hovered into view, hanging just above the roof and allowing Langford a moment to scramble onboard before it rose up above the city and headed north, away from London. Langford was so relieved to see the helicopter, proof that someone, somewhere, was responding to the…crisis… that it took him a moment to realise and protest.

"Flying Officer," he snapped, "where are we going?"

"We're going to the command centre," the pilot said. Langford looked back at the looming towers of smoke; London had millions of people living within the city, and all of them would be caught up in a nightmare. "The Major will brief you when we arrive."

They passed the remainder of the flight in silence, waiting for the journey to end; finally, they came down over a small industrial estate. There was little remarkable about it, right on the edge of London's outlying suburbs, but Langford noticed with some surprise that the entire estate looked as if it had been sealed up tight. It was dotted with antenna and satellite dishes, not unusual in a corporate paradise, but odd to see them in such numbers. The helipad itself was well-concealed; no one looking in with binoculars would be able to see them as they disembarked.

"Right this way," the pilot said, as he shut down the helicopter. He led the way into an empty warehouse, seemingly innocent, but Langford could see traces of oil on the floor and an open door up ahead, leading to stairs, which led down into the ground. "This is as far as Her Nibs will allow me to go."

"Sorry, Landie, but you're not cleared for the remainder of this," a female voice said. "Major-General, welcome to the Classified Joint Headquarters."

Langford shook her hand automatically. Captain Erica Yuppie – if that was who it was – reminded him of Tasha Yar; she was tall, had short blonde hair, and a body that looked deceitfully slight. Her handshake was firm and her blue eyes cold and hard, with only a hint of betraying grimness under the dispassion. Langford wanted to know more; something that could shake a lady like Erica Yuppie was obviously worrying.

"Thank you," he said, automatically, as she led the way into a small conference room. "What is this place?"

To give Erica her due, she didn't seem put out or surprised by the question. "This is the Classified Joint Headquarters," she said. She altered her voice slightly; reciting from memory. "To provide emergency command and control for British forces in the event of a major outrage in the United Kingdom, generally expected to be the Big One; a terrorist nuclear attack. Crew; fifty, commanded by an officer on the reserve list. Status; permanently on stand-by, ready to take over if there is a major interruption of command and control for global military operations."

She smiled, rather thinly. "Or at least that's the theory."

Langford nodded. "How come I never heard about this place?"

"Security," Erica said. "There are roughly sixty people who know about the existence of this place since it was set up in 2018; you may remember that there was a major nuclear threat at the time, from Pakistani nukes. One possible target was London and it occurred to the then Prime Minister that if London was taken out, there would need to be both a command centre nearby – that's here – and another one somewhere out in the country. This place was set up later that year and has continued to run silently until now."

"Very clever," Langford said. "Captain...what the hell is going on?"

Erica's face became grimmer. "I think that you need to hear it directly from the horse's mouth," she said. She picked up an internal phone and spoke without dialling a number. "Lieutenant Sargon, report to the main briefing room."

She turned to Langford. "Lieutenant Aaron Sargon is one of my best analysts," she said. "Like me, technically, he's on the reserve list..."

"And you're more than a Captain," Langford realised. "What is your actual rank?"

"Major," Erica said shortly. "I have the pay and responsibilities of a Major; the rank and uniform of a Captain. There aren't enough Majors for one to vanish without exciting attention."

Langford felt a sudden moment of sympathy for her, mounting her lonely vigil for years over London and the United Kingdom. The door opened, revealing a vaguely oriental-looking young man, slightly overweight by army standards. Headquarters staff officers normally were slightly out of shape. He had short dark hair, a friendly face, but one that was creased with worry.

"General," he said, saluting. "I don't have a proper briefing prepared..."

"Never mind the PowerPoint presentation," Langford snapped. In his opinion, PowerPoint and other programs like it were the worst thing that had ever happened to the military. The security bugs could have been handled, but for sheer confident irritation, it was hard to beat PowerPoint and the other Microsoft products. "Just give me the bad news."

"We maintain a direct feed from MILNET – the PJHQ, the UKADR and so on – into here," Sargon said. "At roughly 1000, the MILNET links started to fail, starting with the European satellites that were supposed to provide us 24/7 coverage of Europe, and continuing with a handful of our own dedicated servers, which came under cyber attack. At the last moment, some of them reported signs of multiple missile launches from home waters, but the system failed before a perfect response could be generated. Ground-based radars, part of the UKADGE, attempted to engage the missiles, but absent the precise targeting details, it was impossible to generate an intercept solution in time. Around – we don't know for certain – three hundred missiles were launched in positions that suggested that we – Britain – were the targets."

"Dear God," Langford breathed. "Who the hell is doing this to us?"

"It's impossible to be certain as yet, but preliminary information suggests that it is the Russians," Sargon said. "They and the Americans are the only people who might have the capability to do this...and, from rather garbled transmissions from France, it seems that we weren't the only ones hit. As far as we know, sir, Ireland wasn't hit, but our communications links are badly fractured and we have only limited contact with our own bases..."

"God damn the EU," Langford swore. He – and almost every other commissioned officer in Europe – had argued against putting all of their eggs in one basket. "That system was meant to be foolproof!"

"There are some very smart fools out there," Sargon said, seriously. He learned forwards. "At least ten missiles came down in London, sir; two of them hit Ten Downing Street and devastated the area. Westminster also appears to have been hit, along with Albany Street Barracks and Cavalry Barracks, where we had infantry soldiers based. We should have a direct line here to Aldershot…and that, too, is gone. We haven't been able to locate the source of the jamming yet – we need to triangulate and our non-radio communications are in tatters – but the reports from Flying Officer Jackson suggest…that we are looking at a total loss."

Langford felt his knees buckle. "There was that session in Parliament today," he breathed. "The Whips were going around saying that they had to go to Parliament, even if they went on their deathbeds; illness wasn't an excuse. They were going to debate the Falklands…"

"Yes, sir," Erica said. "It is quite possible that the Prime Minister and everyone in the line of succession is dead."

Langford swore under his breath. "And the PJHQ?"

"Hit," Sargon said. "Again, it was a bunker-busting weapon, from preliminary reports. The building has certainly been rendered useless."

Langford stood up and paced. "What the hell do we do now?"

Erica looked at him. "Under the emergency protocols, when the country is at war, command of the military and local government devolves upon the senior military officer alive," she said, sternly. The protocols were developed with nuclear war in mind, where the local garrison commanders would work under the local commissioners…something that had slipped since the end of the Cold War, but never mind…and they had never been revoked. Democracy simply didn't get a look in during the planning for total war.

"You, sir, are the senior surviving military officer…and, as such, the powers of government devolve upon you."

Chapter Fourteen

Picking Up The Pieces, Take One

Hitler expects to terrorise and cow the people of this mighty city…Little does he know the spirit of the British nation, or the tough fibre of the Londoners.
Winston Churchill

London, England

"There's nothing on the bands," Sergeant Harold Page said. "Even the BBC seems to have gone off the air."

"I see," Briggs said. "Stay here."

He hopped out of the mobile command post and glanced around. The scene was chaotic; policemen, bodyguards, a handful of survivors from the outskirts of Whitehall and soldiers were milling around, some of them carrying weapons and looking nervous. No one seemed to be in command and, judging from the jamming on the airwaves, no one would have the slightest idea just what had happened. If he hadn't seen the missile, Briggs would have thought that there had been a bomb, or even a gas leak.

He unhooked the whistle from his belt and blew it, loudly. Heads turned to him as he clambered up on a piece of debris; it looked as if it had come from Downing Street. The thought depressed him, even as he saw the eyes of everyone turning to him, looking for instructions or advice. People needed advice in an emergency zone, even soldiers; they needed someone to present a clear threat before training took over.

"I am Inspector Dave Briggs," he said, loudly enough to be heard over the roar of the fires. A distant crackle of gunfire made them all jump; the passage of a jet fighter high overhead drew their eyes skyward. The soldiers clutched their weapons more tightly; the policemen and civilians gave them uneasy looks. Briggs remembered the loudspeaker on the mobile command post and checked his radio. At such range, he could use it even through the jamming.

"In the absence of any contact with higher command" – ignoring the fact that they were standing on the ruins of the highest command in Britain – "I am assuming command of the disaster scene."

The relief in their eyes was not reassuring. "We have to tend to survivors, put out those fires, and work out just what in hell happened here," he said. It was a missile attack, but that meant that someone had had to fire the missile... and he didn't think that terrorists could do that. They were at war. "Policemen, I want you to seal the area completely; move all civilians to Hyde Park or somewhere else out of the way; where is the nearest emergency store of fire-fighting equipment?"

One of the guards raised his hand, almost as if they were at school. "There's a set of hoses down near the river," he said. "It may have survived the blast."

Briggs was improvising and knew it. "Good," he said. He nodded to three Privates who were standing there, looking as if they were desperate for something to do. "You three; go with him and find out what the status of the equipment is." He glanced over at the civilians. "Is there anyone here with medical training?"

Several more hands were raised. "Good," Briggs said. The trick was to look as if he knew what he was doing. "I want you to tend to any injured that we bring out of the building. There's some medical supplies in the mobile command centre and there should be some ambulances and several fire engines along in a moment."

He took a breath as the policemen headed off to carry out his orders. "Who's the senior military officer here?"

There was a muttered consultation and a wounded Sergeant stepped forward and saluted. "I was at the barracks, sir," he said. "We were just going out of the building when we heard the missile and there was an explosion and we came here because the barracks was wrecked. We've been trying to raise higher authorities and no one is answering."

Briggs cursed under his breath. "How many men are there here?"

"Forty, it seems," the Sergeant said. Briggs saw the trickle of blood running down his face and silently cursed; there was no time to spare the Sergeant's presence. "The Captain was trying to organise something at the barracks when the missile hit."

"I see," Briggs said. "What's your name?"

"Sergeant Christopher Roach, sir," Roach said. He started to recite his rank and serial number; Briggs held up a hand to stop him. "As far as I know, I'm the senior survivor from the barracks."

"I want you to send one of your men to the nearest hospital and tell them that we need some medical support out here," Briggs said. He was about to order fire engines as well, when the first of the big red vehicles pulled up, running terribly late. Four more had also arrived; he couldn't help but notice the bullet holes in one of the vehicle's windows. "No; send two, both armed. Deploy the others to cover relief efforts if needed."

Roach didn't argue. "I understand," he said, as he took in the sight. Firemen were spilling out of the fire engine; many of them running towards the Thames with fire hoses, others checking the pressure in the water hydrants nearby. Judging from the general devastation and the collapsed streets, Briggs suspected that the water mains would have been burst by the missile attack. "I'll see to it at once."

He leaned forwards. "You do know that we're at war?"

"I saw the missile," Briggs said, equally softly. There was no time for a panic. "We have to find the Prime Minister."

Roach looked at the ruins. "No chance, sir," he said. "None at all."

The lead fireman came up to Briggs. His nametag read SAM STEIN. "Sir, I assume that you're in command," he said, his voice brisk and under control. "I have to report terrorists near the fire station; one of the bastards took a shot at my people and wounded one. What do you want us to do?"

Briggs gave him an incredulous look. "Put out the fires," he said, shortly. "Have you any contact at all with higher authority?"

"None, sir," Stein said. Briggs felt his blood run cold. "We didn't even get the alert signal; we heard the explosions and then we had to go to the nearest pillar of smoke."

Briggs stepped back as the fire crew went to work. They knew their stuff, he saw; several of them had attached hoses to the fire engines, running towards the river and draining water from the Thames to attack the fires. The fires roared through what remained of the MOD Main Building – he had a nasty thought about ammunition cooking off in there – and refused to be cowed; it fought back furiously. Ambulances arrived under armed escort; doctors and nurses spilled out of them and started to work on the injured. Briggs smiled; he had forgotten the heavy police escort given to the murderer in the nearest hospital, even if he had wanted the man to simply die when he had heard about the cost.

The silence worried him. He should have been able to make contact with New Scotland Yard or one of the back-ups, but the nearest police station had been as isolated as the mobile command centre. There were still occasional bursts of gunfire echoing out over the city and a whispered report of rioting in Regent's Park, the heart of Londonistan. Were they in the middle of an Islamic insurgency? It hardly seemed creditable; sure, there were a few firebrands who openly preached violence, but the vast majority of Muslims wouldn't join a war against the British state, would they? If nothing else, it would put a permanent end to their benefits checks from the welfare state.

The silence…

A gunshot rang out, far too close for comfort; moments later, there was a second shot, and then silence. "That was young Omar," Roach said, checking his radio. The military radios worked at short range, jamming or no jamming. "He just shot back at a sniper and killed him; Omar is a great sharpshooter, best in the unit." He paused. "Not that I would ever tell him that, of course."

"Of course," Briggs agreed. He could see more fires now, spreading up over London, one very nasty fire rising up from the Docklands. "Do you have any knowledge at all of where we might find more authority?"

Roach shook his head. "You're it," he said. There were far too many civilians around, many of them tourists and all on the verge of panic. The London Eye seemed to have jammed; Briggs could see people in the bubbles and knew that they, too, would be panicking. "I only had the barracks and the police stations…"

"I've got something," Page shouted. Briggs was there almost before he realised that his feet were moving. "It's faint, but it's there, on one of the military mobile telephone bands."

The voice was faint. "This is command," it said. "Please identify yourself."

"This is Inspector David Briggs," Briggs said. The voice sounded oddly familiar. "I'm at Downing Street and we need help."

"This is Major-General Langford," the voice said. It became much clearer within moments as both units strove to boost the signal and beat the jamming.

Briggs remembered a tall thin man from the PJHQ; he had been wondering what had happened to Northwood, even to the point of considering sending one of the soldiers there to find out. "Please report on your situation."

"Bloody desperate," Briggs said. The fact that they had made any sort of contact was a massive boost to his morale. Judging from Roach's face, the same thought had occurred to him; he was smiling openly. "It seems as if we're in the middle of a fucking war."

"We are," Langford said flatly. "I need to know; what's happening there?"

"We have the fires more or less halted now," Briggs said. It had only taken a couple of hours to bring them under some form of control. "The entire area's a wreck; we only pulled out a few dozen survivors and they were all on the edge of the impact area. None of them are important people, sir; the Houses of Parliament have been utterly destroyed."

There was a long pause. "There's no hope?" Langford asked finally. "None at all?"

"No," Briggs said. He closed his eyes. "Sir, just who is in charge of the country?"

"Me, it seems," Langford said. Briggs heard the bitterness in his voice and shuddered. "For the moment, you have been confirmed commander of all of the police and other emergency services in London; New Scotland Yard appears to be gone, along with the PJHQ. We'll sort out seniority later. Is there a military officer there?"

"Yes," Briggs said. He passed the microphone to Roach. "You'd better tell him about the sniper as well."

Roach reported in clear and concise terms, sparing nothing, from the details of the missile impact at the barracks to the snipers and gunfire that burst out from time to time over the city. Briggs had studied the snipers that had cropped up in America; a single man with a high-powered rifle and no sense of morals could bring an entire city to a halt for hours. How many were loose within London?

"I see," Langford said finally. "Can you get a bearing on the source of the jamming?"

Briggs looked at Page. "Yes, sir," he said. He tapped commands into the system and recited a bearing. "That's the rough bearing."

There was a pause. "The Russian Embassy," Langford said, after a long moment. Briggs realised that Langford must have taken a bearing from somewhere else and used it to triangulate the source of the jamming. "It figures."

Briggs rubbed his bald head. "Sir, do you think that the Russians are behind all of this?"

"I think that they're the ones doing the jamming," Langford said. "That may not be damning, but any court of law would consider it highly suspicious behaviour at the best of times. Sergeant Roach?"

Roach straightened, as if they were face to face. "Yes, sir?"

Langford sounded too tired to be stern. "Sergeant, how many men do you have now who are armed?"

"Fifty-seven," Roach said. They had been trickling in from the remains of the other barracks; most of them had been helpful, both in providing security and in caring for the injured. Some of them had been veterans of actual fighting; they had understood some things that civilians would never grasp. "I don't have a complete unit, just dribs and drabs."

"It'll have to do," Langford said. "Take thirty men and take the Russian Embassy; shut the jamming down, any means necessary. Tell them that we will try to treat them with the standard respect for diplomatic representatives, sneak attack notwithstanding, but if they don't shut down the transmitter and surrender, we'll bomb the embassy."

"Understood, sir," Roach said. "I won't let you down."

He marched out of the mobile command centre, shouting orders to his men. "General, we need support out here," Briggs said. "Just what the hell is going on?"

"I don't know for sure," Langford admitted. "Most of the command network has been shattered; what reports we are receiving are frequently confusing and contradictory. Once the jamming has been removed, we can hopefully start finding out just what is going on, and then somehow take whatever action we need to take."

"I understand," Briggs said. Several more police officers had arrived, none of them outranking him. London had to be in chaos; the streets were crowded at the best of times, and now it looked as if half the city was on fire. People would be fleeing the city for the countryside, if they had anywhere to go, and looters would be coming out of their holes, intent on enriching themselves. "I just wish I had more men."

The Russian Embassy, like every other Embassy that felt itself to be under threat from terrorists, was much stronger than it appeared from the outside. Ambassador Konstantin Molotov – he had assumed the surname in honour of his private hero – knew that it could be held for at least an hour against a determined force, such as a Chechen resistance group. The thought of what happened to Russians who fell into their hands would keep the guards – all of whom were far more dangerous than their resumes suggested – fighting well past all hope being gone. Molotov also knew that the Embassy, like all embassies, was dependent upon the goodwill of the local population – or at least its government.

Molotov, like all diplomats, had been furious over the fate of the American embassies in Iran, Saudi Arabia and Indonesia. He had been one of the people calling upon the President to support the American War in revenge for the decision of the *Jihadists* to move against the embassies, which were intended to be sanctuaries. The discovery that the embassy was at the centre of Russian war plans hadn't pleased him, not least because, as Ambassador, he could be made to pay the price for the actions of the FSB agents operating behind enemy lines. The sealed orders had been clear; keep the jamming going as long as possible, then request safe passage out of Europe…

And so Molotov had heaved his bulk down to the gates. "This is Russian territory," he said, as calmly as he could. The young man facing him didn't look too steady; he was holding a weapon as if it was a deadly snake. "You have no right to force admittance."

"You have launched a war against us," the British soldier said. Molotov saw the blood trickling down his face and shuddered; it was a far cry from any world he was personally familiar with, nothing to do with the soft words and softer moves of diplomacy. "You are engaged in hostile acts!"

"I deny all such accusations," Molotov said. He realised instantly that it was the wrong thing to say; the young man brought his weapon up and pointed it right at his chest. "Threatening an Ambassador…"

"You've killed the fucking Prime Minister," the British soldier said. "Ambassador, you will open the embassy and order your men to surrender."

The Russian soldiers lifted their own weapons. Molotov waved at them frantically to lower them. "And what happens if I refuse?" He asked. "Russia has a right to guard her territory…"

"If you refuse, my men will keep you trapped in here while a fighter-bomber drops a bomb on your head," the British soldier said. "The jamming will be shut down and you will all be killed." He ran a hand across his brow. "Choose, Ambassador; I have no more time!"

Molotov took a breath. "In that case, I will open the embassy," he said. The prospects of bullets flying anywhere near him terrified him. "I must inform you that my government will protest in the fullest possible terms to your Prime Minister, or his replacement, the United Nations, the European Union and consider taking the strongest action against you personally."

He paused for breath. "Under international agreements, I must remind you that you have no right to harm any of my people and in fact must see to their reparation as quickly as possible through the graces of a neutral country," he continued, hoping that the Englishman would let him finish. "As diplomats, we have rights…"

"Put your weapons down and assume the position," the British soldier said to the guards, cutting Molotov off mid-lecture. Resentfully, the guards obeyed; other British soldiers appeared and scooped up the weapons, guarding the Russians carefully as they were herded into the grounds. The embassy quickly emptied of staff; cooks, cleaners, a handful of girls who were officially typists, but were really there to be mistresses, all joined the soldiers on the ground.

"Now, Mr Ambassador," the British soldier said. "Lead me to the jamming system."

Molotov obeyed.

Chapter Fifteen

Picking Up The Pieces, Take Two

Never has America been more alone in spreading democracy's promise. [...] It is the last country with a mission, a mandate and a dream, as old as its founders. All of this may be dangerous, even delusional, but it is also unavoidable. It is impossible to think of America without these properties of self-belief.
Michael Ignatieff

London, England

"Mr Ambassador, there's a fucking air raid coming in," Captain Douglas McDonald shouted, bursting into the room. "Get into the emergency escape shaft, now!"

Ambassador Andrew Luong didn't hesitate; the access shaft was already unsealing as alarms started to sound inside the American Embassy. He wondered if it was the President's idea of a joke - he had once accused her of being on the rag when she had sent Special Forces into Central Asia to kill a warlord who had been only making anti-American proclamations – but dismissed the thought of a drill; McDonald had sounded far too serious...even scared.

His assistant, Margery Wayne, was even more scared. He ignored her questions as training took over; he took a breath and jumped into the emergency shaft, falling through several floors into the bomb shelter underneath the basement. Through some miracle of science he didn't even begin to understand, his fall was slowed and he popped out the end of the tube as if he had just jumped off a stool. Moments later, a protesting Margery followed, her skirt bunched up around her waist by the air pressure in the tube, revealing her underwear to his eyes. He grabbed her arm and yanked her out of the tube, seconds before McDonald followed, his voice grim.

"All right," Luong said, "what the hell is going on?"

"We just had a FLASH warning from NORAD," McDonald said. "Orbiting satellites have tracked the launch of over three thousand missiles in Europe, with at least two hundred of them aimed into British airspace. We don't have targeting indicators for them yet, but it's a certainty that some of them are going to fall within London. This place is a prime target."

The Marine wasn't even breathing hard, Luong noticed, resentfully. "I see," he said, between pants. His heartbeat was racing so fast that he was surprised he hadn't had a heart attack by now. "What's the hell happened? Are the Europeans at war?"

"It looks that way," McDonald said. "I'm very much afraid that..."

"Targets identified, central London," a Marine called, from the large console that controlled the emergency systems in the basement. If a group of terrorists mounted an attack, standard procedure was to hole up in the bunker and wait for the English cops to arrest the terrorists, after which the Americans could escape. Missiles, on the other hand...Luong knew that a bunker-busting missile would have no problems at all busting the embassy bunker. "I think...Westminster and Whitehall; one fell in Northwood, explosion registered on NORAD's satellites, non-nuke, I repeat, non-nuke."

Luong closed his eyes. His tenure as Ambassador to Great Britain had been a surprise to him, particularly after the infamous rag comment, but he had understood the importance of the President's decision. The United States needed allies, and even if NATO and all of the formal alliances had been dissolved, there was still a great deal of cooperation between the United States and its former allies. It was true that the misnamed and over-exaggerated Embassies War had damaged reputations, but some elements within the various establishments were still willing to work privately with the Americans.

But even that had limitations. If he had had the chance, Luong would have happily strangled Corporal Mike Collins himself; the young fool had cost America far too much. No one, not Hitler, not Yamamoto, not even Osama bin Laden himself had wreaked so much havoc...and the worst of it was that it had been unnecessary. The British might have frowned on prostitutes, but there had been plenty of them near RAF Mildenhall. Collins had never needed to find a young innocent girl, let alone rape and murder her. The crime had shocked England...

Luong had seen the reports, the increasing war waged in Parliament, tearing apart a desperate attempt by the British Government to keep it all quiet until Collins could be extradited properly and sentenced to life imprisonment at His Majesty's pleasure. The American Government had cooperated…but the British media and even some media back in the States had treated it as if Collins had been flown out of the country to safety. The British Government had been forced into retreat after retreat and finally…America had been asked to leave the country. It had been the final act of that government; it had fallen a month afterwards.

Collins had died the same year, murdered in Leavenworth by a fellow inmate during a particularly nasty homosexual rape; as far as Luong was concerned, it wasn't anything like enough. The storm had refused to abate; governments had fallen across Europe, and by the time the storm had started to fade, American forces had been evicted from almost every base in Europe. Horror stories, many of them older than the Cold War, had been dug up and tossed at America; Americans were using Europe, Americans were fighting the war in Europe, Americans were intent on eternally controlling Europe…

The year afterwards, NATO had dissolved permanently.

Luong stared up at the console, saying nothing, as the missiles found their targets. He had had hopes of repairing the relationship with Britain, at least, after he had been appointed to England. It hadn't been easy; the Prime Minister was a committed believer in Europe and had been inclined to allow matters of international concern to slip to Brussels. The European Parliament, overwhelmingly elected by socialists and known anti-Americans, had found America-bashing to be a substitute for its own failed politics. They had passed resolutions that condemned the rise of the American police state, border controls and harsh responses to terrorism, all the while ignoring the growing threat under their own noses. Places like France, and Spain, and even London provided a haven for terrorists…and the European Parliament didn't care. They had even welcomed thousands of known terrorist fighters from Palestine…

A Marine looked up at McDonald, just as the ground shook. "That was at least four impacts in quick succession," he said. "The missiles hit Downing Street and the Houses of Parliament; NORAD's uplink is reporting multiple missile hits across the United Kingdom and several airliners going down in flames. The main power seems to have failed completely, sir; the generator is all that's keeping the embassy working."

Luong took a breath, trying to act ambassadorial and failing. America had warned the British that they were inviting trouble; they had warned the French and the Germans, but none of them had listened. It was easy to blame America for Europe's woes, from the endless trade disputes to the funding provided for terrorists from European Muslim groups. Some Americans could never set foot in Europe without being arrested for war crimes; many more Europeans who had no loyalty at all to Europe would be arrested and charged with terrorism – which carried the death penalty – in America. America had lost some of her innocence…and it showed.

He sighed. "Do we have some idea of who's actually launching the missiles?"

"I think its Russia," a Marine said. His face was very pale, but his eyes were bright. "NORAD tracked at least a thousand missiles coming out of European Russia, others coming out of Serbia and Algeria, Russia's closest allies. Others were launched from submarines and aircraft and only we or the Russians have that kind of capability."

Luong nodded. The Chinese had tried to build it, but Chinese ambitions had firmly sunk after the attempt to seize Taiwan had failed so badly, destroying most of the People's Liberation Army Navy. Luong thought that it would have made the Chinese feel better if American ships and submarines had been directly involved; the proof that the Taiwanese were determined to avoid reunification had proven the downfall of the Communist Government. The Chinese Civil War still raged on.

Margery caught his arm. She was terrified, he realised; she hadn't signed up for being trapped in a bunker. They weren't trapped, it wasn't as if they couldn't get out onto the streets, but he knew that they were probably safer in the bunker until the situation on the ground clarified itself. It shouldn't take long; Britain might have been in the dumps, but it was far from a Third World country.

Her voice was thin and reedy. "What do we do?"

"It's a cliché, but we have no choice, but to wait," Luong said. He held her hand for a long moment until she calmed down. "The Russians seem to have ignored us completely."

He wished he could say that he was surprised. The Russians had been growing more and more powerful, ever since they had recovered from the post-Cold War depression and started to rebuild their country. They had sold arms to everyone who was interested, much to American outrage; Russian weapons had killed Americans in Iran and the Middle East. They had also sold weapons to Latin and South America – he remembered, his blood running cold, the British task force that had been dispatched to shore up the defences of the Falkland Islands – and, in defiance of the Monroe Doctrine, even started a long-term process of upgrading the Latin and Southern American militaries. They had even invited the Central Asian states back to the fold…and many of them had actually rejoined the Russians. They no longer trusted America either.

America hadn't wanted to become involved in the Ukraine situation and had been more than happy to leave it to the Europeans; it was in their backyard, after all. Luong had been more alarmed, however, by the rise in Russian preparations for outright violence; the Russians had said, quite clearly, 'this far and no further.' They had wanted to keep Ukraine within their sphere of influence and that had meant, as far as they were concerned, no foreigners allowed. They already dominated Belarus; the CIA had been privately warning that the Russians intended to support various factions in Ukraine to take control and evict the pesky Europeans. It had surprised them that the Russians had allowed a EUROFOR unit into Ukraine…

Outright missile attacks across the United Kingdom? Luong had a feeling that he knew what had happened to the European forces in Ukraine. The CIA had warned repeatedly about some of the methods the Russians were using to rebuild their country, including the use of forced labour and the genocide of thousands of Chechens. The Russians had just started World War Three.

Luong sat down on a sofa and glanced around. He hadn't spent much time in the bunker and the drab utility of its design surprised him. The embassy itself was very luxurious, but the bunker was cold, if not dark; a collections of weapons were mounted against one wall, just in case a final last stand was required. It was how he imagined a missile launch room in a nuclear silo to look; the pistols so that the crew could take their own lives, rather than die slowly under the rubble.

"I just heard from Vince, on the roof," Rolf Lommerde said. The CIA spook, the main intelligence operative for London, looked grim. "He says that there's fires everywhere and even some gunfire; no sign of an official reaction as yet. There's a great deal of jamming on the British military, police and civilian bands; it looks as if Britain just took one hell of a hammering."

"I think I worked that out," Luong snapped. He didn't like Lommerde; the man was just too slick, even if sending one of his people to the roof was actually a good idea. He glared at the CIA officer with all the disdain a professional diplomat and former National Guardsman could muster. The National Guard had a low opinion of the CIA after a unit had walked into a firefight where the CIA had absolutely, positively, sworn blind that there was no chance of an enemy presence. "Was there any clue at all as to what was going to happen?"

"No, Mr Ambassador," Lommerde said. He sat down next to Luong without being asked. "We tracked a lot of Russian military movement, but we believed that it was intended to convince the Poles that the Russians would act if they were to do anything stupid, such as calling for European intervention if Ukraine actually boiled over into civil war. Other movements were in the same field; one of the most active units was right on Ukraine's eastern border, well out of range to threaten Poland or Europe."

For a moment, the mask slipped and Luong saw the desperation under Lommerde's glib tongue. "He saw one of the places that are burning," Lommerde said. "It was the Regent's Park Mosque, one of the places that we maintain some covert – very covert – surveillance on, nothing that the British would have to take official notice of and prevent us from carrying on. The British Anti-Terrorist Unit knows about it and says nothing; we believe that the British Government knows nothing about it."

He sighed, loudly. "But…that place has always had cells of radicals nearby; the Mosque was taken over by radicals several times. The British cleared them out, from time to time, but they always came back; Mustapha has been known to speak there and – God knows – we've actually tried to have him assassinated while he's been in England. It would be worth it, even if we failed to find a criminal to subcontract the job to, to trade one of our people for him."

Luong ground his teeth. Mustapha was wanted in the United States for connections with the attack that had devastated Oakland. The evidence against him, however, had been gained by 'special means,' or torture, as more-enlightened people called it. The British Government might have let him be taken off the streets, but the Americans had made the mistake of asking the Prime Minister directly…and he had refused. Mustapha continued to spread havoc through Europe…untouched, unmolested; Luong wasn't even sure if the British maintained their own surveillance on him. He wouldn't have been surprised to find out that Mustapha hadn't been watched at all.

"I see," he said. "I don't suppose that Mustapha is dead?"

"There's no information," Lommerde said. "Mr Ambassador; if someone wanted to start a civil war in London's streets, I can't think of a better way to do it."

"My God," Luong said. The sheer scale of the operation impressed and terrified him. "What the hell is going on?"

McDonald came over and saluted, exchanging a brief glare with Lommerde. "I have managed to talk directly to my superiors," he said. Luong rolled his eyes; in an emergency, the superiors were the officers at the Pentagon who supervised the close protection of American representatives around the world. "There are no further missiles heading towards Britain and they have provisionally decided to leave us here, unless the situation changes."

Luong nodded in relief; the thought of an extraction under fire terrified him. He wouldn't have been surprised to know that it terrified Lommerde, or even McDonald, as well; no one would forget the botched operation that had failed to save the lives of the Ambassador to Pakistan, back in the Pakistani Intervention. Perhaps that had been when the rot had finally set into America's geopolitical strategy; who had reasonably expected other countries to play ball when the cost of playing ball could be even higher than not playing ball?

"The President has sounded a military alert and units of the Atlantic Fleet have been placed on alert to launch a covering mission for an extraction flight, if necessary," McDonald continued. "At present, I do not believe that there is any real threat to the embassy, and you are safer inside here than you would be trying to escape in the middle of a shooting war."

"I can't fault the logic," Luong said. USAF pilots had accidentally shot down civilian aircraft during the War on Terror before and he couldn't see British pilots avoiding the same mistakes, particularly if several airliners had indeed gone down. Had they been hijacked, or was it merely a case of a terrorist with a portable SAM launcher? "Did the President have a message for me?"

"The National Security Council is meeting in emergency session fairly soon," McDonald said. "The President has so far not commented, apart from approving you remaining within the embassy and attempting to open communications with the British Government, or what remains of the British Government. Brussels and every other European city appear to have been attacked as well; we can only conclude that these are the opening moves in a full-scale invasion."

Luong found himself grasping for words. "But..."

"It is standard military tactics," McDonald said. "We launched decapitation strikes during the Iraq War, and to some extent during the Iran War. If our intelligence had been better" – he paused to give Lommerde a scowl – "and the legal situation back then what it is now, we would have left the ragheads gasping for breath and utterly unaware of what was going on around them. There is no point in launching such a...brutal series of attacks, sir, unless you intend to go all the way."

Luong felt his legs grow weaker and silently thanked God that he was sitting down. Europe...hell, if all of Europe had been hit as badly, then Europe no longer existed except in name. Somehow, he would have to pick up the pieces and find out who was in charge, before the Europeans lost the unexpected war. What the hell was going on?

"I see," he said finally. "We need to get in touch with the local authorities, somehow; how do we do that?"

Chapter Sixteen

I Told You So!

I don't want to say that I told you so...but I told you so. So there.
Unnamed

Brussels, Belgium

"Jesus fucking Christ!"

The explosion seemed to destroy the entire city. As he drove along one of the roads set aside for government ministers and workers in the centre of Brussels, Colonel Seth Fanaroff yanked the car aside as other cars screeched to a halt or came to a stop, the drivers panicking as the centre of Brussels vanished in fire. Captain Saundra Keshena screamed as the side window shattered, scattering broken glass over her arm; Fanaroff ignored it as he fought to control the car. They skidded to a halt and he shouted at her to jump out, seconds before a massive lorry charged into the road and came to a halt, caught on a crashed car.

"Get down," Fanaroff shouted. He'd seen it before, in Iran; it was almost textbook perfect. He hurled himself at her and knocked her to the ground, covering her with his body, just as the lorry exploded with an almighty blast. A wave of heat passed over him and he realised, that by a miracle, they had escaped serious harm. "Stay down!"

He could hear nothing, not even screams from the wounded...and there *had* to be wounded. He'd seen truck bombs before; they carried plenty of explosives, but they were hardly nuclear devices, and the blast hadn't been that large. Saundra was moving under him, trying to move; her mouth was opening and closing soundlessly. He realised that he had been deafened and rubbed his ears, hoping that they would recover; the strange feeling grew worse and then noises started to penetrate his mind again. He could hear!

Saundra's voice was strange. It took him a second to realise that his ears weren't working right. He rolled off her and looked around, seeing burning buildings and landscapes, right in the centre of Brussels. It had been designed as a multi-billion euro project to create the perfect home for the governing class; slowly, Brussels was becoming a black hole sucking the rest of Europe towards it. Some of the European Defence Commission…

Memory returned and he looked north. Flames and smoke were rising up from the EUROFOR headquarters; the building not only wasn't very secure, but it had not been designed to take an impact, or a bomb. Terrorists had left the European building alone for years, until now; it had failed its first major test. The Pentagon had done much better…and they had had the excuse of not knowing that there was a major threat out there.

"Colonel," Saundra snapped. Her voice sounded much more normal now. "What the hell do we do?"

Gunfire crackled out, not too far away; both of them had their service pistols in their hands before a moment had passed. Both of them preferred the latest version of the Combat Commander pistol, but Fanaroff knew that they had only a few magazines each. The Europeans had been reluctant to let them carry weapons at all and it was only with the understanding that they would only be used in utmost need that they had been issued European licenses. Finding more ammunition would be…problematic; Brussels, like all European cities, was not keen on gun stores.

"We keep our heads down," Fanaroff snapped back. He forced himself to think through the ringing pain in his head; the attack, whatever it was, didn't seem to have an infantry component…at least, not one nearby. American Special Forces would have launched a ground attack to finish off the defenders if they had been fighting a war; the odds were that the terrorists had either decided not to, or lacked the ability to mount an attack. "We have to call in…"

His hand reached down to his terminal and pulled it out of his belt. It was broken; he swore aloud as he realised he had landed on it. Saundra didn't carry one; their secure access to the American Military Datanet had been lost along with the terminal's functionality. Perhaps it could be repaired, in an American lab, but if the destruct system had been triggered, all that would remain of the interior would be powder. He checked his mobile phone and switched through the possible networks; they all seemed to be down.

Saundra was doing the same with her phone. "How the hell can terrorists do something like this?"

"They can't," Fanaroff said. He felt the weight of the pistol in his hand and felt oddly reassured. The Combat Commander was a man-killer, one of the latest versions could even punch through body armour; even the most rabid pro-gun supporter had qualms about allowing them on the streets. The military hated them as well, once some had been reverse-engineered by someone and duplicated in the Middle East; they killed soldiers who had previously had body armour to protect them. "I think that we have a worse problem."

The sound of gunfire was coming closer. "This way," Fanaroff said. He knew the streets of Brussels much better than he had ever let on to Guichy and his cronies; it would only have upset them, or had them wondering if he was a spy for an American invasion. The highest-grossing European film of 2023 had been about an American invasion of Europe and had led to questions in the European Parliament about EUROFOR's plans to face an American invasion; in many ways, it had been as shamelessly patriotic as *Independence Day*. "I think we have to get back to the embassy."

They rounded a corner and came face to face with a scene from hell. Cars, dozens of cars, were smashed and broken by the force of a blast, used as barricades by desperate European soldiers, fighting against hordes of teenage men, screaming insults and obscenities in Arabic. Fanaroff hadn't seen anything like it since Iran; there was a savage glory surrounding the entire desperate fight. The young men seemed completely heedless of their own personal safety; they charged at the Europeans, spraying bullets from AK-47s and launching RPG shells from insanely close range.

"No," Fanaroff said. His lips twitched as he ducked back. "Perhaps we should go the other way."

The entire area had been designed to be a celebration of Belgium's culture, or so he had been told; privately, he wondered if that meant that the natives had no culture, or had stolen it from everyone else. It had been strange and very tasteless, in its way; one artwork that had hardly deserved the name had been a model constructed out of frozen human shit. The commentary from nationalists in Belgium had been bitter; not a single 'real' native had had an artwork accepted. There was a moral in that, somewhere...

"Stop," a voice snapped. Fanaroff glanced ahead; two youths were bearing down on them, lifting AK-47s. He would never forget what the AK-47 looked like; the entire Middle East was awash with them, manufactured everywhere from Saddam's palaces to caves in the darkest reaches of Afghanistan. The Europeans would use the German-designed Eurorifle; the youths had to be unfriendly. "Stop and..."

Fanaroff shot the leader through the head; the young man collapsed to the ground, with half of his head blown clean off. Saundra dispatched the second one, sending him screaming into the next world. His insane giggle suggested that he was hyped up on something, perhaps one of the drugs that some Islamic fighters had been known to take before going into battle. Neither of them had been wearing body armour, nor had they shown tactical sense; something didn't quite add up.

"Guard us," he muttered. If the youths had friends, the shots would bring them running. He checked through the bodies quickly, removing wallets and two ethnic entitlement cards, both written in Arabic, rather than English or any other European language. That meant something, but he had forgotten what; the European Parliament had passed a ruling about native languages two years ago when it came to ID cards. There was nothing to suggest that they were soldiers, just some additional bullets for their weapons and one mobile phone, broken.

"Take the rifle," he said. It had been a long time since he had used an AK-47, but his body had refused to forget; it had once been a survival skill in Iran. He had been holed up in a flat and had had to use enemy weapons to last the night. He hoisted the other weapon onto his shoulder and waited for her to finish before starting the long walk back towards the embassy. "I think that we're in the middle of a riot."

"No shit," Saundra said. "I would never have noticed."

"Just don't let them take you alive," Fanaroff warned. She was holding together better than he'd expected, for a paper-pusher. "There is a fate worse than death."

The side-streets of Brussels were deserted. Fanaroff hoped that that meant that the population was inside, hiding behind locked doors; he suspected that it actually meant that most of the population was joining the rioting. If rioting it was...there was something organised about the attack, rather like insurgencies had been organised in the Middle East. The Mullahs and other clerics had used young men as cannon-fodder; they had run their groups like criminal gangs and taken a cut from the loot. The young men had often proven impossible to control, but…so what? It wasn't the Mullahs who suffered – or, at least, it hadn't been until the last President had signed the Sanction Protocols into effect.

He could hear it, though; the endless drumming of the guns. Some guns were constant, well-known; AK-47s and the handful of knock-off versions that had come out of China and a dozen other countries. Others were larger and more regular, more professional; he wondered just who was firing those weapons…and what they were firing at. A light in the air caught his attention and he saw the trail of a SAM rising up to strike a target he couldn't see; moments later, there were two explosions in quick succession.

"Shit," Saundra hissed. She had tripped over a body; it was a policeman, one with light dark skin. He had been garrotted; something rare in Belgium… and his trousers had been torn down. Fanaroff felt sick; someone had taken a knife to his penis and severed it from his groin. Fanaroff could almost read the story; the young policeman had defied his culture and people to try to make a difference on the streets as a policeman…and had paid the ultimate price. "Sir…how do we reason with these people?"

"You don't," Fanaroff said. It was impossible to reason with barbarians; you could only defend yourself and hope that they would grow out of it. He held up a hand. "Quiet!"

He'd sensed them before he saw them, a line of people, dressed in civilian clothes, but wearing body armour underneath. They didn't look Muslim, he realised; many of them were paler than he himself was, and they moved as if they knew what they were doing. Arabs made bad soldiers, in his opinion; the only decent ones he'd met had been Kurdish warriors before the Turks had set out to kill them all. The insurgents might have had a certain honesty, unlike so many Arab civilians he had met, but they were hardly professional soldiers. None of them would have gotten through Hell Week without being kicked out in disgrace.

The newcomers were professionals…and it struck him, suddenly, just what was going on. The coordination, the weapons, the perfectly targeted attacks...and now commandos. Only one power could do that and had the motivation...the Russians. They had been angry at the Europeans, they could be fairly certain that the United States would not interfere...and they had been making vast military moves. He had thought, the CIA had thought, the DIA had thought that the Russians had only been planning to snatch Ukraine, but then, the Russians were masters at counter-espionage. They had even made Iran far more dangerous by teaching them how to fool spy satellites and probing sensors from the west.

He thought, briefly, about surrendering. If the Russians had really decided to go medieval on Europe's collective arse, they wouldn't want to piss off the United States by shooting two military officers out of hand. He dismissed the thought within seconds; the Russians were much more likely to shoot them and swear blind that it was an accident, or disarm them and leave them handcuffed until they returned. Either way, it was not going to be a pleasant trip back to the States.

The Russians slipped out of sight. He shook his head as Saundra lifted her rifle, instead leading her down the alley towards the embassy. The noise of the guns was getting louder and he realised, suddenly, that the embassy was under attack. The new building had been designed with security in mind, but if the entire city had fallen into chaos, then what would happen to the defenders when they ran out of weapons? He nodded towards a fire escape and scrambled up the side of the building, meeting only a pair of frightened eyes at a window, as he reached the roof.

He froze. There were two men there, firing down towards Embassy square. He pulled his pistol out and shot them both quickly, in the back, watching dispassionately as their bodies fell towards the ground. A third body lay on the roof, quite dead; he showed every sign of committing suicide by sniper. The insurgents had never grasped just how good American snipers actually were; it was amazing what could be done with modern technology and deadly intent. He kept low, knowing that the Marine sniper – if he was still alive – would have no way to know that he was friendly, and peered carefully over the edge.

"Oh, shit," he breathed.

The entire row of embassies was under attack. Terrorists, fighters, insurgents, whatever they were...they had taken over some of the nearby buildings and were using them to fire down into the diplomatic establishments. The American flag was burning; he could see fires flickering in and out of the building as the terrorists concentrated their fire on the Americans. The marines were returning fire with enthusiasm, but Fanaroff could see that the situation was hopeless; the insurgents had mortars and were preparing to start blasting the Americans out of their embassy. The Mexican and Japanese embassies were burning completely; a Japanese girl, half-naked, was being chased around in circles by a group of laughing young men. The Turks…

Fanaroff felt sick, again. There was a large Palestinian population in Brussels, one that campaigned relentlessly for a return to Palestine and the extermination of Israel and America…and Turkey. No Arab would forget that the Turks represented a threat on more grounds than one; not only were they the most loyal allies that Israel had, but they were also an ideological threat. As Muslims, the Turks represented a different call on young Muslim men, one that offered an alternative to that preached by fundamentalists. There could be no mercy…and none had been shown; the male Turkish embassy staff had been crucified. The women…

He looked around, to try to avoid the sight, and saw flames rising from the harbour. There had been a strike, he remembered; the Russian *Gazprom* Corporation had had some of its people demanding extra pay before they unloaded the vast quantities of LNG they carried. He cursed under his breath; it seemed hopeless. The chaos couldn't go on forever, but while it did, escaping the city would prove difficult.

Fanaroff pulled himself back and scrambled down the ladder, holding his pistol in one hand. Saundra glanced up in relief; he explained in a few quick words what had happened and what they were going to do. She didn't argue, although she was obviously ashamed at leaving their friends behind; Fanaroff knew that there was nothing they could do for the people in the embassy now.

"They won't have done all of this in isolation," Fanaroff muttered, as they ran. "They'll have done something to the bases in Belgium and perhaps France and Germany as well…shit, if they have half the radicals up in arms, they'll have the entire continent ablaze."

A distant explosion underlined his words. "We need to find safety and report in," he said. "Have you ever been to the red light district?"

Saundra gaped at him. "Sir?"

There was another brief rattle of gunpowder, and then a large explosion; Fanaroff wondered if the Marines had blown up the embassy rather than let the American staff be torn apart by...well, whatever the hell they were. He knew more about the military situation than Saundra; *she* could hope that Uncle Sam would save them, but Fanaroff knew better. The United States was fully committed to Korea and the Middle East...and was no longer in the habit of helping Europe dig itself out of a hole.

"They brought this on themselves anyway," he muttered. "I went with a guy called Lombardi; God knows what's happened to him. There are plenty of whorehouses that will give a fellow board and lodgings for the night if he has a girl with him; I think it actually has something to do with Arabic boys, girls, and the reaction of their families if they were caught together."

He smiled. "Don't worry, you're perfectly safe with me," he said. Insanely, he felt better than he had in years. "All you have to do is pretend to be my lover."

Saundra laughed. "I draw the line at faking orgasms," she said. Somewhere along the line, the differences in rank had vanished; shared experiences did that in the best of units. "I'll just simper and say 'honey' a lot."

"As long as it's convincing," Fanaroff said. They passed a set of hastily boarded-up shops; the owners were hiding from the people who had once been their customers. Fanaroff didn't give much for their chances; as soon as the embassies fell, the mob would lose its focus and start looting in earnest. "I think we're going to have to hide until we get back in touch with home."

Chapter Seventeen

State of Play

My duty is not affected by what others may or may not do to discharge their own.
Honor Harrington (David Weber)

London, England

They reconvened two hours afterwards.

He had argued, of course; Langford had never seen himself as having a political career, not when a military background was the kiss of death in many parts of the country. He also had a deep respect for democracy, the same democracy that he had tried to export to Iraq and several places in Africa... and a military dictator was anything but democratic. He had been briefed, years ago, on some of the older war plans that the British Government had drawn up when it had had to come to terms with the possibility of nuclear war, but so many of them had been...hopeless. Victory was never an option.

Major Erica Yuppie had been determined...and it was easy to admire her determination to ensure that she carried out her duty, whatever it took. He had looked into her service record – the computers in the CJHQ might have been a closed system, but they had been detailed and read-only – and he could see the signs of an officer with rare promise. She had been an infantrywoman before transferring to higher office, showing skills that would have taken her far, perhaps even to the post he held. Instead, she had been asked to spend her days on a lonely vigil, waiting for the day that Britain was under such threat that the Emergency Protocols had to be activated.

It still stunned him that he had known nothing about it; of the sixty-odd people who knew, fifty of them worked in the CJHQ and had the highest security clearance in Britain. Twenty-three of them had actually been on duty when the missiles started to fall; they had handled themselves very well under their first real test. Erica had recalled the remainder of her staff at once, but as she herself admitted, it wasn't exactly certain that all of them would get the message in time. The communications network was in total disarray…and they dared not risk a security leak.

Erica's concerns had made sense once he had examined the details of the CJHQ itself. If Briggs was to be believed, the Russian missiles had made short work of the bunker and tunnel complex under Ten Downing Street, shattering a network that had been designed to defeat a nuclear attack. The CJHQ was flimsy by comparison, its survival assured more by secrecy than any actual protection; an enemy force that stumbled across it would have little difficulty actually taking the place, although he suspected that Erica would blow the compound up rather than let an enemy take it.

He stood up and paced, glaring down at the briefcase on his desk. There were no more than five copies of the complete Emergency Protocols in existence…and he was looking at one of them, the others would have burned with Whitehall and the Prime Minister. He had read them, seeing the mindset of a different era in the cold dispassionate words of a defence planner, a man who had grappled with the complexities of nuclear war. He had said, clearly, that nuclear war would destroy the government…and the senior officer who survived – or was in direct contact with British forces – held authority. He hadn't planned for a precision strike, like the Russians had carried out, but otherwise the situation fitted, at least until new elections were held. Langford privately resolved to ensure that they were carried out as soon as possible.

There was a knock at the door. "General, please will you come into the briefing room," a young Indian girl said. She wore civilian clothes, but Erica had explained that she handled almost all of the personal facilities at the CJHQ, the only non-career military person cleared to know about its existence. "They're ready for you now."

Langford laughed silently at himself as he stood up. He had wanted to be out there, giving orders and working to bring the country back together again, but Erica had convinced him that he had to be thinking about the overall problem, at least until they found a surviving politician in the line of succession. Langford wasn't hopeful; the Houses of Parliament had been blown apart and there had been no time for an evacuation. His only order, so far, had been simple; he was not to be addressed as Prime Minister.

"Thank you," he said, to the girl. Her nametag read SARA. "Please lead the way."

It was a very short walk; the CJHQ was a tiny complex, certainly compared to some of the vast American complexes that had been built for a global war against terrorists. The main briefing room made no concessions to public opinion; it was both comfortable and functional, if a little shabby. Langford had inspected it briefly and realised that it was almost ideal for a press-free base. There were only three people in the room; Major Erica Yuppie, Aaron Sargon and a man Langford didn't recognise.

They saluted him as he sat down. "Major-General, this is Michael Casey, our expert on EUROFOR and other militaries around the world," Erica said. Langford liked him on sight; he had an air of reassuring competence that he appreciated in people who were telling him vital information. "We have spent the last hour gathering as much information as we can from all of our sources – all of our surviving sources, I should say. The damage has really been quite remarkable."

Sara passed them all cups of tea, checked that they didn't want refreshments, and slipped out of the room. "It doesn't look good," Erica said, as soon as the door clicked closed and locked behind her. "There is little doubt that we have been attacked on a major basis by the Russians, although I admit that there is marginal – very marginal – room for doubt. The assault plan is not something as…deniable as the execution of Alexander Litvinenko, sir; there seems no reason to believe that this is nothing less than a major grab for power in Europe. The attack caught us completely by surprise and was asymmetric; the reports make that clear."

A screen flickered into life, showing Britain; the number of red icons made Langford's blood run cold.

"This is the situation as we understand it," Sargon said. The analyst sounded as if he didn't quite believe his own words; Langford understood his shock and horror perfectly. How had they gotten into this mess? "At roughly 1000 hours, several things happened, starting with the loss of all of the European satellites in orbit and continuing with the launch of around three hundred missiles into the UKADGE. This data is still preliminary; some of the reports come from pilots flying wherever they saw a flash or a faint radar trace, some more may be blaming the actions of other operatives on the cruise missiles. Regardless, we have taken serious losses; all three of the major fighter bases took a pounding, although RAF Coningsby got lucky and took down three of the five missiles aimed at it with TMD systems operated by the RAF Regiment. Other bases weren't so lucky; RAF Leuchars and RAF Leeming both got clobbered, while the tanker base at RAF Brize Norton got badly hit when a fuel tanker exploded. The death toll was pretty heavy; only a SAR base in Scotland avoided getting worked over."

He took a breath. "We had one stroke of good luck," he said. "A Sentry and three Eurofighter Typhoons - and one Eurofighter Tempest – were engaged in a practice run against the French Air Force. They saw most of the attack and are currently providing top cover over Britain – fortunate, as all of the military radar stations got hit. That includes RAF Fylingdales, along with its BMEWS solid-state phased-array radar, which was completely destroyed. As you may recall, successive defence chiefs had provided warning after warning about the vulnerability of the radar; large, immobile, and easy to hit."

"I think the horse has bolted on that one," Langford said. "And the remainder of the UKADGE?"

"There have been at least seven – there may well have been more – incidents of airliners being shot down with handheld SAM missiles," Erica said. "Two came down in London itself; the others are scattered around major airports, such as Manchester, and Edinburgh. The explosions have only added to the civil unrest, sir; the situation is already growing out of control. We have several incidents of truck bombs being deployed against our remaining ground bases..."

Langford held up a hand. "Our remaining ground bases?"

Erica's eyes showed real pain for the first time. "Every major barracks has been hit," she said. "Some of the damage wasn't as bad as it seemed at first sight, but it was still pretty bad; there are thousands of casualties out there. We've been able to get lines out to most of the bases, and now the jamming has gone, we have been able to make radio contact with the surviving bases. According to the preliminary results, we're looking at over three thousand dead..."

Langford just stared at her. "And the naval side is worst," Erica said. "There were at least seven missiles, all designed to inflict major damage, targeted on

Faslane Naval Base, which is part of HMNB Clyde. The destruction was vast, sir; two of our three SSBNs are wrecked. The third, HMS *Vengeance*, was on patrol; she may well have been sunk already. She was due to get back in touch with us in a week; she was ordered to run very silent and deep for a training exercise."

Langford cursed the European Union under his breath. They had insisted on Britain decommissioning one nuclear submarine…and Prime Minister Nicholas Donavan had gone along with them, rather than face the fury of the peace protesters. The two wrecked submarines had cut Britain's deterrent down to one…and if the Russians had been willing to go so far, they might decide that it was worth the risk of engaging the final submarine directly.

Erica continued her damning recitation. "The other naval bases were badly hit as well," she continued. "We have lost over seventeen ships outright and several more have been damaged to the point where they will be effectively useless for combat operations. A destroyer at HMS *Portsmouth* was successful in providing some cover for the port; the Captain took the risk of opening fire and saved the port from much worse damage." She took a long breath. "We lost the *Queen Elizabeth*."

"Billions of pounds, most of our defence fund for several years…just gone," Langford said. The sheer scale of the damage seemed impossible to grasp. The *Queen Elizabeth* had been the pride and joy of the Royal Navy, one of two large carriers intended to finally regain the capability of serious operations after decades of messing about with small carriers that could barely mount a strike force. "What about the Falklands?"

"We have no contact with Admiral Wilkinson at the moment," Erica said. "Almost all of our communications are down, either though physical destruction or through hacking attacks. Most of the civil communications network has been shattered and broken; all over the country, people are panicking. Even in the areas not touched by civil unrest, we have real problems…"

Langford stared at her. "Civil unrest?"

"We have major riots in at least six different cities," Erica said. "Most of them appear to be violence either committed by Muslims or directed against Muslims…and the police. We have some radio contact with police stations across the country, but many of them have been specifically targeted by the mobs, others have been left almost completely alone." She paused; Langford was starting to dread her pauses. "Many of the rioters are very well armed, sir; this is not a coincidence."

"I am really starting to hate the Russians," Langford said. He stared at the display, willing it to suddenly start making sense; how could anyone sort the entire mess out? France in 1940 had looked hopeless, but so had Russia in 1941; quick and decisive leadership had made the difference between disgraceful defeat and a final victory. The Russians were powerful, but they couldn't be invading Britain at the moment, could they...?

He looked up at her. "The forces in Poland?"

Erica looked at Casey. "No word," he said. "We have a status report sent to PJHQ every hour upon the hour; the last one was at 1000hrs. If there was one at 1100hrs, we missed it in all the confusion, but the 1000hrs report stated that there were no major problems. The daily report to the European Defence Commission from General Konrad Trautman, which is copied to us as well, stated no problems apart from a small fight between a German soldier and a Polish civilian. Since then, we have lost all communications with both EUROFOR Poland and the EUROFOR Standing Force in the Mediterranean."

He tapped the display again. "We maintained a regular listening watch through GCHQ of European communications," he said, as close as anyone had ever come to admitting that the British spied on their allies. Langford had never doubted it; the French, Germans and Americans almost certainly did the exact same thing. "However, the Doughnut - GCHQ headquarters in Cheltenham – was hit by the Russians; all functionality was apparently destroyed. Regardless, we have had radio crews attempting to read messages from the continent...and we believe that the Russians have not confined their attentions to us. We have no direct contact with Brussels, Paris or Berlin, but we have been picking up thousands of garbled messages, and some hints that Russian jamming is operating in France and the Netherlands. From what we have detected, we believe that there are major riots going on in France as well, and a call for *jihad* has been detected coming from Algeria."

Langford closed his eyes. "Make finding out what is actually happening there your first priority," he ordered. "Now...what about our military situation? What do we have to work with?"

"We have around four thousand soldiers in units that we have contact with," Erica said. "Many of those are TA reservists who have been trying to report in; in some places, the TA bases have been completely destroyed. We think that there are still more soldiers out there, but they haven't been able to report in to their commanding officers, or have started to look after their families rather than report for duty. Under the circumstances, that's understandable."

"No it bloody isn't," Langford muttered. "Fine; what about the aerial situation? Can we expect air raids?"

"The entire CAA flight control network has been thoroughly screwed," Sargon said. "The Sentry crew have been working hard to get the civilian aircraft out of the air as fast as possible, but it's not easy; we've had at least two crashes that happened because of pilot error under pressure, rather than SAM teams. Airport security agents at Birmingham shot two terrorists with a missile launcher; its all-too-possible that there are others crawling around somewhere, waiting for a target. We have some nightmarish possibilities here; the Russians have long planned to insert agents into hostile countries to launch acts of sabotage against the local government."

Langford shook his head slowly. "The last time we seriously drilled for that was before I was even born," he said. "What happens if...?"

He looked up at Sargon. "And?"

"We have twelve aircraft flying CAP in the air now; we were fortunate enough that the QRA aircraft were launched on the first signs of trouble," Sargon said. "Two more were caught in blasts as the missiles exploded, wrecking runways and hangers alike; the loss rate was quite heavy. Our main problem is that our logistics chain has been shot to hell; we have lost supply bases and stocks without knowing quite what we have lost. Replacing it all is going to be a nightmare...

"We don't see any conventional threat to Britain *as yet*," he continued. "We have tracked some aircraft over France, but they didn't seem to have any serious purpose and were totally unresponsive to radio hails. Some other aircraft were utterly confused; I think that elements in France have been shooting them down, just as they have here. Overall, sir...if the Russians sail the *Admiral Sergey Gorshkov* into the North Sea, we might have real problems countering the threat. In a couple of days, we should know just how bad the situation is; we should be able to call on some help from Europe, at least the French."

"Dear God," Langford breathed. "What have we come to?"

He stood up. "First order, then," he said, trusting them to carry it out. "I want us to mobilise what remains of the Territorial Army, and then prepare to retake our cities, by whatever means necessary. Briggs was talking about problems in London, so I want whatever survived at the nearby garrisons formed up into scratch units and moved in. I want those problems stamped on fast."

"Second; I want as much as possible of the navy at sea," he continued. "I – we – need to secure the sea lanes as quickly as possible, before it occurs to the Russians that sinking a few dozen ships would complete the task of strangling us. Get back in touch with Admiral Wilkinson, whatever it takes. We're going to have to recall his force and forget the Falklands. For now."

Casey was moved to protest. "Sir…?"

Langford swung around on him. "What price the jewel in the crown, such as it is, if the crown itself is lost?" Casey said nothing. "Third…dear God, what do we tell the people…?"

Erica smiled. "You could always tell them the truth," she said. "There are a lot of frightened people out there and they need to know that there is continuity of government and that it's not the end of the world."

"I know," Langford said. "But Major…what if it is?"

Interlude Two

The Price of Inaction

All over Europe, the chickens were coming home.

It started in Paris, where Algerian sleeper cells had worked for years, preparing the revolution. The plan had been simple; supplying the weapons had been even simpler. The Algerians had only a small force of radicals, but they knew that many of their fellow Arabs would join them, while the Palestinians would bring their talents at confounding the Israelis to work against the French. At the designated moment, the call for *Jihad* was sent out and the first bombs started to detonate in the city.

All over Paris, police and government buildings found themselves under attack; the missile strikes had shattered the French command and control systems, preventing a unified response. Algerian sleeper teams seized several important targets, while isolated police and military units found themselves fighting a desperate running battle for survival. They responded with brutal force, allowing racism to surge to the surface, inciting more violence as Paris dissolved into a nightmare of fire and death. The sleepers had planned carefully; before the day was done, they wanted to hold the entire city and proclaim their new world.

The same story was occurring all over Europe. In Spain, long the favoured destination of Moroccans and Algerians, massive bombs shattered buildings and spread panic. Rumours were rife, ranging from the long-dreaded civil war courted by the ETA to a landing of soldiers from America; panic and chaos spread rapidly. The missiles had shattered the Spanish Government, leaving only fire and death in their wake. In Germany, the far-right came out and attacked Muslim and Turkish immigrants, along with Russian guest workers and even American tourists, promoting massive retaliation by the ethnic groups. A savage multi-sided war had begun right in the heart of Europe.

The Russians had inserted themselves into many far-right and far-left groups in Europe; the Algerians had worked hard to control the different Islamic groups. The combination was explosive as the first dominos fell, one by one; attack was repaid by attack and then a full-scale race war broke out.

The police, seen as the enemy by all sides in the conflict, were forced back, often right out of the cities; more than a few policemen, their fortitude torn and broken by multiculturalism, tore off their uniforms and vanished into the night. The terror had taken on a life of its own; no one, not even the Algerians, could control it. It didn't matter, or so the Russian planners had intended; the chaos could only work in the Russian favour.

The Netherlands, the capital of radical Islam in Europe, found itself sucked into darkness as the first bombs detonated. The Dutch had been growing ever more resentful of the population of Muslims within their ranks; no one would forget in a hurry the murder of Theo van Gogh by Mohammed Bouyeri, a Moroccan-Dutch Islamic extremist. Even as Muslim radicals asked the dreaded question – "are you with us or against us?" – of the other Muslims in the Netherlands, the far-right was already on the march. The streets ran with blood.

The civil network had broken down almost at once, first under the impact of Russian missiles, and then under the pressure from Russian commando groups. Unseen, unheard, the Russians moved silently through Europe, taking out targets that could become problems, later. Politicians who showed fortitude were targeted for elimination; weapons' dumps and other military bases were targeted for destruction or capture. In some cases, groups of anarchists snatched weapons and used them on everyone, fighting for their own purposes, while the cities burnt around them. The Russians, untouched, carried on their grizzly work.

A dozen timers ticked down in a dozen ships. The tankers had been stalled in port because of a strike; an embarrassed Russian government had paid their tolls…and Europe had laughed at the Russians who hadn't dared to strike outside free and liberal Europe. Now, the timers reached zero and ships loaded with Liquid Natural Gas exploded, devastating the surrounding areas and forcing the remains of the European emergency services to concentrate on a very different disaster. Isolated, cut off from their superiors, they did what they could, unaware of the real threat.

In the south of France, the explosions were a sign to the Algerian Special Forces units that had been inserted into France two weeks before the war began. Five thousand Algerians had gone to Russia to be trained; seven hundred had returned, each one a lethal killer and a ruthless operative. They moved now as the sky lit up with unholy fire, driving towards the massive refugee camps that had been set up to house the immigrants from Algeria, Morocco and further south in Africa. The French had wanted to return them, but the European Courts had said no; they had remained there, day after day, under guard…

The guards disliked their job and the people they watched over. Some of them did the best they could, some of them abused the refugees, or traded food for sexual purposes. They were hardly the cream of the French armed forces… and there was no reason to expect that they would be attacked in the heart of France. The sudden assault overwhelmed them; the guards killed before they could sound an alarm, and the commandos looked upon those who had fled their country, months ago. Many of them had allowed themselves to be caught.

Weapons had been provided and limited plans made; the makeshift army surged out of the camp, already forming up into groups. The commandos knew how to control brute troops; they had gained respect by killing the guards and they used that mercilessly. Under their leadership, the refugees would take part in the violence, intended to establish the Islamic State of France. None of them knew, nor would they have cared, that the Russian plans were very different. Doubt was not in their mindset; the few dissenters among the male population, those who had been in the camps and had escaped being radicalised, were rapidly dispatched with quick shots to the head. Howling, the army set off towards the burning city on the horizon, the Promised Land that had turned its back on them.

In Britain, the situation was different. In the light of burning cities, far-right groups launched attacks; Muslim groups fought back, the situation made worse by the sight of aircraft crashing and wild rumours spreading across the country. As in Europe, police stations and TA bases found themselves under attack; a string of accidents to gladden the heart of Muhammad Saeed al-Sahhaf occurred on the streets. Manchester, Bradford, Luton, Liverpool, Birmingham and even some parts of London fell into civil disorder and chaos; both sides, once again, were targeting the police as well as any other part of the national government. The chaos seemed unending…

No one knew that, in Poland, it had only just begun.

Chapter Eighteen

A Day That Will Live In Infamy, Take One

There are four hundred neatly marked graves somewhere in Sicily. All because one man went to sleep on the job. But they are German graves, because we caught the bastard asleep before they did.
George S. Patton

Near Warsaw, Poland

"Regarding your response to my request for another infantry regiment, I must say that it is most inconvenient," General Konrad Trautman dictated to his assistant. "I have the task, it seems, of defending the borders of Poland without either a clear mission statement or sufficient force to deter a cross-border raid. As the Polish President has made clear to Parliament, the Russians can rush a force into the border, complete their mission and withdraw, all the while being fairly safe from our interference. Two heavy armoured units are valuable, but they are not suited to the role of a rapid reaction force, while for political reasons Polish units are held back."

He took a breath. "I must say that this is not improving the reputation of EUROFOR in the Polish military," he continued. It was one of his less serious problems…the serious problems were potentially disastrous. "The Poles are fast running out of patience with us and only their dependence upon energy supplies from Russia has prevented them defying us and moving up their own infantry, counting on them to deter any raids. If this happens, Commissioner, I must question the value of both the security guarantee and the Parliament's commitment to Poland. EUROFOR must be reinforced *effectively* or heads will roll."

He smiled tiredly at his assistant. "Sign it and have it sent by courier back to Brussels, marked for the attention of Commissioner Henri Guichy," he ordered. His opinion of Guichy wasn't high; odd, given that most of the

German Army regarded him as Guichy's closest German ally. "Have the courier issued with all of the special permits that he will require to gain admittance into the headquarters."

"Yes, sir," his assistant said.

She saluted and left the room. Trautman watched her go, wishing that he shared her problems; his problems seemed almost insolvable. The EUROFOR organisation had managed to deploy the rough equivalent of two divisions to Poland, backing up the forces the Poles kept ready for action, but they were hardly prepared for the role of securing the borders. The chaos that broke out, from time to time, in Belarus sent thousands of refugees fleeing across the border, some of them with bad intentions towards Russia. The Russians launched raids to capture them…and the Poles were prevented by the European Parliament from securing their own borders, just to avoid provocation. Instead, they had…

They had General Trautman and EUROFOR. Trautman had spent enough time with each of the major units to know that they were hardly prepared for the task; the two heavy armoured units, one from France, one from Germany, were not suited to the task of sealing the borders. If the Russians ever launched a raid with heavy armour, then they might be useful, but otherwise, Trautman was grimly aware that getting them into position would take far too long. He needed more infantry…and it was infantry that the European Defence Commission was refusing to send him.

He scowled at the map. Poland was a large country and it had a long land border, almost impossible to secure at the best of times, one that was crossed regularly by criminals and terrorists as well as illegal immigrants and freedom fighters from Belarus. The Russians called them terrorists and demanded that the Poles hand them over; the Poles themselves would have been happy to comply. European laws, however, were clear; anyone seeking asylum had to be granted at least provisional asylum unless there were very clear circumstances proving that they should be returned. Trautman had read enough of the media's left-wing reporting – and the outraged right-wing independent media – to know that there seemed to be no case where someone would actually be sent back to face justice. If Brussels was prepared to give asylum to people wanted for the bombing in Oakland, there was no way that they would send Russians back to Russia.

There was a knock on the door. "Come in," Trautman shouted. One of the EUROFOR communications officers entered. "Report."

"General, we have a report from the field," Captain Philippe Laroche said. The French officer was mercifully free of the institutional bias of Guichy and his fellow commissioners; most junior French officers were at least as good as their German or British counterparts. The French just had a habit of promoting officers for their political skills rather than their military skills; General Éclair had had political skills as well as military skills, a rarity in any army. "Several border guards are reporting that they can hear engines on the far side of the border."

Trautman glanced down at the map; Laroche pointed out the location. "That hardly seems likely," he said, as he worked through it in his head. "There's no refugee camp near there, just the border guards and an infantry unit."

He glanced up. "Is there anything on the radars?"

He would have been delighted to have taken up the American offer of a direct feed from the American bases in Poland. He would have been even more delighted to have had an American armoured division attached to his force; few countries enjoyed the thought of picking a fight with the Americans these days, not after Tehran had paid the price for the nuclear attack on American forces...even though the *Jihadist* propaganda claimed that it had been in response to the attack on Israel. The European Defence Commission had made its will clear...and Trautman was a loyal servant of Europe.

He was uncomfortably aware that General Éclair would have done it anyway.

"No, sir, just normal traffic," Laroche said. "The Russians keep rerouting aircraft away from Ukraine, but after that lunatic was seen with a SAM launcher, there was little else that they could do. The pilots are getting used to it; we can listen in on their chatter sometimes. The Russians have their standard five-ship air patrol up, but no sign of anything that would be supporting a cross-border raid."

Trautman rubbed his head. He was about to start his first headache of the day. If he sent out the alert, the Poles would be on hair-triggers and end up firing on Russians, or even accidentally firing on European units. If he didn't send out an alert, the situation might get better, but it might also get worse... and if that happened, his forces would be caught on the hop.

"Tell them to get ready to get ready," he said, hoping that the young Dutchman in command of the closest European force would know what he meant. "If we need to support them, then..."

The buzzer sounded. "General, you asked to be notified when the Polish supply convoy arrived," his assistant said. "They're just pulling up..."

Her voice vanished; moments later, the lights and computers faded and died. Trautman opened his mouth to say something and realised that they had had a power cut; emergency systems were coming online, trying to get everything running again, but the small generator that the Soviets had left them with in the base hadn't anything like enough capability to power everything. He had wanted to move in a more modern generator, but the idea had been dismissed as 'unnecessarily provocative.' There were times when he wondered if the entire European Defence Commission was in the pay of the Russians.

"We've had a power cut," he said, calmly. Laroche had drawn his service weapon and was looking around grimly. ""I don't think there's anything to worry about..."

An explosion shook the camp, followed rapidly by a second explosion and a burst of heavy gunfire. Trautman recognised the sound at once; those were Russian weapons. His mouth fell open...and then the window burst as a third explosion detonated, far too close for comfort. He could hear the sound of mortars being fired and rounds impacting within the camp and realised, dimly, that they were under attack.

"Sir," Laroche shouted at him. Trautman found himself on the floor, the cold hard Russian floor, without a clear memory of how he'd landed there. "Sir, we have to get out of here!"

The building shook again. Laroche was making sound tactical sense; they couldn't remain in a building that the Russians – if Russians they were – would know perfectly. Trautman yanked open a drawer and removed his own service weapon, cursing the limited ammunition; if he had to fight, he would only have nine shots before he ran out of bullets. The door burst open and he almost shot the intruder before realising who he was, the commanding officer of the French paratroopers who had somehow been assigned to the base. It had been at that moment that he had realised that the European Defence Commission just didn't care…but now he was grateful. French paratroopers had a tough reputation.

"Sir, we have to get you out of here," the leader said. Trautman struggled to remember the Frenchman's name; Captain Paul Montagne, if he recalled correctly. A service record with details classified beyond even his clearance, but some details of service in Africa and even in an ill-fated attempt to topple the Islamic Government in Algeria had slipped through the cracks. "This base is under attack!"

Another explosion shook the base. "Fine," Trautman snapped, as the paratrooper hustled them out into the corridor. Four more paratroopers, all heavily armed, were securing the corridor, their eyes flickering left and right as they waited for contact with the enemy. "What's happening?"

Montagne motioned for two of his people to go ahead and check out the corridor towards the rear exit of the base. "The Polish Convoy was larger than it was supposed to be, but the guards let the lead truck in the gate anyway, whereupon a truck bomb exploded and killed the guards; two more truck bombs devastated the remainder of the defences. Armed men appeared and launched an attack; I sent the remainder of my people down to the rear entrance to hopefully keep it secure."

Trautman could barely grasp it. Minutes ago, he had been trying to scrape up another infantry unit for EUROFOR; now, he had been plunged into the middle of a shooting war. It was his shame that the closest he had come to a real war had been a peacekeeping mission in the Middle East, before Europe had washed its hands of the whole matter; now, he would be trying to coordinate a response without any means of escape.

His hand fell to the radio he always carried at his belt. It was jammed. "There's jamming everywhere," Montagne reported, as they jogged round a corner into more drab grey soviet-era corridors. Trautman had never liked them; military bases weren't designed by freethinkers, but the Russians had taken the entire concept to extremes and stamped out any trace of personality. "I think that this is happening everywhere."

Trautman remembered the spread-out deployment of EUROFOR's forces and shuddered. He had talked the Poles, several times, out of mobilising their army. If every EUROFOR base was under attack, and he couldn't see this attack as being anything other than the first moves in a war, the Russians were all-too-likely to get quite far into Poland before they bumped into something that could stop them. How far could they go?

He shuddered again; Germany still remembered the Russian hordes looting, raping and burning their way across Germany, in the last war. If some of those tales were exaggerated, and Trautman knew enough to know that folk memory often was nothing of the sort, there had still been enough horror for everyone. Was that what life was going to be like again?

The elevator ahead beckoned him. "Not bloody likely," Montagne snapped. Trautman remembered, embarrassed, that the power was out. They headed down the stairs and came to a halt as a burst of fire shattered concrete and sent chunks of debris everywhere. Montagne didn't hesitate; he pulled a grenade off his belt and tossed it down the stairs, the paratroopers crashing down in the wake of the explosion, firing ruthlessly into the smoke. "Move!"

Trautman had seen carnage before, but the sight of the Russian bodies was something new; they were torn and broken by the force of the grenade. A single Russian was still alive and Montagne shot him, quickly, through the head; Trautman opened his mouth to protest and decided that it wasn't worth the effort. His very survival, and the only chance of organising a counterattack, depended upon his escape from the horror that the camp had become.

He took a breath; more drab grey corridors, more blank walls, more sense of danger, of imminent threat. Part of him was wondering if it was an endless nightmare, or if he would wake up; the sheer level of detail reminded him constantly that it was no dream. His hand felt sweaty around his pistol; he had to keep reminding himself that it was dangerous and that he couldn't put it away or drop it. A voice ahead shouted out a challenge in thick French; Montagne shouted back in the same language. Trautman had prided himself on his command of French, but he didn't recognise the words at all, just the language.

"Come on," Montagne hissed. There was another explosion; this time, plaster and dust drifted down from the ceiling. The vehicle bay was empty; his jeep, he remembered now, had been outside with the other official vehicles, and was either useless or in enemy hands. He wondered if they should surrender, if a surrender would be accepted, but how could they offer it in the midst of bloody chaos? It wasn't possible and he knew it; commando raids tended to have very high casualties because of the chaos.

He looked up at Montagne. "What's the plan?"

Montagne looked around; there were nine paratroopers left. "We're in the middle of the camp," he hissed. Trautman hadn't needed the reminder. "We're going to have to head to the north side, where the exercise and training facilities are; they have to be at the bottom of the Russian list of priorities. We can't get to the barracks by now; unless the Russians have forgotten all they knew, they will be targeting the barracks and the armoury and ammunition dump first, along with the vehicles. Once we're there, we'll cut our way through the fence and escape into the countryside."

He nodded briefly at his men. "Jean, check the side," he ordered. "Come on, sir."

Trautman followed him into the chaos. The camp seemed to be half on fire, half destroyed; the entire place seemed to be in total chaos. A collection of dead bodies, hit and killed by a mortar round or a grenade, lay in front of him as they moved carefully through the smoke, staying low. The sound of firing was drifting over from the eastern side of the camp, the barracks, but the soldiers there would have little in the way of supplies. The European Defence Commission had drawn up the guidelines and Trautman – he cursed himself for a fool – had implemented them; soldiers would not have their weapons unless they were issued from the armoury. The guards were armed, but how long could they hold out alone?

"Some of the lads will have kept their weapons anyway," Montagne said, when Trautman broached the subject. He had had a vague idea that they could retake the armoury and issue weapons. "The modern soldier knows that he could be plunged into war instantly and therefore keeps his weapons ready for action, even if it means a week of fatigues if he gets caught at it."

Trautman realised that the Sergeants and Military Police must have known…and said nothing. As long as the soldiers weren't causing problems, and European soldiers were very well disciplined, they would have allowed the forbidden practice to continue; their failure to act might have saved some lives. The firing was starting to weaken, however; Trautman knew what that meant. The defenders were running out of ammunition…and, once it was gone, they would be hacked apart by outraged Russians. The sneak attack meant only one thing; the Russians intended to be merciless.

A shout, in Russian, brought them back to reality. Montagne fired once, dropping the Russian, and shouted at them to run. Other Russians fired back as Trautman fell to the ground, firing twice towards the shapes in the smoke and haze; he saw flashes of light as the Russians returned fire. The Russians, at least, seemed as surprised as they were to meet them, but they had the advantage in firepower and determination. Laroche was shot four times by a Russian as he struggled to pick some of them off; Trautman shouted in rage as the Frenchman was blown apart, dead in the prime of his life.

"Sir, get out of here," Montagne shouted. The tough paratrooper had been hit, badly; blood was trickling from a wound in his arm. Trautman caught up his assault rifle and fired a long burst towards the Russians, knowing that it was his last stand. He didn't dare be taken alive, not after what the Russians had done to any number of Chechen leaders. They had been forced to broadcast radio messages ordering their people to surrender…and EUROFOR wasn't composed of rogue fanatics. If ordered to surrender, they might just surrender, particularly if he sounded normal. "Sir…"

A bullet shattered Montagne's head. Trautman kept firing, seeing Russians everywhere…and then a burning pain flared through his head. There was an instant of pain, and then he hit the ground, dead. Half an hour later, every European in the camp was dead, a prisoner, or fled into the Polish countryside.

No warning had been transmitted.

Chapter Nineteen

A Day That Will Live In Infamy, Take Two

The art of concentrating strength at one point, forcing a breakthrough, rolling up and securing the flanks on either side, and then penetrating like lightning deep into his rear, before the enemy has time to react.
Erwin Rommel

Polish-Belarus Border, Poland

General Aleksandr Borisovich Shalenko crossed over to Polish territory with a theatrical flourish worthy of George Patton or Douglas Macarthur. The president had understood that his old friend yearned to command the largest military operation in the history of the world, and if he was denied a direct combat command, he would have the pleasure and duty of coordinating the offensive. Around him, thousands of tanks drove into Polish territory, while above him, the streaks of MLRS-launched missiles and jet aircraft lit up the sky.

A group of Polish prisoners sat in one corner, guarded by a bored-looking soldier. Their faces were masks of horror and grief; they had been caught, almost literally, asleep at the switch. A handful of Spetsnaz, wearing Polish uniforms, had entered the customs post and subdued the border guards, almost without firing a shot. The prisoners now stared at the advancing Russian force, their hands firmly secured behind their backs, broken by what they were seeing in front of them. Shalenko ignored them magnificently; their fate had already been decided.

A massive line of infantry-carrying lorries rumbled past him, carrying Russian soldiers who still seemed a little bemused at going to war. They had been drilled relentlessly for months, but they had never been told why, not until the hurried last-minute briefings that had explained what they were going to do. Some of them had deserted under the sudden news; Shalenko had heard that Russian border guards had shot two men trying to make a break for Poland. If another had managed to make it into Poland, he hadn't been able to alert the Poles in time to make a difference; there had only been four Polish aircraft in the air when the missiles started to land. They had been swiftly bounced and destroyed by MIG-41 aircraft.

"General," Captain Anna Ossipavo said. She was his aide, lover and bodyguard, all rolled into one. No one would take her seriously – sexism was still alive and well in most levels of the Russian hierarchy – until it was too late; even the Black Widow herself hadn't convinced Russians that sexism was a dangerous weakness. Shalenko suspected that most of her detractors thought she was a lesbian. "I have the first reports from the observation and assault teams."

Shalenko turned and smiled. They stood together in the middle of organised chaos. He knew what it all meant; none of the Poles, or even most of his own people, would have a real inking of the truth. Four massive Russian forces were invading Poland, crashing into the Polish borders and their unprepared defences; behind the lines, Russian commandos were ripping apart the Polish command and control centres, hacking the proud Polish Army into a screaming mob of tiny units. Some would break under the pressure, some would fight to the death…it hardly mattered. Isolated, they couldn't pose a threat, or a problem.

"Good," he said. The Battlespace Management System would warn him if anything went seriously wrong, but he still needed the details. "What's the bad news?"

"We scored around a seventy percent success rate," Anna said, seriously. "In several places, the Polish guards were alert and killed most of the assault terms before they could detonate their bombs or launch the attack; those teams either retreated or were wiped out to the last man. A handful of Polish aircraft were launched into the air before the missiles destroyed their airbases; they may pose a threat to our advance. The attack on Warsaw airport more or less succeeded, but an airliner was destroyed on the runway and is now blocking activities."

Shalenko shrugged. He hadn't expected that part of the plan to work. "Remind the team leader…"

"His deputy, sir," Anna said. "The team leader was killed in the assault."

"Remind the new team leader that if the Poles do manage to mount a counterattack, he is to destroy as much as he can and run," Shalenko said. There was little point in trying to hold the airport; the Poles had always had an infantry force nearby, and the missiles might not have destroyed or scattered it. If there was a counterattack, the Russians would lose. "And the rest of the news?"

"We have destroyed or crippled around seventy percent of the deployed Polish armed forces, as well as hitting all of their barracks and bases with missiles," Anna said. "The strike team that attacked the EUROFOR camp near Warsaw reported complete success, but they had to mortar the barracks; a mixed force of soldiers was holding out and imperilling the success of the operation. Other strike forces have more or less completed their missions; bridges, dams and command centres are in our hands and the Poles are crippled."

Shalenko nodded. Tanks were far more powerful than they had been in the days of Stalin, but the price tag was high…and not just in money. The Poles would have ample opportunity to slow his forces if they managed to scrape together the coordination to mount counterattacks; a single destroyed bridge could stalemate the invasion for hours. The lighter tanks, using armour developed by the Americans and stolen from them by the FSB, might find it easier to advance, but they were more vulnerable to heavy weapons. The Americans had thought about the problem of engaging insurgents, not another armoured force.

He smiled. "And further in?"

"The assault units that hit Germany and France have reported success as well, although some of them have been lost or at the very least haven't reported back yet," Anna said. "The jamming stations have been emplaced and are being used; that's actually impeding our own operations in some locations, although we still have direct laser links to orbiting communications satellites. The monitors back at Moscow are claiming that ninety percent of the missiles launched at European targets have found their targets, but they're requesting that we prioritise the surviving targets for attention as soon as possible."

"The devil is always in the details," Shalenko said, as a hail of gunfire echoed out over the horizon. There were countless Polish civilians in the area and he felt a little sympathy for the hell that they were about to go through. They were caught in the path of an invading army and that was hell for civilians, particularly young female civilians. He had made it clear to his men that atrocities would not be tolerated – and the penal units had an endless thirst for men – but the FSB units were only marginally under his command. "What about the radio signal?"

"It was transmitted on the general bands, all civilian," Anna said. The message had been pre-recorded by a traitor, the greatest success story that the FSB had had in Poland since the end of the Cold War, a success story so unbelievable that Shalenko had wondered if it was a sting operation. It was amazing what people would do under the threat of having their night time activities revealed to the world. "The message is repeated every ten minutes, in between the jamming; we took out the official radio and other media centres in the opening moments of the offensive. Even if the President has survived our attempt to kill him, he won't be able to get his message out…and really, what can he say that disagrees with our message?"

"True," Shalenko said.

They watched in silence as assault helicopters flashed overhead, heading for targets within Poland, harrying the remains of the Polish Army and EUROFOR to the point where they would disintegrate. Other armoured thrusts were moving to relieve commandos who had seized targets; a handful of FSB units had already been given the task of securing prisoners before they could be sent back into the wastelands of Siberia. Shalenko didn't like that solution, but there was little choice; it was that, or kill them all. The FSB had argued in favour of just that solution, but Shalenko had put his foot down; besides, they might need something to bargain with.

A young officer came running up to them. "General Shalenko, sir," he gasped. Captain Vladimir Ivanov was in the best of health; he had to have run all the way from the helicopter landing pad away from the guard battalion protecting the makeshift base. "We have all of Unit One in position."

"Excellent," Shalenko said. Ivanov was young for his role and seriously under-ranked, not unusual in Russia, but Ivanov's role had been critically important. Unit One was not charged with fighting a war, but preventing one…or at least preventing the war that Russia had started getting out of control. The entire episode had to be handled very carefully. "Come on, Anna; we're going for a helicopter flight."

Anna had protested, of course, but Shalenko have overruled her. It was true that renegade Polish units might be scattered around, and they might have the SAM missiles needed to take down a helicopter, but there was little need to actually *panic*. Russia controlled the air over Poland, the Russian Air Force was reaching out towards Denmark, Germany and even Norway…what possible threat could there be to one helicopter with two attack helicopters escorting it?

Poland was burning. They flew low, but he could still see the fires, the remains of Polish forces that had been caught by surprise by the Russians, or European forces that had been lulled into a false sense of security. Jet aircraft criss-crossed the sky, hunting for the armoured units that the Europeans had dispatched in a desperate attempt to look as if they were Doing Something; when they found a tank, or even a military vehicle, they would take it out with extreme prejudice. The pilot took them even lower as they approached their target, the forces attached to Unit One spaced out around the area, ready and waiting.

"There are no signs that Polish forces have attempted to seek refuge here," Ivanov said softly. The sight of the American base was awe-inspiring, even to Shalenko himself, who knew what it all meant. The base was studded with antennas, radar domes, aerials and all manner of systems, some of them capable of tracking aircraft far into Russia. "The only Polish force nearby has been soundly attacked and dispersed into the countryside."

Shalenko nodded as the helicopter came to the ground; he scrambled out and pulled his cap on as Anna followed him, one hand on the rifle she had on her back. He kept his head low as he accepted some salutes, before walking up the road towards the American base. Speed was of the essence…despite himself, he was going to enjoy himself. This was payback time.

The American guard lifted a weapon as Shalenko approached. "I would like to speak with your commanding officer," Shalenko said, as calmly as he could. His lines had been preset; ironically, they had been preset by the Americans. His English was perfect. "I would…appreciate his presence at once."

The Guard showed no hint of nervousness. "The CO doesn't see anyone who comes with an invading army," he said, making his sympathies clear. "This is…"

Shalenko spoke over him. "This is a base in a war zone aiding and abetting the enemies of my people," he said, speaking the lines from heart. "You will inform you commanding officer that I will speak to him within the next five minutes or the base will be reduced to burning scrap metal. Your choice."

The guard pulled down a microphone from his helmet and subvocalised into it. "One moment," he said, grudgingly. "The CO will be out within a minute."

Shalenko had studied the file on Major Alan Fletcher with care. American – obviously – and regarded as a safe pair of hands for a base in friendly territory. The Americans were more or less prisoners on their own base; the European Parliament had insisted on gaining control and jurisdiction over Americans in Europe who left the base and the Americans had balked. Fletcher looked…harmless; his career had been a solid one, rather than exciting. A paper-pusher, Shalenko decided; Fletcher certainly didn't have the attitude of a Grant or even a Sherman.

"Major," Shalenko said. He made his voice as pleasant as he could. "I must request that you cease all activities and prepare your men for reparation back to the United States."

Fletcher's eyes glittered. "This is an American base…"

Shalenko cut him off. "As your Marine Colonel Vandergrift said to the commander of a Russian research base in Iran, this base is providing aid and support to the enemy," he said. "You have the choice between shutting the base down – on the same terms as you offered us during the Iran War – or having the base destroyed. I need an answer now."

Fletcher seemed to stand a little straighter. "That would be an act of war," he protested. "I certainly have no orders regarding the…incursion on Polish territory."

"And, as your Colonel refused, I also refuse to give you time to consult with Washington," Shalenko said. He leaned forward. "I have four batteries of heavy guns back there, Major; I will pour fire onto the base until it is wrecked and incapable of resistance, and then my infantry will secure the site. You have no means of countering my attack and no means of escape; all you can do is die."

Fletcher seemed to wilt. "This is an act of war…"

"This is exactly what you did to us," Shalenko reminded him. "If you agree to surrender, we will provide free transport back to Washington as soon as the situation permits it, or we can just send you all to the American Embassy in Moscow. You will not be harmed or held hostage; we won't even interrogate you as the CIA interrogated some of our people. After the war is over, we will even transfer everything from the base back to American soil; we won't damage it if you hand it over."

"After you've studied everything," Fletcher snapped.

"Quite," Shalenko agreed. "Also…exactly what you did to us."

There was a long pause. The sound of aircraft could be heard in the distance.

"Choose," Shalenko hissed. "I have no more time. Your radar feed could mean life or death for hundreds of Russian pilots, and I am not going to allow their lives to be risked by your…insistence on rights that are used to threaten Russia. You set the precedent; live with it. What do you want to do; die here futilely, along with all your people, or go back home to Washington?"

He watched Fletcher's mind turning over. "I am prepared to surrender on the condition you allow us to wipe the files first," Fletcher said finally. The self-hate in his tone was remarkable. "If not…"

"You refused to allow us to wipe any files," Shalenko said dryly. That, too, had happened in Iran, although plenty of files had been burned by the Russians before the base was surrendered. "You set the precedent…"

"Washington will not allow this to pass unpunished," Fletcher snapped. They both knew that it was an empty threat. Washington had its hands full with Korea and the Middle East, where thousands of little groups had taken the Second Korean War as a chance to hit the Americans and hurt them. "Very well; I will issue the orders."

"Thank you," Shalenko said. "You have my word that you and your people will remain unharmed."

He tapped his radio; the men of Unit One moved in. The Americans came out of the base in small groups, many of them angry and frustrated, even those who had known that the position was completely helpless. Unit One had been trained carefully; the Americans would not be searched, nor would they be cuffed; they would be interned rather than treated as prisoners of war. They would be the lucky ones; the Turks would agree to take them out and send them to American bases in the Middle East. As for the files…

Shalenko knew that the Americans had made great progress in some areas…and the President knew it as well. The chance to examine the base was beyond price, even though the American inventions might be impossible to duplicate, at least for a few years. Anything that came out of the base wouldn't be useful for the present war, but as for the future…well, who knew what could happen? Russia still lagged behind America and Japan in the high-tech areas and anything that could shorten the space was worth having.

He watched as the Americans were taken away on trucks, heading back into Belarus. "General, I just had a signal from the 2nd Shock Army," Anna said. He heard the note in her voice and smiled; he knew that it was good news. "They have pocketed and destroyed the main Polish force between us and Warsaw."

"Good," Shalenko said. He glanced at his watch; it was almost exactly on time. The remains of the Polish army would either be scattered or prisoners of war; in any case, they would be in no position to dispute with the Russians for a while. It was time to move ahead with the second stage of the plan, before the Poles and EUROFOR gathered themselves into a serious threat. "Is the 2nd Shock still operative?"

Anna nodded. "The Poles were completely disorganised," she said. She held up the terminal for him to see; the Poles had been battered enough to shatter them as a coherent force. "They only lost thirty tanks."

Shalenko smiled. "Then give the order," he said. He had waited a long time for this moment. "The advance forces are to continue the offensive…and the secondary forces are to move on Warsaw."

Chapter Twenty

A Day That Will Live In Infamy, Take Three

Every man is scared in his first battle. If he says he's not, he's a liar. Some men are cowards but they fight the same as the brave men or they get the hell slammed out of them watching men fight who are just as scared as they are. The real hero is the man who fights even though he is scared.
George S. Patton

Near Warsaw, Poland

There was something in the air.

Captain Stuart Robinson could feel it, somehow; the sense that matters were somehow not quite right. It reminded him far too much of Sudan, or of patrolling through a hostile town, the sense that everyone was watching you for just a hint of weakness. The old sweats who had served in Iraq had told him about the feeling from Basra and other godforsaken places in the Middle East; the sense that at any moment the horde of people was going to turn on you and try to kill you.

He shook his head, trying to dismiss the feeling. They were in Poland, in Europe; they were not in the heart of Afghanistan or darkest Africa. Sure, they didn't like the French, or had a long history of fighting the Germans, but they weren't about to carry the feeling onto the battlefield. The only bloodshed between England and France these days had been in the last football match, where two players had smashed into one another without looking where they were going, breaking an entire list of bones. The Poles weren't unhappy to see them, they didn't feel occupied, so why the feeling?

Sergeant Ronald Inglehart felt it too. "I doubled the patrols, sir," he said, without being asked. Robinson knew that he should feel slighted by the Sergeant refusing to seek his permission, but some Captains wouldn't have moved because of a 'feeling.' It didn't make him any happier to know that the

Sergeant was sharing his thoughts; he would have been able to dismiss them if it had been just him. "The sensors have been reporting movement all night from wild animals, but nothing else."

Robinson rolled his eyes. His own guard duty had been spent at a RAF base, where they had been replacing the RAF Regiment for a short period while the members of the regiment, overworked like everyone else, went for training on the newer equipment. The heights of excitement there had been a chance to watch local wildlife through the night-vision equipment – that, and laying bets on who would be the first to get inside Flying Officer Cindy Jackson's pants. The memory made him smile; the female fast-jet pilot had gone through men as if they were going out of season, looking for a different man each night. He'd kept the book; as a married man, he had had no intention of chasing other women.

He frowned. It struck him, suddenly, what was missing. "Jacob, have you had any contact with the Polish command centre?"

Captain Jacob Anastazy looked up at him. He'd been in a mood since Marya had left…with the telephone numbers and emails of half the Company in her pocket. Marya, too, could date a different man a night…and Anastazy had been worried about her. Robinson hadn't cared; as long as his men were gentlemen, he didn't worry about it. Marya was a grown-up girl…

"No," Anastazy said slowly. "Normally, they call me, just to check in."

Robinson exchanged a long glance with Inglehart. Maybe it was just another manifestation of the overworked computer systems breaking down and taking the communications system with it – Microsoft had done half the work, which explained some of the problems, although the European Consortium that had attempted to finish the work had its own share of bugs – or maybe it was a sign that something was actually wrong. He almost felt relieved; they would have something real to face, a problem he could solve. It was bound to be nothing, really.

"Try and raise them," he said. A mischievous thought occurred to him. "Tell them that we want more booze and hookers."

"I bet you have a habit of putting stink bombs in the General's quarters as well," Anastazy commented dryly, as he lifted his radio to his lips and activated it. A screech of static burst out of it, causing him to almost drop it in shock. "Sir, I…that was…"

"Jammed," Inglehart snapped. "Someone's jamming us!"

Robinson felt his blood run cold. Perhaps it was a drill, but that would have been announced, surely. The Poles wouldn't have held any drills without telling people who depended on the communications network…and EUROFOR would have told him if they had intended to take it down.

"Sergeant, get the men into defensive positions," he hissed, removing his rifle from his shoulder and bringing it up into defensive position. "Jacob, see if you can locate any signals, EUROFOR or Polish or…"

"Captain," Lieutenant Benjamin Matthews shouted. The note of alarm in his voice brought Robinson to his side quicker than anything else could have done. The small laptop that served as one of the hubs for the radar they had mounted on the hilltop was buzzing an alarm at them. The display was lighting up with red icons. "We have problems."

Robinson stared down at the screen. It was making his eyes hurt; it was so bright. "What the hell is happening?"

Matthews tapped the laptop. "One moment, everything is nice and normal, from that bunched up and pissed off group of commercial airliners, to the handful of Russian aircraft in the air and…then all hell broke loose. We have aircraft and missiles rising everywhere and coming for Poland – coming for us."

Robinson felt his training reassert itself. "How are you getting the information?" He demanded. He pointed one long hand towards the radar unit. "Is that thing working?"

"Yes," Matthews said. "It's…"

A scream echoed across the sky; a blast of lightning seemed to reach down and touch the radar, which exploded in a burst of fire. Robinson realised dimly that it had been a missile, fired from somewhere not too far away, targeted perfectly upon the radar. It had been a HARM-type missile, he saw; it had homed in on the radar transmissions and destroyed the radar. It was sheer luck that no one had been hurt.

"Get the trucks moving," he snapped. If someone, most likely the Russians, had decided to start something, they would try to take out the CADS as soon as possible. They would want control of the air and the CADS represented one of the latest breakthroughs in air denial systems; even without their radars, they would make prime targets. "I want them to move and then…"

Shooting broke out, far too close for comfort; mortars and grenades started to explode. He threw himself to the ground, rolling towards his guards, as they opened fire on the attackers. The enemy soldiers wore unmarked uniforms and seemed to be determined to kill all of the British soldiers. He heard the noise of helicopters in the distance as the enemy pushed closer; whatever else was going on, this was no minor accident.

"Sir, keep your fucking head down," one of his Corporals shouted at him. They'd done well on the defensive positions, but it was far from perfect; they seemed to be surrounded and taking fire from all sides. "Those sons of bitches are out to kill us!"

"I never would have fucking noticed," Robinson screamed back, as he lifted his rifle. Fire seemed to be coming from everywhere; the enemy was well-versed in using territory for concealment. He fired at a shape in the woods and had the pleasure of seeing it topple to the ground, screaming as it died. A thought struck him and he swore. "They're in the fucking river bed!"

"Done and done," Inglehart said, sounding as if he were having the time of his life. The burly sergeant pulled up an entire belt of grenades, unhooked one, and tossed the others towards the dry bed, sheltered from the fire of his people. Seconds later, a stream of explosions and screams announced the end of a handful of enemy soldiers; mortar bombs began to fall in the British position. "Sir, we're going to have to take that fucker out!"

"Take four men," Robinson snapped. He hated positions like this; every infantryman learned to dread them. They were fighting at almost point-blank range against an enemy who was both well-trained and experienced, something that was rarer than outside observers suspected. There was little strategy about it; they would fire at whatever targets they saw, until they were all killed. "We'll cover you."

He took a moment to note the path that Inglehart had taken and opened fire, joined by the chattering noise of the SAW as the cook put down the ladle and opened fire with the weapon he was rated to use in combat. Robinson remembered the jokes about sending the cook to the enemy to poison them all and realised that they were silly; the chattering of the SAW would send many of the enemy to hell with lead poisoning. Flames and smoke were beginning to rise from their camp where they had emplaced the tents; the enemy fire had started to take a toll of the defenders. He shuddered to think of what would have happened if they hadn't suspected that something was wrong.

An aircraft flashed by, high overhead, heading west. He wondered who was flying it, which side it was on; there seemed to be no way of flagging the pilot down and calling for help. The aircraft might be Russian, or it might be Polish, or…there were just too many possibilities for him to grasp. It didn't matter anyway; his world had shrunk to fighting and killing, or dying in place. Surrender just wasn't in his blood.

Hazel's face flickered once across his mind, and then he devoted himself to returning fire. An explosion, far too close for comfort, marked Inglehart's success against the enemy mortar; green-clad figures leapt towards his position and were mown down by the defenders. Others kept pressing closer with grenades; Robinson shot a man in the chest and was astonished to discover that he had survived; the body armour had been much better than he had thought. The wounded man staggered away and he shot him neatly through the head.

A voice shouted at them in English as the rain of bullets slowed. "Surrender or die!"

"Fuck you," Robinson shouted back, to cheers. "Fuck the lot of you!"

Inglehart jumped back as the enemy resumed firing and this time added a second mortar to the bombardment. Robinson laughed as a shell struck the ruined radar unit, shattering something that was already impossible to repair into something even more impossible to repair. One of his men who had a sniper's badge crawled up a tree and picked off a handful of enemy soldiers before being shot out of the tree himself. His body crashed to the ground.

"And your mothers," Inglehart added, firing away like a madman. "Fuck them and your sisters and your grannies and your…"

"Helicopters," Matthews shouted, loud enough to be heard over the firing. Robinson realised that he was using one of the loudspeakers. "Incoming helicopters!"

Robinson turned his head and saw them; four helicopters, black and hanging in the air like angry angels. There was no mistaking them; they were Russian assault helicopters, each one armed to the teeth. He'd seen briefings on them; deployed to Afghanistan and Chechnya, they had been feared by the insurgents and underground fighters alike. They would make short work of his position and he didn't have anything that could touch them except...

"Ben, tell me that you can kill those bastards," he shouted. The Russian attack seemed to have tailed off as the helicopters drew closer; the British took the opportunity to pick off several Russians who had unwisely exposed themselves. "Tell me that or we'll have to make a break for it!"

"Trust me," Matthews shouted back. "Have I ever lied to you?"

"How the fuck would I know?" Robinson demanded. He thought again of Hazel; what was happening to her in the new world? What would happen to her? The black helicopters were racing closer now; it wouldn't be long before they opened fire. "Just kill those cock-suckers..."

The first CADS opened fire. The roar was deafeningly loud, much louder than a Stinger missile or a Yank missile; the line of light seemed impossibly fast as it slammed into the lead helicopter and blew it apart. The second opened fire, then the third; the first finished off the fourth helicopter. It was the only helicopter to fire a shot; the missile struck one of the CADS and blew it away, sending red-hot shrapnel everywhere.

"Fuck the lot of you," Matthews shouted; his voice gleeful. Robinson laughed as Matthews shouted out his victory. "Who's your daddy, eh?"

There was a final round of firing and the attack finished, as quickly as it had begun. The enemy soldiers faded away into the woods and vanished, watched warily by their British enemies. Robinson felt as if he had run a ten-mile race in minutes; his breathing was coming think and heavy, the strange rush of combat fading as the danger ebbed. He forced himself to think and think hard; what the hell had just happened?

"Status report, right bloody now," he snapped at Inglehart who saluted and turned to count the cost. The soldiers had all performed well; some of them had just had their first dose of a real fight. It had been surprisingly clean, compared to Sudan; the enemy had been quite honourable, in their way. "Jacob, find out who they are!"

"CADS Three is a complete write-off," Matthews said, looking grim. He too was coming down from the rush of combat. "The missile punched into the truck and detonated; there's literally nothing left of the crew." He paused. "We can't stay here."

"I worked that out," Robinson said. "What do you think is happening?"

Matthews picked up the military-grade laptop and opened it. It might have been slower by several orders of magnitude than most civilian machines, but it was tough; a group of soldiers had once used it for a football and the machine had been undamaged. The radar feed might have been gone, but it still had its memory; it had recorded all that the radar had seen.

"This is what we were seeing, just before the first missile," Matthews said. "Notice how quickly everything changes and compare that to our position behind the lines. We were not in the path of a cross-border raid, sir; we were deliberately targeted, along with plenty of other targets in Poland. If they attacked us, they attacked more or less half of Poland, perhaps all of Poland."

Robinson looked east. Columns of smoke were rising in the distance. "This is war," Matthews said. "They intended to destroy us, both removing your force off the balance sheets and destroying the radar; my CADS are designed to act as a passive radar sensor as well, and it's reporting that there are very few radars still operating in range. The attack we beat off is going to report that we are still alive and that we still have two CADS…and then they're going to come searching for us."

Robinson desperately started to look for a hole. "But…they sent the helicopters here against the CADS," he protested. "Do they know…?"

"They do now," Matthews said. "The original version of the CADS had the radar and the missiles mounted on the same truck; the Russians might just have assumed that we had the same kind of vehicles and launched an attack using helicopters. It hardly matters, sir; we cannot stay here."

Robinson nodded. "Get your vehicles moving at once," he ordered. "I'll get the men ready."

"We lost twenty-one, with seven injured," Inglehart reported, as the CADS roared to life behind them. Robinson cursed; that meant that half of his strength had been killed. "We also lost three of the lorries; all of them were taken out by enemy mortar fire…"

"Have the wounded moved into the remaining lorry and prepare to move out," Robinson snapped. "Jacob, anything?"

"There's nothing on the handful of bodies," Anastazy reported. "Sir, I don't know for sure, but those were definitely Russian helicopters and they were…"

"I know," Robinson said. There was no drill planned for any such incident; the closest they had come to planning for a full-scale Russian attack was a plan to cut off a major cross-border raid. "We have to move out, somewhere west. If we can't get in contact with higher authority..."

"I got something," the radioman called. "There's a signal, in Polish..."

Anastazy listened carefully...and paled. "No," he said. "It can't be...its Molobo!"

Robinson wanted to slap him. "Translate it," he ordered. Anastazy's country might be under threat, but he cared more for the lives of his soldiers, the men under his command. He needed every possible source of intelligence and Anastazy was the only one he had. Whoever Molobo was, he had to be connected to the Russians somehow. "I need to know what they're saying!"

Anastazy took a breath. "Citizens of Poland, this is an emergency announcement," he recited, as the speaker started to repeat himself. "There is a military and civil emergency going on; remain in your homes and stay off the streets. Do not venture outside. Do not attempt to use telephones, radios or other methods of communication; all communications must be reserved for the emergency services. Whatever you see or hear, stay in your homes; do not put yourself and the lives of your friends and families in danger. Electric supplies will be restored as soon as possible. Further information will be relayed to you as soon as possible; continue to listen on this frequency and ignore every other frequency. I repeat; these are very dangerous times. Stay in your homes."

The message began to repeat. "Jesus," Inglehart breathed. Robinson shook his head slowly as the sinister import of the message began to sink in. "What the hell does it mean?"

"Isn't it obvious?" Lieutenant Benjamin Matthews snapped. "The Russians are invading Poland...and we're caught in the middle!"

Chapter Twenty-One

Strike from the Sky, Take One

I love it when a plan comes together.
The A-Team

Polish Airspace, Near Szczecin

"Are you sure that this is actually working?"

Captain Boris Lapotev shrugged. "So far, there's been nothing since we lost contact with the ground," he said. "The Europeans put all their eggs in one basket, and what part of the civil aviation network the missiles didn't fuck up got fucked up by the cyber attacks. We're just a group of harmless civilian aircraft who are meandering blindly along towards Szczecin-Goleniów Airport. What could go wrong?"

Colonel Boris Akhmedovich Aliyev, who knew much more about the overall plan than Lapotev, said nothing. It was possible, if not particularly likely, that one of their own commandos on the ground would launch a SAM at them...and any of the countermeasures built into the aircraft, if used, would give away their real identity. It might not matter, not with the confusion on the ground, but it was better to be safe than sorry. On the ground, the five hundred commandos under his command were dangerous; in the air, they were sitting ducks for enemy aircraft.

He glanced back out of the cockpit. The aircraft had once been a fairly normal Boeing 747, before the Russian Air Force had gotten their hands on it and handed it over to the GRU. Now, it looked like a normal jetliner, acted like a normal jetliner, but it had carrying space for over a hundred commandos and their equipment. They could have packed more into the aircraft, but he knew that if they were lucky, they could take the airport, and if the Germans or Poles had time to react and dig in, they were all about to die. Everything depended upon the Europeans being fooled.

They'd taken off in the early hours of the morning, replacing a set of aircraft that had been coming the long way around Ukraine, something that had become routine after several years of chaos and the occasional explosion. Russia had bent over backwards to ensure that the pilots, crew and passengers of those aircraft had felt welcome on their brief stopover in a Russian airport, but the last time had been different. Passengers and pilots had been herded off their aircraft; the IFFs had been quickly copied and a new flight of aircraft was on their way, to all intents and purposes the same as the aircraft that had landed...at least from the outside observer's point of view. The long flight had been nerve-wrecking – they'd seen at least one vast explosion in the distance – but the combination of jamming, limited contact with other aircraft and panic on the ground had prevented anyone asking questions that Lapotev couldn't have answered.

"Roger that, Speedbird-Seven," Lapotev said. Aliyev covered his mouth to conceal a smile; anyone who knew the actual pilot's voice would blame any misunderstandings on the jamming. "We confirm no contact with anyone on the ground; have you any contact at all?"

He thumbed the radio off and grinned. "Everyone is completely confused and doesn't have the slightest idea of what's going on," he said. "Some of them might try to land at the airports anyway, even without radio contact."

"I had limited contact with Dresden, Ukraine-Four," Speedbird said. Lapotev had identified it as a British aircraft, intending to fly into Poland before all hell had broken loose. "They're warning of terrorists with missiles and rioting on the ground, and then we lost contact again."

Aliyev said nothing. He couldn't remember, offhand, if Dresden was a target or not for the commando teams, but the airport would certainly have received a dose of missiles, just to ensure that it didn't start helping military aircraft into the air. Dresden had played host to a large immigrant community, he remembered; perhaps some of the FSB's attempts to spread rioting had actually worked there. He scowled down at the final update from an operative in Szczecin; there had certainly been no sign of any military presence at the airport, but standard European procedure was to put all the airports on alert...if they knew that there had been SAM attacks elsewhere in Europe. One of the problems with such attacks was that it was impossible to know just how well you had done...his force might have an easy fight or run headlong into a battle they couldn't win.

Fortune favours the brave, he reminded himself. There was no questioning the bravery of his men. They had served together in the worst of war zones, which had allowed them to weed out everyone who might have let them down at the worst possible time. Poland should be an easy target compared to some places in Central Asia. *Who dares...wins...most of the time.*

Speedbird-Seven was talking again. "I have radar and aircraft coming into Poland," he said. He was still on the verge of panic; his radar had to be seeing the first thrust of Russian aircraft into western Poland. There would be fighters and transports heading in everywhere now. The plan was coming together. "What is going on?"

"I think that there have been a few terrorist attacks," Lapotev said. "I think that if we are patient, we will know what to do pretty soon."

Aliyev smiled at him. That wasn't likely.

Lapotev unkeyed the radio and scowled. "I feel like just telling him the truth," he sneered. "Commercial pilots; cut them off from their daddies and they go to pieces."

Aliyev smiled. "How much longer?"

"Twenty minutes," Lapotev said. "If they try to order us away, we'll keep going anyway and claim communications failure."

Aliyev nodded. "Twenty minutes," he shouted back down the aircraft, to the commandos who were performing the final checks on their weapons. They were all ready to move; the aircraft crew would launch their supplies into the air after them before turning to flee back towards Russia, or a secured airfield in Poland. "Twenty minutes before we do or die!"

They cheered.

The MIG-41 appeared out of nowhere, almost before *Staffelkapitän* Mayer realised that it was there, a testament to the Russian Air Force's improved skill at stealth aircraft. The MIG-41, known as the Flatpack to its NATO observers, fired a missile at Mayer's aircraft and then swung into a long evasive pattern itself. Mayer fired a single ASRAAM missile from his Eurofighter Typhoon back at the enemy and evaded the Russian missile though a series of hair-raising manoeuvres, trying to avoid being shot down. The Russian pilot was less lucky; Mayer saw him trying to escape the missile, but failing.

The entire encounter had taken less than a minute.

Mayer stared down at his onboard display and silently cursed to himself. He was one of the lucky pilots who had managed to get off the ground, but he was starting to wonder if it had been lucky at all. *Jagdgeschwader* 74, his fighter wing of the Luftwaffe, had been placed on alert status when someone had reported a terrorist waving a portable SAM missile launcher and threatening commercial traffic. As the first reports of SAM attacks on civilian aircraft came in, the QRA aircraft, including Mayer, were launched into the sky…and then all hell had broken loose. The base, in Southern Germany, in Bavaria, had been attacked by cruise missiles. Moments later, it had seemed that the entire command net had gone down.

Mayer and his three wingmen had consulted and decided that the *Vaterland* was under attack. Their onboard systems had reported the sudden spurt of cruise missiles that was flying over Germany, some of them heading towards towns and cities. The four fighters had engaged the cruise missiles, but then they had finally received orders from a different airbase; they were to attempt to determine what the hell was going on. Moments later, that airbase too had vanished off the net…and the Eurofighter's sensors were reporting explosions on the ground, big explosions. Meyer had feared nuclear war, even as cold logic reminded him that there had been no EMP pulse; the Eurofighter would have fallen out of the sky if an EMP had struck it.

No, he had decided; *they were under conventional attack*.

Meyer had issued his subordinates with orders, each aircraft to a different region, and separated, heading over Poland. The Poles should have challenged him before he crossed the border, even at supersonic speed; they were paranoid about German aircraft. Meyer, who had had a grandfather who had served in the *Luffwaffe*, rather understood their concern, but something very bad had happened. The cruise missiles alone added up to only one answer. They were at war and only one power had the means and the motivation to hit Germany.

Russia.

As he'd flown north-eastwards, he had attempted to raise the Polish air traffic controllers, only to discover that most of them were off the air. His radar had picked up a massive flight of transport aircraft, heading out of Russia towards Poland, but he had refrained from engaging them; he still wasn't exactly sure what had happened. He saw smoke and flames reaching up from targets right across Poland, which meant that the cruise missiles hadn't just been aimed at Germany. The main Polish military airfields, Biała Podlaska, Cewice and Częstochowa-Rudniki, seemed to have been hit; there didn't seem to be any Polish aircraft in the skies at all. Commercial traffic had to be panicking; they would be flying through suddenly very hostile skies… without the slightest idea of what was going on.

Meyer himself wasn't sure that he knew what was going on.

"*Jagdgeschwader* 74-9, you will listen to the code words," his radio crackled suddenly. Meyer's heart leapt; he wasn't alone! Someone knew where he was and what he was doing! The voice was young and dreadfully nervous, and he could hear a French accent underlying the German, but it was a contact. "Please respond; alpha-tango-theta-napoleon."

The Eurofighter's onboard database provided a match; a French AWACS aircraft that had been intended to take part in a small exercise with the British. It all seemed to belong to another world now, not the nightmare of fire and death that had crashed down upon Europe, when everything had seemed so safe and tranquil. He was more relieved than he could say to hear the voice…and then it dawned on him that the voice belonged to a kid, a very junior officer. Dear God…had the French been hit as well?

"This is *Jagdgeschwader* 74-9," Meyer said, and gave his details. "Update me."

"I…everything's gone to hell," the young Frenchman said. The voice made him think of the French cadets who had defended their academy back in 1940, years ago. "We were on patrol, then someone launched SAMs at us and our escort sacrificed himself to save us, but we can barely talk to anyone and the network is failing badly! There are civilian aircraft trapped in the sky and we can't even talk them down because the bases are out of service and there are terrorists in the airports…"

"Not terrorists," Meyer said. He remembered the brief deadly encounter with the Russian fighter. "Russians."

The Frenchman didn't argue. "Can you do a radar sweep?"

Meyer had thought about that; he needed intelligence, but lighting up the radar was one way to guarantee that every Russian in the area would know his location. He could pick up the sweeps of the French AWACS now – it struck him that it might be the only AWACS left in Europe – and knew that he didn't dare refuse. That AWACS had just become the most vital aircraft in Europe.

"Operating," he said. He smiled suddenly. "What's your name?"

"Lieutenant Jacques Montebourg," the Frenchman said. "It was meant to be my first command and..."

Meyer could fill in the details himself. The French would have given young Montebourg a chance to prove himself, unaware that he would have to deal with a real emergency. The radar sweep had been brief and powerful, but it depressed him; there were hundreds of aircraft in the air, some of them clearly warplanes. There was no sign of his former wingmen.

"I hope you got all that," he said, grimly. "Do you have a place to land?"

"I don't know," Montebourg said. He sounded tired. "The base where we are normally stationed is in flames, and Paris is on fire; there are airliners nearby unable to land because of the terrorists. Sir...where the hell do we go?"

Mayer stared down at the data. There was a pattern there, aircraft that... were not panicking. They'd come out of Russia, he saw; they were heading towards Germany, and western Poland. There was something about them that worried him; he was sure, looking at it, that they were suspicious.

"Look at them," he said, detailing his suspicions. "What do you think they're up to?"

The kid, to give him his due, didn't hesitate. "Can you investigate?"

"I'm going to have to," Mayer said. "Watch as long as you can, then head for Britain unless you can get an airfield in France."

He rolled the Eurofighter over and launched the bird towards the unknown aircraft, noting in passing that their IFF signals didn't match their behaviour. If they were in denial, they should have been preparing to land...but they weren't. They were going to fly over Szczecin-Goleniów Airport, almost in formation. The implications worried him; Szczecin-Goleniów Airport was in the west of Poland, near Germany and the German border. It was one of the places that had been marked as a possible emergency landing site for the

EUROFOR air support squadrons…and should have been outside the realm of targeting possibilities for any attacker. The faint suggestions of aerial combat, further to the east, suggested that the Russians – if Russians they were, but who else could they be? – were winning. "I am going stealthy now."

"Good luck," Montebourg said.

The Eurofighter was not a pure stealth fighter, not like the newer fighters that had been produced by the Americans, the Japanese and even the advanced Eurofighter Tempest. It did have a very small radar cross-section and, without any active transponders, should have nothing calling serious attention to itself. If there were ground forces below that were friendly, in other words not Russians, they might try to shoot him down because he wasn't broadcasting an IFF signal. There wasn't a choice; he didn't dare draw enemy attention until he knew what the hell was going on.

Air traffic started to grow larger as his radars started to look further into Poland. Normally, the skies would be stacked with commercial airliners, but now there were only military transports…and he could see smoke rising from dozens of different places on the ground. Meyer had a sudden sense of what had happened to the commercial jets and shuddered; the Russians would have just shot them down and never worried about the loss of life.

His sensors recorded everything as they grew closer, preparing to relay them back to Montebourg. A Russian Mainstay – a Beriev A-50 AWACS aircraft, one of a hundred the Russians had produced and heavily modified over the years – was operating in the air over Poland, protected by a swarm of Russian fighters. Other heavy Russian transports seemed to be dominating the skies over Poland, while tankers and bombers floated around, picking on targets as they chose. The sheer scale of the effort was daunting…and the lack of any effective opposition was chilling. Had the Russians secured so much control that they could fly so close to Germany without fear?

He cursed softly as another flight of Russians headed into Western Poland, their escorts peeling off and returning to the tankers for refuelling. The entire area was lit up by hundreds of different air-search radar systems, watching out for possible attackers, and he realised that if he went any closer, he would almost certainly be detected. A flight of Russian transports rose into the air from Poland, heading back towards Russia, and he realised that he was looking at the greatest airborne operation in human history. By the time the Poles rallied, they would be defeated; it was neat, elegant, and almost unstoppable.

They're going to land at Szczecin-Goleniów Airport, he realised. No one in Germany would have the view that he had of the invasion, not until it was too late...and unless Montebourg managed to make contact with someone before the AWACS ran out of fuel, it would never be useful to anyone. He risked a microburst transmission, sending the data back to Montebourg, and then turned to see the unknown aircraft. *Right on the border of the Vaterland...*

The mystery aircraft were drawing closer and closer to him; he tried to hail them and received no response, not even a nervous pilot wondering what the warplane was doing, so close to a civilian aircraft. They looked civilian, he saw, as he swung the aircraft over the jet liner, except...there was something wrong.

"Shit," Lapotev hissed. The alarm in his voice was unpleasant. "He has us; he'll see the false images and then he'll kill us."

"Take him out," Aliyev snapped. There were only five minutes until the jump began. A single Eurofighter could not be allowed to ruin it, not now; he wouldn't allow it. He would sooner die than fail Russia. "Kill that bastard!"

Lapotev flicked a switch. "Done," he said. The airliner shook, but if it was from the missile or the passage of the Eurofighter, Aliyev couldn't tell. "You'd better get back and ready to jump."

Ping...!

For a long moment, Mayer's mind refused to grasp what had happened; the airliner, the innocent-looking airliner, had lit off a short-ranged military-grade air search radar, more powerful than the one that the MIG-41 he'd killed had carried. He had never seriously contemplated firing on a civilian airliner, not even if he had to prevent a repeat of September 11th and he hesitated. Fatally. The missile blasted away from its hidden launcher...and struck the Eurofighter before he could react. Mayer's life came to a sudden end…as the first paratroopers began to fall on the airport far below.

The Battle for Szczecin-Goleniów Airport had begun.

Chapter Twenty-Two

Strike from the Sky, Take Two

I can picture in my mind a world without war, a world without hate. And I can picture us attacking that world, because they'd never expect it.
Jack Handey

Polish Airspace, Near Szczecin

Hans Cooper loved the airport.

His father had taken him on a visit to see his family in Germany and Poland, a long holiday that was a chance to reconnect with relatives that he hadn't seen for years; the ten-year-old had been delighted and only wished that his mother had been able to come. Hans had begged his father to take him to each and every one of the airports they passed, and their relatives had been more than happy to provide transport. The airport in western Poland - Szczecin-Goleniów Airport – was no different; he had even been able to stand on the balcony and watch the aircraft come in to land.

The chaos that had broken out had passed unnoticed by Hans; he had little interest in anything but the aircraft, including the massive jumbo jet that had been taxiing onto the runway before the chaos had begun. There were thousands of people milling about in the airport, but Hans only had eyes for the aircraft…including the fighter that had flown overhead at very low level and disappeared into the distance. A Polish policeman was trying to shout orders, only to be drowned out by the crowd, and Hans barely noticed. The flight of aircraft high overhead held his attention.

His father had bought him a pair of binoculars. Some airports had been reluctant to have him use them on their premises, for reasons that made no sense to him or his father, but the Poles had allowed him to use them…or, at least, they hadn't tried to stop him. Hans was of the age where limited defiance was the 'cool' thing to do, but at the airport, he was wrapped up in the joy of seeing the aircraft. He could see the aircraft…and then the aircraft started to launch paratroopers out into the air.

"Dad," he shouted, delightedly. "Those are paratroopers!"

Hans had studied military aircraft as well with a child's fascination. He knew what paratroopers were; it was his dream, if he failed in his first dream to become a fighter pilot, to become a paratrooper and jump out of planes all day. His guidance counsellor had pointed out that it was a hard and dangerous life, and not all of it included jumping, but Hans had been determined. Besides, his dad had said that he was ten years old…and that was really too early for the schools to be trying to fix him with a career path.

He heard the screams and shouts from behind him as the parachutes fell through the air, heading towards the ground, and laughed at them. What possible danger could there be? Weren't the grown-ups caught in the excitement of the moment? Hans whooped with joy as the parachutes opened, revealing the men below as their fall slowed almost to a standstill, just above the runways. It was exciting, almost like the air show he seen when he was younger; there was nothing to match the sight of aircraft and men doing cool things. His father was tugging at him, trying to get him to move, and Hans refused to budge. He wouldn't lose the chance to see what was about to happen.

"Move," his father said. His hand impacted firmly with Hans' rear. Hans squawked in outrage – his father rarely spanked him and then only when he was very bad – and tried to struggle. His father was much stronger and pulled Hans away mercilessly; he opened his mouth and started to bawl. "Hans, we have to move!"

The parachutists had landed, their parachutes drifting away; Hans could see them as they formed up rapidly into units, a perfect display of formation landing. Alarms were going off everywhere, but to him it was only part of the excitement and he cursed his father for trying to get him away from the sight. It wasn't fair…

And then the shooting started.

Szczecin-Goleniów Airport was no different to Airport One, at least in general concept; long runways, terminals and two control towers. Aliyev was unimpressed as the long fall towards the ground slowed sharply and his feet touched the ground; it would be almost impossible for the Poles to defend it unless they had an entire regiment dug in around the terminals. There hadn't even been any shooting; the attacks on Airport One had been far more dangerous than Szczecin-Goleniów, so far.

"Form up," he snapped, trusting his subordinates to know what they were doing. "Advance!"

Alarms were sounding everywhere, but there was no sign of any real resistance at all; the shock and awe of their sudden arrival should paralyse the defenders long enough for them to lose...if there were any defenders. The intelligence reports had stated that there was a stand-by anti-terrorist unit in the airport, one with military-grade training and equipment, but it wouldn't be any match for his people.

The parachutists broke into a run as they charged towards their targets. A handful of dark-clad figures lifted weapons and tried to fight, overcoming their shock; the Russians mowed them down and kept coming. Aliyev took a second to check their bodies and realised that they had been security guards, completely outmatched by real military people. The terminal rose up in front of him, frightened eyes peering out through massive glass windows, somehow unaware that his men could come right through the glass. The strike teams moved fast and threw their grenades; the glass shattered, sending fragments flying over the civilians. Many of them screamed as glass cut into their bodies; Aliyev had no time at all to worry about them. It was vital that they took the airport largely intact.

The other parachutists fanned out as they crashed into the terminal. Civilians scattered in front of them; a policeman lifted a weapon and fired once at a commando, who took the shot on his body armour and only staggered backwards. Aliyev felt for him; the impact felt like being punched in the gut, even if he had been lucky enough to escape real physical harm. He should have escaped such harm; the weapon the Pole had fired hadn't been a serious pistol at all. Aliyev's team shot him down anyway.

"Everyone get down on the floor, hands on your heads," he bellowed, and cracked the skull of a fat aggressive German who started to shout at him. His wife, equally fat, threw herself to her husband's side and tried to tend to him, until Aliyev ordered her to lie down with the others. There were hundreds of civilians in the airport, he realised as they fanned out through the building, along with employees and workers. They were sheep in front of his men; only a handful even tried to hide. They were dragged out and placed with the others as the reinforcements rushed into the terminal. The remainder of their supplies would be landing now…and then the aircraft would be heading back to Russia.

Aliyev and his men were on their own.

"Listen," he bellowed, in Polish. He would repeat himself in German and English in a moment; the sight of a small boy, weeping, reminded him far too much of Groznyy. "This is a military emergency; anyone who refuses to follow our orders will be shot. Follow orders and we promise that you will not be harmed, nor will you be killed, raped, hurt or forced to help us. Remain calm; parents, keep your children calm and everything will be well."

He repeated himself in two other languages and then led his main unit up the stairs towards the control tower. The airport had two, redundancy was built into the system, and he was certain that the Poles would be screaming for help as loudly as they could. He knew that both of the nearby barracks had been hit by missiles, but there was no telling how much damage had actually been done until it was too late; he was uncomfortably aware that he might find out when the Polish infantry launched an attack. The stairs had been blocked; several shots rang out as they approached.

"That's the antiterrorist unit," Captain Alexander Vatutin muttered. Aliyev had given command of the preliminary work to his most trusted subordinate. "They've dug themselves in and we can't get up the steps without using grenades."

Aliyev scowled. Grenades meant that they risked damaging vital equipment, but there was no choice. He muttered orders and the team deployed, each one holding a light fragmentation grenade; at his command, they hurled them into the stairwell, and then charged as soon as they exploded. More gunshots rang out, but the firing was no longer perfectly targeted; the commandos shot the Poles before they could recover from the grenades. A handful of Poles tried to escape and were mercilessly shot in the back; Aliyev led the charge towards the second locked door, leading into the control room.

He grinned and knocked. A female voice called out a question in Polish. "Who is it?"

Aliyev forced himself to speak Polish again. "It's the team," he said. "You're safe now and you can open the door."

"Fuck off, Russian," the woman shouted back. Aliyev shrugged; it had been a long shot, but it had been worth a try. She probably knew all of the members of the antiterrorist team by heart, perhaps even cock size, the nasty part of his mind whispered. "We're calling for help and you'd better be gone when it comes!"

Aliyev nodded to two of the commandos, who placed small charges on the door and melted through the metal. There were screams from inside as the metal ran like water and the door was kicked in; he saw seven terrified men and women…and one woman, sitting in the centre of the room, trying to look confident and failing miserably. She would have been a beauty in her youth; the sullen defiance on her face twisted it into the realm of ugliness.

"Everyone, hands in the air, now," Aliyev barked, as the commandos charged into the room. There was no resistance, but they didn't dare take chances; they grabbed the operators, secured them and left them tied up on the floor. Some of the civilians were whimpering; like most civilians in their position, they were used to the idea of emergencies taking place a long way away. "If you attempt to resist, you will be shot!"

He checked the consoles quickly. The civilian wavebands had been jammed, but they were still intact; the emergency power generator in the airport had taken over from the main power supply, which should have been cut off by the missiles or a commando strike team. It hardly mattered; they had radar units, but no easy way of using them to get instructions to the handful of European fighters that had managed to get into the air. Emergencies were things that happened to other people, far, far away. They would have prepared for a terrorist attack, but a full-scale military assault?

Aliyev sighed in relief.

"You won't get away with this," the commander said. Her voice spat defiance. "They'll come and kill all of you."

"Maybe," Aliyev replied, unwilling to banter. The team wouldn't have hesitated to break her if she had been a serious problem, but for all of her defiance, she was nothing but a nuisance. He lifted his tactical combat radio and smiled. "All units, report in."

He listened as the reports trickled back. The commando teams had seized the hangers and aircraft inside intact, although one of the aircraft was out of service and had been in the middle of being repaired when the fighting had begun. The fuel dump under the airport had been intact, but it hadn't been quite as full as they had hoped; Poland had been having a semi-permanent fuel crisis since 2020, when Russia had started to get serious about using the fuel supplies for political leverage. It was ironic; if they had sent the Poles all the fuel they needed, aircraft landing at the airport could have been refuelled for much longer. As it was…

He shook his head. It wasn't something that he could alter now. They had to work with what they had, not with the world as they would like it to be. Other teams had secured the fence surrounding the airport and reported that all of the cars on the road had been turned back; hundreds of additional prisoners had been taken as they tried to escape the airport. That was unfortunate; the news would be likely to spread further before more reinforcements could arrive, but again, there was nothing to be done about it.

"Secure the perimeter and get the prisoners back into the terminal," he ordered. He turned quickly to the pre-prepared operators. "Get in touch with higher command and inform them that we have secured the airport and are ready to receive transports."

"Yes, sir," the lead operator said. They had trained for a week on terminals that had been rigged up to look exactly like the terminals they worked with now; they moved with practiced ease to set up the system and issue orders over the Russian communications network. Far behind the lines, aircraft were waiting for the order to take off and transport their units to the airport, where they would become a dagger aimed at Poland and Germany.

The Polish operators watched in horror; for some of them, it was becoming increasingly obvious what was happening; the nightmare of Russian invasion and occupation had returned to Poland. Aliyev felt no sympathy; he had fought long enough in Central Asia to hate those who held protest marches and wrote long detailed articles – mainly with the facts made up – about what they called genocide. Aliyev had been there; it hadn't been anything like that.

He swung around to glare at the Sergeant. "Our causalities?"

"Seven down, three injured," the Sergeant reported promptly. "A handful of men landed outside the airport fence and had to make their way in by foot."

"How embarrassing," Aliyev said. The men would be the butts of their comrades' jokes for weeks, although he wasn't that annoyed; the operation had had a certain amount of friction built into it, after all. He had expected much more to go wrong than actually had; if the European pilot had fired on the aircraft, he could have lost a third of his force. He looked down at the prisoners. "Bring them."

Ignoring protests, the soldiers picked up the Poles and carried them carefully back into the main terminal, where they were dumped on the ground. The follow-up units had secured all of the adult civilians, male or female; the children sat next to their handcuffed parents, staring at the armed Russians with wide terrified eyes. The feeling of dread and fear was almost amusing; for the first time, Aliyev understood the rush of power that hostage-takers felt. He had killed many hostage-takers in Moscow; the thought that he might have something in common with them terrified him. He ground his teeth; he was a professional soldier and that was the end of it. Terrorising and population control was the task of the FSB.

"Bastards," he muttered under his breath.

"We searched the entire terminal thoroughly, sir," a Captain reported. He didn't salute; salutes were forbidden in combat zones, not that the commandos were big on such gestures anyway. It wasn't considered insubordination. "There are no more hiding civilians or workers; we had a man injured trying to bring down a Polish policeman."

Aliyev scowled. The fate of the policemen had already been decided. He glared around at the prisoners and saw how few of them could meet his gaze; they had clearly decided to keep their heads down and hope not to be noticed. Most of them were tourists, not soldiers; there was no real need to terrorise them still further.

Captain Alexander Vatutin appeared. "I have deployed the SAM teams to cover the airport and moved units into combat position to defend the airport terminal if there is a low-level probe," he reported. "The cars will make excellent barricades once we get them moved into position."

"Good," Aliyev said. It was time to see to the long-term fate of the prisoners. "Has the prison detachment found a suitable spot?"

"The rich capitalists' car park," Vatutin said. "It's got a fence with barbed wire. We couldn't have done it better if we had planned it that way."

Aliyev nodded and coughed for attention. "Good morning," he said, mischievously. The prisoners looked up at him, their eyes terrified. "For those of you who haven't realised, a state of war now exists between Russia and the European Union. Unfortunately for you, you have been caught in the middle; I have to hold this airport and you, I fear, are in the combat zone. I would dearly like to just throw you all out of the gate, but you would tell the Polish authorities what is happening, so that is not an option."

He repeated himself in German and English, and then continued. "None of you are combatants and I intend to keep you out of the firing line as much as possible," he said. It was almost true; the security staff, the policemen and the two survivors of the antiterrorist team would never see their homes again. The others would have to wait until the Russians knew who they were, and then they would either be released or sent out to prison camps somewhere in Siberia. "My people will be moving you out to a makeshift prison in the car park; I strongly advise you to cooperate with my people, rather than trying to resist. If you need attention, tell them; we will do our best to look after you..."

He paused. "But understand this, I will not allow you to threaten my success here," he concluded. "If you cause trouble, you will be shot."

He nodded to the Sergeant. "Take them away."

Chapter Twenty-Three

Prisoner of War

The Geneva Conventions are a wonderful idea that are completely impractical and unenforceable.
Christopher Nuttall

Near Warsaw, Poland

The first thing that Caroline Morgan knew about the war was the explosion.

"Stay here," Captain Loomis snapped, before Caroline could say anything. She had been interviewing Hannah Loomis, a female infantry captain, as to the role of women in the military. Hannah, a fearsome figure, had been more than willing to talk, although she had dismissed some of the common knowledge about women in the military as feminist or sexist nonsense. The real state of affairs was quite different.

"If you're in the military – worse, if you're in the military as a woman – you have to behave as one of the men, within reason," she had said, much to Caroline's surprise. "You have to eat with them, sleep – and I don't mean sex, I mean sleep – with them, crap with them, fight with them, kill with them…and generally act as one of the men. You're either one of the boys or you're queen for a year…provided you act like it. Some women go mad for sex because there's only one woman and fifty-odd men and they can get whatever they want if they reward the men with sex, some women go ice queens…frankly, if you give it up for one guy, it'll tear the unit and your reputation apart."

Caroline hadn't really understood. "You can be one of the guys; eat, sleep, shit, talk about women…or you can be a slut," Hannah had said. "It's really a case of not creating tension within the group; as my first Sergeant put it, you don't want brave stupid young men rescuing brave stupid young women rather than getting out there and kicking the shit out of the enemy. Have one woman with one man and plenty of other men who aren't getting any…well, that's a recipe for trouble." She laughed. "Oh, and being brave helps as well."

Caroline didn't feel very brave as a second explosion rocked the camp. She had wanted to call Hannah back as the young Captain fled the room, pistol in hand, but she hadn't quite dared. It was something far less…congenial than the time she'd spent with the soldiers on distant deployment near Warsaw; they'd been friendly and relaxed, particularly with Marya. Caroline had felt distantly ugly in comparison, even if she had had a string of boyfriends back home. Marya was still sleeping the effects of the alcohol they'd consumed off; Caroline had swallowed a de-tox pill, cleared away the effects of the drinking, and gone back to work. She hadn't expected to be caught in the middle of a war zone.

The sound of shooting was growing louder. She glanced around, frantically, as the noise grew louder, finding only a small table to hide under. The windows shattered and she dove for cover, crawling under the table and praying aloud to God to help her out of her position. She felt the reassuring shape of the terminal in her pocket – a direct link back to the BBC in London – and activated it. The signal refused to form; there was absolutely no contact with the BBC at all.

A voice was shouting something defiant in French; seconds later, there was another explosion, much louder than any others. Caroline whimpered as the noises grew louder and louder; she could hear shouts in a language she couldn't understand. Something bad was going on; the thought that it might have been a drill was rapidly dismissed as wishful thinking. No one, as far as she knew, would be crazy enough to fire off live ammunition during a drill, particularly not into a room where a civilian was trying to work. Something thudded against the side of the building and she cringed again before realising that it hadn't killed her; she could hear the approaching rumble of engines… and then the sound of a tank's main gun.

She scrabbled at her terminal, trying to use it for one of its more secret functions. The BBC had kept them quiet over the years; it was also capable of scanning nearby radio bands and trying to record and play them back. She didn't understand why no one knew about that – the technology's capabilities had been in the public domain for over a year – but it would work in her favour; she scanned the different radio signals nearby, only to hear more static and bursts of Russian. She didn't speak Russian; she couldn't make out at all what was actually happening.

Something new flickered into the radio, on one of the civilian bands. It should have been a Polish radio station, now it was something else, something sinister. "*Citizens of Poland, this is an emergency announcement,*" it said. "*There is a military and civil emergency going on; remain in your homes and stay off the streets. Do not venture outside. Do not attempt to use telephones, radios or other methods of communication; all communications must be reserved for the emergency services. Whatever you see or hear, stay in your homes; do not put yourself and the lives of your friends and families in danger. Electric supplies will be restored as soon as possible. Further information will be relayed to you as soon as possible; continue to listen on this frequency and ignore every other frequency. I repeat; these are very dangerous times. Stay in your homes.*"

Caroline felt her blood run cold as yet another burst of shooting echoed out over the camp. She was far from stupid; the message had to mean that something had really gone wrong, and she was in the middle of a camp that was under attack. She felt for her press pass carefully, hoping that she still had it safe; that would get her out of trouble if the Russians caught her. The sound of a helicopter rose in the air; a dark shadow fell over the window for a moment, then the noise of rockets being launched echoed through the window. The helicopter was attacking targets in the camp!

She clicked the terminal off and pocketed it, then tried to decide what to do. The shooting was dying down, but she didn't know who had won; she didn't know anything at all that might tell her which way to run. She thought about trying to sneak out of the camp, but that only worked in movies; the heroic stars always had three things going for them that Caroline didn't. They had a sympathetic scriptwriter, perfect grooming and chest sizes that could only be described by resorting to imaginary numbers. They always found a guard who could be seduced, or turned out to be lesbian vampires, or had something else up their sleeves. She had no military training; until recently, she had never seen a gun. What could she do?

The voices were growing closer, shouts and barks in an unfamiliar language. She listened carefully and felt her blood run cold; she was almost sure that that was Russian being spoken. She spoke German and French in addition to English; it was none of those languages, but something very different.

It wasn't Arabic, or another Asian language; it was something else, very different. Her second boyfriend – before he had embraced the Buddhist way of life – had once taken her to see a Russian show; it sounded very much like that. It sounded as if the Russians had won the fight.

The door exploded inwards and two black-clad men entered, their weapons raised and ready for a fight. Caroline cringed backwards, but there was little real cover and they saw her. One of them barked a command at her in Russian as their eyes met, but she didn't understand him. He motioned with his rifle, but she was too terrified to move; fear had turned her legs into jelly. She was bitterly aware that Hannah – what had happened to her in the fighting? – would have handled it better, but she was so scared. She couldn't even breathe!

The lead soldier grabbed her arm and roughly pulled her out of her hiding place, pushing her against the wall and ignoring her protests and gasps of pain. His hands roughly, but quickly frisked her, removing everything from her pockets, from a pair of pens to the terminal and her notepad, both of which he dumped on the table and left for later. He found her ID card hanging around her neck and inspected it briefly before leaving it; Caroline was too scared to speak. Her hands were quickly caught and secured behind her back with a plastic tie; she was left leaning against the wall, her eyes blurred with tears she could no longer wipe away, while the Russians searched the room, removing anything that even looked dangerous. Caroline had once attended an inquest into an overzealous police officer who had confiscated a microwave on the grounds that it had computer chips inside; the Russians made him look like an amateur. Their paranoia seemed to have no limits.

She focused on them; knowledge was power, as her boss had once said to her. They were both young and very strong; she could practically see the muscles rippling under their black uniforms. She knew what happened to American servicewomen who were captured by insurgents in the Middle East; was that about to happen to her? The insurgents tended to leave newspaper men and women alone, particularly European journalists, who tended to support them, but who knew what the Russians would do? Her mind kept chasing its own tail; she had thought about rape, every woman did at some point in their lives, but she had never really believed that it could happen to her. Her sexual favours were hers, as far as she was concerned; the choice about whether or not to bestow them was hers…except, perhaps, it was no longer hers. They were both young and strong; they could take her with ease.

One Russian made a comment to the other and they both stood up. Almost before she could react, they were holding her and hustling her out the door, through the corridors and past several bodies lying in the dirt, weapons dropped where they had fallen. The stench was appalling as they passed what had once been – she thought – a man; was it even possible to have that much blood in a human body? Surely the chunks of gore belonged to several people; that couldn't all be one person, could it? She was panting as she tried to force her legs to work; she was certain that the Russians would hurt her if they had to force her to move, or perhaps just carry her. She was completely at their mercy.

She tried an experiment. "Where are you taking me?" She asked in English, and then in mangled French and German. "*Là où êtes vous me prenant? Wo Sie mich nehmend sind?*"

There was no answer, not even a hint they understood her. She couldn't understand them; they only spoke quickly, almost as if they suspected that she could understand them and were trying to confuse her. They reached four more armed men, guarding what had once been the entrance to the camp, and she winced; the Russians had definitely won the fight. Leaning against the corner, a massive wound in its chest, lay the body of Major-General John McLachlan. The Russians were collecting ID cards from the bodies and comparing them to a list; one of the guards examined her ID card with interest, and then compared it carefully to her face. Caroline almost laughed; she had been made up perfectly when the photograph had been taken, with a nice dress showing just the right hint of cleavage. Now…she shuddered to think of what she looked like; her hands tied, her clothes disorganised, sweat and the smell of fear rising from her body.

The Russian Commander looked up at her. "You are Caroline Morgan, Press Reporter?"

She was so relieved to hear a voice speaking English that she almost wilted. "Yes," she said, and forced her mouth to speak further. "Sir, I am a non-combatant in a war zone and…"

"At the moment, you are a prisoner of the Russian Army," the Russian snapped, cutting her off. He barked a series of commands to her captors. "You will be held until we decide what to do with you. Failure to obey promptly any orders given to you, of any nature, will result in sentence being passed against you and you will be shot. Do you understand?"

She nodded fearfully, her face smarting from imaginary blows. "Answer me," the Russian barked, his voice digging right into her soul. "Do you understand?"

"Yes," she stammered. She stood in front of him, helpless, broken; unable to do anything, but obey. "I understand."

The Russian nodded at her two commanders, who marched her outside into the camp. It was no longer what it had once been; half of the buildings had been destroyed, or were burning merrily away. EUROFOR had been caught by surprise, but the French, German and British defenders of the camp had sold their lives dearly; she could see the dead bodies of Russian soldiers being prepared for return to their homeland. There were other dead bodies being gathered as well; European soldiers and commanding officers, all being checked by the Russians for their identity. She realised, dimly, that the Russians knew everything about the camp; they even had a list of the soldiers, right down to the lowliest infantryman. How had they done that?

A dead body caught her attention; for a moment, she stared at it without being able to understand why it had caught her, and then her eyes traced the curves of her body and the swell of the breasts. Half of her head was missing, but there was no mistaking her; Captain Hannah Loomis had gone down fighting with her men. Her escorts made what sounded like crude comments, directed at the Russians who were gathering the bodies; they made rude gestures back at them. Caroline would have given anything to know what they were saying; were they accusing the gravediggers of necrophilia-type practices, or were they commenting that they had a live woman?

The training field had impressed her when she had seen it for the first time; a large field where games and exercises could be conducted at the same time, larger than two football fields. Now…now armed Russians stood guard around a handful of prisoners, all sitting on the ground and securely tied. Her own hands were aching as the plastic tie dug into her wrists, but she didn't dare try to draw attention to it. The prisoners all looked downcast; their ID cards prominently displayed around their necks. The Russians had not only caught them, they knew who they had caught.

"Caroline," a voice shouted. Caroline looked up to see Marya's face in the small group; her clothes had been torn in a number of places that she was sure weren't accidental. The Russians who were holding her pointed and made more rude comments; Marya's nipples could be seen poking out the holes in her blouse. "Oh Caroline, thank God!"

One of the Russian guards inspected her ID again. "You will remain here until ordered to move elsewhere," he said. "Do not attempt to move, whatever the reason; you will be moved to a proper detention facility soon enough. If you disobey any orders, or attempt to leave, you will be shot. Do you understand?"

Caroline nodded. She had learned her lesson. "I understand," she said. A worrying thought struck her. "What if we have to go to the toilet?"

"We will arrange toilet facilities as quickly as we can," the Russian said, with a bored tone. Caroline guessed that he had been asked the same question by each of the prisoners. "Sit down, talk quietly if you must talk, and wait."

Her escorts pushed her down next to Marya, winked at her, and left. Caroline almost missed them; they, at least, hadn't taken advantage of her. Closer now, Marya's face was streaked with tears; the Russians who had caught her had taken advantage of her before she was brought to the makeshift pen. She nodded towards a group of Russians wearing green uniforms and looking very grim; they almost seemed to be prisoners themselves.

"That one there tried to...take me," Marya whispered, her voice breaking. "Caroline, what are they going to do to us?"

Caroline remembered a vague report about Russian punishment battalions. Instead of court-martialling soldiers who were brought up on charges, the Russians gave them a month in the penal units, where they would do all the dangerous tasks, such as mine-clearing without detection gear or charging into a heavily-defended bunker with explosive satchels. If they survived the experience and the dangers, from both the enemy and their own former friends, they were returned to their units. Most of them would never dare to re-offend.

"I don't know," Caroline said.

She glanced briefly at their fellow prisoners, mainly injured soldiers, their eyes showing that they were trapped in their own purgatory. They had suffered the shame of being taken prisoner in what might very well be the first battle of World War Three; what would happen to them in the future? The

Russians would not mistreat media reporters, she hoped – and tried to ignore the fact that Marya had been abused – but they would be merciless to the soldiers. The Geneva Convention was a joke to everyone these days; everyone, but the European Military Commission and the European Parliament. Had they not charged some soldiers in Sudan with breaching the Conventions?

She shook her head. "I just don't know," she said. She looked around again; the penal soldiers were digging graves and bodies, European bodies, were being dumped in the graves. Helicopters and jet aircraft were flying overhead, heading west; they seemed to be caught in the middle of a full-scale invasion. "I just don't think that it's going to be pleasant."

Chapter Twenty-Four

The Long Way Home

In the Soviet Army, it takes more courage to retreat than advance.
Stalin

Near Warsaw, Poland

"I think we have to make some decisions," Ca0ptain Stuart Robinson said, as the small force stopped two miles west of the attack site. They had remained as quiet as they could, ignoring the enemy aircraft passing overhead, although Matthews had argued that they should have engaged them with the CADS. "Our position is not good."

The mysterious and ominous radio message had been repeated every ten minutes, on the main Polish radio channel, interspersed by jamming. Robinson had tried several times to get in touch with someone higher up the chain of command, but the radio systems seemed to be completely jammed except at short-ranges, and the satellites seemed to be gone. Matthews had sworn blind that the laser communications system should have been working perfectly; the satellite, for whatever reason, was refusing to respond. The implications of that worried Robinson.

They had worried him enough to order Matthews to make a very quick low-powered radar sweep from time to time. Passive sensors had recorded bursts of Russian activity that seemed designed to hunt down European units; the low-powered bursts had revealed flights of heavy Russian transports heading into Europe. The sense of threat, of being watched, had followed them from the scene of the ambush; Robinson was no longer inclined to dismiss the feeling at all. It affected them all; the soldiers spread out, as if they were launching a probing attack rather than just marching to the nearest base. They held their weapons at the ready, eyes scanning the horizon; as far as they were concerned, they were in bandit country.

He gathered Anastazy, Inglehart and Matthews together while they took a short break. "We are more or less out of communication with anyone higher up," he said, as they smoked cigarettes. He had smoked as a teenager, in defiance of the ban on smoking; only Hazel had forced him to break the habit. Her threat of no sex if he so much as looked at a cigarette had forced him to quit; now, he found that he needed one just to keep a clear head. "We know that there are Russians roaming the country and plenty of Russians in the air. What do we do?"

It wasn't normal for any commanding officer to call a council of war, but there was little choice; he had both Matthews, his nominal equal, and Anastazy along as well as his soldiers. Both of them looked worried; Anastazy because it was his country that was under attack, Matthews because he had lost one CADS and might lose more if the Russians caught them. Without its active sensors, the CADS was much less effective as a system, but using active sensors might have been like calling up the Russians and inviting them to launch a missile at their position. So far, they'd been lucky; Robinson didn't want to press his luck.

Anastazy spoke first. "We're not that far from Warsaw," he said, nodding towards one of the looming pillars of smoke. The soldiers had seen over nine massive pillars of smoke rising up into the sky, several of them near places they had known to hold other soldiers. "We could head towards the city, find out what's going on..."

The noise of a distant aircraft made them all jump. "I think that that would be the worst possible option," Matthews said. He was no coward – he had proved that in several encounters before the ambush – but he sounded distinctly worried. "I was studying the Russian aerial manoeuvres and they're flying heavy military transports to the west...and they wouldn't be doing that if they thought there was a serious risk of ground-fire. They're big bastards; we saw them during the Russian flight to Algeria and they're capable of carrying hundreds of men, or even light tanks. Where are they going?"

He picked up a map and showed it to them. "There are several large airports in the west of Poland," he said. "If the Russians managed to mount a sneak attack on us, they might have done the same for the airports; it was the type of threat we planned to counter back in the NATO days. With communications shattered, or at the very least badly damaged, they could reinforce before any local defenders could mount a counterattack. Once they do that... they expand their areas of control and cut off any forces that try to retreat out of Poland."

Anastazy glared at him. "What are you suggesting?"

"We have to fall back," Matthews said. "We're too exposed out here, sir; they have the power to trap and destroy each part of EUROFOR before we can build a proper defence line. I know that the 7th Panzer is up there somewhere" – he nodded in the direction of Warsaw – "but they will have been hit as well, and if we move too openly, we'll be seen and hit from the air."

Robinson stroked his chin, feeling the impact of tiny pieces of stubble. It had been too long since he had shaved, even though he had had the opportunity; Hazel would have been annoyed with him. She had never liked kissing his stubble. The thought of his wife made his heart ache; she had to be worried out of her mind. The BBC would probably be screaming that the British had lost the war already and had to get back to Britain before it was too late.

"We have your two vehicles to protect us from air attacks," Anastazy said. "We have a duty to Poland."

Robinson held up a hand. "Sergeant?"

Inglehart looked wary. "I think that Captain Matthews is right," he said. His face twisted with the bitterness of retreat. "We're down to thirty active fighters and two CADS, not enough of a force to make a difference on our own." He peered at the map. "There was a Polish training facility out here, if I remember correctly" – Anastazy nodded – "and that's only twenty miles in the direction of Germany. If they're active and they know something useful, we can decide what to do then; if not, we head back towards Germany and hopefully encounter other European units."

Robinson nodded. "Jacob, I can't order you to come with us, but your chances of survival will be much improved if you are with us," he said. "Please... will you come?"

Anastazy nodded once.

The drive would have taken only half an hour at most in a car. Keeping to the back roads, well away from civilisation, it took over two hours, not least because of the walking soldiers, rather than using the truck. Robinson had considered pausing at a Polish farm long enough to requisition a second lorry, but they would already be targets for Russian high-attitude aircraft or reconnaissance satellites; he expected that the Russians would know that they were still out there somewhere. They heard aircraft from time to time, even saw a few, but most of them seemed to be concentrating their attention on Warsaw. They heard explosions echoing out in the distance...

Robinson looked at Anastazy, walking with his head bowed, almost as if he were a prisoner. The Pole was walking away from his duty, and even if cold logic supported the decision, it didn't sit well with him to run away. Robinson had read several books where the United Kingdom had been invaded and he had often wondered; what would he do if he was faced with such a choice? Would he abandon Edinburgh – and Hazel – to regroup somewhere outside the city, or would he desert his mates and see to the safety of his wife? How could anyone be asked to make such a choice?

"I'm sorry," he whispered. Anastazy either didn't hear or didn't respond. "I wish it could be different."

Silently, he cursed the Prime Minister under his breath; had he already been thrown out of office in disgust? Everyone had been saying that everything was fine...except those who used the Internet and other media to try and fight the culture wars. The experts had been predicting that the current government would remain in power, but the rise of tension within Europe might have surprised them all; would a far-right party be elected into power soon? The French National Front had been hotly tipped to win the last general election in France...only the assassination of their leader had torpedoed their campaign. Might it have been different?

He shook his head. There was no point, now, in wondering over what might have been.

"Shit," Matthews snapped. Robinson felt his head jerk up as the CADS started to rotate their missiles into firing position. "We have two Russian fighter-bombers, I think; closing in on us and targeting..."

His voice broke off as two black shapes skimmed along the ground, almost at treetop level, dropping their bombs on what looked like a harmless field. Robinson almost didn't see it, but the single SAM rising up from the field was impossible to miss, not like the hail of rifles being fired at the Russian aircraft. The Russians were rising now, banking as they caught sight of the CADS...and Matthews fired. Two streaks of light marked the rise of the missiles; two massive explosions marked the deaths of the fighters, revealing their position to the enemy.

"We'd better keep moving," Inglehart muttered. "Whoever is there may have to wait."

Robinson shrugged. "I think I want to know who they are, first," he said. "We might need their help."

Anastazy was shouting in Polish; the reply came back in German. "They're Germans," he said. He sounded as if he couldn't decide to be relieved or angry. "God alone knows how they got here."

The Germans turned out to be the remains of an infantry unit that had been positioned in a camp to the south of Warsaw.

"They attacked us at the same time they hit you," the leader said. Major Cajus Bekker was a short grim man with a deadly scar running down his face and an air of competence that Robinson rather liked. "They hit us with bombs, and then missiles struck the barracks and FAE bombs completed the massacre. Nearly seven hundred men, all wiped out in a few moments; we decided that we had to head for Germany before the noose tightened."

Anastazy leaned forward. "The noose?"

"The Russians are moving," Bekker said. "We were lucky; we had a communications van along and we managed to talk briefly to a handful of Poles using the more obscure bands before the jamming caught them. There are two major Russian thrusts developing and they're moving to cut off Warsaw and destroy as many of our units as they can."

Robinson felt his blood run cold. If they had stayed where they had been, they would have been destroyed as well. They had stood off a small commando attack, but how could they have stood off an attack with tanks and rockets? He glanced to the east and heard more aircraft and distant explosions; the front of the war was moving on fast.

"We must have been noticed and they had a go at us an hour ago," Bekker continued. "They killed the communications truck and more of my men, then we lost them, and then they found us again and would have killed us all, if you hadn't interfered."

"Sheer luck," Robinson said. "Did you manage to make contact with EUROFOR higher command?"

"Not a peep," Bekker said. "My tech thought that the satellites had been destroyed as they weren't responding to her and that's supposed to be impossible, but as we don't have any communications truck any longer, we can't continue to try to get a response."

"We couldn't raise the satellites either," Matthews said, from his perch. He had been supervising the reloading of the CADS, but he had warned Robinson privately that they didn't have that many missiles left. "We're supposed to receive a permanent data download from them, but in the absence of anything useful coming from them, the only thing we can assume is that the satellites are destroyed or otherwise out of service."

Anastazy looked up. "I have a duty to my country," he said. "Once we reach the training base, I will leave you and join whatever unit was on duty at the time of the war, and take the fight to the Russians."

Robinson didn't bother to argue. "We can't stay here," he said. If Anastazy had made that choice, he would respect it, even if he believed that it was a stupid choice. How could one man, or even a small Company, change the face of the war? "Hopefully, they'll be wary about sending more aircraft after us, but if they want to find us, they could send infantry after us."

"They must have bigger fish to fry," Matthews pointed out. "We're only two CADS and thirty soldiers, hardly war-winning material..."

"It hardly matters," Robinson said. "I intend to get to the German border and hopefully find out what is going on there. Major...what do you and your men intend to do?"

Bekker gave Anastazy a grim look. "The same," he said. Robinson winced; he had been hoping that perhaps Bekker had known something that they could use to strike back, or at least get back in touch with higher command. The presence of a hidden armoured division with air support would have been a nice surprise, but the only two European armoured divisions in Poland were likely to be under heavy attack. "The sooner we move, the better."

They passed through several villages as they drove onwards. Anastazy insisted on stopping long enough to tell the villagers what was actually happening; all they'd heard had been the Russian radio broadcast telling them to remain in their homes. For farmers, that wasn't an option; they had to keep working or the farms would go bust. Anastazy spoke, bitterly, of European farming regulations that had been driving the farmers out of business; taxes, more red tape, everything that farmers dreaded wrapped up into one. The Russians needed food; Robinson wondered if the Russians would make the farmers grow as much as they could, or would they simply collectivise the farms as they had in the days of the Soviet Union.

He looked to the east. Was there any resistance at all? His force, and the remains of the German force, was on the run…and they hadn't seen a single friendly aircraft. If the Russians had really been landing behind Polish lines, they might run into Russians in front of them as well, and that would be even worse. The question of fuel continued to nag at him; European units could take all kinds of fuel – the only real benefit that had come from integration – and they had taken some from the villages, but what happened when they ran out? Matthews had warned that they might have to leave the CADS on auto-engage and abandon them; there seemed to be little choice.

He turned his head to the west and kept walking, one step at a time.

In no particular order, Natasha Belova was brown-haired, beautiful enough to set hearts fluttering even as a child and one of the smartest Russian women on the planet. She had won a scholarship at age twelve and had spent ten years in America, learning from the best, before spending a year in Japan, finally returning to Russia to share what she had learned in the field of computer science with her fellow Russians. Natasha had been one of thousands of Russians who had studied abroad, spies in all but name; she had taken what the Americans had shown her and used it to benefit Russia.

She stood, now, in the centre of the American base and smiled. The soldiers of Unit One had searched the base and removed a handful of documents, but their commanding officer had told her that they were more or less useless. Captain Vladimir Ivanov had cursed the Americans, assuming that they had destroyed files, but Natasha had reassured him; the Americans had merely kept most of their information in their computers. The handful of books, articles and porn magazines were hardly vital strategic information. It was the computers, all around her, that were important; she could hardly wait to get inside them and see how the Americans had made them tick.

She touched one and the screen lit up. The Americans used sensors on their computers these days; the system would probably recognise that she wasn't cleared for any information and refuse access, but that hardly mattered. The screen lit up...and showed nothing, nothing at all. A moment passed, and then an image of a Jolly Roger appeared, a tiny primitive GIF straight out of the early years of computing.

GUTEN MORGAN, INGLANDER SCRUM, printed on the screen. YOU HAF NO WAYS OF MAKIN ME TAK.

Natasha laughed...and then swore as she sensed that something was wrong. She touched the side of the computer and felt something, an odd otherworldly tingle, passing through her arm. Muttering under her breath, she pulled at the panel, which came off. It should have refused to be opened, but it opened...and a massive cloud of dust billowed out at her. She jumped backwards, sneezing; the dust had caught in her throat. She gagged, reaching for her water bottle, and washed her mouth out before looking back at the computer. A terrible sense of doom overtook her.

"Shit," she breathed. Only a few components, ones that she was sure had been home-produced, were still active; somehow, the remainder of the computers had been reduced to dust inside their cabinets, without letting her sense that anything was wrong. She opened a second, then a third, and then a fourth; it was the same story with all of them. Whatever the Americans had done, it would be impossible to recover any data or even more than a little useful data. "Bastards!"

Her grand triumph had just turned to dust.

Literally.

Chapter Twenty-Five

The Advance on Warsaw

Warsaw is burning. Warsaw is fighting its enemy in this last mortal battle. All the promises let us down, the help did not arrive. Lack of food and lack of potable water paralyses and weakens. Yet we fight: with the enemy, with the fire and with the epidemics. Everyone is fighting. Whole city is tied in this mortal struggle. You send us letters of compliments and best wishes from London and Paris. We don't want wishes any more, nor do we await your help. It's too late for help. Before it arrives there will be only rubble here, a corpses-covered, levelled terrain. What we await is revenge. We expect that you will start fighting one day, just like Warsaw is.
Stefan Starzyñski

Near Warsaw, Poland

"The Americans screwed us!"

General Aleksandr Borisovich Shalenko found it hard to contain his fury, made worse by the fact that he knew that he had been the one who had concluded that they had managed to successfully take the American base intact. Major Fletcher had stated that he wouldn't destroy any files…but he had already done it, somehow. The report from Natasha Belova, who had almost been in tears, had been clear; they would get nothing from the American systems, but dust.

"That's one way of looking at it," President Aleksandr Sergeyevich Nekrasov said. Shalenko felt his heart sink; the Russian Government had a long history of blaming the messenger, or the commanding officer, for any mistakes, even if it hadn't actually been their fault. Nekrasov was different, but at that moment, the remembrance that terror and death were very close was chilling. He had promised to secure the American base…and Fletcher had been laughing at him behind his weakness. "Still, we could hardly expect the Americans to roll over."

Shalenko understood, once again, the frustration that led to atrocities. He had spent years rebuilding the professional Russian army and he had trained them, as best as he could, to avoid committing atrocities. He wouldn't hesitate to cause a civilian slaughter if the civilians were in his way, but he shrank from mass slaughter for no good purpose. It was the task of the pacification units to continue preparing Poland – and the rest of Europe – for integration into the Russian Federation; they were criminals and Kazakhs, not true soldiers. They would also have Warsaw, once he took it; they were only in theory under his control.

His lips twitched. If they caused his supply lines to be broken, he'd kill them all personally.

"The Americans said that they would destroy nothing," he snapped. He paused; Natasha's report had been clear and concise, and it had reported an impossible precision of devastation. The computers had looked intact when he had walked through the base; Natasha had claimed that only the interior, part of the interior, had been damaged. The Americans had even engaged in a little taunting. "They broke the terms of their surrender!"

"The Americans have made it clear that the destruction was carried out as soon as Operation Stalin actually began," Nekrasov said, coldly and very calmly. The chill in his voice worried Shalenko, even if it was not directed at him personally; the President seemed angrier at himself than anything else. "Under the circumstances, we could hardly treat them as surrendered prisoners who grabbed guns and started to shoot."

He held up a hand before Shalenko could say anything. "No, we will honour what we told the American Government, through their Ambassador; the men will be returned to America though Turkey, which has agreed to take them," he continued. "The loss of the computers and the other systems there is irritating; my people here can't figure out how it happened. One thought is that the Americans somehow caused the molecules in the computers to come apart, but how…? No one seems to know."

Shalenko nodded. "Mr President, one day we will be able to do it ourselves," he said. "Did Unit One find anything of interest apart from American porn magazines?"

"Not much," Nekrasov said. They shared a mischievous grin before Nekrasov was all business again. "What is the current status of the offensive?"

He could have downloaded it from the Battlespace Management System, Shalenko knew; his friend wanted his impressions, not the cold dispassionate figures. "We have secured most of our targets for paratrooper drops and supply lines," he said. "The Shock Armies are spreading out to push deeper into Poland while the smaller armies are preparing to take Warsaw and secure the city. Once that is completed, we can turn our attention further north and link up with the northern prongs."

Nekrasov nodded once. "And resistance?"

"We smashed most of their forces on the ground in the first few moments of actual combat," Shalenko said, proudly. "A number of isolated units stood their ground and fought to the death, a handful more started to flee back to Germany. Air resistance has been almost non-existent; we have lost a handful of aircraft to ground-based systems and one accident at a captured airport. So far, there is no sign that the enemy has begun to organise coordinated resistance or even a general withdrawal. It will become harder from here, of course, but we have smashed most of the forces they would use against us."

"That is acceptable work," Nekrasov said, as they shared a glance. "What about the civilians?"

Shalenko winced. "There have been thousands of injuries or deaths," he admitted. "Around twelve of our men have been remanded to the penal units on charges of rape and, in one case, shooting a child by accident. The general population in areas we occupy are staying in their homes, out of sight; there's a lot of panic further west, despite our radio broadcasts. I fear that there will be more deaths before we have finished."

"Remember, it is the human capital that we need as well as the land," Nekrasov said, seriously. "Some elements of the population will resist us, and when they do they will be eliminated, but the general population must remain as unhurt as possible by the fighting. Please bear that in mind."

"Of course, Mr President," Shalenko said. "Have you made that point to the FSB as well?"

"Yes," Nekrasov said shortly. "They have the task of purging enemy society of unfortunate individuals, but otherwise they are to behave themselves, or you can have them for the penal battalions."

Shalenko nodded his head. "Then with your permission, I will return to supervising the fall of Warsaw," he said. "Once the city has fallen, we can resume our offensive west."

"The enemy tanks are advancing," the spotter's voice murmured. The tactical combat communications system lent a faint air of unreality to the entire scene. The distant sound – and sometimes not so distant – of long-range gunfire and rockets could be heard in the background; it was just like an exercise, with one very real difference. They could get killed in Poland. "They'll be on your position in five minutes at most."

Captain Guntar Markus was scared, much as he hated to admit it, even to himself. He had been deployed to Poland as part of a large force of Eurotanks, mainly German-crewed. The Poles hadn't been that welcoming, even though they had largely overcome their fear of Germany from the last war; EUROFOR's failure to deter the Russians from pushing the limits had shamed the Poles. Markus had never expected to be part of a very real war; he had never fired his Eurotank's main gun in action before, outside drills. No one had expected the Russians to launch a major attack.

The German commander of the Eurotank division had been a martinet; it had saved Markus's life. The orders from Camp Warsaw had been to spread out the division, even though any natural-born tank crewmen knew that that was inviting disaster, in order to provide some support to the Polish forces near Warsaw. There had been little point in it; the 7th Panzer was well out of position to either guard the border or provide reinforcements. As far as he had been able to tell, their task was really to hold the Poles' collective hands.

His commander had seen it as a good chance to engage in some training and sent Markus – and a force of six tanks – out on a training drill. Two hours after they had started their stealthy manoeuvres designed to practice an advance against an unsuspecting foe – the irony was killing him – the skies had echoed with the sound of thunder…and lit up with the flashes of explosions. The Eurotank's systems were among the best in the world; Markus had a ringside seat as Russian shells crashed down on Polish and European positions…including the command post for the 7th Panzer. The jamming had made it impossible for Markus to request orders, until they had established a brief link with EUROFOR Command, but there had been no orders. Moments later, they had even lost that link; there was no way to know what was going on.

There *had* been some intelligence, albeit very limited. The Russians had launched a major offensive…and they were targeting the mobile forces with air strikes. The European tanks, designed to be stealthy, had been missed, or at least Markus's small unit had been missed. He'd forced down the rising flow of panic and sent out his small Polish escort to act as spotters, knowing that all he could do was delay the enemy. At least his position was good for that, if nothing else; there was no longer a serious uplink to EUROFOR Command. His men had tried to contact higher authority…and failed completely; it was almost as if they were the only human beings left in the world. Only a handful of helicopters, heading west, had passed the tanks…and the tanks had remained unnoticed. Markus was pleased; they might just have a chance to hit the enemy a major blow.

The Polish road leading into Warsaw would be a major angle of attack for the Russians, Markus was sure; it was basic tank tactics to ensure that your forces could move as quickly as possible, and trying to take tanks through the mixture of woodland and marshes was a recipe for disaster. If he tried to move his own tanks, even though his Poles knew the region much better than any enemy unit could know it, they would be certain to be spotted, but if they kept their heads down, they would be unlikely to attract attention. They would have a chance…

"Understood," he muttered back into the tactical microphone. The entire system used a low frequency that was supposed to be undetectable by any known ELINT system, but Markus knew better than to trust it completely. A burst of radio or radar energy could strip away their protection within seconds, leaving them exposed to Russian precision bombing, perhaps even missile fire. The attack on the command post had been ruthless; he didn't hold out much hope of being able to surrender if the Russians caught them. "Move."

He checked his vehicle's batteries again. The power cells that were changing the entire face of the world – and might have played a role in precipitating this attack – were supposed to be rechargeable from any power source, from other tanks to a main power grid. In theory, even without recharging their systems, they could have made it all the way across Poland, but he suspected that that was very much a best-case scenario. If they had to power the tank's impressive array of systems, the power drain would become critical much faster…and once they ran out of power, they would be stranded. One hand caressed the service pistol he wore at his belt; if necessary, his men would try to make their way across country. Someone, somewhere, had to be organising resistance. He was sure of it. The Russians couldn't have killed everyone in Europe.

"Shift in the background noise," the gunner muttered. He was also the EW officer for the Eurotank; the three-man crew had had to have special training to cope with all of the requirements, even with the massive automation that had been installed into the hull. The passive sensors, thank God, didn't trigger Russian alarms. "There's a Russian drone up there, watching for trouble."

"Think good thoughts," Markus murmured. The tank's optical sensors were peering down the road now; the audio sensors were reporting the noise of oncoming vehicles. He wished that he could say that he was surprised that the Russians had a drone overhead, but it was standard practice; the Russians had stolen the plans for the American Dragon Eye micro-drone and improved upon it. "Prepare to engage the enemy."

Suddenly, he saw them…and he felt a spurt of cold rage. Part of him had never quite believed in the threat, even though he had known what was happening; war in the heartlands of Europe seemed a nightmare from the preceding century. He saw, now, the black shapes of the latest, most modern, Russian tanks, and shuddered. They were at war. The Russian T-100 tank was known for being as capable as a late-model Abrams tank, with optional versions for amphibious and anti-insurgency operations, but he was certain that he was facing a tank designed for offensive warfare. There would be no insurgency in Poland, at least, not yet; the Russians wouldn't issue the anti-insurgency tanks until much later. He was facing the cream of the Russian Army.

"Bastards," he hissed. Two Russian helicopters, anti-armour and ground support units, he suspected, could be seen floating in the distance and coming towards his people. The Russians weren't acting as if they knew that the EUROFOR troops were there, but it could have been a trick; he forced himself to remain calm, waiting for the first chance to hit the Russians a major blow. The line of Russian tanks seemed endless…and unstoppable. "*Bastards!*"

He checked the gunner's panel quickly. "Choose your targets," he muttered. Little strands of laser light, connecting each of the tanks to one another, flickered out, designating targets. The Russians would probably detect a laser targeting system, but one wasn't needed for the Eurotanks, not at this range. The Russians were still coming along, watching for trouble, but unaware of the presence of his tanks. "Stand by…"

The image of the lead Russian tank grew in front of him. "Fire!"

The Eurotank was the result of seventy years of armoured warfare experience, much of it British, American or German. It barely shuddered as it fired a main antitank shell towards the enemy tank, catching it completely by surprise. The gunner didn't hesitate; even before the shell had struck its target, he was swinging the barrel of the main gun around to engage a second target and…

Six Russian tanks exploded. The high-energy shell had been developed to defeat the latest armour; they punched right through the Russian tanks and exploded. He saw the turret of one of the Russian tanks exploding into the air, wrapped in a wreath of flame, and come crashing to the ground. The gunner fired a second shot, then a third…and then the Russians started to turn their own guns at terrifying speed.

"Get us out of here," Markus snapped. The driver didn't need to be told twice; he hit the engine and the tank leapt backwards, heading as quickly as it could down the hill. The foliage seemed to explode as a hail of Russian fire cut through the woodlands that had hidden the tanks, but only one of Markus' tanks was hit and destroyed. There were no survivors. "Move it!"

A Russian tank crested the hill, its guns already searching for a new target; two of Markus's tanks fired and disintegrated it. The passive sensors were blinking up alerts; the Russians were sending in their helicopters to cover their tanks, which would be moving around the hill, trying to outflank the

Europeans. The driver kept them moving as fast as they could, trying to get out of firing range, while Russian infantry appeared holding antitank weapons.

"I think we made them mad," the gunner remarked.

He fired at them with the tank's machine guns. Russians fell under his fire or dived for cover, trying to escape the machine guns, as the Russian helicopters swooped down. The Eurotank's sensors were working completely now; it fired an automatic missile at the first Russian helicopter, blowing it apart in a sheet of flame. The second helicopter fired a stream of rockets at the tanks and killed two of them, roasting their crews inside the flames. A Russian tank burst out of nowhere, narrowly missing Markus's tank with a high-explosive shell; they destroyed it with a single shot. A second tank was hit in the treads and skidded to a halt, but he realised that its main gun was still working.

"You're telling me," Markus said, as the tank reached the road. The driver gunned the engine and the tank drove rapidly away from the encounter, the crew knowing that they had only a limited amount of time before the Russians gave chase or called in a close-air support aircraft to finish the surviving two tanks off. "Get us to the next firing point!"

He found himself very calm, even as the Russians stopped their pursuit; he'd faced his first major encounter with the enemy, and survived. Over half his force had died, but he had survived...and he promised himself that he would exact revenge for what the Russians had done to his crewmen. A shadow fell across the tank and the sensors screamed a warning...just as the Russian attack helicopter blew the Eurotank away.

The road to Warsaw lay open.

"Excellent work," Shalenko murmured, as he watched from the command vehicles. The remains of the 7th Panzer had dug themselves in well, but they had exposed themselves to his fire when they engaged his lead units, and he had far more tanks than the European forces. He didn't understand it; the Europeans could have built thousands more Eurotanks for the sums of money they had spent upon their headquarters, but they had chosen to waste the money instead. He could only be grateful; the Germans had handled themselves well...as had the French, further north. If they had had more tanks, air cover, and advance warning, the attack would have bogged down.

"General, the advance units are requesting permission to enter the city," Captain Anna Ossipavo said. "They believe that resistance will be minimal."

Shalenko nodded. "Remind them that they are to use the minimum force consummate with the survival of their commands," he said. He looked towards the burning city; smoke and flames were rising into the air. "The President wants Warsaw fairly intact."

Chapter Twenty-Six

A Stillness Upon the Sea

There seems to be something wrong with our bloody ships today.
David Beatty, 1st Earl Beatty

HMS *Churchill*, Mediterranean Sea

"Still nothing?"

"No, sir," the communications officer said. "There's nothing from EUROFOR HQ, Marseilles or PJHQ."

Captain Adam Ward scowled. HMS *Churchill*, a *Jean Monnet*-class surface control destroyer, had been assigned to the Standing Force in the Mediterranean Sea, attempting to block the flow of immigrants to France, Italy and Spain. It seemed more like a public relations job than anything else; the Standing Force was more armed and equipped to fight a major sea battle, rather than blockade a coastline. They could have done it perfectly if they had been allowed to engage every target they saw and generally treat it as a war, but no, the European Union had to be civilised about it. That meant that every ship had to treat the enemy – and the crew referred to the immigrants as the enemy – with respect; Marines had to board their ships and turn them back, sometimes under gunfire.

He scowled. It wasn't a public relations job; it was a public relations disaster. When new immigrants were picked up and escorted to the camps in France and Spain, it was a disgraceful failure on the part of the French Admiral Bellemare Vadenboncoeur; when the fleet actually boarded a ship, it was a disgraceful display of French bullying – as if all the ships in the fleet were French. The *Churchill* had been designed for major-level combat, not for a blockade; it showed in the way the crew reacted to their mission. They would have preferred to have gone with the Falklands Task Force.

The display flickered as a handful of aircraft appeared, heading out from Algeria. The Islamic Government in Algeria endlessly blamed the Standing Force for all Algeria's woes, that and the French. The Algerians had driven the French out years ago, well before Ward had even been born, but the new government was fond of issuing threats against the fleet from time to time, just to remind them that they were there. The Algerians were encouraging people to flee their country, or so Intelligence said; it was amazing how many Muslims wanted to flee the Islamic paradise. Algerian Radio told of a day when they would rule all of Europe, but they had been saying that for so long that no one took it seriously.

He looked back at the communications officer. "Has the Admiral issued any orders?"

"No, sir," the communications officer said. Admiral Bellemare Vadenboncoeur was a fairly competent, if uninspired, naval tactician, one of two Admirals who were considered to be Europe-rated. The other was German and in the Baltic Sea. Vadenboncoeur knew what he was doing, but didn't have the Nelson Touch; he wouldn't take risks with any of his large ships if he could avoid it. "There seems to be a great deal of confusion, but no real answers."

Ward grimaced. The European communications network was supposed to be perfect, but it had failed before; the fleet was used to that. What they were less used to was losing all communication with their bases in France, Spain and Italy. The *Churchill* had been trying to raise Gibraltar – still British despite the best efforts of Spain and the European Commission, which had been in session for five years arguing – but they had had no luck either.

"Damn it," he muttered. "When are they going to get their heads out of their asses and tell us what to do?"

It wasn't the navy he had joined, not now; working with Europe was a confusing mass of rules and laws that rarely jibed together well. Twenty-seven heavy combat ships, forty smaller craft...all meshed together and expected to work as a team. To give Vadenboncoeur his due, he had immediately started a program of training and exercises, but their real mission seemed to eat up too much of their time. Ever since the Americans had moved the Sixth Fleet out of the region, the European Union had called itself the master of the seas...and that meant patrolling. From Grecian waters – Turkey wouldn't even consider letting them into Turkish waters – to Gibraltar, the Standing Force patrolled and hoped that they would never have to face a real emergency.

"Captain, we may have a problem," he said. "There are nineteen aircraft, now heading out from Algeria towards us…and they're bombers."

"Warn the flag," Ward ordered automatically. Admiral Vadenboncoeur probably knew already, but standing orders were that all intelligence was to be shared as soon as it was developed, just in case it wasn't known to the commanding officers. "Do we have any ID?"

The Algerians sent, from time to time, MIG-29s and other Russian-bought aircraft to harass the Standing Force; they always presented a possible threat. The Arabs were lousy pilots, but there was no questioning their bravery; they would sometimes do something so utterly brave and stupid that no one from the West would anticipate it. The fleet had orders to avoid a confrontation with the Algerians if possible; land-based air cover would provide protection if the fleet needed it. The three carriers had only a minimal air group loaded.

"Flag acknowledges," the communications officer said. "We are authorised to go active."

"Finally," Ward said. He grinned across at the sensor officer. "Bring up the sensors and let rip."

The *Churchill* had the most advanced sensor suite in Europe. It was so powerful that it could cause problems for other ships who were too close, or worse. The radars started to sweep the skies, hunting for possible enemy aircraft; it was the loose equivalent of shouting 'hey stupid' at someone. The Algerians couldn't miss it, even if they had their own sensors dialled down to nothing; it would literally shake their aircraft.

"Captain, there are more aircraft in holding patterns in Algerian airspace," the sensor officer said. "I think they're up to something."

His voice broke in astonishment. "*Jesus Christ*!"

Ward stared as the display suddenly exploded with icons. Missiles, some of them tactical cruise missiles launched from submarines, were being fired… and aimed directly into Europe! There were hundreds of them, some being fired from far too close to the fleet, and they were heading right for their targets. At such short range, with so little warning, they would almost be impossible to intercept. The Algerians couldn't do that, could they? They only had a handful of submarines the Russians had dumped on them and none of them carried cruise missiles.

"Sound general quarters," he snapped. "Clear for action; link us into the other ships and get moving!"

The who and why were unimportant at the moment, he told himself firmly; the only certainty was that they were at war. Someone had just launched a massive pre-emptive strike on Europe...and it didn't take much imagination to realise who it had to be. The Russians; who else could it be? He forced the thoughts down and turned to his display.

"Captain, the Algerian aircraft are closing," the sensor officer reported. "I'm picking up limited targeting emissions, Russian-spec; they're coming to attack us!"

It was almost unbelievable.

"The flag is warning them off," the communications officer said.

Ward cursed; Admiral Vadenboncoeur wouldn't have the stones to order the fleet to open fire unless there was a clear threat...as if hundreds of cruise missiles didn't present a threat. They were spread out and vulnerable – damned politicians – and the best they could do was hold off the attack. His ship was coming to life around him as it prepared to enter its first combat operation, but he knew that it was too late. The enemy would almost certainly get in the first blows.

Admiral Daniel Sulkin was having similar thoughts. His aircraft had been sold to Algeria only a year ago; a handful of the latest version of the old Backfire bomber, an aircraft that had worried NATO badly back in the days of the Cold War. The Algerians had been keen to arm themselves to the teeth, fearful of American intervention into their Islamic paradise, and the Russians had been keen to give them whatever they wanted; they'd had plans brewing for Algeria. The Algerians couldn't fly the aircraft without assistance, but the Russians had trained their own naval strike groups on Backfires...and, when the time came, the Algerians had been more than happy to allow the Russians the honour of flying them.

His unit had arrived in Algeria two months ago, something that had relieved him when he had seen the condition of the aircraft; it seemed that Arabs still cared nothing for more than basic maintenance. The Russians had sold them thousands of older tanks; half of them were unserviceable after a year, while three of the Backfires had had to be written off and cannibalised to get the others working. The Algerians hadn't even understood the problem; as far as they were concerned, the aircraft were fine. Sulkin had known better; they would have only one chance to get the major blow in before the Europeans could react.

"That's the enemy fleet," his coordinator said. "The main ships have been targeted with heavy weapons and missiles; the submarines will move in afterwards."

Sulkin nodded. His command mainly consisted of submarines and aircraft; the heavy ships had remained in the Black Sea. The Turks hadn't commented at how many submarines had passed through their waters; Sulkin hoped that that meant that the Turks were onboard, or at least neutral in Russia's favour. The Europeans had been quite rude to them, shattering their dreams after the Turks had bent backwards to honour their obligations; they owed no love to Europe. They would never fully trust the Russians either, but the Russians, at least, weren't hypocrites.

"Good," he said. "Prepare to attack."

The enemy fleet was lighting up; sensors activating and powerful radars starting to sweep the skies for his aircraft. They would see them, of course; the anti-radar foam that coated the Backfire was far from perfect, even without the other aircraft around and the disturbances they were creating in the air. The question was simple; would the Europeans fire first? If not, he would have the chance to get into firing position and engage them from ideal range; if they did, he would have to launch at once, even though success was still fairly certain. Sulkin was a perfectionist; he would be satisfied with nothing less than the destruction or scattering of the European Fleet.

He also knew about the second stage of the grand plan. The Algerians had to be successful…but not too successful. If they were too successful, the Russians would end up engaging their own allies, just to prevent them from compromising the objectives of Operation Stalin. In the long run, Sulkin knew that the Algerians were likely to suffer the same fate as the Chechens, but that would have to wait; for the moment, they were useful.

"Two minutes to ideal engagement range," the coordinator said. They were approaching at Mach Two; the European radars had locked on. The odds were that they were within European engagement range as well; his aircraft were far more vulnerable to European missiles than their ships were to his missiles, even if they were newer antiship missiles capable of damaging an American carrier. They had been tested in Iran; the Iranians had actually managed to damage an American carrier with one of them. They were tricky targets to hit. "The enemy is hailing us."

Sulkin pulled down a set of headphones. "...is your last warning," a voice crackled, in English. It was more or less the official language of the seafarers around the world. "If you do not break off your attack, we will open fire; this is your last warning."

"Too late," Sulkin said. He smiled grimly as the final seconds ticked down. "Fire!"

The aircraft buckled in the air as it launched its first missile, then its second, then its third, all heading towards their targets. The European ECM wasn't online; even if it were, it wouldn't have made much difference. The sensors in the missiles were far more capable than the Europeans could have guessed, particularly if they still thought they were facing Algerians. The Russian-maintained Backfires could have fired all of their weapons at once, but he had thought it best to ripple-fire from the Algerian-maintained aircraft; a single mistake and the aircraft would have exploded in the air. His other aircraft were firing as well; thirty aircraft, each launching four missiles...there were one hundred and twenty missiles heading towards the European fleet.

"Bank, bank," he snapped, as the Europeans returned fire. They had to have been on a hair-trigger; they might even have fired first by microseconds. Their missiles were faster, too; a Backfire disintegrated in the air, then a second one was damaged and fell towards the sea, the pilots ejecting just before their aircraft smashed into the waves. "Take us out of here!"

Two more Backfires fell, but Sulkin was safe; his aircraft had been missed. The Backfires dropped flares and other countermeasures – the trade of ships for aircraft worked in their favour, but he would have preferred to have kept the aircraft himself – and evaded more return fire. They had succeeded in their mission; all they had to do was escape. That would be easy.

The Europeans would have a far harder task.

"My God," the sensor officer snapped. "Sir, there's over a hundred missiles coming towards the fleet."

"Clear to engage," Ward snapped. "Get your head out of your arse and kill those missiles! Priority target; leave the aircraft to the air defence frigates!"

The *Churchill* rocked as it fired counter-missiles into the air. Its CIWS opened fire as well, killing two missiles; he allowed himself a moment to hope that the fleet could beat off the attack with little loss. The air defence ships had been targeted first, he saw; a French frigate and an Italian destroyer were struck and blown out of the water before they could reprioritise their weapons. They had attempted to wipe out the attacking aircraft and paid the price. Two more ships were struck, even as a warhead exploded far too close to the *Churchill* for comfort; he realised that they hadn't been the target. The *Churchill* was small beer compared to the bigger ships.

The bridge fell silent as the fleet fought for life. The *Principe de Asturias* was the first to be hit, but the *Charles de Gaulle* and the *Cavour* rapidly followed her as the missiles slammed into the side of the ships and exploded. Smaller ships died, but the carriers burnt; they died slowly, in terrible pain. Ward could only watch as the merciless bombardment continued; the Standing Force, proud masters of the sea only half an hour again, was being torn apart.

"The Admiral has been confirmed dead," the communications officer said. The bombardment was ending, but only three ships remained undamaged… and seven more remained floating, but damaged. The remains of the *Charles de Gaulle* were still floating, but the carrier was a burning wreck; it wouldn't be long before it sank. He wondered briefly what that would do to the environment, before realising that it hardly mattered; there were worse issues at hand.

"Captain, we have more aircraft coming over the sea from Algeria," the sensor officer said. His voice was rising with alarm. "I think they're going to try to finish the job."

Ward made his decision. If they were at war with Russia, they would be hunted down if they remained in the Mediterranean; they would almost certainly be caught before they could make it to the Suez Canal and the American positions there…and if the Americans weren't in the war, they might intern the ships rather than let them go back to Britain. Escape through Gibraltar would be risky, but he could think of no better idea; if nothing else, they should be able to make contact with higher authority at the rock.

"Weapons, engage anything that comes near us and looks like a threat," he ordered. The ROE hadn't been written with a full-scale sea battle with Algeria in mind. "Communications, inform the other ships that we are returning to the rock and ask them to come with us; if not, wish them the best."

"Aye, aye, sir," the communications officer said. There was a long pause. "They're scattering, Captain."

Idiots, Ward thought. But he understood; how could a Frenchman, or an Italian, leave the sea when they could make it back to their bases? "Helm, take us to Gibraltar, best possible speed," he ordered. "Communications; I want strict communications silence, understand? From now on, we're hunted animals."

To all intents and purposes, EUROFOR naval forces in the Mediterranean had ceased to exist.

Chapter Twenty-Seven

The Fall of Warsaw

It is part of the traditional law of war that, in case of a siege, a city may have its food cut off and civilians attempting to escape may be fired upon, even killed, to drive them back to eat up the food. This is cruel to be sure, an "extreme measure" as the U.S. Army's manual on the subject admits.
Tom Kratman

Warsaw, Poland

Shalenko watched dispassionately as the Russian forces slowly invested the Polish city. Warsaw had once seen two brutal uprisings against the Germans, and the Polish forces had been trickling into Warsaw ever since the first blows had been struck in the war. It actually worked in his favour; the Poles would have thousands of their soldiers trapped neatly in a pocket, which he had surrounded before preparing to reduce it.

Modern war hadn't changed city-fighting much. The Americans had taken Baghdad easily; they had just been able to walk in with only a handful of causalities. Holding the city had been a different matter. The fight for Qom, in Iran, had rivalled Stalingrad; after the first nuke had detonated, neither side had been interested in showing quarter. Even today, Qom was still partly ruins.

"Ensure that our broadcast continues to go out," he ordered. The sound of fighting was getting louder; the last thing he wanted was more civilian deaths than he needed. "Inform Nikita that he can begin the offensive as soon as he is ready."

"Yes, sir," Anna said.

"Citizens of Poland, this is an emergency announcement," the voice said, over the radio. "There is a military emergency in progress. Remain in your homes.

Do not attempt to interfere. Do not use the telephones, radio transmitters or the Internet. If you require medical assistance, stay calm; help will come to you. Do not disobey this warning. Listen only on this channel for further instructions. There is a military emergency in progress."

Zyta Konstancja hit the button hard enough to almost break her finger. The radio had been one of a set intended for transport to some third world hellhole or another; her sister had worked for Polish International Aid before the local government had evicted all western aid workers. Her sister had been upset, even before Zyta had gone to work for her own living; she had always wanted to aid people who had needed help. Melania Kazimiera hadn't been put off by what had happened to some aid workers, but Zyta had been privately relieved when the workers had been sent home.

Melania was older than Zyta, mother of two children, both born after she had returned. Zyta had, on impulse, gone to stay the night with her sister…and then the 'military emergency' had begun. The Polish television stations had gone off the air, along with most of the power lines to the city, but rumours spread fast; the Russians had invaded Poland. The news had spread quickly; Melania's husband had gone off to join up with the rest of his army unit, wherever it was. Everyone, Zyta included, had been terrified when Russian aircraft had bombed the city; their precision weapons had taken out most of the government buildings. They hadn't heard anything from her brother-in-law yet.

Melania's voice was very tired…and terrified. If it hadn't been for her children, Zyta suspected her sister would be a nervous wreck, but she was trying to put on a brave front. There had been some riots in the streets – no one seemed to know whose voice it was on the radio – and the police had tried to contain them, but most people were trying to stay at home.

"Zyta," Melania asked, "when is this going to end?"

Zyta glanced down at the television. It was supposed to be permanently linked into the global information systems; the modern media depended upon them to function. The builders were more than just a television company, no matter what its detractors said; it relied completely on the Internet and the developments in compressing and transmitting streams of data right across the world. Critics might have sneered that left or right-wingers could have their information adjusted to their personal bias, but anyone who subscribed could access a massive store of information. The global network was overloaded; the help service had been unable to regain anything beyond the single bland radio transmission. .

"I don't know," she said. The rumour mill had reported that the Russians had invaded and sacked Tallinn, in Estonia, only to report moments later that it had been a peaceful entry into the city. She didn't think that it was possible for word of anything from that far away to spread so quickly; it might have been a mistake or a lie or...

A distant rumble of gunfire echoed across the city. There had been noises in the distance all though the night, some of them carried by the wind, from explosions to heavier weapons. The power failure meant that most of the city's support services had failed; after the first riots, most people remained indoors, out of sight. Zyta knew that that wouldn't last either; she'd followed the advice of her sister and checked their food supplies. They had, if they were lucky, enough for a week; once that time had passed, they would have to venture out into the streets to find food.

And hope that we can pay for it with money, she thought. Most citizens of Poland used credit or debit cards for larger sums of money, except the banking computers would have gone down along with the power supplies. She had a debit card, one that would be useable right across the world, but if there was no power, she might not be able to use it. If not...the thought of trading her body for food was disgusting, but she had her two nieces to support; if she had to do that, she wondered if she would. *I think that...*

A scream echoed across the sky, followed by a series of explosions. They sounded far too close for comfort; the Russians seemed intent on scaring them to death. Someone was moving outside, running down the deserted streets; she'd heard some of the men in the apartment block talking about taking weapons and going to join the defenders. Few of them had placed any faith in EUROFOR - or at least the Germans – and they had wanted to aid the defenders. She could only hope that they were only trying to appear tough; they might have been assholes who had kept eyeing her, but they didn't deserve to die. More explosions followed, nasty sounds; Melania whimpered as the sun rose.

"I'm going to the top," Zyta said, suddenly. Her friends had advised them to find a bomb shelter if they could, or to remain inside, but there hadn't been any shelters or basements anywhere nearby. She had been told to stay off the roof – it wasn't safe at all – but she couldn't stay in the apartment any longer. "Stay here."

She left the room before Melania could stop her, stepping into the apartment corridor and heading for the stairs. The elevator had been out ever since the power had failed; she could only hope that no one had been caught inside when it died. There were no lights, not even emergency lights; the only illumination came from the windows. One of them was broken, leaving glass scattered all over the floor; a faint smell of urine rose from one corner. Wrinkling her nose, she walked quietly up the stairs; there could be any number of human animals around. She hadn't seen a police officer in hours...and she hadn't felt in so much danger since a nasty incident when she had been younger. The sense of threat was almost overwhelming; she almost stopped before pushing her way up the final flight of stairs and bumping into the final door. It was locked.

She almost broke down into giggles, then saw the opened padlock and removed it, before opening the door properly and stepping out into the open. The smell of smoke hit her first, almost before she saw anything; the smell was drifting right across the city. Smoke...and something else, something she was almost reluctant to place a name to; she sensed the body almost before she saw it. The landlady had kept a small garden on the roof of the apartment...and someone had shot her. Her body lay in the middle of the garden, stone dead. Zyta checked it, closing the eyes automatically, and stood up.

"My God," she breathed. The sight was overwhelming. Words threatened to fail her as she turned, trying to grasp the entire scene. "What is happening?"

It was like a war zone – no, she corrected herself, it was a war zone. She couldn't see any actual soldiers, but she could see smoke rising from the east, with aircraft flying high overhead. The aircraft were large, they seemed to be like jumbo jets, but very different in purpose; they were unloading weapons down onto the ground below. Zyta had very good eyesight; she could see one of the bombs, a massive black speck, falling towards the ground...and expiring in a thunderous explosion.

Moments later a force of Russian jets thundered by, at very low level. A missile reached up to touch one...and it fell out of the sky, slamming into a building and exploding, the others retreated, launching their weapons down towards the source of the missile. Light flared up within the city; the force of the missile's impact shattering buildings and killing hundreds underneath. The noise of an alarm echoed across the city, and then it died; she could hear shots from the battle outside.

She stared, suddenly heedless of her own safety. The shooting seemed to be coming from right outside the city, far too close to her; she saw a force of helicopters diving down and firing at what she hoped was a defence line. Explosions flared up, time and time again; she hoped that it was better than it looked. It looked as if there would be no one left when the Russians had finished; flames were already spreading through some of the newer parts of the city. Sections built after Poland had become independent again were on fire; she wondered if the Russians had targeted them deliberately, just out of spite.

The building shook. She fell to her knees as a missile detonated, far too close for comfort; a massive Russian aircraft had just blasted a building. She'd seen, very briefly, Polish soldiers on the roof; the Russians had flattened the entire block. She forced herself back to her feet, only to see that things had become much worse; Russian helicopters were moving over the city...and a massive cloud of smoke and fire was advancing into the city. The Russians were directly assaulting the city, she realised; the defenders had been forced back into the city, some of them breaking and running. Civilians were running as well; she could see them fleeing the fighting that had suddenly enveloped their lives, hundreds, thousands...perhaps more of them cut down in the streets in a haze of blood and gore. The Russian military machine had come to stay; she saw a helicopter flying low...and firing a spread of rockets into a building. She couldn't hear as much fighting any longer; the shooting seemed to be dying down as the Russians brought up their heavy weapons and pounded the defenders...

Silence fell.

It was as if someone had turned off a switch. She could still hear Russian aircraft in the sky, see Russian helicopters hovering high overhead, but the shooting seemed to have stopped. She felt relieved, wondering if the war had suddenly come to an end, then felt cold. The shooting had stopped because there were no longer Polish soldiers to shoot at. Even Russians wouldn't shoot bullets around at random; Poles might maintain their distrust of Russians, but they weren't stupid. How else had they gotten away with it for so long?

...And perhaps they wouldn't want to trigger a rebellion in their rear. She clung to that hope with all the enthusiasm she could muster; the thought of how bad a Russian occupation could be was terrifying. She'd heard what some of the older people had said, talking about their childhoods when Stalin's hordes had pushed one bad master out of Poland and replaced the Nazis with the Communists. The Russians had been fellow sufferers under the Nazi yoke, but they had shown no mercy to Poles. Polish women had been raped; Polish men had disappeared in the night or had been pressed into service, fighting for Stalin. She shuddered; there was no reason to expect the Russians to be good masters, not after the way they had acted last time.

A new sound echoed through the streets. It was dull, a long engine rumble, mixed with metal and clinking notes. She wondered what it was, even as a long burst of gunfire echoed out and faded almost as quickly; had the fighting started again?

"Tanks," a voice said from behind her. "There are tanks coming our way..."

Zyta jumped and tried to pretend that she hadn't; she turned to see an older man standing behind her, looking into the distance. She felt a spurt of fear; he was older, larger and probably stronger than her and Polish society seemed to have broken down completely. If he had evil intentions, she knew that she wouldn't be able to stop him from doing whatever he wanted to do, but he seemed intent on watching the scene as it unfolded.

She saw them, now; massive black machines, moving along in a single line, escorted by green-clad men holding assault rifles. The blocky tanks bristled with weapons, some of them armed with machine guns, others with the more familiar heavy weapons she knew; they advanced carefully, prepared for trouble. She tried to imagine that they were Polish tanks, but she couldn't cling to the belief; there could be no mistaking the markings on the front of the lead tanks.

They were Russians.

"My God," she said, as the next sight came into view. "What's going to happen to them?"

A line of men – and a handful of women - were marching behind the tanks; no, not marching, they were almost slouching. They looked beaten, defeated; they had their hands firmly cuffed behind their backs and were escorted by Russian soldiers. Some of them were injured, blood pouring from their wounds; others just kept their heads down and tried not to be noticed. Some wore Polish uniforms; others wore civilian dress. The civilians seemed to be the most brutally wounded, but there was no mercy; they all had to march. The women looked traumatised; had they been punished in the oldest way? Some of them had had their uniforms ripped and torn; they shuffled along, their eyes lowered. They looked terrible.

"They're prisoners," her new friend said. His voice was bitter. "The Russians don't like people who dare to resist them, particularly people out of uniform; that entire show is meant to humiliate us and remind us that we have been beaten. It's also a warning; that could happen to you as well."

He sighed. "Once again, years of independence have come to an end," he said. "God damn the European Union!"

Zyta looked up at him. "Who are you?"

"Names would be a bad idea at the moment," the man said. He winked at her; she noticed that his hair was shading towards white. "I was here the last time the Russians were, back when Jaruzelski was in power and we were starving. The Russians...well, some of them blame what happened to the Soviet Union on us Poles and think that if they crack down on us, they won't fall again. Names would really be a bad idea, Zyta."

Zyta started. "You know my name," she pointed out. "It would be fairer..."

"Fairness is a foolish concept," the man said dryly. The line of Russian infantrymen seemed never-ending. "The world is full of people who would like the world to be fair, and it would be a nice thing if the world was fair, but the truth is they want the world to be fair in their favour. 'Fairness' is only valued if you think that 'fair' will give you what you want."

He smiled grimly. "And, on a different note, what you don't know, you can't be made to tell," he said. "I wonder if the Russians will remember me from last time."

Zyta blinked. "Last time?"

"Never mind," the man said. "Call me Jacob, if it helps. I dare say we'll see each other again."

"I hope so," Zyta said.

"Good girl," Jacob said. "Now, go back to your sister and stay calm; we'll talk again in due course."

Zyta nodded again and stepped back to the stairs. They were covered in dust and pieces of plaster from the explosions, almost ruined. She picked her way down carefully, until she reached her floor; the smell had, if anything, grown worse. She held her nose and stepped into her sister's apartment; Melania looked up at her, her face very pale. Zyta stopped dead as she took in the sight; a set of bullets had smashed through the window and broken objects. She knew that they had been very lucky.

"There's something new on the radio," Melania said. Her voice was shaking. "You have to hear it."

Zyta looked at the radio. The message was repeating constantly. It wasn't long before she heard the beginning of the message. "Citizens of Poland, this is Minister Molobo, the senior surviving government elected official," it said. The voice sounded cracked and broken. "Our position is grim; the Russian response to the unprovoked German offensive launched into Belarus, using our bases, has resulted in the occupation of our capital city and most of our country. The Germans, having sabotaged the military systems they themselves gave to us, have fled, leaving us alone."

Zyta and Melania exchanged glances. *Unprovoked German offensive?*

"The Russians have assured us that their occupation of a number of vital positions within the country is only temporary," Molobo's voice continued. It gave no sense that the speaker knew that he was speaking nonsense. "The Russians, at the request of the elected Polish Government, have taken over the defence of Poland from the German hordes. All military units are ordered to report at once to the nearest Russian military outpost, where they will be issued new orders for the offensive against Germany..."

Molobo spoke on, but Zyta wasn't listening. "He's mad," she said. "No one is going to buy that line of...shit."

Melania looked back. "That's not the problem," she said. Suddenly, she started to break down; Zyta placed a hand on her shoulder. "What's going to happen to the children?"

Interlude Three

Blitzkrieg

It was happening everywhere.

In Poland, as Warsaw fell and was rapidly garrisoned by a specially-trained and prepared FSB security unit, the Russian forces regrouped and headed west. The airports that had been targeted for assault and capture had never been so busy as Russian airborne forces were rushed in and reinforced, expanding the zone of Russian control in the rear of the Polish lines. The captured bridges and vital points, held by small commando teams, were relieved by the ground forces as they advanced; only a handful of commando teams had been wiped out. The Baltic States, attacked without warning, fell almost at once.

The remains of EUROFOR, surprised, shattered and bombed relentlessly, were forced back. Isolated units, unaware of anything outside their own zone of responsibility, were forced to either surrender or fight to the last man. Many units were destroyed or captured before they even knew that they were in a fight; other units began the long process of straggling back towards Germany and – hopefully – safety. Many of the retreating units were attacked from the air, others ran into Russians in the west of Poland and fought final desperate battles; only a handful of survivors escaped the chaos. The remainder of the Polish army scattered into the countryside, their leaders realising that they had no choice, but to go underground and wait. Hundreds deserted to return to their families, hundreds more took up their weapons and made a brave and futile last stand, or prepared the cities for war.

It didn't matter. With the exception of Warsaw and a handful of other cities, the Russians were content to merely surround them and wait for them to surrender. The Russian planners knew that city-fighting would eat up their armies; they were prepared to wait until the population either starved or surrendered. The task could be handed over to the less well-prepared and armed units; the main body of the Russian force was needed further west. As Poland fell under Russian control, Russian forces reached the borders of Germany and pressed west.

In the Baltic Sea, Russian bombers, submarines and missiles had already crippled or destroyed most of the European navies, often before they knew that they were under attack. Massive explosions devastated German ports and bases, Russian aircraft were everywhere; the survivors made a desperate break for Norway, or even Britain...and the Russian Navy followed in its wake. Copenhagen had been torn apart by rioting, unaware that Russian naval infantry were hiding in a handful of massive merchant ships; they now burst out of their ships and seized ports and supplies largely intact. The Russian Navy had been on the move since the start of hostilities; now, a massive force of transports, under heavy escort, docked in the captured ports and unloaded an entire invasion force. The remainder of the city quickly fell and the Russians fanned out; in many places, their presence was welcome to the citizens, who had been caught in the middle of a nightmare. Rioters, looters and insurgents, many of whom were still brandishing placards carrying images of strange cartoons, were crushed without mercy; the survivors were shoved into prison camps and left to rot. The remains of the Danish Armed Forces melted away.

All across Europe, the scene was nightmare and horror; entire cities had been torn apart by rioting and street fighting between different groups. The ordinary citizens hid themselves as best as they could, wondering how their lives had changed so rapidly in the space of a day, and wondered what was happening to their governments. Many of them, dependent upon the welfare state, stayed and waited for someone to Do Something, unaware that there was hardly anyone left to do anything. The hardier stock took what they could and fled into the countryside, hoping to find somewhere where they could hole up until it was all over. The death toll of those unable to survive long without support, of one kind or another, grew ever larger; the survivors called on the army to save them from the nightmare...

The armies were scattered and in disarray. The political leaders were dead, in most cases; a handful had been snatched off the streets by Russian commandos for later use. In Germany, some officers struggled to pull together a defensive line, crippled by their lack of useful information and the endless bombing as Russian fighters and bombers ventured further into Germany. As they became aware that Denmark was falling, some officers ordered a retreat before their flank could be turned; many of their soldiers were unwilling to retreat with the fatherland in danger. Often unaware of each other, barely able to keep their forces together, the remains of the armed forces strove to hurt the enemy before they were destroyed.

It was happening everywhere. A French infantry company that had been on manoeuvres was lucky enough to react to one of the insurgencies in France, but completely unprepared for what they found. An attempt to put the whole matter down as quietly as possible failed as they came under attack from heavy weapons carried by Russian and Algerian commandos. They shot back ruthlessly and tried to fight their way out, only to be trapped and killed when they ran out of ammunition. Algerian forces were landing in Spain and France; the remains of the Police and the armed forces found themselves under attack from two sides at once. They marched to the sound of the guns…and failed to realise the existence of the real threat. They would spend themselves, with their shattered supply lines and what equipment they had been able to save, against the diversion. The real threat was grinding into Germany.

Europe no longer existed. All that was left were thousands of isolated police and soldiers, trying to hold out against the fall of night. Refugees were everywhere, clogging the roads; Switzerland sealed her borders as thousands of refugees, their eyes wide with helplessness and fear, unaware of anything beyond their own little worlds, tried to find safety with the Swiss. The Swiss police and army were rapidly reduced to shooting refugees, just to keep them back; they had no room for more immigrants.

Europe no longer existed. The politicians were dead. The police were gone. The population in some places found themselves struggling for life, in other places unaware that anything was going on; the social contract that had bound Europe together was breaking apart. Ethnic violence grew even worse as the Russians pressed their advantage; Europe no longer existed as a functioning group of nations.

The only exception was Britain.

Chapter Twenty-Eight

Standing Alone

The more I live here in Western Europe, the more I am impressed by the sense of decay; not the graceful and dignified decay of an oriental, but the vulgar and sordid decay of a bankrupt cotton-mill.
Henry Brooks Adams

London, England

"I'm very glad to hear from you, General," Ambassador Sir John Kevin O'Brien said, through the secure link-up from London. His face, old and dignified enough to fit a traditional lordly image, was lined with worry. "How bad is it?"

Langford briefly recited the military situation in Britain. "Given time, we could pull the country back together, stamp on the trouble-makers, and hold elections," he said. "The question is simple; will we have that time?"

Sir John looked worried. He had been Britain's Ambassador to Washington for several years, after committing the ultimate sin of disagreeing with the Prime Minister and his own Party in public. He couldn't be sacked for that, but the Powers-That-Were hadn't considered Washington an important post; they'd given him the role of Ambassador to America. Sir John was popular in Washington, but even he couldn't hide the torrent of anti-American abuse coming from Brussels, or smooth over some of the issues regarding terrorists in Europe.

"I've been talking to the President," he said finally. "The Yanks have agreed to provide us with some of their up-to-date intelligence, mainly from satellites; this blindsided them as well and President Kirkpatrick is taking it very seriously. At the same time, for political reasons, there is very little that they can do to support us openly; the military situation is grim."

Langford rubbed his eyes. He had managed to snatch two hours sleep last night; the strain was starting to wear him down. "They're not going to get involved?" He asked. "What about their bases in Poland?"

Sir John shook his head. "The Russians rolled out the red carpet for Major Fletcher and his men, even after they somehow disintegrated their computers," he said. "They're already on a flight to Turkey with a great deal of free vodka. The Yanks are heavily committed in the Middle East and Korea; the only military move they have made is to send the 101st Airborne Division to Iceland, at the express request of the Government. The Russians have been claiming that the entire situation is purely defensive..."

"Bollocks," Langford snapped.

"...And that the European Union started it," Sir John continued. "The main problem is that Europe is not particularly popular in the States these days; the average Joe Sixpack on the street thinks that Europe is a host for terrorists and Eurabia is just around the corner. The Americans are still considering the matter; it looks as if the President may want to intervene, but she won't get any support from Congress or the Senate."

He sighed. "The other countries that might have been able to help have their own problems or aren't interested," he said. He was now *de facto* Foreign Minister; Langford wondered if it was the first step towards a government-in-exile. "The Turks...well, we asked them to honour their old NATO commitments towards securing and closing the Dardanelles, but they told us that it was an internal European matter and they weren't going to interfere. If the chaos in the Balkans gets worse, General, they may intervene, but they're... more than a little mad at us – at Europe, I mean. The Russians have apparently offered them everything from economic support to military assistance and even some territory in Central Asia; for the moment, they're staying out of it.

"Israel said pretty much the same, except they included a little gloating about the Palestinian problem," Sir John continued. "David – that's President David bar Elias – told us that it was our problem and we had to deal with it ourselves. Even if they had agreed to support us, they would have problems helping...and in any case, they're the best friends of the Turks. Canada condemned the Russians in no uncertain terms, but they don't have much of a military, while both Australia and New Zealand are on the other side of the world..."

"So, in other words," Langford said carefully, "we're on our own?"

"Some things may change," Sir John said. "The fall of Warsaw galvanised Polish opinion in the United States; the same goes for the various Baltic States and even Denmark. The American President has promised that she will try to free up resources to help us with everything short of direct American armed involvement, but that will be tricky; they're rather committed at the moment."

"So you said," Langford said. The intelligence alone would be more than merely helpful, but he was far too aware that the British Army had taken a battering, the Royal Navy had lost far too many ships...and the Royal Air Force had been almost wiped out. The RAF had claimed that they would need 200 modern fighters to cover the United Kingdom Air Defence Region; they had around nineteen fighters currently active, and more that it might be possible to repair in time. "Please keep pressing them."

Sir John held up a hand. "General, I am aware of the issues, but...I would like permission to return to Britain," he said. "My place is with you."

Langford shook his head. "I understand," he said, "but we need you there. If worst comes to worst, we will need you there to serve as Prime Minister of a government-in-exile. Whatever happens, I won't leave Britain."

Sir John looked resentful, but he nodded. "One other point," he said. "What have you told the people?"

Langford sighed. It was something that he had been trying to avoid considering. "I'll have to make a broadcast tonight," he said. "It's been a day; there's a lot of frightened people out there."

"Yes," Sir John said. "I'm one of them."

The connection broke.

Langford sat down and yawned. He had hoped, more than he had dared admit, that there would be a cabinet minister out there, someone who had survived and could take the role of Prime Minister. If Sir John had been in the line of succession, he would have had him back in Britain so fast that he would have had jetlag for years, but he wasn't and he was far more important over in America. He had also hoped that the Americans would help – even the Russians would have hesitated before firing on American ships and aircraft since the Americans had become a lot more assertive in the world – but he hadn't expected much. There wasn't much that could be spared.

There was a quiet tap on the door. "General?"

"Come in," Langford said, recognising the voice. Sara pushed the door open and entered the room, looking disgustingly fresh and cheerful. Langford almost laughed tiredly; just for a moment, homicidal thoughts had crossed his mind. When it was all over – if it was ever over – he would go on leave and sleep for a week. "What can I do for you?"

"The Major has asked me to tell you that the analysts have finished going through the data we received from the Americans," Sara said. "They're ready to brief you now."

Langford nodded and allowed her to lead him into the briefing room. Major Erica Yuppie, Lieutenant Aaron Sargon and Captain Michael Casey were already there, their faces grim. Even as Sara brought them their coffee and tea, Langford realised that it had been bad news; the American satellites could penetrate the fog of war surrounding Europe. They would now know the truth; he prayed that they would be ready for it.

"Well, General; it doesn't look good," Erica said. Even her spirit seemed quelled by what they had discovered. "As you are aware from the garbled messages we have been receiving, Europe has been invaded by the Russian Federation. Prior to now, we had no clear information, but plenty of rumours; now we know just how bad it is." Her hand tapped the map. "It's disastrous."

Casey took control of the display. "The Americans noted that the Russian ASAT satellites engaged the European satellites as soon as the invasion actually began, cutting our communications and orbital reconnaissance capabilities right out of existence. All thirty-seven European military satellites are gone; NASA tracked them as either falling out of space or heading into decaying orbits, scattering debris everywhere. Regardless of the exact details, none of the satellites are functioning…but the American satellites are unaffected. The story they tell is terrifying.

"At roughly the same time as we suffered the missile attack, our units in Poland and the other European units – and Polish units deployed from their bases – came under massive attack, mainly through commando assaults and missile bombardments," he continued. The map of Poland was starting to look as if it had been developing measles as the attack fanned out. "The vast majority of the attacks were actually successful; the handful of survivors in the border regions were rapidly wiped out or captured by the Russians as they surged across the border. The general breakdown in communications meant that units that should have mobilised at once to counter the threat often knew nothing about it until they were under attack themselves and therefore unable to deploy. The Americans note that many units fought bravely, but were overwhelmed by superior firepower; the Russians smashed through them and moved onwards."

He paused for breath; the map expanded outwards to show Europe. "Missile attacks were launched against almost every country in Europe – Switzerland was the only major exception – and they were far too successful. Following, there were riots and revolutions, even small insurgencies, in dozens of places across France, Spain, Italy and Germany, as well as the Netherlands and Denmark. You will remember that various figures in the intelligence services were warning that real trouble was brewing, and were ignored by the governments. These insurgences have caused great loss of life and, worse, tied down various military units that should be engaging the Russian forces.

"The matter was made worse by Algeria, which launched an attack on the Standing Force in the Mediterranean Sea," he said. "The Standing Force was more or less completely devastated by the attack, which we believe was actually carried out by Russian pilots, and only a handful of ships escaped to head to Gibraltar. The Rock itself came under heavy shelling from Morocco – the Moroccan Government has also taken the opportunity to recover Ceuta and Melilla, and we believe that Peñón de Vélez de la Gomera will also fall – and our ships were lucky to escape into the Atlantic. They've headed for Britain, including some other European ships, and we will give them what support we can.

"Algeria, in the meantime, has declared war on France and is sending in troop transports," he concluded. "The French are fighting back savagely, but they have been shattered into individual units and the Algerians are trying hard to pour more petrol on the fire. As the French get their act together – if they do – the Algerians will have far less success, but we believe that the real threat is from Russia."

He sat down, breathing hard. "The latest reports were that Warsaw had fallen and Denmark was on the verge of falling," Erica said, tiredly. Langford made a mental note to remind her to get some sleep afterwards. "With the Russian positions all through the west of Poland and Denmark, we expect that Germany will quickly be invaded and what remains of the German forces driven back. We have been unable to make contact with the German authorities; the only European authorities we have heard from are the Dutch, who put their Royal Family on a boat and sent them here. From vague reports, Norway is also threatened with invasion; the Finns have been hit as well, but so far the Russians don't seem to have pushed into Finnish territory. The victory will be won or lost in Europe."

Langford shook his head slowly. He was familiar with vast battle plans, most of which were drawn up by amateurs and 'clever' – i.e. they would fail as soon as someone actually tried them in real life. Hitler's grand plan for the invasion of Russia had run into problems almost as soon as it had begun… and yet it had come far too close to success for comfort. The American plan for the invasion of Iraq had worked fine, as far as it went, but even that had run into problems…and as for some of the lunatic plans people came up with to interfere in the Chinese Civil War…

"I see," he said finally. The sheer scale of the Russian attack was terrifying. "What do you believe will happen next?"

It was Lieutenant Aaron Sargon who answered. "The Russians have secured the Baltic States almost without a fight," he said. "They captured thousands of tons of shipping and they're pressing it into service, just as they are pressing into service thousands of civilian aircraft. That will complicate their logistics to some degree – they will have captured fuel, but there is no way to know just how much – but as they bring more of their own men into the battle, they will have the transport to land them in Denmark and work their way into Germany from two sides, or work their way around the coast to the Netherlands, Belgium and France."

He scowled. "It would be a perfect target for submarines or aircraft if we could deploy them up there," he said. "The Russian navy has moved several sub-hunters into the area and is deploying the transport convoys with some heavy escorts. As for aircraft, they have deployed mobile air-search radars everywhere, and you can bet that they'll be backed up by the latest ZSU missile launchers. With so much of our AWACS capability, even with the French…"

Langford held up a hand. "The French?"

Erica blinked. "You were sent an email about it," she said. "A French AWACS landed in Dover; scared the shit out of the airport crew as they thought that it was Russian and it couldn't get in contact with anyone on the ground. We barely saw it from the air before it came in to land; the radar network is shattered." She smiled. "And there's this plucky little French Lieutenant, barely twenty years old if he's a day, trying to do his duty and give us all the records from his plane before he collapsed."

She allowed her smile to fade. "We put them all to bed and dug up a reserve crew for the aircraft," she said. "The French boy wants to talk to someone in authority as soon as possible."

"I'll see him," Langford said. "Now..."

Sargon nodded. "We don't have the capability anymore, if we ever did, to launch an air attack into the teeth of those defences," he said. "A single stealth Eurofighter Tempest might get in there, but the damage it could do would be limited, and we have only one tanker left to support it; no ELINT aircraft any longer. We may get more aircraft coming out of Europe, but at the current state of play, I doubt it."

He looked at the map. "I believe that the Russians will push into Germany as soon as they can," he said. "That won't be more than a few days at most. Once that happens, the remains of the defences will crumble and our units there will be trapped."

Langford stroked his chin. "You do not believe that it can be held?"

"The Germans have been scattered, just like the Poles and the French and...well, us, except we don't have more than a few dozen commandos running around on our soil to worry about," Sargon said. "There's no longer any coordination; I am certain that the German soldiers will fight, but they won't be able to hold a defence line for long in the face of Russian firepower. As you know, the European militaries operate on a 'just-in-time' basis when it comes to supplies; the Russians hit the three main supply depots on the continent. The Americans say that the explosions set off the nuclear sensors.

"Bottom line, sir; they're going to run out of ammunition," he concluded. "I have no doubt that the Russians will push them before they can even begin to get production lines set up; as you know, ammunition production for the larger and more powerful weapons was always on a scanty basis. One of the factories for the Knife antitank missile, for example, is now behind enemy lines in Poland. It will take weeks, if we are lucky, to expand production and by then..."

"The Russians could be eating cheese and drinking Chateau Picard in Paris," Langford said. "Can't we hit their supply lines?"

Sargon shook his head. "With what? We don't have the assets or the bases to launch such attacks from British soil…and with the situation on the ground becoming so nightmarish, we don't have bases on the continent any more either. I believe that the only option we have is to recall all of our remaining units on European soil and attempt to get them to Britain before the Russians crush them."

Langford eyed them. "You're advocating that we abandon our allies," he said. It was so hard to think, so hard to grasp; his head was hurting and he wanted to sleep desperately. "We made commitments…"

Erica spoke sharply. "General…with all due respect, that no longer matters," she said. "EUROFOR HQ is gone; the Americans think that Islamic rioters destroyed the building after the missiles hit. The united command system is down and there is no hope of getting it back up. There may be still vast assets on the ground, in theory, but we cannot get them to work together; in reality, there are merely pockets of resistance in a swarm of panicking humanity."

She took a breath. "Europe has fallen already," she said. "It's only a matter of time before the Russians move onwards and complete the task. If we don't get those men and their equipment back as quickly as we can, whatever it takes, we will lose them, permanently."

Chapter Twenty-Nine

Reds Under The Bed

I have here in my hand a list of 205 names that were known to the Secretary of State as being members of the Communist Party and who, nevertheless, are still working and shaping policy in the State Department.
Joseph McCarthy

Edinburgh, United Kingdom

Hazel had spent the evening in a state of near-terror.

Morningside was normally one of the quietest places in Edinburgh. Where there were places where street fetes and parties were the norm, Morningside operated on the basis of quiet-is-best. Hazel was barely old enough to remember the millennium celebrations at the turn of the century; her husband had been a toddler at the time. Now…now Morningside seemed to be caught in the middle of a nightmare; there were alarms, bangs and shouts going on all over the place…and the sky was burning. Every time she peered towards the centre of the city, she could see smoke rising from the crash site and…

She had been sick, repeatedly, as soon as she had entered the house. Her husband had told her something about emergencies and she hadn't been a military wife for so long without learning something herself, but chaos and gunfights on the streets of Edinburgh were something new and terrifying. She'd been able to have a brief word with her neighbour, who'd told her that there had been an explosion in Colinton, near the barracks, and she'd almost fainted before realising that Stuart was safe in Poland. She was almost grateful; he would have been spared the chaos on the streets.

The television had failed along with the power. Stuart had given her a small military-issue field radio; one not for transmitting, but receiving; an emergency model that had been popular for a few years after Oakland. The British

Government had designated a channel as the Emergency Broadcast Channel, with the advice that people should listen to it as soon as an emergency happened, but every time she'd tried to use it, it had failed. There had been literally nothing on the airwaves; she wasn't even certain if anyone was in control. There were no policemen patrolling, no soldiers with guns; the civilian population seemed to have been completely abandoned. It reminded her far too much of the *Dies the Fire* film that she'd watched back when she was dating Stuart, with the civilians abandoned to whatever fate the gods decreed for them.

The night had passed slowly. There were places in Edinburgh that were rough and violent and she allowed herself to hope that the police and soldiers were dealing with them. Perhaps Morningside was peaceful enough to prevent them from having to make a major deployment, or perhaps…she refused to think about the other possibilities. Her father had been out of town for the day; he was probably worried sick about her, but there would be no way to get back to Edinburgh.

Hazel had paced and paced. The news she had received had made her day, literally, but now she was worried; what happened if she died, in Edinburgh, alone and unnoticed. The government-issue booklet on preparing for emergencies, generally considered to be useless even as toilet paper, had been no help. *Stay in your homes unless you are in immediate danger*, it warned. *Help will come to you.*

It had been hours since the air crash and no help had come.

Once again, she picked up her mobile phone in-between dozing fitfully through the night. It was recording no signal, no sign at all that there was anyone else out there. The landline telephone had gone completely as well; she had attempted to fire up the Internet-attached computer and remembered, moments later, that there was a power cut. The battery-operated laptop, connected to the telephone line, failed to connect to the British datanet.

Morning dawned, and with it, footsteps and voices upstairs. Her heart had started to race – Stuart had warned her that when the Police were gone, the looters came out to play – and she had started to head for Stuart's gun cabinet before realising that it was only the two lodgers, returning home. She was relieved; Stuart had told her the combination to the gun cabinet, but had warned her never to touch the weapons unless it was absolutely desperate. They'd all heard tales of political correctness gone mad, from the driver who had had too much to drink before an accident, and had taken someone to the hospital only to be charged with drunk driving, to the farmer who took pot-shots at thieves, only to be charged with manslaughter.

These days, being a Good Samaritan would only land a person in jail. It wasn't worth the risk; something important had died in British culture when that landmark case was fought, won and lost. No one would come to help someone screaming for help any more, nor would they even call the police; it just wasn't the world her father had been born into. The Britain that had stood alone against Hitler was no more.

She opened the door to the back stairwell and walked up quickly. She was more concerned about the two Russians than she was prepared to admit; they were both strangers to the city and the influx of Slavic refugees had not been warmly welcomed by the Scottish public. She would have bet that there was a lot of violence going on; whatever the lying cheating politicians in the Scottish Parliament had claimed about immigrants being useful for the economy, she knew that there weren't enough jobs for the British, let alone foreigners. She opened the door and peeked into the living room; both men had their backs to her. She coughed...

...And then she saw what they were assembling on the table. It was dark and shiny, glittering metal; it was a weapon of some kind, a genuine military weapon. There was none of the simple workmanlike design of the shotgun, or even of the revolver; the weapon looked intimidating beyond belief. The two men jumped as she coughed, spinning around; Sergey Ossetia grabbed up a pistol from the table and pointed it at her, moving faster than she would have believed possible.

Her mouth fell open. No words emerged.

Rashid Ustinov moved like lightning. Before she could react, he caught her and swung her around, pushing her against the wall. She opened her mouth again to scream and he pushed his hand against her throat, preventing her from breathing in more than a little air. Ossetia snapped something in Russian – she couldn't understand it at all – and Ustinov snapped something back, then pulled her away from the wall and pushed her over the table, far too close to the strange weapon. Strong hands caught hers and pulled them behind her – she couldn't even gasp in pain – and then tape was wrapped around her wrists, securing her hands behind her. A moment later, her legs were taped together as well and Ustinov lowered her gently to the floor.

Hazel fought for breath as two sets of cold blue eyes stared down at her. She was terrifyingly aware of her own vulnerability, her own weakness; they could kill her at any moment and she couldn't even crawl away. She opened and closed her mouth, feeling silly even as she tried to regain control of her body; she wanted to scream, but she didn't dare.

She asked a question instead. "Who are you?"

Ustinov stared down at the blonde woman and felt...conflicted. The rush of power he had felt as he had forced her into submission – never mind that she wouldn't have posed a real threat to him and his training anyway – had manifested in a wave of lust and desire. He knew that he could indulge it without compromising the mission more than it had already been compromised, but he refused to give in to that desire. His father...

Ossetia checked out Hazel's part of the building quickly. If she'd had friends staying, if they had fled the building as soon as they heard the struggle, they would have had to assume that their base was compromised. Ustinov allowed himself a moment of pure relief when his partner reported that everything seemed fine; Edinburgh was a strange mixture of chaos and stillness, as if a storm was about to break. They'd seen thousands of people trying to get out of the city; only a handful of people had been trying to come into the area. Anyone would think that they thought that there was something to be scared about.

"It's clear," he reported. He looked down at Hazel; it didn't take a mind reader to know what he was thinking. FSB soldiers got some special perks that ordinary soldiers didn't get, starting with first access to the brothels that the rear units would set up in their path. "Sir..."

Ustinov shook his head. "No," he said, in Russian. Plenty of English men and women would know that '*nyet*' was Russian for 'no' – perhaps Hazel would recognise that he had spared her from a fate worse than death. She looked up at him, her eyes wide with fear; he hadn't even answered her question. She was probably wondering what they were going to do to her.

He switched back to Hazel and spoke in English. "Are you all right?"

Ossetia spoke before she could answer, in Russian. "Sir, we do not have time to spend coddling her," he snapped. "Use her and eliminate her, or just..."

"Silence," Ustinov said. He turned to Hazel. "Are you all right?"

"I'm pregnant," Hazel said. Her voice was broken, sore; he'd pressed at her throat to prevent her screaming and it had damaged her throat. It would recover, eventually, but for the next few hours it would be hard for her to talk. It took a second for the impact of her statement to crash down on him; *pregnant*! "I missed my period and I wondered and I went to the nurse and she told me and...oh god, what are you going to do to me?"

Her voice broke off somewhere between a sniff and a sob. Ustinov stared down at her, his mind churning; his own conception was the product of rape. His mother, who had raised him despite the disapproval of almost all of her family, had been caught in the middle of a terrorist action – the occupation of a building in Moscow. She had been blonde herself, and beautiful then; one of the terrorists had raped her several times and then saved her life when the Spetsnaz launched their attack to liberate the building. She had named him after her father, who had been shot in the head several times by the man who would later marry her; the Spetsnaz Captain who had brought the young Ustinov up as his own. His stepfather, who had gone on to be one of the planners for the occupation, had told him that if he went into the occupation corps, he would be doing the same as had happened to his mother...and Ustinov had been determined to avoid such a fate.

Ossetia looked up at him. "Sir, with all due respect, she is a security risk," he said. "One scream at the wrong moment and we will be caught before we can carry out any more attacks."

Ustinov winced. The plan had been for them to lie low for a week, get a handle on the situation, and then either carry out further attacks designed to incite chaos or find a way out of the city and then the country. He knew, now, that Control had launched more attacks than even he had guessed... and the hints from his stepfather of something really big being about to happen came back into his mind. What had happened...and what would happen?

Ossetia was waiting for him to make a decision. Ustinov cursed under his breath; the British would be quite within their rights to shoot the pair of them if they caught them, and while Ustinov didn't fear death, he did want it to mean something if – when – they died. He was right...and yet, he didn't want to kill Hazel if it could be avoided. If he could keep her alive without compromising the mission, he would do so, even if Ossetia disagreed.

"I need to talk to you," he said, to Hazel. "We don't want to kill you, but we will if we have to, so we need you to listen."

He paused. How much did he dare tell her? "We're Russian soldiers," he said, shortly. "We were sent here by our superiors to fight a guerrilla war against your people. We don't intend to remain here – in this building - much longer, but while we do, you present a serious risk to us, understand?"

She nodded fearfully. Ustinov felt for her. Feelings were dangerous on a mission, his trainers had warned him, but he could no more abandon them without obvious danger than he could cut off his own penis. She was a pretty woman, and she was pregnant; it was that, more than anything else, that drove his decision.

"We're going to have to keep you secure here for a week," he said. Her eyes went wide. "We can't risk having you running around unsecured, so we will put you in the basement, but we will take care of you. In exchange, we want you to remain quiet and not draw attention to yourself; once that is done, we'll free you before we leave. Do you understand?"

Hazel had new tears in her eyes. She was about to start an ordeal…but she would survive it, unlike either of the two Russians if they were caught. They'd managed one strike because the British hadn't expected it; now, they'd be lucky if every place that was worth hitting didn't have an armed guard. They would pick their targets carefully, but it would be difficult and dangerous.

She nodded. "I understand," she said. "Please…do what you like to me, but please don't hurt my baby!"

"I don't see how we can hurt her without hurting her baby," Ossetia muttered, in Russian. "Sir, are you sure…"

"Yes," Ustinov said shortly. "I want you to check the radio again; I want to know what the party line is on all that's happened."

He picked Hazel up, ignoring the fear in her eyes and the feel of her body pressed against his, and gently placed her on the sofa. The radio they'd bought had a battery and an automatic scanning system; they had already picked up broadcasts calling every policeman, fireman, medical worker and soldier back to duty, the latter told to report to police stations if they couldn't report to their barracks. The transmissions had been low-powered; he had wondered if that meant something to the British, or if some transmitters had just been destroyed.

"I have something," Ossetia said, exploring the civilian bands. Ustinov had spent nearly ten minutes ensuring that he had everything worked out, while Hazel's fearful eyes had watched him as if he was about to rip her jeans off and take her on the couch. "It's a transmission on the emergency frequency."

He saw Hazel's eyes flicker with interest. "Let's hear it," he said. "I want to know what the British have to say about what's happened."

"Citizens of Britain, this is an emergency announcement," an unfamiliar voice said. "Please stand-by for a message from Charles Langford, the current head of government. Please listen to the message and inform others of its contents. Please listen on this frequency, every hour on the hour, for updates."

There was a pause. "Citizens of Britain, my name is Major-General Charles Langford, the Chief of Joint Operations," a new voice said. It sounded dreadfully tired. "It is with a heavy heart that I must confirm to you that Great Britain is once again at war. Many of you will have seen chaos on the streets, many of you will have watched in panic as missiles and aircraft came down, many of you will have been injured in the first strikes of a war launched by Russia against the western world. These strikes have killed many, including the Prime Minister and the Members of Parliament."

Ossetia chuckled darkly. "Russian forces have invaded Poland, Denmark, Germany and Norway," the voice – Langford – continued. "We are under no direct threat from Russian forces, but the chaos on the streets must be stopped. Under the Emergency Protocols, I am declaring martial law over the entire land area of Great Britain; the chaos will be stopped. We are working as hard as we can to restore power and water supplies to large parts of the country; I must warn you that there may well be further shortages of what we consider to be essential to our lives. Please do not panic; we are working as hard as we can to save your lives.

"I am also recalling anyone who has served in the military, the police, the fire service and the medical services," Langford said. "Please report to your nearest police station where you will be given instructions on what to do. For anyone not caught in the chaos, please remain in your homes; if you have wounded, please tend to them as best as you can. We are working to restore services as quickly as possible."

There was a pause. "Seventy-five years ago, our country was at war with Nazi Germany," Langford concluded. "The war was long and bitter and there were times when we wondered if we would ever see the end of war, but finally the long night was lifted. If we work together, now, we can walk through the darkness and know, once again, a world at peace."

The radio seemed to pause again. "That was an emergency announcement," the first voice said. "Please listen again, every hour on the hour, for further updates…"

Chapter Thirty

Back on the Streets

When the news reporter said; "Shopkeepers are opening their doors bringing out blankets and cups of tea" I just smiled. It's like yes. That's Britain for you. Tea solves everything. You're a bit cold? Tea. Your boyfriend has just left you? Tea. You've just been told you've got cancer? Tea. Coordinated terrorist attack on the transport network bringing the city to a grinding halt? TEA DAMMIT! And if it's really serious, they may bring out the coffee. The Americans have their alert raised to red, we break out the coffee. That's for situations more serious than this of course. Like another England penalty shoot-out.
"Jslayeruk," on LiveJournal

London, England

"Are you really the Prime Minister now?"

"Something like that," Langford said. "What about you?"

Inspector David Briggs ignored the sally. "Because I want you to know that I'm not exactly comfortable with it," he said, as he studied the tired General. Langford hadn't said where he had based his new government, if government it was, and Briggs hadn't wanted to ask. The General looked as if he needed sleep, not more problems. "I don't think that the military should be running the country."

Langford looked too tired to argue properly. "I don't think I should be running the country either," he said, through a yawn. "If my leave had been a week later, I would have died at PJHQ, instead of...finding some remnants of authority and using them. Inspector, I would love to hand the damn job of Prime Minister over to some damn politician and get back to doing what I was trained to do, like defending the country, but..."

Briggs caught him almost before he fell. "I think that we should both sit down," he said. It had been two days since the missiles had fallen and he'd barely been able to snatch some sleep in the back of the mobile command unit. "Is it really as bad as it seems?"

"It's pretty bad, yeah," Langford said. A policewoman brought him a cup of strong coffee; he sipped it with some pleasure. Briggs eyed the sight with some concern; Flora's coffee was not for the faint of heart. Langford was drinking it as if it were water. "Between you and me, we may not be able to extract many troops from Europe before it falls to the Russians. If we manage to pull together our infrastructure, we might just have a chance, but…it's not exactly easy to repair the results of years of work in a few weeks."

His lips twitched. "I didn't come here to drink coffee, good as it is," he said. "I need to know; just how bad is it in London?"

Briggs laughed bitterly. "Where would you like me to begin?"

"The civil population and the police," Langford said. "I have to know."

Briggs sighed. "The Metropolitan Police, last week, had around thirty thousand officers and other personal, from parking wardens to close-protection experts," he said. "Numbers have been falling for years ever since…ever since policemen started to die on the streets and the politicos did nothing. The merger with the City of London Police did it for many policemen and they went elsewhere; the massive rise in surveillance technology didn't make up for the lack of policemen on the streets. There are some places, sir, where I wouldn't have wanted to go without armed back-up; there are gangs, ethnic groups, religious nutters…"

The frustration spilled out as he spoke. He spoke about endless political compromises, endless attempts to appease this and that minority interest, all the while seeing good policemen driven off the streets, charged with racism and sexism and something-ism, while watching people losing respect for the police. The most popular movie in Britain had been one about a rogue policeman who killed criminals; it might have been banned, but anyone could have downloaded it from an internet server. It said something about the state of Britain that that had been what people wanted…

And no one had made a stand. If they had made a stand, it could have been prevented, or even handled before hundreds of people got hurt, instead… right-wing groups had attacked left-wing groups, or ethnic groups, and they had struck back; despite several bans, the number of guns on the streets was higher than ever…and they were used. The Police couldn't even prevent some crimes; honour killing was on the rise, and the girls no longer dared escape to the Police. What good would it have done?

"Many people are cowering indoors, while others are out on the streets, looting and having fun," Briggs concluded. "I have around twenty thousand people left after the bombings and the riots and the policemen leaving their posts and seeing to the safety of their families. None of them expected to be caught up in a war zone, sir; in some places, it is a bloody war zone."

"That will have to stop," Langford said, coldly. "These riots; I'm convinced that they were intended to prevent us from acting quickly to aid anyone in Europe. The TA has been called out and I intend to use it to prevent the riots from getting worse."

Briggs shook his head helplessly. "And then what?" He said. "Are you going to have them all mown down in the streets? The problems are not going to go away just because we have smashed one riot; are you even going to use live ammunition?"

"They're using live ammunition," Langford snapped. "Inspector, what's morale like with your boys?"

"Terrible," Briggs said. "I told you; none of them expected to be caught up in a war zone."

"We have two options," Langford reminded him. "The first is to let the riots burn themselves out, devastating parts of our country and draining our manpower, the second is to squash them as quickly as we can. There are people we need in London, people cowering in their homes because of the chaos. What choice do you make?"

Briggs looked down at the floor. "That's not fair," he said. It was almost a child's cry; he had no patience for lawbreakers, but to turn the military loose on them…? "These are not the days of Judge Dredd, sir…"

"No," Langford agreed. He nodded towards the country-wide display; they hadn't been able to take over a police station as a general headquarters yet, not with all the chaos surrounding the city. "What choice is there?"

"Deal with the riots, then," Briggs said. He scowled. "Are you married?"

Langford shook his head. "I am," Briggs said. "It was a long and happy marriage, and we rarely argued, even if we had some quarrels over money. We were talking about quitting, you know; we were talking about leaving and heading out into the country somewhere, because the cities were no longer safe. Since the missiles fell, I have been unable to talk to her and…God, I don't know what's happened to her…"

Langford winced. "I never found the right woman," he said. Briggs had to smile. "Use the secure communications net; give her a quick call, once everything is set in motion here. Another reason to put an end to the chaos as soon as possible; once we end the violence, we will be able to reunite thousands of families."

Briggs nodded.

Sergeant Christopher Roach had no sympathy for the rioters, not after losing several of his people to snipers on the first day. Roach, who had found himself commanding a scratch company consisting of seventy soldiers who had been scattered and separated from their units, had spent two days securing the Houses of Parliament – or what was left of them – before being issued new orders. They were to join the force sealing off Brixton, and then end the rioting, whatever it took.

His orders, he was pleased to see as his men deployed, along with armed policemen and riot control squads, had been written by someone who actually understood the tactical realities of combat. Only a politician could come up with orders that included the contradiction of an armed advance and no casualties on either side, but the orders from the new government were refreshingly clear. He was to use limited force unless his men faced deadly force, in which case he was to return fire and crush the insurgents. Roach, like many other infantrymen, had found himself facing the possibility that one day a new government might order them to put an end to the lawlessness on the streets; he had welcomed the thought after yobs had killed his granny instead of finding something useful to do with their lives.

"Sergeant Roach, reporting," he said, to a harassed looking police officer. The other policemen seemed either pleased that the heavily-armed soldiers were there, or nervous around them, regarding them as more violent than the criminals they frequently had to arrest. "We're ready to move in as soon as possible."

"And not a moment too soon," the officer said. Roach nodded; he could hear shooting from the distance, some of it seemingly aimed into the sky. The gangs were at war; some of them would have noticed the police cordon and laughed at it. What could the police do to them? "Those folks want to get back home..."

He cocked a finger at several dozen people, waiting and watching the soldiers with nervous eyes. They were mainly Indian or Africa; Brixton had been an African area before a careless government had also organised thousands of Indians to move in as well, perhaps in the unspoken hope that they would kill each other off. Roach had no doubt that the last government – which had died along with Downing Street – would have screwed the immigrants if it could have done; the British people had been growing less and less tolerant of immigration over the years. They wouldn't be allowed to return yet, he had been told; everyone who came out alive would be held in a makeshift detention camp until their identities could be discovered and their future decided.

Three helicopters flew overhead, police helicopters; Roach admired their bravery. The police knew – they had to know – that some people on Britain's streets had access to SAM missiles; they'd been used to shoot down at least a dozen airliners. The police pilots were risking their lives in aircraft Roach wouldn't have taken into harm's way if it could have been avoided, but they carried out their duty faithfully. They deserved better than the scorn of the population.

"THIS IS THE POLICE," loudspeakers bellowed, the racket setting the birds to flight. The thunderous voice echoed across all of the area; everyone in Brixton would hear it. "MARTIAL LAW HAS BEEN DECLARED. COME OUT WITH YOUR HANDS HELD HIGH OR RISK BEING SHOT. THIS AREA IS UNDER THE PATROL OF ARMED MEN! ANYONE CARRYING A WEAPON WILL BE SHOT! THERE WILL BE NO FURTHER WARNING!"

Roach turned to the officer. "Do you expect any response?"

"There are people in there who don't dare to leave," the officer said, bitterly. "The real hard men won't surrender and won't let anyone else from their groups leave; we might have some people coming out, but they won't be serious hard cases."

Roach waited. A handful of women, of all races and creeds, were inching their way out, keeping their hands firmly in the air. One of them crumpled as a shot rang out; Roach snapped an order to his sniper as the young man carrying a rifle took aim at a second woman. A shot rang out and the enemy sniper fell to the ground, dead.

"Nice shooting," Roach commented. The surviving women fled towards them and the police met them, escorting them to one of the waiting pens where they would be held until they could be moved to the detention camp. More were coming now, women and a handful of men; they kept their hands in the air. One woman, completely naked, drew appreciative whistles from some of the soldiers; Roach asked and discovered that she had thought that she would be mistaken for a suicide bomber unless she approached naked. She was quickly loaned a coat and sent to the pens. "I think that..."

More shooting flickered out in the area. "That's the gangs about to start shooting, I think," the officer said. He glared down at a terminal he held in his hands. "The bastards smashed all of the cameras as soon as mob rule appeared on the streets."

Roach felt his teeth grind together. "Give them the final warning?"

The Police officer muttered into his radio.

"THIS IS THE POLICE," the helicopters bellowed again. "ARMED OFFICERS ARE ENTERING NOW. ANY RESISTANCE WILL BE CONSIDERED A CRIMINAL ACT AND PUNISHED UNDER MARTIAL LAW. YOU HAVE BEEN WARNED!"

Roach lifted an eyebrow. "You have no idea," the officer said, "just how good it feels to be able to make clear statements like that."

Roach nodded. "Put the engines in gear, lads," he ordered. "It's time to move."

The Floid vehicles had been hastily retooled for Sudan when it seemed likely that intervention was going to be required, but had never been sent as the famine and uprising had happened before they were ready to deploy. They had then been considered white elephants by the Ministry of Defence, who had shoved all fifty production models into a warehouse near London and forgotten about them. A soldier who had driven one remembered them and mentioned it to his commander; a quick check had revealed that the warehouse had escaped harm and the Floids had been quickly recovered. They had been built for city-warfare; it would take a heavy RPG to damage them even slightly, while they were armed with non-lethal weapons as well as machine guns. If the...rebels, insurgents, criminals, whatever they were...had something that could damage them, Roach intended to call for a helicopter strike rather than risk his men.

He had been tempted to play music as they advanced, something to both warn the insurgent gangs and reassure his men, but had dismissed the thought. They needed to remain alert; this was unconventional warfare, but as dangerous as anything else the British army had ever done. They had plenty of experience; the only question was if they would have the resources to do it properly. One by one, buildings were checked, searched, and secured by the police; a handful of people who had been found hiding, terrified, had been cuffed and sent to the rear. He didn't have time to play it gently; experience had taught him that people who looked harmless often weren't when it came to the crunch.

A gunshot rang out, and then another; the bullets sparked off the armour of the lead Floid. Roach felt his lips twitch; it wasn't an unrealistic computer game, where enough hand-weapons could make a real difference to a tank, but real life. He would have loved to have brought a Challenger tank or even a Eurotank along; the insurgents would probably have taken one look and surrendered. It would have been a shame about the roads, but...

"Enough," he snapped. The entire building seemed to be infested with armed men. He nodded to the driver of the lead Floid. "Bring it down!"

The vehicle inched forward, more and more bullets pinging off its armour, and pressed against the side of the market. It had a far more powerful engine than it really needed; all of that extra power was used in pushing against the weaker wall. It slowly buckled and twisted inwards, shattering as the driver hastily yanked the vehicle backwards to avoid being crushed under the rubble. The entire building was weakening rapidly; a handful of people fled out with their hands in the air. They were rapidly cuffed, marked as known insurgents, and sent to the rear. Others came out firing and were shot down before they could find their targets and hit a single soldier.

The hours ticked on. One by one, the strongholds of resistance were reduced mercilessly; those that refused the call to surrender were attacked until they either surrendered or ended up dead. Roach wasn't in a taking prisoners mood; some of the bodies they encountered hadn't been killed by his men, but had taken some time to die at the hands of the insurgents. He had had to threaten one of his men with his gun to prevent him shooting all the prisoners after they found a raped woman's body; it didn't help that he shared the man's rage.

An explosion made him blink. He had been rotating his own people though the battlezone, inserting more soldiers as they arrived; somehow, he had ended up as the local military commander. He wasn't sure if that meant that he was the senior officer – and that was worrying as he was only a sergeant – or if someone had decided that he was doing a good job and left him in place. The radio buzzed and he answered it absently; it felt as if they had been fighting for hours.

"Sarge, you have to come see this," one of his soldiers said. "We just stumbled across it in this dump."

Roach nodded and headed over to the half-wrecked building. The remaining insurgents had been trying to escape for hours, heading right into the teeth of the policed cordon, where they had been forced to surrender or die. There was fighting in other parts of London, but this particular fire was well on the way to being put out.

"Here I am," he said, as he entered the building. It had once been a gay bar and had been savagely destroyed on the first night of the war. Dead bodies were scattered everywhere; a handful of trained people were trying to find identification on them, identifying them for posterity. "What do you have to show me?"

"This," the soldier said. He pointed to a pit in the floor; Roach looked into it, expecting to see bodies, and saw, instead, guns. Lots of guns, many of them of Russian design…and modern. Not AK-47s, but modern weapons, including a Yank missile launcher. If they had been used by trained people, Roach realised, they could have made the Battle for Brixton much more violent…

He scowled. There were enough weapons to take half of London.

"Now, that's curious," he said. He assumed a detective pose. "If these weapons were here, why didn't any of the gangs use them?"

"My name is not Watson, sir," the soldier said. "Perhaps they didn't dare use them…"

"I doubt it," Roach said. "If they didn't use them, then they didn't know they were here to use, which means...someone else put them here." He skimmed through the collection of weapons. "I wonder what's missing from here...and who took it...and where it went; those are the questions we have to answer."

Chapter Thirty-One

War in the Air

If you don't know who the greatest fighter pilot in the world is...it isn't you.
Fighter Pilot saying

Over France

"Charlie-one, you are cleared for departure," the controller said. "Good luck and good hunting."

Flying Officer Cindy Jackson hit the thrusters and the Eurofighter Tempest raced down the runway, lunging into the air as if it were keen to come to grips with the foe. Her threat receiver showed no problems, as it had done for the five days since the war had begun with the treacherous attack on the airbases that were intended to defend Britain, and the download from the orbiting AWACS reported only limited air traffic as far east as Denmark. The civilian aircraft had been grounded, or shot out of the sky; the remains of the French and German air forces had been destroyed, along with much of the RAF. The handful of surviving aircraft had made their way to Britain.

"This is Charlie-one," she said. "I'm going dark now; see you on the flip side."

The Eurofighter Tempest was a new aircraft, one of only six in existence...and perhaps now only one of three. The project had been so expensive that the European Union had had to share it with the Japanese and Australians, something that was ironic as Japan and Australia had been having a handful of minor political disputes. It had been intended to create a fighter superior to the American Raptor...and, to be fair, the project had succeeded. If only the aircraft could be made cheap enough to equip an entire squadron...Cindy would have been delighted; the RAF would have had a truly 21st Century force.

She scowled down at her display as the aircraft raced further into the darkness. The politicians had cut the RAF's budget, time and time again, and the result had been a fleet of aging aircraft and low morale, which had led naturally to low personal. Hundreds of trained RAF officers had taken the option of going to America, where the Yanks needed fighter and bomber pilots in their endless war, others did their duty with ever-diminishing resources. Cindy had been one of the latter – she loved her job – but even she had been missing a challenge. The thought gnawed at her, no matter how silly it was; had the Russian attack happened because she had been wanting a challenge?

The Tempest's real strength lay in its stealth. Although it was capable of travelling at supersonic speed, it was almost impossible to detect on conventional radar sets, although some of the latest American equipment had been designed to detect some of the non-American stealth aircraft. The Americans had learnt a harsh lesson during their war with Iran; Russian radars were capable of detecting some of their stealth aircraft, and directing ground fire onto the targets. The Tempest could, in theory, fly through Russian air space without being noticed; in practice, it might not work quite as well as the scientists had kept claiming. She half-hoped that she would be detected; the chance to put a missile into a Russian fighter and avenge some of her dead comrades would be too good to miss.

She clenched her teeth as the memories returned. She had always been a tomboy; when other girls had been putting on make-up, she had been learning at her father's knee – her father had been an engineer with a passion for flying. Her mother had died when she had been very young and her father had never remarried; his only child had taken care of him in-between acing her Standard Qualification Tests and living a nightlife that would have had the Romans green with envy. Her father had taught her far more than she had ever learned at school; by the time she was twelve, she had been doing advanced maths in her head, and knew what she wanted to do with her life. The opportunity had come when she had joined a flying club, and then the RAF itself; they had been delighted to have her.

The memories refused to vanish. She had lost her virginity at thirteen, had her first steady relationship at fourteen, lost the bastard at sixteen and since then had had a string of boyfriends and girlfriends, playing the role of fighter jock to the hilt. She was fond of claiming that she had slept with more women then all of the men in the squadron put together; it was a way of relieving stress. The RAF could be dangerous; it didn't help that the pilots knew perfectly well that many of the aircraft were older than they were. The Tornados had been intended to be removed from the RAF's flight line years ago, but a handful remained; some of them had even served in the Gulf War. Like everywhere in Europe, Britain's interest in its military had been waning for years…

She checked the download from the French AWACS. The French mission commander, a young Lieutenant barely out of diapers – as the fighter pilots called very young officers – had flown all the way from France to Britain as the chaos enveloped France. The people who had briefed her had said that they figured the French would beat off and kick Algerian arse, but the Russian pressure from the east was growing ever stronger. As the Russians probed west from Poland and south from Denmark, it seemed likely that they would defeat the Germans as well and then crush onwards into France; intelligence didn't believe that it was part of the Russian plan to allow the Algerians any part of France.

The Russians had been busy; her threat receiver warned of at least seventeen large and powerful ground-based air-search radars, sweeping the sky for threats, almost certainly backed up by ZSU missile launchers and fighters further to the east. If the Russians had managed to overrun a Danish fighter base that could be repaired quickly, they might even manage to have fighters operating from Denmark, which would reduce their reaction time significantly. American satellite information revealed that the Russians were using commandeered civilian ships to expand their foothold; most of Denmark had fallen before they even knew they were under attack.

"Time to move," she muttered to herself. "Here goes nothing…"

The Tempest lowered itself still further as it approached Denmark. The aircraft was supposed to be silent, but Cindy had never fully trusted the assurances that it couldn't be heard from the ground. There were two known ways to stealth an aircraft – although there were persistent rumours that the Americans had invented a third, but if there was an aircraft that stealthy no one had seen it – and the Tempest used both of them. The aircraft was designed to both redirect radar energy away from the enemy sensors, through the shape of the design, and absorb radar energy through its coating. In theory, even if the Russians caught a sniff of her presence, they would have problems actually locating her enough to launch missiles at her; the radar return would have shown her as further away than she actually was. In practice…there were a lot of radars operating in the region she was heading towards, and the Russians would have almost certainly linked them all into one coordinated system. If they got a response, they might well be able to determine her rough location…

Her display blinked up a warning; there was a small group of medium-sized freighters under her, heading towards Britain. She wasn't surprised; the news of the Russian advance was now common knowledge throughout Europe, even though most of the media channels had gone down, and thousands of Europeans were trying to escape. Those lucky enough to be near the shore were trying to get onto ships; she'd heard that someone on the French side had detonated a bomb in the Channel Tunnel and blocked all ingress. She didn't want to think about what it would have been like for anyone caught under the seabed when the bomb detonated. The Royal Navy was badly over-stretched; some of the freighters would probably try to dump their human cargo near Britain, forcing them to swim to shore or die, and then head back to collect more refugees. Other Captains, older and wiser, were heading for the United States; they didn't want to be caught by the criminal gangs or the Russians. The Russians would probably have been nicer; they would only have pressed the Captains into service.

The entire North Sea was one vast no-man's-land. She'd watched the satellites reporting on the small Russian fleet of ships that had landed in each of the major Norwegian ports, permanently closing them to shipping, but not expanding any further. It didn't take a genius to understand why; the Russians might have been nervous about the prospect of American intervention landing in Norway, but they couldn't have the manpower to take all of Norway at the same time as Germany and the rest of Europe. The ports might even be retaken by Norwegian forces; the delay was all that mattered to them. Russian and British submarines hunted each other through the North Sea; there had been hundreds of tiny encounters that had resulted in the loss of one or more ships for both sides.

She focused her attention on her sensors as she came up on Denmark. She had taken the precaution of avoiding ports as much as possible, but it was still an intimidating sight on the display screen; the Russians were busy. Their radars revealed the presence of other aircraft to her sensors;

there were hundreds of aircraft in the air, many of them either coming from Russia, or leaving Denmark to return to Russia. She did the maths in her head; the largest troop transport aircraft the Russians had built could carry one thousand soldiers, if they didn't mind only limited equipment. A hundred of them could land a hundred thousand troops in a single flight...and the Russians built their equipment to last. It might not be as advanced as the European or American equipment, but most of it would hold out long enough to land thousands upon thousands of enemy soldiers behind the lines. The ships...there were hundreds of ships, some of them military, but most of them civilian...

The sheer scale of the invasion terrified her. The Russian radars didn't seem to have seen her, but she could detect Russian fighters on patrol and banked to avoid them as her sensors faithfully recorded everything they saw. Denmark itself was dark, with only a handful of lights showing, but she could see the glare of lights from the Russian-captured ports from a far distance. The unloading was going on throughout the night; she wondered if they had captured enough civilian traffic to help them move all of their supplies to their units. Hamburg had either fallen or was on the verge of falling; when it did, the German units that had survived would be destroyed.

It wouldn't be long before the Russians reached the Netherlands and Brussels, she decided. Under her breath, she muttered a curse on the European bureaucrats who had driven EUROFOR to disaster as she hunted for more intelligence. She would have liked nothing more than to have led a force of Eurofighters and heavy bombers into the area to wreak havoc, but that was impossible. Thanks to the politicians, the RAF had lacked the firepower to do that even before the missiles had taken out most of the force. The remaining units were being conserved; everyone knew, even though no one had spoken of it directly, that Britain itself was under direct threat for the first time since 1940.

"A single bombing run," she muttered, wistfully. The Argentines had tried that during the Falklands War – she wondered if they would try again with the British distracted by the Russian War – and they had caused real problems...and would have caused worse if they had worked the tactic out properly. She would have volunteered for the flight; a single very low-level bombing run, right over those ships and ports and airports that had been pressed into service. She might even have got very lucky and hit an ammunition ship; an Italian port had been wrecked by just such an explosion, back in the Second World War. "Why not..."

She banked the aircraft, heading for Germany; the Tempest felt almost disappointed to be taken away from a possible encounter with the enemy. The German countryside was dark and almost completely unlighted; the only bursts of light were explosions as Russian bombers prowled, looking for targets that they could drop heavy bombs on. What they lacked in precision they made up for in enthusiasm; they dropped very heavy bombs without wringing their hands over the civilians who got caught up in the blasts. If those civilians had demanded a real defence capability...

Ping! The moment of lock-on was a complete shock to her; she banked the Tempest without thinking about it. The Russian Mainstay had somehow gotten a sniff of her and was bringing up more search radars, hunting for her... and three of its friends were also bringing up their own radars. They had to suspect that she was a stealth aircraft – a non-stealth aircraft would have been detected well before – and would be sharing data; the green sweeps of their radar waves passed across the Tempest...and locked on. The sheer power was burning through her coating and ECM; the scattered bursts of radar energy would force them to triangulate her position, but they could do it. No...they would do it; she had no doubt at all that they would succeed.

"Lock-on," the flight computer warned. It had the voice of her father, something that she had considered funny at times, but now it just seemed like a sick joke. If only the lawsuits forbidding the use of voices without permission hadn't gone through..."Alert; Russian radars have locked on..."

"Tell me something I don't fucking know," Cindy snapped. The Mainstays might carry some anti-aircraft weapons themselves – the Russians were paranoid, with reason – about their AWACS – but she was well out of their missile range and there was no way that such an aircraft could intercept her themselves. No, they would send in the fighters, unless through sheer ill luck they had set up a passive ZSU system below her. "Find me their fighters..."

"Alert; enemy fighters detected," the flight computer said. "Three fighters; flight characteristics suggest MIG-41 Flatpack aircraft. Suggest evasive action."

"Go fuck yourself," Cindy snapped, remembering the one time she had sworn as a teenager in front of her father. He had forced her to wash her mouth out with soap. Enemy radars were coming on all over the area and the Russians would have a fair chance at getting a shot at her, even if she fled at once. She checked the weapons the Tempest carried; she might well have to fight her way through the Russians if they attempted to engage her. "Order; prepare data dump."

Everything that the Tempest had recorded had been saved firmly in its computers. If she believed that escape was impossible, she would trigger the transmission and send everything back to the AWACS orbiting far over the North Sea, betraying her presence in one burst of radio activity. As she turned the aircraft and hit the afterburners, the Russians closed in, while their radars kept a firm track on her flight path. They didn't look as if they were going to be reasonable about it and let her go.

"Bastards," she muttered, as the flight computer reported missile locks from the Russian fighters. "Real bastards!"

She jinked rapidly, breaking the locks, and threw the Tempest into a long dive and turn, coming up facing the Russian fighters. She uncovered the firing key and depressed it, trusting in the ASRAAM missile to achieve a more permanent lock-on using its own systems. A Russian fired at the same time and she dodged the Russian missile, even as her missile scored a direct hit and blew the Russian aircraft out of the sky. The third Russian aircraft achieved lock-on and fired; she evaded through a series of daring and desperate manoeuvres, feeling her body ache as the gravity forces pulled at her.

Her flight computer was screaming at her; the fight was inching out over the North Sea and they had to make their meeting with the tanker, or else they would run out of fuel and fall out of the sky. The Tempest was so classified that she couldn't allow it to fall into Russian hands; the MOD had ensured that the aircraft had a self-destruct linked to the ejection seat. She glared down at her threat board, finding a Russian fighter trying to lock on to her, and launched her second missile at it. The Russian fighter jock threw his aircraft into a crazy dive and avoided the missile with ease. She forced herself to think; how many missiles did the Flatpack carry? She couldn't remember…

The Russian fighters broke off. For a moment, she wondered if it was a trick of some kind, or if they had run out of missiles and she hadn't noticed, and then she saw the three Eurofighter Typhoons flashing towards her position. They had been escorting the AWACS; the controller had vectored them towards her, just to save her from the Russians. It had been a risk, but none of the remaining RAF fighter pilots would leave a comrade in trouble; they had too few pilots to lose one when she could have been saved.

"It's good to see you," Cindy said sincerely, as the Typhoons fell into escort formation around her. She would be running on vapours by the time they met the tanker, but she was certain, now, that she would escape the Russians. There would be other chances to even the score a little, before the close of play. "That was a tight spot there."

"Tight as a virgin's cunt," her rescuer agreed. Cindy laughed bitterly. "At least you managed to hurt the bastards. We don't even get to do that."

Chapter Thirty-Two

Backs to the Wall

Here is the answer that I will give to President Roosevelt: We shall not fail or falter; we shall not weaken or tire…Neither the sudden shock of battle nor the long-drawn trials of vigilance and exertion will wear us down. Give us the tools and we will finish the job.
Winston Churchill

London, United Kingdom

The map on the wall showed Britain's death throes.

"Explain it to me again," Langford said, as calmly as he could. He felt slightly better, even though he had reprimanded Erica for ordering Sara to slip him a sedative with his coffee; there might have been something that only he could deal with. "Why are we having problems?"

Rolf Lommerde flinched. He had problems with soldiers, particularly armed soldiers; he had reacted as through the soldiers who guarded the small building were wolves, with him cast in the role of the sheep. He had been on the verge of ivory-tower status, but unlike many academics, he had real experience in handling problems; he had coordinated some of the relief efforts that had taken place in England following the flooding of 2020.

"It's complicated," he said. The government had never appointed a military supervisor to Lommerde's headquarters during the flooding; he had been able to pretend that the soldiers working on the relief effort didn't exist, or were just policemen in funny uniforms. "It would take a long time to explain…"

"I'm a smart guy and I have until my staff decides that it's time for me to be briefed," Langford snapped. He knew how to delegate and he had a good staff who had actually prepared for country-wide emergencies, but there were just too many fires that needed to be put out. "Explain it to me in layman's terms!"

Lommerde took a long breath. Langford wondered with a hint of uncharacteristic malice if he had ever been called upon to explain anything in anything but jargon and buzzwords before, or if he had just dazzled his listeners with babble. It wouldn't have been difficult; the government the Russians had destroyed had been long on buzzwords and short on action. The bastards had left him with a terrible mess to sort out before the Russians started to attack Britain directly again.

"Think of a city as a black hole," Lommerde said finally, his jaw working frantically. Langford smiled to himself, he was probably wondering if Langford would have him shot for failure. He was perfectly safe from *that* fate, but there was no need to tell him that; he might break out more buzzwords. "It sucks in supplies and so on from the countryside, power stations, water stations and so on. Each city needs thousands upon thousands of tons of supplies to work properly; the newsagent on the corner must be replenished every few days, just to ensure that they maintain their business. Understand?"

Langford ignored the hint of derision in his tone and nodded.

"Good," Lommerde said. "Now…the Russians hit us pretty badly, destroying several power plants and transformers; I dread to imagine what would have happened if they had targeted nuclear plants specifically, but they left those alone. This caused a lot of panic and disruption; the supplies in supermarkets and shops were often removed by desperate people, or at the very least sold out rapidly. Worse, they hit Europe and devastated the supply chain there."

He took a breath. "As you know, sir, the European Union regulations stated that we had to purchase most of our food from Europe, as they purchased items from us," he continued. "Those supply lines have been broken more or less completely, while we cannot get replacements quickly from other sources, such as America or South America. I have taken the liberty of sending purchasing agents to several possible sources with authority to buy food supplies, but that may come with a political price tag. In any case, we are dependent upon food sources in Britain itself, and those are rather short."

Langford reminded himself that Lommerde did actually know what he was doing. "We had stockpiles of food supplies during some parts of the

Cold War, and stockpiled more after the first bout of heavy flooding in 2007," Lommerde said. "There are also the locations in the supply chain; food doesn't appear magically, and for every box of cereal in the stores, there are several in the supply line. Some of them have been looted, but others have been abandoned and my people have been able to recover them. Non-perishable food sources, or at least items that last longer than a week, have been recovered in great quantities. The real problem lies in the stuff that is perishable; milk, unfrozen meat and so on. Matters are not helped by the disruption of supply lines; some of the cities had problems because they had run out of water supplies, and then out of things to drink. We've had examples of truly awful behaviour, such as people eating pet food, but we are likely to get most of the population through the first month, providing that we maintain control."

Langford smiled. "I remember military cooking," he said. "There were times when pet food would have been a vast improvement."

"Ah...yes," Lommerde said. His face was a study in contrasts. He wanted to believe Langford's comment at face value, and yet he didn't quite believe it; Langford wasn't exactly joking. Food supplies had sometimes gotten very short indeed at Basra. "The real problem lies in the long-term survivability of the country."

"I see," Langford said. "Because we can't get supplies from outside?"

"Among other things," Lommerde said. "Some items, milk for example, can be obtained; most of that still came from British farms. Other supplies are going to be harder to replace, sir; we got a lot of our meat from Europe...and the farmers weren't happy about it. The supermarkets pretty much exploited the farmers and...well, what they grew wasn't what we actually needed, as opposed to wanted." He paused. "With me so far?"

Langford held up a hand. "Why can't they just produce what we need?"

"Two separate reasons," Lommerde said. "The first problem is that they will need to sow fields that were allowed to lay fallow...and growing will take time, months even under the best of conditions. The second reason...I don't know if you noticed, but the economy has collapsed. Much of our trade was with Europe and, at the moment, we're getting almost nothing from the continent, and so businesses start to take losses. We didn't see much of this in the first few days, because most people were keeping their heads down, but I expect that pretty soon the unemployment level will rise sharply. The trade wars with America did plenty of damage and the sudden loss of Europe will only make the damage worse; sir, this is uncharted territory for us, for any First World economy."

Langford rubbed his head. "We did it in the Second World War," he said. "Why can't we do it again?"

Lommerde scowled. "Several reasons," he said. "We had time to prepare for the Second World War, most of our trade was with the Empire and the Americans, and the Americans were willing to extend us credit. They basically screwed us after the war, economically speaking, but they allowed us to survive in wartime. Now...there's no preparation, the sea-lanes are even less safe than they were in 1940, and a lot of people are thinking that money's worthless. I've had reports of farmers using shotguns to try to defend their fields against mobs and farms being eaten out, all within a few days. Farmers...just don't want money any longer."

Langford steepled his fingers. "All right," he said. "What do we do about it?"

"We have to ration food, and quickly," Lommerde said. "If we can ensure a proper system of food distribution, we can at least put a lid on the panic for a few weeks and win us time. The NHS has actually been working much better in the last two days; your order to forget the red tape has worked a small miracle, aided by the thousands of medical workers who came back to help the injured from the attacks. Given time, we can restore much of the country to normal, but..."

His voice tailed off. Langford lifted an eyebrow. "But what?"

"In the long term, General, we may be looking at a long depression at best, and depressions breed desperation," Lommerde said. "You may expect to see real trouble on the streets before too long, much larger than you have already seen and even handled, in most places. The mass of unemployed and unemployable was a serious problem for the government even before the war began, when they were fed from the welfare teat...but now, we can't maintain the welfare teat at all. The best we can do is give them rationed food, but..."

Langford had been wondering about that. "We might have to conscript them," he said, seriously. Many people on the dole would have worked if they could have worked, others were lazy teenagers who had never got into the habit of actually working. The Army had been forbidden to recruit in many areas; that would have taken its own toll on the unemployed. If only they had been able to pay soldiers more...he shook his head; it was a dead issue now. "There are no arms, but muscle alone would be useful; could you help with that?"

"I don't like it, but...I guess there's no choice," Lommerde said. "The Social Service and the Job Centres can help finding people; we can always tell them that their rations depend on them, at least the young males, making themselves available for service. We don't have the resources to track them down, however, if they refuse to take service..."

"Do what you can," Langford said. "The emergency services may have to use their labour if the soldiers are needed to actually fight. Hamburg has fallen, and with that, the Russians are in a position to expand their control along the North Sea coastline."

Lommerde's eyes went wide. He was far from stupid, after all. "General... do you think that they could reach Britain?"

Langford hesitated. "It would be a formidable undertaking," he said, soft-pedalling it as best as he could. The Russians would have to secure all of France before they even thought of trying to leap across the Channel, but with the French distracted in the North, they might well manage to secure France within a month. It all depended on just how much control they thought they needed; would they want every last problem terminated, or would they settle for holding the vital points and waiting? "I don't think that we need to worry about that for a while."

"But this is *Britain*," Lommerde protested. "Such things don't happen here..."

Langford thought about that as the helicopter carried him back towards London. No one had understood that the Russians were planning an invasion of Europe, even if there had been hints and signs of possible trouble. Europe had *known* about the capabilities of the Russian forces, Europe had *known* about Russian plans for the Cold War invasion that everyone had feared, but Europe hadn't put all the tiny bits of information together. They had pushed at Russia, in the Ukraine, in Serbia, in even North Africa, without a thought as to the possibility of a violent Russian response. The FCO had considered that the Russians were just pontificating from time to time, and if their views were taken into consideration, they wouldn't cause trouble.

He scowled. The American data made it clear what the Russians had been planning…and why they had even made friendly overtures of their own. The EUROFOR unit from Sweden, in Ukraine, had been attacked brutally, just like the EUROFOR forces in Poland, and crushed without mercy. The survivors, he was sure, would have been shipped into a prison camp somewhere. The Irish unit had been luckier; they had scattered into the countryside, but how long could they survive without supplies? The Russians had plenty of allies in Ukraine; already, they were handing over security duties to them and moving more units towards the west.

It was the same story in the Balkans. Serbian units had attacked the EUROFOR forces in the Balkans, and then moved on into Kosovo, where they had promptly started to remind the natives of why they had been chased out in the first place. The Balkans had been caught up in the war; aided by Russian aircraft, the remaining EUROFOR units fought a desperate battle to survive, some of them even surrendering to the Russians, rather than face the Serbs. Years of humiliation demanded blood; there were even reports that Turkish forces were considering a move into Greece. Thousands attempted to flee to Italy, only to discover that the Italians had their own problems; the Libyan forces that had attempted to attack Italy had discovered that the Italian military reputation was nonsense. The fighting raged on…

"Welcome back, General," Sara said. Her eyes were lowered; she had to know that he hadn't been happy about being sedated. "Was your trip successful?"

"Yes, and no," Langford said shortly. He didn't want to discuss it. "Are they in the briefing room?"

Sara nodded and led him to the room he was starting to slowly, but very surely detest. The CJHQ had never been designed for long-term occupancy and it showed; the work on establishing a proper seat of government was going slowly, even though it was obvious that something would be needed, if only to give the Russians something to shoot at. If they found the CJHQ, they would launch a missile at it…and the CJHQ was not designed to take a bombing. A single JDAM would put it out of use permanently.

"General," Erica said. She looked tired; she hadn't taken a sedative herself. Langford made a mental note to order her to take one after the meeting; she didn't look as if she could remain on her feet for much longer. "I have the latest report from both Britain and Europe."

Langford lifted an eyebrow. Had they at last managed to make contact with someone in authority? "The good news is that we managed to make contact with a French General, in the south of France, and warned him about the dangers of the Russian offensive," she said. "The bad news is that he cannot disengage from the war against the Algerians; they're not that competent, compared to the French forces, but there are a lot of them and Russian aircraft are providing a lot of support. The entire south of France is going to be devastated; the same, more or less, goes for Spain and Portugal. We had an emergency transmission up-linked from Gibraltar; the Governor doesn't believe that they can hold out for much longer under the shelling. Everyone on the Rock is stuck."

Langford could see it now; the Russians would let the Algerians and the Moroccans serve as cannon fodder while they finished off the Germans, and then turned on their allies. The Russians had no time for radical Islam; the Algerians would discover that the Russians had stuck a knife in their backs. A handful of Russian submarines could close their shipping lanes permanently…and the Algerians would never know who was really responsible.

"It gets worse," Erica admitted. "The Russians have turned the German flank and have captured Hamburg; that suggests that they could push down into the Netherlands, and once they do that, we won't be able to extract any more forces from Europe. I think we have to redouble our efforts to call them all out and extract as many Europeans as we can as well."

She paused. "We have managed to make contact with our surviving units and ordered them to pull out," she said. "Most of them will try to bring their allies along with them, others will have issues with abandoning their people, but I feel that we will be able to pull out around a thousand British servicemen and around twice that many Germans and Frenchmen. The main problem would be the equipment; it would be tricky to pull that out unless we get a secure harbour."

"Dunkirk again," Langford said. "Can we secure a harbour?"

"I believe that we could secure several places in Belgium," Erica said. "The Russians will still need several days, perhaps even as long as a fortnight, before they reach the Belgium coast. Once we get some Royal Marines into the ports, some of which have been badly damaged, we should be able to start taking people out." She paused. "There is a case that doing that is like declaring war on Belgium."

"Ridiculous," Langford snapped. The thought actually made him laugh dryly. "Do we have any contact with anyone in Belgium?"

"No one whom we recognise," Erica said. "There are still thousands of garbled messages, but from the panic, there are no traces of the civil government at all. The real danger is that we might have to take thousands of refugees as well…hell, we should try and take as many as we can if we can use them to fight."

Langford looked up at the map. "Can we spare the resources?"

"We won't be committing anything more than a large Marine force," Erica said. "Seven hundred men won't make much difference to the situation inside Britain, which may have taken on a darker tone." She scowled. "Sergeant Roach found a large cache of weapons in London, during the clear-out operation. The interesting thing is that none of the survivors from the area knew that it was there."

The implications were obvious. "We have Russians underground somewhere," Langford concluded. "Do we have any idea as to who?"

"We knew that they had commandos on our soil," Erica said. "The point is…there were enough weapons there to make taking and holding a medium-sized city possible, for a while. The question is…how many more of them are out there?"

Chapter Thirty-Three

The End of the European Dream

Do not confuse "duty" with what other people expect of you; they are utterly different. Duty is a debt you owe to yourself to fulfil obligations you have assumed voluntarily. Paying that debt can entail anything from years of patient work to instant willingness to die. Difficult it may be, but the reward is self-respect. But there is no reward at all for doing what other people expect of you, and to do so is not merely difficult, but impossible.
Robert A. Heinlein

Near Madgeburg, Germany

"Let me get this straight," *Generalmajor* Günter Mühlenkampf snapped. His voice was understandably annoyed. "You are basically heading to the English Channel, whatever else happens, and I am invited to take my men and come with you? Right?"

Captain Stuart Robinson nodded once, briefly. The retreat from Poland had been nightmarish, even with the addition of a handful of other stragglers from Germany, France and even Spain. Mathews' brief low-powered radar sweeps had revealed an enemy aerial presence that dwarfed anything they'd seen on exercises, or even when the Americans had moved into Iran. There had been thousands of aircraft in the sky, from fighters on patrol to transports moving Russian soldiers forward to the battlezone. They'd kept their heads down and inched west.

It hadn't been easy. They had had to shoot down a Russian bomber that had located them and that had brought more attention to their general location; the 'Devil's Cross' aircraft, the Russian copy of the A-10 Warthog, had hunted for them with deadly determination. Luck had been with them; the Russians had missed them, that time. A day later, they had stumbled into a Russian patrol; the Russians had been just as surprised and both sides had broken off the contact after a brief exchange of fire. They had reached a German military camp only to discover that it was in ruins; they had decided to avoid the cities and keep moving. Along a deserted *autobahn*, they had encountered German Military Police, who had escorted them to Mühlenkampf's camp; Robinson had taken a deep breath of relief before realising that the Germans were in worse condition than his men.

Mühlenkampf had explained it, on their first meeting; the Germans had received the main brunt of Russian malice. Robinson, who had been in Poland, had his doubts about that, but it hardly mattered. The *Bundeswehr* had been battered right from day one; a combination of riots and insurgencies in the cities, mixed with air and missile attacks. Mühlenkampf himself had been lucky; as far as he knew, he was the only surviving German General Officer...and the seven hundred men under his command, all from scattered units, the largest surviving German body. He had been bitter; he'd managed to pull together a larger force, but some of his units had caught the attention of Russian bombers and been pounded into scrap.

Robinson had held out hope...until he had seen Mathews' success, linking to a civilian satellite that had been able to provide directions for linking into an American military communications satellite that had been loaned to Britain. The laser-link had been established and a great deal of information had been downloaded, more than Robinson would normally have expected from anyone. The Russians were grinding their way into Germany from two directions at once...and unless his force moved now, they would be caught and destroyed.

"Yes, I suppose you could put it that way," he said, turning back to Mühlenkampf. The German had an unfortunate name for many reasons; he didn't deserve to be abandoned. He felt shame, mixed with an odd combination of impatience; the men under his command deserved better than to be thrown away in a fruitless last stand. They would fight like mad bastards if they were cornered, but he wanted to avoid a last stand if it was even remotely possible. "Orders are orders."

Mühlenkampf glared at him. "The Fatherland is under attack," he said. He didn't seem anything like old enough to remember the long period of Soviet occupation and East German repression, but his father-in-law didn't look that old either. He wondered briefly what had happened to Hazel and her father; the military link didn't allow them any time for personal messages. He could only hope that she was safe. "I have a duty to defend it."

Robinson stared around the camp. It didn't look like a military camp, something that probably worked in its favour; the Russians had bombed, for no apparent reason, a German Boy Scout camp. It had probably looked like a military camp from the air or some reason like that; even the Russians wouldn't have killed a few dozen children if they had known that that was what they were doing. Mühlenkampf's camp had a handful of heavy tanks, all carefully camouflaged, a few dozen smaller vehicles, some of them without fuel, and the British CADS. The handful of soldiers from other countries brought even less to the coming confrontation.

On cue, a rumble of thunder split the air.

He had studied the downloaded information and passed all of it onto Mühlenkampf. His own experience with military matters had convinced him that the Russians were running the risk of friction – the effect of small failures acuminating to make operations delayed or impossible – but it looked intimidating on the map. The Russians would either cut Germany in half or they would seal the escaping British units off from retreat; if that happened, it would be time for a last stand. He had no illusions; the most his force could do was slow the Russians down for a few minutes.

"Answer me a question," he said finally. "Can you defend it?"

Mühlenkampf's face worked furiously. Robinson felt sorry for him; the admission that the Germans couldn't stop the Russians for long had to cost him badly. His force had no communication outside their local area; they might be able to slow the Russians, but in the absence of real air cover, they would get pounded and crushed. There were no supply lines, no reinforcements; he had requested that the Americans provide communications to other German units, but there were only a handful of organised units left. The jamming made it impossible to call up the reserves, or even offer an amnesty to deserters who returned to duty.

"I have my duty," he said finally. "My men are all volunteers; they decided to stay with me and fight."

"Come with us," Robinson insisted. The Russians would notice them leaving, but they had the CADS for air cover; they might even pick up other anti-aircraft units if they looked organised. "We can get to Britain and use it as a springboard to regain Europe..."

"Don't be foolish," Mühlenkampf said, dryly. Robinson was reminded helplessly of Captain Jacob Anastazy; the Pole had left them when they had encountered a scratch force of Polish infantry, preparing to head underground to continue the struggle at a later date. "Unless the Americans get involved...and thanks to our lords and masters, that's not likely to happen...Germany is lost."

"We don't know if that is what will happen," Robinson urged. "There's a Frenchman trying to pull together a defence line in France. You could add your forces to that..."

"If we get that far," Mühlenkampf said. He shook his head. "Do you remember the Iraq War, or Iran?"

"I was barely teething at the time," Robinson said. "I thought German units weren't involved in the fighting..."

"There was a small mission sent to observe the Yanks at work," Mühlenkampf said. "They dominated the skies" – he nodded upwards – "rather like the Russians are dominating our skies, and had weapons that could pick off a single tank from high attitude. The tanks I have here, as far as I know, are the last tanks in Germany...and if I try to move them to England, we will be seen moving and destroyed."

He nodded towards the east. "That information you brought has the Russians coming down the nearby *autobahn*," he said. "We don't have enough explosives to take down any of the bridges and I don't want to waste tank shells, but we can ambush the Russians, slow them down, keep hitting them until we run out of fuel, abandon the tanks, and then go underground. It won't be long before we can set Europe ablaze with resistance to the Russians."

Robinson hoped that he was right. Aldershot had bashed some military history into his head and he could remember that resistance had been a hit-or-miss affair in the Second World War. The history books had argued backwards and forwards about how important the role of the various resistance groups had been, but it would be a long time before Mühlenkampf could build up the resources needed for an underground war. Unlike Iraq, Europe had no massive stockpiles of basic weapons, left around for just anyone to take; Mühlenkampf would find gathering weapons difficult, at least until the Russians got careless.

"I wish you the best of luck," Robinson said finally. "I have my orders."

"Yes," Mühlenkampf said slowly. "Do you think that you can get the CADS back to Britain?"

Robinson had wondered about that. "You want me to leave them here," he said. "Can your people operate them?"

"They're EUROFOR-standard vehicles," Mühlenkampf said dryly. "There will be soldiers who know how to use them in my force."

"I'll see," Robinson said. He saluted and wandered towards one of the groups of soldiers, mainly British and French; they stood up and saluted as he approached. They looked tired, battered, and shocked; none of them had really anticipated a weeklong nightmare that wasn't over yet, if it was ever over. "At ease..."

They relaxed. "We have finally some orders from home," he informed them. The sense of relief was easy to sense. "We have been ordered to make our way to the coast and hopefully board a ship to return to Britain, in preparation for the time when we will return and kick the Russians' arse." There were some tired chuckles. "The main body of the Germans intend to remain here and fight; I ask now, does anyone want to remain here and join them?"

There was a long pause. "I'll take that as a no," Robinson said. "Be ready to move out in one hour."

He saw Captain Mathews working on one of the CADS. "We have a problem with one of the engines," he said, shortly. "I think there was something wrong with the last batch of fuel."

"It doesn't matter," Robinson said. "General Mühlenkampf has asked that we leave the CADS behind when we move, as they will be far too easy to spot from the air. If one of them is almost immobile..."

"Yes," Mathews said. He paused. "I think that he's right; we do owe him the best chance we can give him...and, anyway, with these engines we might not get this baby to a ship."

"I asked the others if anyone wanted to remain behind," Robinson said. "What about you? Mühlenkampf thinks that his people can operate them, and they could just flip on the auto-fire program; do you want to remain behind?"

Mathews hesitated. "I don't know," he admitted. "I'll feel like a heel for running out, but it would be a futile last stand for all of us, so...if I have to die, I want it to be worth something."

"I know," Robinson said. Mere words seemed inadequate. "We're taking the two lorries as far as we can, so get there in an hour with your men, if they don't want to remain behind. I'm going to report to Mühlenkampf and let him know."

Mathews lifted an eyebrow. "You're not going to tell them back home what we're doing?"

"Of course not," Robinson said, bitterly. "It would only upset them.

Mühlenkampf was studying a tank when Robinson found him. The Germans had had one lucky break; they had recovered a fuel tanker that had been disabled by a Russian attack, but through sheer luck the fuel hadn't exploded and added to the damage on the roads. The Russians had strafed several civilian vehicles by accident; all over Germany, people would be running out of fuel. Robinson didn't want to even think about the effects on civilians, caught up in a meat-grinder; the fools who said that war was glorious had never seen the effects on those caught up in the fighting. Robinson had known the job was dangerous when he had taken it; the civilians had not even been consulted about the war.

Of course not, he thought, as Mühlenkampf stood up. *They would have voted against it and did vote against it, but there is no point in passing resolutions in favour of being vegetarian if the wolves are of a different opinion…*

Mühlenkampf's eyes were bitter. "Well?"

Robinson ignored the tone. "You will have the CADS," he said, fighting down the sense of shame at abandoning both Mühlenkampf and the CADS. "Captain Mathews has agreed to leave them for you – incidentally, something that our orders technically forbid. We also have something else for you; we're taking one of the satellite phones from the CADS, but the other will remain with you. The American intelligence information will be yours for a while."

"They'll cut me off eventually," Mühlenkampf predicted. "If they don't get involved, they won't want to be in the position where they have to say no to me, so they'll cut me off, just like they do to every group that trusted them and outlived their usefulness."

Robinson held out a hand. "It's been interesting," he said. Mühlenkampf snorted, but took the proffered hand anyway. "I do wish you the best of luck; give them hell, from me."

The sound of an aircraft echoed in the far distance. "We'll do the best we can," Mühlenkampf said. He scowled. "One of my runners has reported Russian tanks probing towards us, so if you don't mind...?"

"We'll be on our way," Robinson said. He led the way towards the two lorries; a handful of soldiers had volunteered to remain behind, leaving him with twenty-one soldiers, and the redoubtable sergeant. The German lorries were open-topped, something that would allow the soldiers a chance to jump for cover if they were detected and attacked; a covered truck might be harder for the Russians to notice, but if the Russians decided to blast it on general principles, his men would be roasted before they could escape. "Good luck, sir."

He waved as the lorries started their long trip to the west.

They never saw one another again.

The *autobahn* was massive, large enough to hold four lanes running in each direction, and almost completely deserted. Mühlenkampf watched as his force settled into its position, waiting with inhuman patience for a chance to take a shot at their tormentors. The original series of *autobahns,* it was generally believed, had been started by Hitler, but that wasn't true; Hitler had only taken an idea from the previous government and run with it. They had thought in terms of military vehicles moving from west to east; later governments had kept one eye on the military possibilities, until the threat from the east had vanished. Europe had built new roads, linking Europe together...and the Russians were using them to invade. Their tanks would smash up large sections of the road, but they wouldn't care about that; they only cared about speed and the desperate requirement to get as far into Germany as possible.

Mühlenkampf ground his teeth as he waited. He had seen how political correctness had ripped through the *Bundeswehr;* there was no longer pride in serving Germany. A law had been passed, forbidding his soldiers to wear their uniforms in public; young Germans tried to avoid the military as a career, fearful of being disdained in public by their fellow youths, particularly the girls. The *Bundeswehr* was hardly the *Waffen-SS* – they were professional soldiers who acted in a professional manner – but they were shunned. Their fellow professionals respected them; what did it say about Germany when they had more respect from foreigners than their own people? What did it all mean anyway?

"Enemy in sight," the tank crewman shouted. The first Russian tank had appeared…with the sun in their eyes. The Germans had worked hard to camouflage their tanks, but the half-blinded Russians would have more problems seeing them. "At least seven tanks and escorts!"

Mühlenkampf nodded. The Russians had launched a light probe, hunting for resistance; they had helicopters closing in as well, hunting for any resistance on the part of the Germans. They had to be nervous; the Russians, too, respected the German Army. They were probably told tales of how a single SS tank had held up an entire Allied attacking column in the last war with the Germans. Perhaps they had nightmares about Germany; they had certainly worked tooth and nail to keep Germany divided for nearly fifty years.

"Fire," he ordered calmly.

The Leopold tanks fired as one; seven Russian tanks exploded. The smaller Russian vehicles scattered, returning fire; he silently thanked God that he had had the foresight to place his infantry out of sight. Their bullets glanced off the tanks, which returned fire with machine guns, saving their limited stock of shells for worthier targets. Another Russian tank appeared and three of his tanks fired, shattering it under the combined impact of their shells; Mühlenkampf laughed aloud as Russians scattered under his fire. For a moment, he could believe that he was in control…

The Russian helicopters swooped down…only to run into the fire of the CADS. They exploded in midair, their pilots blown away in the second of the missile strike; flaming wreckage fell on the remains of the *autobahn*. He saw a Russian officer barking orders into a radio and knew what was happening; he barked a quick order of his own and laughed as the Russian staggered and fell, half his head missing. The sniper had hit the target perfectly. His tanks were moving backwards, trying to break contact before the Russians managed to react…

He was still laughing when the first missiles from a Russian MLRS truck landed on his position and blew him to bits.

Chapter Thirty-Four

Stockholm Syndrome

[Stockholm Syndrome] is named after the Norrmalmstorg robbery of Kreditbanken at Norrmalmstorg, Stockholm, Sweden, in which the bank robbers held bank employees hostage from August 23 to August 28 in 1973. In this case, the victims became emotionally attached to their victimizers, and even defended their captors after they were freed from their six-day ordeal.
Wikipedia

Edinburgh, United Kingdom

Hazel carefully tested the bonds that bound her and smiled.

She was still terrified, but as her two…lodgers, the two Russians who had shot down an aircraft and killed thousands…had checked out the basement, she had realised that she had a chance. They'd left her tied up on the sofa, listening to the buzzing of the emergency channel, as the Russians searched the house from top to bottom, looking for a place they could imprison her. She had been shaking like a leaf as they left her alone, but no amount of straining had loosened the tape that bound her hands; it wasn't like it was in the movies. She hadn't been able to understand them either, but she was sure that the younger one - Sergey Ossetia, if that was his real name – had wanted to rape her; the older one had prevented him.

She had listened, fruitlessly trying to search for meaning in what might as well have been nonsense to her, as the Russians argued, and then started to search the house. She had wondered about the weapons, and what they would do if they found her husband's small – and technically illegal – collection. They hadn't seemed too worried about it when they found them, but they had been careful to lock them somewhere in their rooms, before searching her and removing her keys, phone – which was useless anyway – and even her small make-up case.

"I think that the basement would be best," Rashid Ustinov had said, after they had completed their search. Hazel had almost flinched before the first burst of hope crossed her mind; it was just possible that they would make a mistake. "Hazel; remember, we will let you go once we are finished here, but if you give away our presence, we will have to kill you."

Hazel had nodded; Ustinov had pulled out a small kitchen knife and carefully sawed the tape from her legs, releasing her and helping her to sit up on the sofa. She gasped in pain as the cramp stuck her; Ustinov massaged her legs gently until the worst of the pain faded, and then helped her to her feet. Her hands were still bound, but she had felt oddly safe with him, now that the first and worst moments were over. Ossetia eyed her as if he thought she was trouble; she concentrated on looking harmless while thinking about what she could do.

Stuart had taken her, once, to a course on hostage situations. There had been several officers' wives kidnapped by one terrorist group or another, before British troops had largely been withdrawn from the Middle East. It had been worst for the Muslim soldiers, who were pressured by their co-religionists to abandon the armed forces or lose their families, but others had been at risk as well; Stuart had insisted on her learning about the dangers…and the first moments were always the worst. She could not fight, she couldn't try to escape; the kidnappers might not be experts, but panicky amateurs. Once the dangerous moments were over, she could try to get the kidnappers to see her as a person, rather than a thing; she seemed to have succeeded at that already. Ustinov, for whatever reason, was treating her almost kindly.

He held her arm to steady her as he took her down into the basement. It was hardly the spider-filled dudgeon of slave girl movies, but a warm room that they had considered turning into another bedroom before the war had begun; Ustinov seemed fairly pleased with the arrangement as he searched the room again, just in case there was anything useful in the boxes they had dumped in the basement. There was nothing, Hazel knew; the junk they had dumped in the basement was useless. He carefully sat her on the floor and made his mistake.

"This should hold you fairly safely," he had said, as he attached handcuffs to the pipe on the wall. It was a useless pipe, as they had found out when they moved in; it literally did nothing, not even carrying water or gas. It was fairly simple to attach a handcuff to the pipe, release her hands, and attach the other end of the handcuff to her right wrist. She would have to sit on the ground, but it was better than being left permanently tied up with tape. "We will take care of you."

"Thank you," Hazel had said. He had been as good as his word, even though the bathroom facilities had left something to be desired; the four days she had spent in the basement hadn't been completely bad. The two men had provided her with several plates of food, from sweets to more healthy options; they had even provided her with some books from her collection while they waited. They had been determined to keep their heads down for several days while the chaos faded off the streets, just so that they could start it up again at some moment that suited them.

"Food," a voice said, glumly. "There should be enough here for a while."

She glanced up the stairs as Ossetia descended, carrying a small plate of canned beans and sausages. She was rapidly growing tired of the fare; unlike almost everyone else in Edinburgh, the two Russians had known to stockpile food to avoid shortages. His gaze flickered over the handcuffs, paused long enough to worry her on her breasts, and then fell to the tray in his hand.

"Thank you," Hazel said, as Ustinov appeared as well. The older Russian looked grim. "What's the matter?"

"We have an interesting opportunity," Ustinov said, seriously. "We may have to leave you alone for a while."

Hazel winced. She didn't want them to get the impression that she would be delighted by them being out of the house…and, truthfully, if she had been wrong, she would be trapped if something like a fire happened. Stuart hadn't been too worried about fires in their house, but normally they didn't even play bondage games. They had three ways out on the ground floor, but only one way out of the basement.

"Don't worry," Ustinov reassured her. "We'll be back in a couple of hours and we have turned off the gas. What could go wrong?"

Hazel smiled. "What's the news?"

Ossetia smiled darkly. "The European forces are crumbling and our forces are sweeping towards the English Channel," he said. "Hamburg and Berlin have fallen, while the French are fighting barbarians and ignoring us. Victory is certain, don't you think?"

Hazel wasn't sure if he was telling the truth. "I don't know what to think," she admitted. "Has the power come back on permanently?"

"Yes," Ustinov said shortly. "Didn't it occur to you why the lights were on?"

Both Russians laughed. "We'll show you the news later today, or perhaps a movie," Ossetia said. "That assumes that you understand the news..."

Hazel flushed. Let them think of her as a dumb blonde if they liked. "I do," she assured him. "I would like to see it."

"Later," Ustinov said. He held her eye for a long moment. "Don't do anything stupid."

She waited patiently until they both left, closing the door behind with an audible slam, and then forced herself to wait for ten minutes, listening very carefully for signs that one of them had remained in the house. She wouldn't have put it past one of them to have tried to trap her, even if they *knew* she was trapped; neither of them seemed particularly stupid...but there was nothing. She shrugged off the blanket and considered the pipe carefully, remembering what Stuart had said when they had taken the house. The pipe looked as if it were firmly in place – and Ustinov had made certain she couldn't just slide the handcuff off the pipe – but she knew that it was very lightly fixed behind the plaster walls. She took a breath, lifted both of her feet to the wall, and pushed as hard as she could. She held the pipe and pulled, her legs pushing against the wall, feeling something starting to give...

The pipe disintegrated with an audible *crack*. She fell back and landed hard on her rear, feeling her bottom bruise under the impact, but she was free! It was a matter of moments to pull herself together and run for the stairs; as she had known, there was no lock on the basement door and the Russians hadn't had time to fix anything to add to her woes. Why should they have? They had *known* that she was firmly secure and at their mercy. The house no longer felt friendly, or welcoming; she half-thought about trying to find one of Stuart's guns before remembering that the two men had locked them away. She had had days to plan what to do; she grabbed her coat and fled the house, onto the streets. The street was almost deserted, as always, but she knew her way; she had to find a police station and find help.

She slowed to a walk as she rounded the corner and lost herself in side streets. Part of her...didn't want to betray Ustinov, although Ossetia was a danger to everyone in Edinburgh. Ustinov had spared her life; Ossetia, she was mortally certain, had wanted to rape and kill her. She paused to think, trying to decide, but the thought of her husband forced her mind to focus; what would Stuart want her to do? If Ossetia had been telling the truth, Stuart, like her, was in the middle of a war zone; he might even be dead. Cold rage burned at her, forcing her onwards; the police station wasn't that far from where she was. All she had to do was keep putting one foot in front of another and…she would reach them. She would find help.

An old man appeared in front of her. She sensed him wrinkling his nose; after so long without a proper bath, or even proper sanitation, she had to smell pretty bad. He wasn't a fine-smelling person himself; the absence of water supplies for a day had probably had all kinds of nasty effects…

But his voice was kind. "Are you all right, love?"

"Yes," Hazel said shortly. He couldn't help her; the police station was right in front of her. It dawned on her suddenly that she had no proof, nothing that she could show them; would the Police believe her when she told her story? She staggered into the police station and came face-to-face with a grim-looking Police Sergeant, his face scarred by some great heat; he looked as if he should be in hospital. "Constable, I…"

Her legs buckled and she collapsed on the floor. "I've got you," the Policeman said. His voice sounded as if it were coming from a far distance; her vision blurred, and then stabilised as she pulled herself back together. "I'm Sergeant Adams, of the Edinburgh Police, recalled to duty since the war began. Are you all right, love? I can call the nurse if you want, or even a doctor, although our doctor has been tending to victims of the airplane and we might have to take you to hospital."

Hazel burst into giggles. Adams reacted smoothly and called a nurse from the depths of the police station, who tended to Hazel's arm, which had been squeezed tight by the handcuffs, as she told her story. They didn't believe her at first, until the nurse pointed to the injuries on her throat and wrist; she was still covered in plaster dust from the wall and the pipe. One of the older Police officers had some experience with Special Forces and recognised the injuries…and then the Police got very interested indeed.

"Form a line with your documents and national insurance card," a voice bellowed, in front of the job centre. Ustinov watched dispassionately as thousands of young Scottish men, some of them old enough to be doing a real man's work, lined up as if they were about to be put in front of a wall and shot. The grim face of the Scottish Sergeant standing near the side of the building was easy to read; the young men could use some military discipline. Some of them were listening to music on their headphones, others were looking around as if they were searching for a way to escape; their nightmare was hard work and people ordering them about.

He carefully pulled himself back from the window before he was seen. The radio broadcasts on the emergency channel had been clear and to the point; every young man who had been on the dole was being conscripted into work battalions to help repair the damage that Britain had suffered during the first stage of the war. Failure to respond to the call was not an option; a welfare-dependent person – as the radio had put it – would receive no rations or other supplies if they failed to report for duty, or even face arrest. There had been the promise of a week to report, but Ustinov was pretty certain that most of them would be bending their minds trying to think of some way out of the nightmare; they were trying their hardest to avoid the sergeant's disgusted gaze. The thought of actually being shot at...

He nodded once as Ossetia appeared at the end of the stairwell; they would have to move quickly if they were to take advantage of the opportunity. A simple bomb would destroy the job centre and the recruits; Moscow had been very clear on the need to hit the British where they lived. Britain, he had been told, was unique; they would have a chance to pull themselves back together before it was too late, something he hadn't understood until he had seen the news reports of Russian armies grinding their way into Europe. The very fabric of British society had to be attacked...and if the young men who were conscripted felt that there was a chance that they would be blown up... they would be more reluctant to report. Even better, more of the population, normally law-abiding, would be reluctant to force them to report.

"Time to go," he said, already cataloguing what they would need. If they were really lucky, their attack would be blamed on a terrorist group, but even if it wasn't, it would hardly matter. All that mattered was attacking the very fabric of British society; Iraqis had known for years that Saudi Arabia was behind their woes after the American Invasion, but they hadn't been able to muster the determination to rebuild and crush Saudi, because the insurgency kept burning away at their new fabric. His force had been trained in destabilisation; a single car bomb could do the work of thousands of air bombs if placed in the right place. "Once we get back, we'll find a way of using Hazel's car to take a bomb past the job centre."

Security in the heart of Edinburgh and around the aircraft crash site was pretty heavy, with nervous armed police officers patrolling some parts of the streets. There were fewer cars on the streets; posters had already begun to appear, printed off by some wag, about the need to conserve fuel. IS YOUR JOURNEY REALLY VITAL? One asked; GO HOME, HENRY – ALL THE VILLAGE KNOWS YOUR JOURNEY IS NOT IMPORTANT, another warned, with the image of a beaten middle-aged man being kicked off by a railway guard. Edinburgh was slowly coming to grips with the thought that it was at war; as he turned into the street that held Hazel's house, he saw other signs of panic. Some of the buildings near their building had been abandoned the day after the war began; he'd watched the people going with only a few suitcases, abandoning the rest to the looters.

"Home again," Ossetia commented dryly. They climbed out of the car and locked the doors. There was a droll tone in his voice; after they bombed the job centre, they would have to change their base before some bright spark with a CCTV system and supporting footage put everything together and found them. "Are you going to feed your pet…?"

Ustinov opened his mouth to reply, and then he saw them; men appearing from the houses, weapons held high. They weren't police; they held themselves with an easy confidence, an ease of motion, an awareness that they were the best, that screamed *Special Forces* at him. Somehow, they had been detected; somehow…

"HANDS IN THE AIR," a voice bellowed, loudly enough to shake the entire neighbourhood. They had to have all been evacuated; somehow, the British security forces had managed to get into position without them even noticing that they had driven right into a trap. If they had still been in the car, escape might have been possible, but in the time it would take to get back in, they could be killed several times over. "THIS IS YOUR LAST WARNING…!"

Ossetia snatched up his pistol and fired once towards one of the figures; a sniper bullet blew the top of his head off, before he could even hit one of the SAS soldiers surrounding them. Ustinov stared at them, calculating, and knew that it was futile; he could only get himself killed, not even taking one of them with him. They had him directly in their sights and he knew it.

Carefully, he raised his hands above his head and waited for the end.

Chapter Thirty-Five

Rats and Sinking Ships

The problem with collaboration is that most people will never collaborate...until it seems to be the only rational choice. If the wind changes, the collaborators find themselves facing their outraged countrymen...in many cases merely for having tried to do the best they can. It is not given to humanity to know the outcome in advance – sometimes, it seems as if the best choice is to sell out for the best terms you can get.
Christopher Nuttall

Moscow, Russia

The terminal was dark and cold.

Prime Minister Zdeněk Kundera of the Czech Republic waited with as much patience as he could bring to bear on the situation. A kindly, almost scholarly man, Kundera knew that he was not cut out for the interplay of political power and naked violence that determined the future of most of the world, but then, the Czech Republic had never intended to play a major role in the world. The Czech Republic had been willing to commit itself to the European Union, but it had never imagined that it would be called upon to fight a serious war; commitments to peacekeeping missions and the occasional EUROFOR operation had been the limits of its involvement...until the 1st of June.

Kundera remembered the terror as missiles crashed into Prague, only sheer luck keeping him safe as buildings had shattered around him and the remains of his close-protection detail struggled to get him to safety. That had been found on a military base that had been lucky enough to survive almost intact; Kundera had found himself Prime Minister in the middle of a war. The President was dead; nearly a third of the Czech Armed Forces had been wiped out in the opening shots. Kundera had struggled to try to pull a defence together, but it had seemed futile; the sheer violence of the Russian attack into Poland and later Germany had stunned him. He knew where he was debating in Parliament, or making points in front of the cameras; he was completely out of place in a war zone. Russian aircraft were flying in and out of his airspace, and he was unable to issue orders…

And then the Russian Ambassador had appeared. Kundera had never liked the Russian Ambassador; he was too…slick, with an 'I know something you don't' attitude that grated on Kundera's own sense of the appropriate. It had been obvious since the missiles had fallen what he had known that Kundera hadn't known…and his role in the disaster that had overtaken the Czech Republic was obvious. Polish refugees were flooding into the Republic's territory…and Russian soldiers wouldn't be far behind.

"Go to Moscow," the Ambassador had said, after an agonising session of insincere pleasantries and half-hidden gloating. "They'll meet you there, perhaps offer you something you want, an end to the war you didn't expect."

Kundera had stared at him, wanting to throw it back in his face and not quite daring. "Or what will happen to the Republic?"

The Ambassador had leaned forward. His breath smelt terrible…or was Kundera imagining it? He had never considered that he would be in the position, one day, of accepting or rejecting what was an ultimatum in everything, but name. Russian forces were only ten kilometres away from the Polish border; his military officers had warned him that they could be halfway to Prague within a day, and the Czech Republic had nothing that could stop them. Kundera knew that he had no choice, but to listen; he just wanted to block out the screams.

"They're prepared to offer you a place in the new world order," the Ambassador had whispered. There was nothing subtle about it at all; there was none of the nuances and polite inanities that Kundera knew and loved. "If you refuse the offer, as generous as it is, your country will not like the second offer at all."

And so Kundera stood on the tarmac in the dark, waiting. He understood the reason, of course; his briefers had worked desperately to brief him on what the Russians might do to convince him that further resistance, such as it had been, was futile. The wait was one tactic, a less-than-subtle way of informing him that President Aleksandr Sergeyevich Nekrasov did not consider him important enough to arrange for either rooms, or an immediate meeting. The cooling metal of the aircraft that had flown him to Moscow, escorted all the way by Russian fighters, ticked in the night; the crew remained inside, wondering if they would ever be allowed to leave again.

Kundera waited…

A black car detached itself from the shadows and headed towards him. Kundera refused to allow himself to show fear as it came to a halt near the aircraft, the rear door opening to reveal a strikingly beautiful woman with long blonde hair and an almost perfect body. Her eyes were cold and distant, however; she eyed Kundera as if he were a mouse and she were a cat. Kundera kept himself calm; the woman, whoever she was, wouldn't be the one making the decisions.

"Welcome to Moscow," she said, in flawless Czech. "I am Colonel Marina Konstantinovna Savelyeva, aide to President Nekrasov. I have been ordered to escort you to his presence at once."

"Thank you," Kundera said, calmly. A Presidential Aide could hold vast influence, but she wouldn't be the official face of the Russian regime. "I look forward to meeting him."

Marina opened the door for him and motioned him into the car. The inside of the car smelled leathery, a smell that reminded him oddly of the car he'd used on his wedding day. The vehicle itself hummed almost silently as Marina sat next to him, commenting from time to time on places within Moscow; the city seemed to be almost bursting with curiously ordered life. On one corner, a blue European Union flag was being burned; behind it, American and British flags were already being prepared for the fire. Kundera realised that he was being shown everything purposefully; the Russians were trying to intimidate him.

It was working.

"As a mark of respect for your status, we have decided that you can pass through the security checks," Marina informed him. Kundera heard the almost-hidden mocking in her tone and winced; it was a blatant slap in the face, a reminder that the Russians didn't take him or his country seriously. "I will take you directly to the President in the War Room."

Kundera had never visited the Kremlin before and, after hearing about some of the humiliation that Czechoslovakian leaders had suffered there, had never wanted to visit in his life. Marina's brief tour of the strange, very... *Russian* building hadn't been reassuring; the building was almost alien to his eyes, a strange mixture of different elements, all devoted to power. Marina's running commentary had surprised him; some of the artworks on display had been looted from the Warsaw Pact countries and long believed lost. The Russians had had them all that time.

"This is the War Room," Marina said finally, as two doors opened in front of them. The room was dominated by a massive plasma screen, showing Europe...with a massive wave of red light moving over the continent, heading west. Marina said something, but Kundera missed it almost completely; the sight before him terrified and awed him. If it was reliable, Denmark and over half of Germany had fallen, and there were Russian advance teams as far west as France and Norway. He *knew*, now, that a global shift in the balance of power was taking place; Russia had shattered Europe for the foreseeable future. Even if the European forces rallied...

"Perhaps the Prime Minister would care to hear a briefing from my military leaders?"

Kundera turned, slowly, and came face to face with President Nekrasov. The leader of the Russian Federation seemed more amused than anything else with Kundera's sudden paralysis; he didn't seem inclined to make a diplomatic incident out of it. Then, Kundera reasoned, why should he? He already had most of Europe in the palm of his hand. He hardly needed an excuse to send the Russian Army into the Czech Republic.

"That won't be necessary, thank you," Kundera said, after a long moment. "I understand what is happening."

"Splendid," Nekrasov said, his Russian seemingly soft, but with a hint of pure steel underneath. The presence of four bodyguards paled as Kundera took in the sight; there was no mistaking the leader in the room. If they had all been naked, still there would have been no mistaking it; Nekrasov was the master and they all knew it. "We will repair to one of my private rooms and discuss...matters."

Kundera followed him into a smaller room, trying to grasp an image of Nekrasov in his mind; his sheer personality swallowed up little details like face and body. Nekrasov was shorter than he had expected, or than he had seemed in the photographs that had been sent around the world after his rise to power.

His stocky body was topped with a head of white hair, almost as white as snow. His handshake, as he waved Kundera to a seat, bespoke hidden strength.

This is a very dangerous man, Kundera thought, as Nekrasov took a seat facing him. Marina stood at the rear of the small, comfortable room, her hands crossed below her breasts; the bodyguards remained outside the room. *I can't relax, not even for an instant...*

Nekrasov played the gracious host. "Would the Prime Minister care to dine with me?" He asked. He sounded almost jovial. "Or perhaps something to drink? Coffee? Tea? Vodka? We even have some fine wine that the President of France sent me last year, if you would prefer it...?"

"No, thank you," Kundera said. "I would prefer to get down to business."

The transformation was frightening. The jovial host vanished, to be replaced with a cold-blooded calculating soul, eyes studying Kundera as if he was a hunted animal. Nekrasov stared at him for a long moment, perfectly calculated to unnerve, perhaps even unman, him, before nodding slowly and leaning back in his chair. It was a chilling display. The knowledge that Nekrasov could do almost anything he liked terrified Kundera to the very depths of his soul.

"Let me discuss military realities," Nekrasov said, very softly, but no less menacing. "I have ten divisions in a position where they can roll into your country and brush your defenders aside. I have hundreds of bombers that can be over Prague in an hour, reducing your capital to rubble, and you are powerless to prevent it. I have a large occupation force of FSB soldiers who will occupy your country and ensure that the Czech Republic takes its orders from Moscow and Moscow alone.

"These are the parameters of our conversation," he said, after a chilling pause. "I would like you to bear them in mind at all times. It will make this so much easier.

"We started this war for various reasons, partly to gain revenge for various European acts that were against Russian interests, partly to gain access to European resources that we need for the future. The military balance of power is so firmly on our side that we can guarantee the occupation of Europe as far west as the Pyrenees within a month at most. The shift of power is impossible for any state, even America, to alter; the balance of power is firmly in my favour. Do you understand me?"

Kundera stared at him, feeling as if he had been bludgeoned to death with a club. There was no diplomacy, just a calm recital of military power; the threats unstated, but barely hidden below the surface. There was no need to spell out the 'or else' – a little imagination suggested possibilities that would be too nightmarish for anyone to grasp. The Czech Republic was at his mercy.

"I understand you," he said, softly. "What do you want?"

The genial host was back. "Splendid," he said. The cold-blooded strategist returned. "The choice is simple; the first option is that you agree to sign an alliance with the Russian Federation, bringing the Czech Republic into a new alignment with Russia. The second option is that you refuse…in which case, those ten divisions will roll into Prague and impose our own order."

Kundera felt cold. "I would need more information," he said. "What would be the terms of the alliance?"

Nekrasov smiled, once again the genial host; Kundera wondered – and then pushed the thought aside because it was too terrifying – if Nekrasov was mad. He switched between friendliness and coldness with terrifying speed…and he controlled a vast country. Kundera's mind refused to escape that thought; it kept running around in his head.

"It's quite simple," he said, after a moment. "You would permit us to take what steps we deem necessary when it comes to securing the territorial integrity of the Czech Republic. Your forces will assume a subordinate position to our own and accept orders from our commanders, assisting us to move forces through your territory into Austria, should it become necessary, and prevent your people from blocking the roads, unless you want us to do it…?"

Kundera shook his head.

"Your foreign relations will be placed firmly in our hands and all other alliances will be dissolved," Nekrasov continued. "You will continue to hold internal authority, but we will have the right to veto or suggest laws as we choose. You will permit us to take what steps we choose against those of your people who practice the Islamic faith. In time, your factories and people will become part of a new economic alliance, devoted to rebuilding the continent and once again creating a powerful European force."

Kundera tried for an even tone. "And what will you do for us?"

"We will ensure that your government remains in power," Nekrasov said, still genial. "Should your people refuse to carry out some of the steps we might take against the Muslims, we will be quite happy to carry them out for you; I'm sure that many of your people will welcome them. We will even consult with you before we use any of our new rights."

The words didn't disguise the reality; Kundera knew exactly what he was being told – cooperate and collaborate, or your country will be crushed. The vague comment about 'consultation' meant nothing; once there was a Russian army in the middle of Prague, the Czech Republic's independence would be at an end. He licked his dry lips, carefully marshalling his thoughts; he wanted to be clear on a few details before making any final decision…as if he held that right still.

"I have three conditions," he said, carefully. Nekrasov said nothing, only watched him as a spider might watch a fly, trying to escape a web. "The first one is that you do not require Czech soldiers to take part in any offensive operations against our allies…our former allies."

Nekrasov nodded. "That should be acceptable," he said. There was a darker hint in his voice. "Next?"

"Second," Kundera said slowly, "I want a guarantee that Russian soldiers will behave themselves in the Czech Republic. The behaviour of Russian soldiers during the Cold War meant that there could be no lasting bridges built between us and you; they looted and raped at will."

"I will ensure that the commanders in the field know that such behaviour will not be tolerated," Nekrasov said, after a long bitter moment. "It is a shame that Alex was not interested in such a posting; he can be relied upon in such matters."

He shook his head slowly. "Very well," he said. "So…what is number three?"

Kundera almost lost his nerve. "I do not want you to commit genocide against the Muslim population of my nation," he said, taking a deep breath. He had a grim suspicion that that would be one of the demands that could not be discussed, or modified. "I have responsibilities to them as well as the others in the Republic."

Nekrasov looked at him for a long moment. "You have tolerated the…vermin who were responsible for atrocities like Belsan, Stalingrad and worse in my country," he said. "The problem that faces both the Americans and ourselves took root in your countries; just ask the French if you don't believe me. Do you believe that we will pass up a chance to get at them and burn the cancer out?"

"You're talking about living people," Kundera almost cried. "They're flesh and blood, not...cancer cells in a living body. They're people too..."

"So were the children that died in Stalingrad," Nekrasov said. It was the cold-eyed one who looked down at him. "That is not up for discussion; we will not kill them all, but we will ensure that they can do no further harm. Will you sign the agreement?"

Marina produced a sheet of paper from a hidden printer. Kundera scanned it rapidly; it had been updated already to reflect his requested compromises... all except the Muslim one. He looked into Nekrasov's eyes and saw his future; he could sign, serve, and do the best he could for his country, which would become merely a subordinate state of the Russian Empire, or he would never return from Moscow. A Russian occupation government would move in, take over, and do whatever it liked to the helpless civilians caught in their grasp. He could try to do what he could to help his people, or he could make a stand on a point of principle...and make no difference whatsoever.

Nekrasov was waiting patiently. "I agree," Kundera said finally. The document was written in both Russian and Czech; he read them both and noted that they were the same. The bitter taste of ashes was in his mouth. He had gone to Moscow as Head of Government of an independent state; he would return as a Russian pawn. There was no longer any choice at all. "Where do I sign?"

Chapter Thirty-Six

The Way Home

Wars are not won by retreats
Winston Churchill

Brussels/Ostend, Belgium

"Wake up, sweethearts," a voice called from outside the door. "It's time for breakfast!"

Colonel Seth Fanaroff rubbed his back as he pulled himself off the floor and to his feet. The brothel they had found had accepted the story that they were lovers – in defiance of various US Army regulations on fraternisation – and had been quite happy to take American dollars once they had established a link-up with an American bank. The catch was that they had to share a room, and, as a gentleman, he had insisted on sleeping on the floor. Being a gentleman was starting to look like a really bad idea.

"Time to get up," he called, gently poking Captain Saundra Keshena in the shoulder before averting his gaze as she sat up, hands reaching for the pistol she had concealed under the pillow. She had been having nightmares about the desperate flight through the city to the brothel in the Red Light district; Fanaroff, who had been through several wars and dangerous situations, had taken it more in stride. "We have a long day ahead of us."

It was a lie, he thought; they had managed to get back in touch with the States, only to be told to sit tight and wait. They were the only two Americans, it seemed, to have survived the fall of the embassy; the United States would be looking for a way to extract them, but Fanaroff wasn't hopeful. The best plan he had so far was to wait for the Russians to arrive, make themselves known to the Russian commander, and ask for reparation. The Russians might have returned the crew of the ABM stations, but he didn't know if they would be willing to repatriate two lone Americans in a city that had descended into chaos. Brussels was a confusing mass of factions; he didn't understand how the water supplies had come back on, let alone how the city intended to survive the next few weeks. Large parts of the city had burnt in that first terrible day.

He splashed a little water on his face; the madam – Madam Rose - had insisted that they conserve water as much as possible, even to the point of filling bathtubs with the liquid and forbidding more than basic washes; who knew what would happen to the water supplies in the future? One of the other groups, an Islamic group that had managed to establish itself, had attacked the Red Light district in a fit of holy zeal…and the criminals had kicked them out with extreme violence. The Red Light district held some of the nastiest characters in Brussels…and they had been, in their own way, patriotic. Every man was against his neighbour, but it was every inhabitant against an outsider; the police had never come into the Red Light district on official business. It wouldn't have been healthy.

Saundra was rubbing the side of her head. "Is there any news from home?"

"No," Fanaroff said, shortly. "It looks as if we have to stay here."

Saundra looked good as she dressed; his treacherous mind was too tired and sore to exercise proper discipline and banish the thoughts. It was only the two of them; they had remained chaste, but their relationship had developed well beyond senior-junior.

Madam Rose met them as they descended the stairs. "Morning," she said, shortly. Her face split into a strange leer. "There's breakfast on the table; help yourself, and then get back to bed."

"Thank you," Fanaroff said, as he took Saundra's arm and guided her to the table. There was a massive pot of porridge on the table, something he had only had in England before; he took a small amount and filled Saundra's bowl to the top. She needed her strength more than he did. "Any news from the outside?"

"Very little," Madam Rose said. "There was a call for you on the phone; they want you to call them back as soon as you have had your breakfast."

Fanaroff took a long breath. "Why didn't you call us at once?"

"I don't interrupt my customers when they are using the facilities, even if they are well-paying customers," Madam Rose said tartly. "People who come here come for privacy; they don't come for my conversation." She slapped her belly. "I may have a belly that people come miles to see, and a strong right arm that some men find impossible to resist, but they don't come for my conversation."

And perhaps you wanted to try and get something out of them first, Fanaroff thought dryly. Madam Rose was a desperate woman, after all; her girls and herself would be caught in the path of the Russian advance, if what they had been told was true. Fanaroff was still having problems coming to grips with it, but if it was true, the German Army had been scattered and was in full retreat, assuming that it was still in existence. Fanaroff had reviewed the old war plans from the cold war; there would be no reinforcements from the other NATO allies, not now. The Germans were in real trouble.

"I'll call them after we have finished eating," he said. He wasn't that hopeful; as far as he knew, there were no American assets that could be used to extract them, and the British had their own problems. He had thought about trying to get into one of the airports and stealing an aircraft, but without any IFF transponder, one or the other side would probably shoot them out of the sky. "Is there any other news?"

"I'm starting to think that it might be time to get out of the city," Madam Rose said. "What about you?"

Fanaroff couldn't disagree. The criminal gangs had secured vast food supplies – and the girls had an easy way of paying for them – but everyone knew that it couldn't last. There seemed to be no government trying to pull everything back together again…and it seemed an impossible task anyway. The city had collapsed into a dozen semi-independent fiefdoms; it reminded him too much of the old *No Man's Land* Batman movie.

But he said nothing. As soon as he had finished his breakfast, he picked up the satellite phone and carried it upstairs to their room, allowing Saundra to activate it while he remembered some of the identification words. The satellite phone might work using American satellites, but it was hardly a secure system; his controllers had been reluctant to give him too many details because the Russians might well be listening in to the transmissions. It made him long for the lost terminal; if he had had that, they would have had no problems at all in downloading information from the military datanet.

"This is Fanaroff," he said shortly, and recited a string of identification numbers. "I understand that you wanted to talk to me?"

"Certainly," a droll Texan voice said. "Who played George Washington in the university play you took part in back in 2010?"

Fanaroff had been surprised the first time he had been tossed such a question, a moment's thought had explained why. It would be harder for a Russian imposter to figure out the answer in time to matter. "That was Shawn O'Neil," he said, remembering. Fanaroff had wanted that part; but he had lost the draw and played Arnold the Traitor instead. "Do you have anything useful for me?"

"Friends of ours have been busy in Ostend," the voice said, without bothering to comment on Fanaroff's tone. "We have talked to them and they have agreed to pick you and your lady-friends up and get you back to mother if you get there within a few days. Failure to get there within five days may result in you being left to your own devices."

Fanaroff took a second to unravel everything. Something was happening at Ostend; he guessed that the British had secured the small port and city, and they were willing to extract him and his 'lady-friends' – perhaps Madam Rose and her girls, if she had talked to the controller first – if he made it there. He scowled; the real problem with improvising a code was that it would be easy to either make it blatantly obvious, or confuse friends as well as enemies.

"I understand," he said. If he were wrong, there would be a chance to steal a boat and set sail for England anyway. "Is there a lower limit?"

There was a pause. "The day-tourists are moving in now," the controller said finally. "I would recommend haste; mother may have popped her clogs earlier than we thought."

"I understand," Fanaroff said again. "I'll call you later."

He closed the connection and thought for a long moment, then turned to face Saundra. "If I understood that bastard properly, we have a chance to get out if we can make it to Ostend," he said, grimly. "I guess that the invitation includes Madam Rose and her girls…if they will come with us, if not, just the two of us." He grinned. "Unless you wish to stay, of course…"

"Not bloody likely," Saundra said. She looked less mussed than he did; Madam Rose would have made a fearsomely effective drill sergeant, unlike some commanding officers he'd met who had insisted on shaving every day, despite low water supplies. "I don't want to stay in this place any longer."

"Come on, then," he said. "Let's go see Madam Rose."

He explained the situation as clearly as he could to her. "We have one chance and you're included in the offer," he said. "We can't let anyone else know, because there would be panic; are you interested in coming?"

Madam Rose laughed. "I have been thinking about joining one of the boats leaving Belgium for England," she said. "I'll come with you, if the girls will come; if not, then…I can't leave them here."

"She's a very strange woman," Saundra muttered, as Madam Rose headed off to organise the girls. She hadn't liked the thought of staying in a whore-house, even if it had been safe and fairly secure; female soldiers and officers were rarely comfortable with the chain of brothels that appeared everywhere that soldiers lived and worked. "What will happen to her if she remains here?"

"Die, probably," Fanaroff muttered back. "Pussy is cheap in desperate times; someone might take the girls and leave her to die. This is her best chance to get out and she knows it."

There were nine girls in all; seven of them native to Belgium, one whose family had come from darkest Africa, and one who had been from an Arab family that had thrown her out for premarital sex. She had been very lucky, the more so because Madam Rose had found her and offered her a job before she starved to death on the streets. She was apparently popular with the clients; Madam Rose had claimed with some pride that she brought in more money than the others put together. The conversation had gone downhill from there.

"Jade wants to return to her family," Madam Rose said finally. "The others are willing to come with us. We have a truck and enough fuel, I think, to reach Ostend; keep your weapons visible and we won't have any trouble."

Fanaroff said nothing as the girls were loaded into the truck; Madam Rose herself took the wheel. They would be victims if they were caught by the Russians; he had seen some of the classified files of what had happened in Chechnya as a warning to all other Muslims in Russia and the CIS to behave themselves. There were rumours that the Russians had even begun a breeding program to breed loyal Russians who could blend in perfectly with Central Asia – and the new government had offered bounties and rewards to women who had more than three children who were pure Russian – and the girls would be treated as nothing more than whores. It was strange; most of the girls were quite well-educated, in their own way, and yet they had earned more lying on their backs than holding down a proper job.

He clutched his weapon tightly as the truck started to move out of the city. The criminals had cleared a path out of the city, but parts of the city were still in a state of lawlessness; in the future, he wondered what the Russians would do when they reached the capital of the European Union. He didn't think it would be pleasant. The girls fell silent, lost in their own thoughts; Fanaroff almost understood their concern. They were leaving all that they had ever known and as for him...

He would never see the city again.

The helicopters swooped low over the beaches and came in to land; a dozen heavily-armed soldiers jumped out of each one and fanned out across the beaches, which were almost deserted. A handful of people who had been nervously waiting for their boats to England screamed and panicked as the soldiers fanned out, running towards their targets as the first ships appeared, launching landing ships towards the beach while the advance guard raced through the facilities, rapidly securing their objectives and holding position. 3 Commando Brigade had arrived at Ostend.

"All targets secure, sir," Captain Bellamy reported. The Royal Marines had had to put the mission together almost on the fly, but they had done well. The heavy equipment would be landed as quickly possible from the ships. "The civilians seem very pleased to see us."

"I'm not surprised," Marine Colonel Patrick Trombly snapped. The civilians might have escaped some of the chaos, but the criminal gangs who had been trying to use Ostend as a place to send refugees to England had been terrorising the entire region as they offered their services...at the cost of everything the refugees owned. The Royal Navy had been working hard to steer the refugees to camps in Britain; some of the criminals had been literally dumping the refugees overboard as soon as they were out of sight of the coastline, and then coming back for more. "Remind the advance parties that they are not to go into Ostend itself; I'm not wasting lives fighting people in the city."

"Yes, sir," Captain Bellamy said. "There's more refugees than we expected..."

He snapped out orders as more units arrived on the beach, heavy anti-aircraft units and light tanks, improved enough that they could exchange blows with Russian tanks on a fairly equal basis. They would be disintegrated if the Russians hit them, but they would get in at least one punch first; Trombly wasn't happy about having them, but if the Russians reached them before they managed to pull out, they would need their firepower just to buy themselves a fighting chance.

"Have them kept well away from the beaches," Trombly said, grimly. He had been on the ground during the retreat from Sudan and knew what would happen; desperate refugees would overwhelm his men through sheer weight of numbers if they thought that they were being abandoned. "We can pull out some refugees if we have time, but the main problem is withdrawing the remains of British forces before they get overwhelmed."

He stared down at the display on the terminal in his hand. Major-General Langford had put out a request to shipping, and even he had been surprised at the response; hundreds of smaller ships had volunteered for the mission to Ostend. Britain's merchant marine was no longer what it once had been; the attempt to replay Dunkirk would be much harder than it had been back in 1940...and that had not been easy. The Royal Marines had studied Dunkirk extensively and knew that repeating it would be tricky; the Germans had allowed the British the time they needed to escape. The Russians...might not make the same mistake.

The skies were clear; that wouldn't last. Higher command had decided that if the RAF made a serious commitment to covering Ostend, the Russians would realise what was happening sooner and bring the full weight of their air force to bear on the evacuation ships. The nightmare would have no end; if the Russians managed to sink a dozen heavy ships, the remains of the British forces would be trapped on the shore. He needed time...and Marine Colonel Patrick Trombly knew that time was the one thing the Russians wouldn't give him.

A soldier ran up to him and nodded once; Marines were forbidden to salute anywhere where there might be an enemy sniper, looking for targets, such as senior officers. "Sir, the Yanks are here, and ten cunts," he reported. "They were coming down the road when they met us..."

Trombly smiled. He hadn't expected that that part of the mission would have worked; Belgium seemed to be as chaotic as the remainder of Europe. "Have them all checked, searched, and then moved to one of the helicopters returning to Britain," he said. He smiled at the thought of the poor American explaining his travelling companions to his own people back in the States, or even in Britain; perhaps the girls were important, but he doubted it. "All we have to do here is wait."

"Yes, sir," the soldier said, and dashed off again.

"Well, fuck me rigid," Captain Bellamy said. "You know...I really thought that would fail and they wouldn't make it..."

"Let's just hope the government drives a hard bargain," Trombly said grimly. The thought of what might happen if – after – Europe fell worried him. Britain was weaker than it had been in centuries. "This is not going to end well."

Chapter Thirty-Seven

Breaking the Back

The German is either at your throat…or at your feet.
Winston Churchill

Hanover, Germany

The Lord Mayor of Hanover was a weak man.

He had, Shalenko knew, been lucky enough to be out of the city when the missiles had blown the New Town Hall of Hanover to bits, and had somehow been able to calm most of the rioting in the city…for a few days. The chaos had started again as the Russian Army had blown through yet another desperate last stand and started its march on Hanover; hundreds of German soldiers and reservists had dug into the city, daring the Russians to enter. They had no supplies, no hope in the long run, but if they could smash up his forces…

It had been the reservists' presence that had allowed the Lord Mayor, Paul Steiner, to put an end to some of the chaos. Hanover had a large community of different ethnic groups and the chaos had seriously damaged half of the city, but the German soldiers had managed to put most of it down, or at least contained it to some sections of the city. The Russian soldiers who had surrounded the city had started to turn back refugees; Steiner had been forced to face the unpleasant fact that his city would starve before too long…if the Russians didn't attack it and reduce it to rubble.

"You have an obligation, under the Geneva Convention, to let civilians go," Steiner protested, when he came to meet the Russian besiegers. "You can't keep them trapped in the city…"

Shalenko smiled. He had read the FSB's briefing on the Mayor carefully. He had been a stout Green, someone who could always be counted upon to pass laws concerning the environment in Germany…and a total novice when it came to military matters. Steiner had been considered a safe pair of hands for Hanover by the Greens; there was no way that they would have allowed him into the rarefied heights of German National Government, or even the European Parliament.

"Actually, I can," Shalenko said. "The Convention doesn't actually say *when* I have to let them out, does it?"

He took no pleasure in ensuring that the city was starved into submission – or death – but it was better than feeding his men into a meat-grinder. The British might have joked about being sporting enough to let the enemy do the killing, but Shalenko had always considered the joke disgusting; his soldiers were a priceless resource. Hanover wasn't a threat, but if the Germans had some armoured units in the city, they could come out and hit his rear.

Steiner said nothing. Shalenko's lips twisted; *Felix* Steiner had been an SS officer and a brave fighter, commanding soldiers in battle personally. His distant descendent had none of the spine that had allowed Felix Steiner to stand up to Adolph Hitler himself. He was at home with the law…but the law was gone, replaced only by the invading army and the Russian occupation forces that were either occupying cities, or surrounding them and waiting for them to surrender. Shalenko wouldn't have given much for the fate of the Germans who had to be forced into submission; the FSB units had a reputation for brutality.

"I am quite within my rights to let them all starve to force you to surrender," Shalenko said calmly. "You must understand; your position is hopeless, there will be no forces coming to your relief, no force that can break the blockade around your city. I will fire on your people if they attempt to leave… this is not Qom, when various factions tried to fly in supplies to the city and the Americans refused to fire on them. Your position is hopeless."

Steiner wilted. "I understand," he said. Shalenko wondered what advice he had been getting from the German soldiers trapped inside the city. "What do you want?"

Shalenko started to tick points off on his fingers. "First, you will tell your soldiers to lay down their arms and surrender," he said. "We will treat them decently provided they surrender and assist us to disarm any surprises that they might have created for us; any further resistance will be considered a breach of the agreement and responded to with maximum force. Second, you will disarm your policemen and order them to assist us in keeping the city calm; our units will take up policing duties as soon as possible. Third, you will warn the civilian population that any resistance, either in the form of an armed attack or civil disobedience, will be treated as a breach of the surrender agreement and punished harshly. Finally, you will provide us with all possible assistance in working Hanover back into the national infrastructure and using it to support the advance."

Steiner stared at him, trying to deny reality. "And if we refuse?"

"We will take your city by force and sack it," Shalenko lied cheerfully. He would wait for them all to starve if he had no other choice; FSB units could maintain the blockade when he moved his armoured and infantry units west again. "I invite you to consider just how many of your people would die if I stormed the city."

Steiner's face was pale. "In that case," he said finally, "I will surrender the city. Please be aware that the behaviour of your troops will be recorded for possible future action by international agencies such as Amnesty International and…"

"And exactly what do you think they can do about it?" Shalenko asked dryly. "My soldiers will behave themselves, or they will end up in the penal units; the FSB troops, on the other hand…"

He smiled. "Better keep your people under control."

"That went well," Captain Anna Ossipavo said, as the bent back of the Lord Mayor headed back towards his city. "Colonel Boris Aliyev has arrived and is asking for an immediate meeting with you."

"Is he?" Shalenko asked. Aliyev had done well in Poland, but since the airport had been relieved by the armoured units of the 2nd Shock Army, his unit had been on the sidelines, waiting. Shalenko guessed that Aliyev wasn't happy about that; the man was a soldier though and though. "I need a briefing first."

Anna nodded as they walked back towards the command vehicle, carefully concealed in a thatch of trees. "The forces probing into the Netherlands are reporting that the city of Wilhelmshaven has fallen to our forces, although there is a great deal of uncoordinated resistance in the Netherlands itself, some of it from Muslim factions that we armed, as opposed to the remains of the Dutch forces. We have pushed to within ten kilometres of Switzerland, but as per your orders, we haven't gone any closer to their border."

Shalenko checked the mental map in his head and smiled. Switzerland had retained its neutrality and its paranoia about outsiders; every Swiss was still expected to have a gun and training in how to use it. It would take fifty divisions to hammer the Swiss into submission and the planners had decided that they could leave the Swiss alone for a while, perhaps even permanently if something satisfactory could be worked out. The Czech Republic's decision to switch sides had started the dominos falling; entire countries were considering what they could gain from offering their submission to the Russian Federation.

"The worrying point is that the British are up to something in Ostend," Anna continued. "The Royal Marines made a major landing there two days ago; we believe that they secured the area and are using it to evacuate what they can of their forces and perhaps other European forces as well."

Shalenko bit off a curse. The British forces had been chased back across the continent along with the other European forces, but if they managed to get across the Channel, it would be several weeks before the final stage of Operation Stalin could be mounted; they would have the chance that the rest of Europe had not. If they pulled out and rearmed the other European forces, the Russians might find themselves facing a resistance movement in their rear before they were ready to deal with it.

They reached the command vehicle and Shalenko immediately reached for a map. The Germans had used that terrain before to slow up an invading army; the Allies had had to grind their way through the terrain step by step. The Dutch could do any number of interesting things to slow an invading army; if there were German forces digging in, they might even buy the British enough time to complete the evacuation.

The display was warning of new threats. A French force was slowly pulling itself together in Lorraine, near the French border, the last significant force on the European continent. The French were scoring some successes against the Algerians; the odds were that the French command either didn't know anything about the situation in the south, or the damned Americans had tipped them off to the real threat. They would be short on fuel and ammunition – their logistics train would have been shot to hell – but they had to be crushed while they presented such a tempting target…

Anna paused as a signal came in. "That's the Germans laying down their arms now," she said. "The occupation units are requesting permission to enter the city."

"Granted," Shalenko said, still thinking. For the first time since the campaign had begun, he had too many tasks and too few men in the correct position to handle them...and there were political implications. If he crushed the French force that was massing in Lorraine, he would be able to overrun the remainder of Europe, but if the British forces, such as they were, got away, the conflict would become a lot harder to bring to a successful conclusion. "Order the reconnaissance units to press on towards Belgium, advancing as quickly as they can; let me know what resistance they meet. The main force is to prepare to advance into France as soon as it can be organised."

"Yes, sir," Anna said. "What about Colonel Aliyev?"

Shalenko scowled. "I'll see him now," he said. He climbed out of the command vehicle and glanced around; he could hear the distant noise of the occupation forces moving into Hanover. It would be a dangerous few hours for everyone involved; a single shot could lead to a slaughter. That would be very bad for the future; the important matter was to ensure that they were firmly in control of their territorial gains before imposing their own system on Europe.

Aliyev was standing, watching a line of tanks advancing onwards towards France, heavy helicopter support flying overhead, searching for targets. The paratrooper looked tired, but still professional; in his uniform, he was one of the deadliest men that Shalenko had ever seen. He was proud of Aliyev; the man had had a difficult mission and had carried it out flawlessly. If the Poles had been just a little quicker to react...

"Colonel," Shalenko said. It was the first time they had met since the war began. "You did well in Poland."

Aliyev snapped off a salute. "Sir, with all due respect, my men and I need a mission," he said, insistently. "We are losing our edge just standing around doing nothing."

"I was unaware that this was the sort of army where officers chose their own missions," Shalenko said, eyeing him darkly. Aliyev showed no reaction; the elite rarely showed any reaction to such issues. "Your unit is irreplaceable."

Aliyev stared at him. "Permission to speak freely, sir?" Shalenko nodded once; the President's determination on never shooting the messenger had sunk in to every level, with the possible exception of the lowest ranks. "My unit needs to continue fighting, not sitting around while others die; we could take an airport in France or..."

"That will be accomplished by smaller groups, those that have been left intact," Shalenko said. France had two armies left, one of which was tied down in the south; it would be crushed once France itself had fallen. "The insurgency in France destroyed several airports and the French have been unable to rebuild or repair most of the damage."

He shrugged. "We will be taking over airports and using them, but we will be doing that with more precision than we were doing in Germany and Poland," he continued. The trick would be to ensure that the Algerians had their backs firmly stabbed before they realised what was happening; timing would be everything. "Your unit will have another mission, fairly soon."

Aliyev looked hopeful. "Ostend?"

Shalenko smiled. Had the news spread that rapidly? "No," he said. "Ostend may have to be handled by the air force alone, although we will be looking for places where we can insert paratroopers if we can; the British have had two days to dig in and the Royal Marines are experts in such combat. It's not a pleasant thought – that's what Hitler did wrong as well – but there may be no choice unless the units probing into the Netherlands can reach Ostend in time to slam the door firmly shut."

He rolled his eyes. "And there are other problems as well," he admitted. It was important that Aliyev understood what was at stake. "Wear and tear on the equipment for one. If we can smash the French force in the north, we've won in France; the FSB can finish the task of securing France. It's butcher's work; the bastards will enjoy it. Once we can take a breath, we can prepare for the next part of the operation - Operation Morskoi Lev."

Aliyev lifted an eyebrow. "Sir?"

"You'll be briefed later," Shalenko assured him. The sound of jets rapidly rose and fell in the distance as they raced west, or perhaps east; the Russian Air Force was slowly expanding its control over Germany and had even skirmished with the remains of the RAF. "Just believe me when I tell you this; it will be the greatest mission of your career."

He watched as Aliyev saluted him and departed. Aliyev had had a nasty fight in Poland; a Polish infantry unit had managed to respond to the capture of the airport and attacked brutally, almost forcing the Russians out of the airport to certain death. The paratroopers had been banged up by the time Russian aircraft had arrived to save them from defeat; hundreds of their civilian prisoners had been killed in the exchange of fire.

The reports Shalenko had read made grim reading. Aliyev had taken the failure to protect the civilians personally; he had intended to keep his word to the civilians and had failed. A small boy, whose enthusiasm about aircraft had been a joy to his harassed father, had lost his life to one of the bursts of fire. No one knew who had killed him, even though Russian propaganda would claim that it had been the fault of the Poles. He hadn't deserved that…

Shalenko could only hope that Steiner would behave himself. The FSB security units were a law unto themselves under any other commanding officer; only his close friendship with the President gave him additional authority over them. If the Germans started to act up, the FSB would give them hell; FSB General Vasiliy Alekseyevich Rybak had made that clear. Bastard.

"General, the air force is sending more jets into the Belgium area," Anna said, coming up behind him. Her face was concerned; she knew, as well as he did, that the process of conquest was still hanging in the balance. If the French managed to stop them…then…then Shalenko would have to bring up additional firepower and keep digging at them until they were broken. He had enough firepower to reduce a city to rubble; he could afford to take the time to ensure that it was ready to be deployed against the targets. "They're confident that they'll close the sea-lanes."

"Hah," Shalenko commented. "Contact the Navy; I want them to recall Admiral Daniel Sulkin and his aircraft from Algeria, so they can start hacking away at the British ships. If I can't get at the bastards on the land, I want to close their only line of escape."

"Yes, sir," Anna said. She paused. "The President would like you to know that Austria and Slovakia have both prepared themselves to accept our terms, Austria with a little more reluctance, but with the chaos in Italy spreading out of control, they're likely to accept our security guarantee and the price that goes with it. Occupation forces had reported that we have secured most of the targets in Germany; once we have breathing space, we can start bringing them back online."

"I'm not worried about that at the moment, Anna," Shalenko said. He stared up into the sky, seeing the trails of Russian aircraft high overhead. "I'm worried about the logistics of the war effort. Our supply lines are still pretty weak, even if we have press-ganged Germans and Poles into driving lorries for us, with the promise of payment afterwards."

And their hands handcuffed to the wheels, just in case they have any clever ideas, he added silently. The FSB was full of nasty tricks like that. "If we lose our supply lines, we will be in serious trouble."

"The FSB is confident that it can keep the supply lines open," Anna said. She was trying to cheer him up; he appreciated it even as he found it cloying. "It won't be much longer before we can advance into France and finish the war."

"That won't be the end," Shalenko said tartly. He allowed his voice to darken as he gazed in the direction of Hanover. There were thousands of Germans in the city and not all of them would be reconciled to the new world order for a very long time to come. "It will merely be the end of one campaign. The occupation and integration will come next and that is going to be very difficult indeed."

Chapter Thirty-Eight

Dunkirk, Round Two

We were all flying around up and down the coast near Dunkirk looking for enemy aircraft which seemed also to be milling around with no particular cohesion.
Douglas Bader

Ostend, Belgium

"Sir, look out!"

Captain Stuart Robinson didn't hesitate. He took one look into the air, saw the shape closing in on them, and threw himself out of the truck, rolling as he hit the ground hard enough to hurt badly. The deafening noise as the Russian aircraft opened fire stunned him; he covered his ears and fought to keep low as the lorries exploded and the Russian aircraft banked away, mercifully not bothering to strafe the British soldiers on the ground.

"Fuck," Robinson hissed, as he checked himself out. Nothing was broken, thankfully, but his body ached. He hadn't felt so bad since his first day at the training camp. "Anyone hurt?"

Sergeant Ronald Inglehart was looking down at one of the soldiers. "He's dead, sir," he said, as he checked the body and removed the tags. Robinson took one look at the body and knew there was no point in hunting for a pulse; the man's chest had been literally punched through by a bullet. "Chris came all this way with us and..."

Robinson forced down his own feelings. They had been lucky, driving mainly at night to avoid Russian aircraft, but they'd had to move faster to pick up their ride home and the Russians had caught them. It was a bloody miracle that they hadn't lost more men; the handful of tiny injuries and two broken bones looked a small price to pay for getting home...if they managed to make it home without losing any more men. The once-proud EUROFOR had been reduced to hundreds of bands of stragglers, trying to make their way back home; he wondered what had happened to *Generalmajor* Günter Mühlenkampf and the remains of his force. Had they made the Russians pay for their attack on Europe?

"We have to start walking," he said. They had passed several bunches of refugees, people fleeing into the countryside and trying to escape, others heading towards the coast in hopes that the Royal Marines would pick them up as well as the British and European soldiers. "We can't stay here."

"Sir," one of the soldiers protested, "can't we bury him?"

Robinson knew what cold logic dictated they should do. The body should be abandoned. But he couldn't bring himself to do that, not now and not ever.

"Quickly," he said, hunting for a spot where the body could be buried quickly. Inglehart and Mathews organised a digging party; seven soldiers worked rapidly to bury their fallen comrade, before they started the long march to the west again. "I don't think that we have much time."

"No," Mathews muttered, as they started walking. "Have you been listening to the aircraft?"

Robinson thought about it. "I think I understand," he said finally. "There are air battles going on as well, aren't there?"

Mathews nodded. "Back in 1940, the Germans threw a lot of air power at Dunkirk, but failed to close the door on the escaping forces," he said. "The Russians will be coming with everything they can bring to bear on us, and you know that the handful of Germans we passed won't be able to slow them down for long. They have weapons the Germans could only dream about; all they have to do is sink a few larger ships and...we're fucked."

A nightmarish hour passed as they walked onwards. The temperature was rising quickly, becoming almost tropical; the noise of unseen battles in the sky echoing around them, the occasional sight of an aircraft flying east or west forcing them to duck for cover. Robinson hoped, from the noise, that the RAF was beating the shit out of the Russians, but he knew something about the balance of power in the air. The RAF was likely to be doing the best they could, but the Russians would have more aircraft and more resources. It would be a nasty confrontation...

"Halt," a voice bellowed, in English. The accent was pure cockney. "Identify yourselves!"

"Captain Stuart Robinson," Robinson called back. "Identify yourself."

"Captain Roberto Grey, Royal Marines, 3 Commando," the voice called back. "Remain where you are; we must check your identity before we can proceed."

"Oh, joy," Sergeant Ronald Inglehart muttered. "It's the Royal Latrines."

"They're the best we have at the moment," Robinson reminded him dryly. The Royal Marines came out of hiding and revealed themselves; there was no mistaking their uniforms or their attitude. If they were Russians, they were doing a very good job of pretending to be British soldiers; they carried themselves with a mixture of competence and confidence. His mouth fell into a smile. He recognised one. "Bob!"

Sergeant Bob Patterson stared at him, and grinned. "Captain Robinson, as I live and breathe," he shouted. The tension drained away; Robinson had felt his men preparing for a desperate last stand. It would have been typical of the unexpected war for his men to die in a brief battle with friendly forces. "We kicked your arse at Salisbury Plain!"

"And we kicked yours in the Highlands," Robinson shouted back, remembering a mock war game that had ended with everyone falling into a bog. A lot of friendships had been forged that day. "How do we get home?"

"We check your biometrics first, and then we send you back," Grey said firmly. He was a dour-faced man; Robinson pressed his fingertips to the scanner he held and sighed in relief when it cleared his identity. He had had no doubt that the Marines would have opened fire if there had been a single mistake. "The British soldiers can pass, but the non-British have to go unarmed."

Robinson opened his mouth to protest. "Sorry," Grey said quickly, "but we have already had one case of an infiltrator – we think he was a Russian in Dutch clothing – and we dare not risk another. This operation is working on the margins as it is..."

"I see," Robinson said. "Jean, everyone..."

The foreigners surrendered their weapons reluctantly; Robinson motioned to his men to take them. Grey saw and decided not to argue. "Now," Robinson said, as an aircraft flew overhead. "What do we do?"

"Follow the road to the west, around the towns and city, and head to the coast," Grey said. "One of the other Marines will show you where to go to board one of the ships; the Russian bastards managed to fuck up the port and so we have had to improvise. Once we get you back to England, you'll be debriefed and given new orders."

Good thing we didn't keep the CADS, Robinson thought, thinking about Hazel. She had to have been worried sick about him in Edinburgh; how much did the citizens know about the war? They started the long walk towards the west feeling much better than they had in weeks; one of the soldiers even began to sing a long and filthy song. Others called out equally obscene requests; Robinson didn't bother to stop them as they encountered a second Marine patrol, which pointed them down onto a beach that had been torn apart by tanks and other heavy vehicles. He could see two more CADS positioned to provide air cover; as he watched, one of them launched a missile towards a low-flying aircraft that had appeared out of nowhere, sending it crashing into the city.

Inglehart sounded stunned. "What about the civilians?"

Robinson said nothing. The civilians had paid the price for their government's failure. A handful of Marine medics gave basic medical treatment to his injured men; they had walked all the way to the beach without complaining, or needing to be carried…not that he would have abandoned them, of course. They were too important to be abandoned by their fellows.

"The boat will carry you to the larger ship," a harassed looking Marine Colonel said. Robinson hadn't realised how few soldiers had made it out of Poland, let alone Germany; he couldn't see more than a few hundred soldiers being prepared for the trip across the Channel. "Once you're onboard, find somewhere to sit and keep out of the fucking way, understand?"

Robinson nodded. "Yes, sir," he said. They were almost home. "We won't cause trouble."

"Charlie-one, you have four enemy fighters, closing in," the controller reported. "Suggest that you engage."

"I would never have thought of that," Flying Officer Cindy Jackson sneered, as she pulled the Eurofighter Tempest into an attack vector. Four

Typhoons followed her; the remnants of the RAF seemed to consider her a pretty good flying officer, even if they didn't share her high opinion of herself. The Russian fighters were approaching at high speed, forcing her to turn to engage them; if they had a chance to commit themselves to a bombing run, they could wreak havoc. "Charlie flight, choose your targets and dance!"

She fired a single ASRAAM, all-too-aware that the RAF was running short of advanced weapons, at the lead Russian aircraft. The Russian tried to evade, failed, and was blown out of the air by the missile; two more fell before the final aircraft could launch its own missiles towards one of the Typhoons. They were still having problems tracking the Tempest; their Mainstay aircraft were holding well back, terrified of the CADS on the ground and the SAS officers that had scattered through the countryside, armed with Stingers and other SAM missiles. Other Russian aircraft appeared, launched their missiles from long range, and then retreated, forcing her to hold back her fliers to prevent them giving chase. The Russians not only had a massive SAM belt established to protect their own forces, but they also had far more aircraft and missiles; every time she fired a missile, she dug into a rapidly-dwindling stockpile. Worst of all, the Russians had pulled a surprise out of their bag; their countermeasures against BVRAAM missiles had been improved to the point where guaranteeing a kill was much harder.

"Several more Russian bombers approaching on attack vector," the controller injected, interrupting her private thoughts. She cursed as one of her pilots was blown out of the sky by the final Russian aircraft before it fled the battlezone; the Russians didn't have to stay and fight. The RAF was badly overstretched; the Russians could keep dancing in, forcing her to burn vital fuel and missiles to react, and then duck back under their SAM belt. Heavy Russian bombers had been trying to raid the Royal Marine positions on the ground; only the Dutch damage to their own dikes had prevented heavy Russian armoured units from reaching Ostend. "Engagement vectors..."

"I know," Cindy snapped. She yanked the Tempest around and raced for the bombers, hoping that they wouldn't sense her presence until it was too late; there was so much radar energy boiling around that she had no idea just how well the Tempest's stealth systems were holding up. They might see her coming, or they might not react in time to prevent her; the ageing Bears wouldn't have the best equipment if the Russians were using them to draw out British fire. "Closing in..."

The lead Bear launched a spread of missiles; some targeted on the Royal Navy ships and transports, some targeted on the beach defences. Cindy cursed and activated her cannon; the Russians wanted her to spend her missiles on the Bears, but she had only one missile left and she didn't dare waste it. The Bears seemed unaware of her presence, then she saw the tail-gunner swinging up to target her; she cursed again and fired a long burst into the rear of the Russian aircraft, sending it crashing down towards the sea. The others were scattering now, their deadly cargo launched; she took down two more before twisting away and allowing the others to escape. She was down to only a few rounds left and she would need them later. Other Russian fighters were closing in on her position. If they hadn't known where she was before, they certainly knew now...

She hit the afterburners and the Tempest flashed away from the Russian aircraft. They didn't bother to give pursuit; they were watching as the Russian missiles lashed the ships, some of the warships successfully covering themselves with their CIWS, others being hit and sunk; Cindy had heard that the Russian submarines had been chased everywhere around Britain, perhaps in preparation for another coordinated missile strike. The Royal Navy had deployed almost all of its remaining ASW units to the evacuation effort; the Russians seemed to have picked up on the hint and kept their own submarines away.

The sky lit up as a massive liner, pressed into service, exploded. Cindy had wondered if she would ever have the chance to sail on the MS *Queen Victoria*; she would never have the chance now as the explosion tore the ship apart, along with the people who had been packed onto her decks. The slaughter would be horrifying, she knew; the Royal Marines would have lost dozens of their people on the ship. The Russians had something else to answer for...

"I require a top-up," she said, as the Tempest headed away from Belgium. She had been fighting for what felt like hours and it was starting to show; the RAF had too few planes and too few pilots. The fuel supply on her aircraft was running low; she needed to refuel or head back to base, one of the handful of airfields and airports that the RAF had managed to press back into service. "Control; please supply vectors to the tanker..."

"Understood," the controller said. The French commander of the aircraft was cute; Cindy had been hoping to make his acquaintance at a later date. He wasn't *technically* a squadron-mate, after all. "Flight vector is...*fuck*!"

Cindy saw it all on the download. Five missiles had been launched, from *Britain*; aimed at the tanker and its three escorts. The tanker had been over British soil, it had been believed to be safe; surprised, the escorts took too long to react, or to drop flares. Two missiles found their target and impacted directly with the tanker, sending it crashing to the ground in flames. The explosion would have been heard for miles!

"No," she said, unable to face the cold knowledge of what had happened. It might have been a disastrous case of blue-on-blue, friendly fire, but she doubted it; the day that the Russians started flying tankers over British soil was the day that the war was lost. It had to have been a deliberate act; someone down on Britain was working for the Russians...and had just pulled off the most successful strike of the war. "Control...?"

There was no choice, she knew; the RAF would have no choice. "All aircraft, retreat," Air Marshall Bentley said, before the AWACS could say anything. His priority would be to save as many aircraft as he could before they started to run out of fuel. The Eurofighters, whatever their other virtues, were fuel-guzzlers. "Return to the nearest airbase and await further orders."

"Bastards," Cindy hissed, as she swung the Tempest around. The RAF had ceded control over the battlezone to the Russian Air Force...and that meant that the people on the ground were fucked. "Real bastards!"

"I just had an update from the headquarters," Captain Bellamy said, grimly. "The RAF has been driven out of the battlezone."

"We knew that it would happen," Marine Colonel Patrick Trombly said, as calmly as he could. They'd pulled out over a thousand soldiers from several different countries, including six hundred British soldiers; the thought of just how many had died in the fighting, or remained trapped behind enemy lines, made him wince. The RAF had held its own in the fighting, but everyone had known that it was just a matter of time. He'd pulled out most of his vehicles hours ago, just to ensure that they got home. "What's the latest from the SAS?"

"The Russians are closing in," Captain Bellamy said. "Captain Grey was requesting permission to engage them directly..."

Trombly shook his head. The Royal Marines had had a busy couple of days, setting up as many ambushes and booby-traps for the Russians as they could, unloading all of their considerable bad feeling on the hapless Russian soldiers. The Russians outnumbered the marines and had artillery support; the bombing was bad enough, but once they brought up their heavy guns, the Marines would be ground down and wiped out. They had won all the time they could...

"Send the recall signal," he said. The SAS soldiers would melt into the countryside; hiding and reporting in using satellite transmitters locked into American satellites. They would report on what the Russians were doing until they were pulled out or the Russians caught them. "Remind everyone that if they miss the boat, they will have to follow the emergency procedures...or swim to England if they are really desperate."

He scowled. His Marines had swum the English Channel more than once, certainly more than they had ever admitted to publicly, but that had been under ideal circumstances. Would tired and battered Marines be able to make the same swim at a far longer distance from friendly shores? He felt bitter; a handful of his men had volunteered to remain behind as a rearguard, fighting until the end, but there had been no choice. They all had to be pulled out; they were going to be needed.

"And set all of the CADS on auto-engage," he said, as the Marines came running back to their transports. Many of them had seen to it that the Russians would get a few unpleasant surprises as they tried to recover British equipment; others were silent, contemplating not only defeat, but also the possible future for their own country. "We may as well give the Russians something to worry about as they close in."

He clenched his teeth. "It's not as if they have had anything else to worry about..."

Chapter Thirty-Nine

The Battle of France

France is invaded; I am leaving to take command of my troops, and, with God's help and their valour, I hope soon to drive the enemy beyond the frontier.
Napoleon Bonaparte

Lorraine, France

"They're on their way, *Mon General*," the young officer said. He seemed painfully young for his role. "They're sending in aircraft and helicopters."

Lieutenant-General Vincent Pelletier nodded once; his command post had been carefully hidden with all the professionalism that the remains of the French Army could mount, hidden from Russian bombers. France had gone for seventy years without hostile bombers dropping bombs on French territory; now, it was as if seventy years had been swept away and Hitler's legions had returned to terrorise the population. Pelletier knew that the fight was probably futile, but if…if he could give the Russians a bloody nose, if a provisional government could assume the reins of power, if…if…there might be room to save something from the wreckage of France. If…

Pelletier had been on an exercise when the Russians had launched their first attack, and then the streets of Paris and several other cities had dissolved into chaos, forcing him to try to bring together the remains of several French units to try to put an end to the chaos. He had done well, he knew he had, but it hadn't been enough; his manpower had been so sharply reduced by the combined pressure of missile attacks and the insurgency – which had been specifically targeted on military and police personnel – that he had barely been able to save Paris. By the time he had battered a multi-sided insurgency into submission, or at least quiescence, the German line had broken and hundreds of refugees had started to stream into France, finally providing him with some intelligence on what was happening to the east. Two weeks of fighting an insurgency had taken a bitter toll; his forces had been drained of most of their ammunition and supplies…and what stores they'd had had been hit or looted by the rioters. The air force was non-existent…and, as for the Navy… well, most of the ships had either gone to try to cut the Algerian supply line, or had been destroyed in the opening attacks.

"Order our forces to deploy," he said. "Tell every man that…France expects every man to do his duty."

It was a British quote, but he couldn't think of one that was more appropriate. He had done the best he could, hoping that the Russians would outrun their supply lines, or the Germans would pull off a miracle, but it was not to be. His forces had been shattered and rebuilt; there hadn't been anything like the time he had needed to create a proper army. He had even thought about offering the insurgents amnesty if they agreed to join up, but he knew that the Russians would just have brushed them aside, even if they could be trusted. The French reserves had been allowed to slip too far; his force would do what it could, but it wouldn't be enough. He had dug in near Nancy…and all it would take to shatter his defence line was the Russians coming in from Belgium, even if French soldiers had done what they could to smash up the approach routes.

There was nothing to do now, but wait. It would only take the Russians a few hours to reach the defence line; he hoped that he understood their strategy properly. His army was the last major obstacle that they would face before Spain; they had no choice, but to attempt to engage him. He had prepared as best as he could for the worst…and he had a sneaking suspicion that the 'worst' was about to happen…

How had it all happened? Pelletier turned it over and over again in his mind; how had it happened? There were parts of France only just beginning to wake up to the fact they were at war, other parts torn apart by one insurgent faction or another, from four different Islamic factions to students, nationalists and even socialists. The President was dead, the Prime Minister was dead; Pelletier couldn't even use the nukes without the codes that had been lost when the emergency command centre had been bombed. France had failed to grasp a nettle, she had failed to either repair her damaged society, or to take precautions against an insurgency. They had believed themselves safe, invulnerable; they had been proven spectacularly wrong. They had concluded, rightly, that no insurgency could long succeed…but it hadn't mattered; the Russians had used the Islamic groups as cannon fodder. They had soaked up French bullets that would otherwise have been fired at Russian soldiers.

Pelletier forced himself to sit back calmly. It would all be over soon.

"Fire," General Shalenko said.

The Russians had moved up twenty-five MLRS units and hundreds of heavy guns, all transported through a largely undamaged German rail network, most of which hadn't even been damaged by the fighting. Unlike in Britain, the German transport network had been left more or less alone – although the weight of thousands of heavy tanks was taking its toll – and it had been rapidly pressed into service, with the unwilling help of thousands of Germans who had been told that it was a choice between working or starving. The guns fired…

Russian satellites had pinpointed the location of most of the French defenders near Nancy, a large French city; the French had done a fairly good job of getting their forces into position to stand their ground. Shalenko knew better than to think that the French would simply run at the first shot; the Russians might well have done the French a favour by wiping out the higher command of the French Army. Political skills had been rewarded; military skills had been considered of secondary importance, at best. General Éclair had been that rarity, a competent general who was also a more-than-competent politician; had he survived Sudan, EUROFOR might have been able to recover in the opening days of the war and fight back successfully. The French armoured units would be almost immobile now, their fuel and weapons supplies limited; he had to remind himself not to assume anything. They could have used civilian fuel in their tanks…not that it would have mattered.

He covered his ears as the weapons fired, launching thousands of missiles and shells into the air, firing in long rippling salvos. The Russians had taken the original design and run with it, improving on the idea and adding some refinements of their own. Every minute, the Russians would launch thirty rockets towards the French position, reloading and attacking again as quickly as they could, while the heavy guns would aim for more specific targets, using satellites to watch the battlezone. The return fire was limited and badly coordinated; only one MLRS was struck by a French shell and blown to kingdom come by the blast. Counter-battery radars zeroed in on the location of the French batteries and pounded them, blasting their operators and their guns to dust. It had been a French General – Shalenko couldn't remember who – who had said that 'fire kills;' the French were learning, once again, the truth of that maxim.

He tapped a command into the terminal that Anna held. Neither of them could hear each other under the noise of the guns. The command was simple enough; the battle had been planned beforehand, and so far was all going to plan. That wouldn't survive for long, but Shalenko intended to push his advantage as much as possible. The command echoed through the network; ADVANCE!

Lieutenant Jean-Paul Foch felt his bones rattling as the Russian attack shook their line of makeshift bunkers; the pounding seemed never-ending. His unit had been shattered by the first Russian attacks and pulled back together with several other units, a company that held only fifty men, now assigned to holding a section of the line. Foch, who had only joined the Army because it offered more excitement than most jobs in France, was trembling; no one had ever expected that they would be fighting through France again…and he had now fought two different sets of enemies.

The bombardment was slowing; some of his men were twitching masses on the ground, despite the kicks from their comrades and the burly sergeant who had taken Foch under his wing. Foch's ears were ringing; he could barely hear the shout of alarm as the first soldier crawled to their vision tube and peered out, seeing the advancing Russians closing in on their trench. Foch had prepared as best as he could – the sergeant had been a mass of good ideas and some discipline for the soldiers – but it was still terrifying as the soldiers rushed to their firing positions; the Russian bombardment had devastated the landscape. Foch had been born in Nancy; he didn't want to think about what might have happened if some of the Russian shells had landed in the city. His three sisters lived there; one of them had never come home after the chaos began, the others had only been able to talk to him once before the Russians had started to move towards France. They had told him to run, to save himself; only the thought of failing the sergeant had kept him at his post. He would not run while he could hold himself in place.

He caught the sergeant's eye and held up three fingers. He could still barely hear and knew that the others would have been deafened; the sergeant passed him a flare gun that they had liberated from a naval store as they had completed the task of suppressing the insurgency in Paris. They had planned for being temporarily deaf – at least he hoped it was temporary – and the green flash would be the sign to open fire. He watched the Russians as they moved forward, carefully watching for mines; Foch just wished that they had had any to emplace. France had only a few mines stockpiled and all of them had been designed for use against tanks; the various treaties against mines had robbed France of a desperately needed defence system. They had tried to rig up some mines, but they had all been primitive; they had probably been disabled by the bombardment.

"Fire," he shouted, at the top of his voice, firing the flare into the air. It burst in a green flash of light; his soldiers opened fire, catching the Russians almost completely by surprise. A dozen Russians fell to the ground with lethal wounds, others threw themselves down and scrambled back as quickly as they could; mercilessly, the French defenders mowed them down before they could escape. A handful tried to throw grenades, but they fell short, blasting holes in the barbed wire. He muttered a curse under his breath, wishing that he could hear himself; the Russians would be back at any moment.

"Sir," a voice whispered, right in his ear. The sergeant had to have bellowed at the top of his voice to be heard through the damage; Foch had heard tales of veterans from various wars who had never been able to hear again. The sergeant was pointing towards rising plumes of dust; for a long moment, Foch didn't understand what he was looking at, and then he understood…just as the first armoured monster appeared, heading right towards the trench. The Russian tank was massive and seemingly unstoppable; the soldiers wavered as bursts of machine gun fire tore into the trench. "Here!"

Foch grinned as the sergeant passed him one of the Knife missile launchers, rapidly activating the missile launcher and putting it to his shoulder, taking a bearing on the tank. The Knife had been another joint European project, but unlike most of them, it was loved by all soldiers – not least because it had escaped being tagged with the irritating 'euro' prefix. The missile was reputed to be able to burn through the frontal armour of an American tank; he hoped that it would make short work of the Russian monster that was closing in on them. The Russian tank was painted green, he noticed; the driver was swinging the machine guns around…

He fired; the force of the rocket launcher pushing him backwards as the rocket screeched out of the launcher and directly into the Russian tank, which glowed red and exploded as its ammunition detonated. The soldiers whooped and concentrated on mowing down the Russian soldiers who had revealed themselves following the tank; the sergeant was carrying another Knife instead of a heavy machine gun, watching for more Russian tanks appearing to try to attack them. A second tank appeared, and then a third; Foch reached for the second flare gun and prepared to use it…

The sergeant caught onto his arm. The red flare gun was the signal to retreat. The first enemy tank was grinding up towards them as the sergeant passed Foch the Knife and picked up a bag of explosives that they had been using to set booby-traps and makeshift mines everywhere, hefting it in one strong hand. Foch stared at him for a moment, and then a burst of fire brought him back to reality; he fired the second Knife on one quick motion, even as the sergeant threw the bag of explosives and detonators under the third Russian tank. There was a savage explosion; the Russian tank was blown over by the blast, rolling over and over until it caught fire and burned merrily away. More Russian soldiers had appeared, this time with mortars and other light weapons; the Frenchmen kept their heads down as the rounds started to fall near their trench.

Something at the corner of his eye caught his attention. Foch swung around to see a black aircraft, flying close to the ground, closing in rapidly from the west. The black cross of the aircraft seemed to be hanging in the sky as it closed in…and opened fire, shredding his men like paper dolls. Foch opened his mouth to call a retreat…and hot bursts of pain tore through his body, and darkness swept him away in its comforting embrace.

"We are breaking through the main defence line," Anna said. Shalenko nodded; the casualties had been heavier than he had expected, but the French had almost no reserves. Their only armoured units had moved out to engage the Russian armour and been picked off by Russian bombers; far too many Frenchmen had retreated into the nearest town, where they were engaging the Russian soldiers in house-to-house combat. Russian bombers were roaming the skies unchallenged after the first hail of SAM missiles; everything that even looked suspicious was targeted for destruction. "The commander of the 2nd Shock is requesting permission to exploit the breakthrough."

"Granted," Shalenko said shortly. The breakthrough had to be exploited as quickly as possible; the French Army had proven itself a tough opponent and if it managed to retreat into Nancy, he would have to flatten the town to kill them all, or starve them out in a long siege. "Has there been any progress on locating the enemy command post?"

"Intelligence believes that it has a rough location," Anna said. "Do you want it targeted?"

"I want a commando team to move in," Shalenko said. They had sent several hundred additional commandos behind French lines, waiting for opportunities like this one. "I want the commander alive if possible."

He turned his attention back to the advance.

"Inform the reserves that they are to move back into the pre-prepared defences at Nancy," Pelletier ordered, as calmly as he could. "I want…"

The sheer violence of the Russian attack had stunned him; it was the Second World War fought with modern weapons, and total command of the air. One of his handful of armoured units had been picked off from the air without having a chance to take a shot at the enemy. He could bleed the Russians out in Nancy; perhaps the remaining citizens would forgive his memory, one day, for the devastation that was about to be visited on their city.

There was a burst of fire from outside. He cursed as his subordinates grabbed weapons; they all knew what that meant. Russian doctrine called for decapitating the enemy force as quickly as possible; he was only surprised that they hadn't ordered a bomber to take a JDAM and blow the command post away before anyone knew what had hit them. The remaining French SAM missiles had been fired off against other bombers and there were no more left to contest the air. The command post shook as grenades – he had been in the infantry; he recognised the noise – detonated, sending chips of plaster falling down from the ceiling. The Russian commandos burst in…and some of his people raised their weapons, preparing to fight to the end. There was a series of quick shots and the armed personnel fell to the ground, dead. Blood and gore scattered everywhere…

"Which of you is the commander?" The Russian snapped. Pelletier saw his fate in that instant; collaboration, infamy beyond anything heaped on any past Frenchman, the treason to end all treason. He didn't delude himself; he might have been wearing battle-dress instead of a fancy uniform, but the Russians would know who he was once they compared his face to their files. There really was no other choice; Pelletier had never fancied the role of Darlan and his fellows for himself. "If the commander makes himself known to us…"

Pelletier was still raising his pistol when they shot him through the head. He died with a smile on his face, laughing at them; they had failed, in the end, to take him prisoner and ruling France would be just that bit harder. The final thought before darkness failed to quell the smile; France had made her last stand…

And lost.

Chapter Forty

Alone

Goodnight then: sleep to gather strength for the morning. For the morning will come. Brightly will it shine on the brave and true, kindly upon all who suffer for the cause, glorious upon the tombs of heroes. Thus will shine the dawn. Vive la France! Long live also the forward march of the common people in all the lands towards their just and true inheritance, and towards the broader and fuller age.
Winston Churchill

Near Dover, England

The line of soldiers looked bedraggled in the rain as they stumbled into barracks that had been hastily prepared for them. In the semi-darkness, they looked beaten, broken; Langford would have liked to have believed that it was only an illusion. The British Army, one of the toughest and most professional armies in the world, had had its collective arse soundly kicked…along with the French, the Germans and the Poles. They all knew that, even if the civilians hadn't quite realised yet; the scale of the defeat had been almost total.

Langford looked up at Erica. "It's confirmed, then?"

Erica nodded once. She wore no parka, nothing covering her short blonde hair; rain dripped through it and pressed it to her skin. "HMS *Vengeance* missed its radio call," she said. "The Americans are looking for it, but I think we have to assume the worst; the nuclear submarine has been lost with all hands."

"Along with the missiles," Langford said. He looked down towards the other members of the party, half-hidden in the darkness. "You know what this means, of course?"

"Yes," Erica said grimly. "Any hope that we might have of threatening nuclear attack to force the Russians to break off is more or less gone. We got rid of the other weapons under the European convention on nuclear weapons;

the absence of mushroom clouds over France suggests that the French have also lost their control over their nukes. Now that Paris has fallen…"

Langford stared down at the tattered soldiers. "Just how bad was it?"

"We recovered around a thousand soldiers, four hundred of them from other European countries," Erica said. "Major-General McLachlan had nearly twenty thousand soldiers under his command; we recovered barely six hundred of them before the Russians drove us out of Ostend. There may be other groups trying to get home, but for the moment, we must assume that they are either dead or prisoners of war."

Langford sat down on the nearby bench and tried to come to grips with it. The British Army hadn't suffered such losses in a single campaign since…offhand, he couldn't remember a single campaign that had claimed so many lives. Iraq and Afghanistan, Libya and Pakistan had claimed around nine hundred between them, before the new government had abandoned the Americans and scuttled for safety in political appeasement; had there ever been such losses since the Second World War? The First World War was strewn with blood, even if there had been less shed than politicians claimed these days; there had been no war since 1945 that had claimed so many lives. The Germans and the French would have taken far more causalities; their territory had actually been invaded directly…

Invasion…

"They're going to be coming for us next," he said, very softly. He had had the thought before, but until recently it had refused to materialise in his head as a possibility. "We never planned for invasion; the possibility wasn't even considered."

Erica nodded grimly. "We have been studying the attack the Russians used on Denmark and Norway," she said. "They would have some problems applying it to us, but they could do it, in theory…and if they managed to land, they would be able to rapidly reinforce their forces and advance towards London."

She paused. "They might even have some help," she said. "That woman in Edinburgh gave us a break, but…"

Langford scowled. "The prisoner told us nothing?"

"I don't think he knows anything," Erica said. "Oh, the Russians did a lot to prepare him for interrogation and possible torture, but we borrowed some of the American manuals and drugs and worked on him. He may be hiding some details, but…he knows nothing beyond the existence of someone called Control who gave them their final orders, and vanished. He may well have been killed in the first round of hostilities, which would be quite ironic, but in any case their orders were to continue to attack until they were caught, or ordered to extract themselves."

She paused. "He didn't even know that the Russians were planning to invade Europe until he heard the radio reports," she continued. "Imagine; thousands of them, still running around the country, striking like they did at the tanker. What happens if a few of them take up position near a RAF base and launch more missiles?"

"We have to find them," Langford said. "How did they get here anyway?"

"Russian workers hired by a shell company," Erica said. "The Security Service was trying to look into the paper trail; guess what happened to the people in charge of the company?"

Langford took a wild guess. "Trapped in Russia by the war?"

"And their records destroyed," Erica said. "There were hundreds of thousands of Russians coming to Britain to work; if even a tenth of them were agents, we have an entire underground invasion on our hands."

"Have them all rounded up and moved to the detention centres," Langford said, hating himself. "We can sort them all out later."

He shook his head. He had always thought that detaining people without trial was un-British, even if it had been the only way to handle international terrorism. The unfortunates who had already been detained had either been offered a chance to make up for their crimes by serving in the army, or had been told that they would remain there until they could be sent to America to face charges there. The known terrorist Mustapha had been caught, much to everyone's surprise, and he would be out of the country in a week.

"Most of them will have gone underground by now," Erica said. She scowled. "Someone very well placed must have been organising this for years."

"I don't think that the last government needed the help," Langford said bitterly. He ran a hand through his hair. On its own resources, Britain couldn't rebuild its army before it was too late, not the vital equipment, at least. Many of the factories for constructing smaller weapons, such as rifles and pistols, had been hit, although those were fairly easy to build, given time. The aircraft and tanks…it could take months before any new aircraft came off the assembly line; once they ran out of spares, the entire RAF would be grounded pretty quickly. "How many soldiers can we assemble here?"

"Around thirty thousand, at most, counting the TA," Erica said. "The initial losses were heavy, particularly in units that were in their barracks at the time; we have to get what we have left into a coordinated force and replace the equipment – I think we also have to call back the Falklands force now, without further delay."

Langford nodded bitterly. "See to it," he said. "I think we need to draw up a plan for resisting an invasion."

A sonic boom split the air; everyone knew that it wouldn't be long before the Russians started air attacks in earnest, securing command over the sea and as much of southern England as they could. He wondered what had caused the boom; a RAF fighter on patrol, or a Russian fighter preparing to enter the UKADR and thumb its nose at the British. With stockpiles of advanced weapons so low, the British could not afford to engage every probe unless it came over the mainland…and by the time the two AWACS tracked the probe as coming in over the mainland, it might be too late to respond.

He looked along the beach to one of the men standing there. "We also need to do something we should have done a long time ago," he said. "We have to ask for help."

Erica nodded. "I'll return to headquarters and start making the preparations," she said. "If nothing else, we need to evacuate this whole area; I don't think that the Russians would dare land anywhere else. Too many variables."

Langford watched her go, and then sped up his own walk. He had asked the two men ahead of him to come to see the return of British forces; it was the easiest way he could think of to stress how serious the situation had become, at least in British eyes. The older man turned as Langford approached; Ambassador Andrew Luong looked almost as tired as Langford felt. Colonel Seth Fanaroff had been briefing him on what had happened in Brussels; the United States had already lost over four hundred lives to the war, many of them in the first day of the fighting. The Americans who had made themselves known to Russian forces had been sent back to America; Langford ground his teeth at the thought. A few atrocities would have made his task much easier.

"Ambassador," he said, as he took in the two men. Fanaroff had brought back his assistant and ten women, nine of whom were prostitutes who had devoted themselves to ministering to the soldiers. The civilian population had done what they could as well, but many of them had just stayed inside, keeping themselves to themselves, seeing to their families first. "May we have a word?"

Luong nodded once. "It doesn't look good," he said, before Langford could say anything. "I don't understand; why did no one ever see this coming?"

"Water under the bridge," Langford said. It hardly mattered now. "Ambassador; Britain needs help."

"I thought you might ask that," Luong admitted. There was a long pause. "It may be politically impossible to provide more than limited support."

Langford closed his eyes for a moment. "Give us the weapons and we can win," he said. "Ambassador, have you considered what the Russian conquest means for America?"

Fanaroff nodded before Luong could speak. "The Russians intended nothing less than conquest, and now that the remainder of France is being brought under Russian authority, it won't be long before they come here," he said. "Once that happens, they will be almost impossible to remove without a war that will make World War Two look like a child's tea party."

"The American public is generally not inclined to take the long view," Luong said, more to Langford than to Fanaroff. "The President may agree with you, but you must know that the American Army is heavily engaged in both Korea and the Middle East. The supplies that used to be based here are gone; even if we were prepared to send troops, they wouldn't be capable of being more than…speed bumps for the Russians."

He paused. "There is also a good chance that political opinion would be so strongly against intervention that the President will be able to do nothing," he continued. "You know, you must know, exactly what Brussels has said about America…"

Langford shrugged. "And Washington has said *what* about Brussels?"

"Washington isn't the place that needs help," Luong pointed out dryly.

Langford felt real despair for the first time.

The American shrugged. "I want to help, I want America to help, but it may be impossible both politically and practically. The average Joe Six-pack in the US is probably cheering on the Russians and wondering what the Russians will do to all the terrorists who have managed to make themselves into media darlings in Europe, so that they could never be sent out of the country to face trial. The Russians in control of Europe may end the flood of poison money; informed opinion may want to wait and see if the Russians improve the situation…"

"Which won't happen if the Algerians get control over the south of France," Langford said. "I was under the impression that Algeria was on your list of states to knock over and repair."

"It was, but not for a few years," Luong said, grimly. He met Langford's eyes. "I will go to Washington to plead your case." He held up a hand. "I would not, however, advise hope; the most I think that Washington will be able to give you is supplies and some additional support, maybe even a few additional tankers and aircraft if they are available."

"Anything would be welcome," Langford said. He stared over the grey sea towards France. "At the moment, if the Russians land, we will lose. If that happens, you will be unable to repair the situation without hideous losses."

Hazel hadn't known what would happen to her in the days since she had found the police station and betrayed the two Russians. She had been interrogated repeatedly by policemen and people in plain suits she guessed were from MI5, digging out every last fact about the Russians that she knew. Her information, she had been told, had been very detailed and very useful, but the Russians had been careful to lay false trails. The attempt to trace their allies, assuming that they had allies, had failed; Hazel had been warned that it would be a long time before she could go home. The Russians might want revenge for the betrayal.

Instead, she had spent several days being moved south, into England. The people escorting her hadn't explained why she was being driven along deserted motorways, taking their time as they drove south; she had merely had to remain with them until they reached Dover, where she had been booked into a B&B. No one knew she was there; she hadn't been allowed to talk to her father and the telephone system was still out of commission. Dover had been under a curfew; the police and armed soldiers were patrolling the streets, preventing anyone being out at night. It had seemed like a strange place to hide; Hazel might have been only a civilian, but she was certain that Dover was the closest place in England to Russian-occupied France.

"It's a surprise," her escort had said, and refused to say anything else about the reason for coming. Hazel had reluctantly accepted it, but the B&B was boring; the owner was one of the owners who insisted on treating each and every guest like a potential thief. She had been reluctant to loan Hazel a DVD player, she had been reluctant to loan her books, or even make-up and other womanly supplies; it was no surprise that there was no visitor's book. If she had been visiting of her own free will, she would have left the day afterwards; the woman had been very resentful of Hazel's escort, who had insisted that the woman provide lunch and dinner as well as breakfast.

A car drew up outside; Hazel wondered if it was her escort, coming back to take her somewhere else. Moments later, she heard angry chatter downstairs; the woman had to be angry at whatever was happening, but she didn't seem to have any choice in the matter. Someone came up the stairs, walking very lightly, and then there was a knock at the door.

"Come in," Hazel shouted. Her mouth fell open. "*Stuart!*"

He stood there, tired, dressed in muddy clothes and with three weeks of stubble on his face, but it was him. Hazel was across the room, flinging her arms around him, before she even realised who it was; his body felt wonderful in her arms. There was a rightness to it that made her melt, even before his lips met hers in a long lingering kiss. Messy as he was, it was no trouble at all undressing him and pulling him into the bed the grumpy woman had prepared for her; it had been too long since she had felt him inside her. He felt wonderful.

The morning afterwards, they had a long shower together, made love again, and then lay together in bed. "So, what happened to you?" Robinson asked, his voice carefully nonchalant. "I only heard a few rumours..."

"I'm *pregnant*," Hazel squealed, remembering. She was gushing and couldn't help herself. "Oh Stuart, it must have been that last night..."

He looked oddly mixed between joy and worry. "It may not be a good world to have a child," he said, and told her everything. The deployment, the surprise attack, the long retreat through Europe...and finally the trip on the commandeered liner from Ostend to Dover. "I honestly don't know what's going to happen next."

"Me either," Hazel said, as she told him her story. She left out a handful of details he didn't need to know, but she told him proudly how she'd broken the pipe and used it to escape, revealing the existence of the Russians to the police. "Then they brought me here..."

"It must have been a reward for you," Robinson said finally, shaking his head. His face had become deathly pale. "I thought you were safe..."

"I thought *you* were safe," Hazel said, and started to cry. They fell into each other's arms again. "I was thinking of you all the time, thinking that you would be safe and..."

Robinson just held her and said nothing.

"So," Hazel said finally, "how long do we have?"

"I was told two days," Robinson said. He shook his head grimly. "I may be in some trouble; I left a valuable pair of vehicles with the Germans and some people want me and Ben in serious hot water for it. Under the circumstances, I should be fine, but..."

He grinned. "I think that I'll be assigned to the defence force here," he said. "And I think that you're going to get your cute ass back to Edinburgh or somewhere safe after the end of my leave."

Hazel stood up. She enjoyed the way his eyes followed her breasts; it gave her a sense of power. "I am not going to leave you again," she said, firmly. Was that a tear she saw in his eyes? "I will find somewhere nearby and stay near you..."

"Hazel, it's not safe," Robinson said, and pulled her close. "Please..."

For a few moments, everything was right with the world.

Interlude Four

The End of Europe

The defeat of the French near Nancy spelled the end of Europe.

In the Mediterranean, Russian submarines received coded transmissions and went into action. Hidden under the waves, they wiped out the ships that Algeria had used to transport their soldiers to France, both the remains of their professional army and the holy warriors fired with faith. Tens of thousands died, unaware of their ally's treachery; the Algerian conquest of France faltered and died. The French had been fighting back with increasing desperation and savagery, their professional training making up some of the difference in numbers; now, the French finally had a chance to cut off and destroy the remaining Algerian forces.

Malta had fallen in the first hours of the war; Algerian forces had invaded Corsica and Sardinia, but rapidly discovered that the natives had their own reputation for bloody-mindedness. The Algerians, cut off from their supply line, held on grimly; the resistance movement bided its time and prepared the final blows. Sicily, invaded by a mixture of Algerian and Libyan forces, became a bloody battleground as the Italians fought back desperately, or tried to escape to the mainland. Italy itself was no longer safe; the chaotic war was shattering the very fabric of Italian society. The Pope's call for peace was swept aside as Italy descended into ethnic conflict; in many places, priests even called for a crusade against the Islamic forces. When Russian units walked through the Czech Republic and Austria and entered Italy, they were almost welcomed as saviours.

The Russian enclaves in Norway were rapidly expanded, even as Sweden and Finland agreed to enter the new Russian Federation on very favourable terms. The Russian President had a sneaking respect for the Finns; they would be permitted considerable autonomy provided they remained out of trouble. The Swedes, less well regarded, were forced to enter on Russian terms. The Norwegians had had two weeks to get organised, but open resistance was futile; the remains of the Norwegian Army and thousands of civilian volunteers melted into the mountains and prepared themselves for an underground war.

For France, the Russians had a different fate in store. Paris fell, three weeks after the war began; the Russians walked into the city after the provisional government tried to escape to the south, to the other war zone. As cities were surrounded and forced to surrender, insurgent leaders came out, expecting to be greeted as allies. They were surprised when specially trained and prepared FSB units snatched them, cuffed them, and in many cases rewarded them with a bullet to the back of the head. Other insurgencies and isolated French units struggled to hold out; the Russians secured the locations they needed and surrounded hotspots of resistance. They could be handled later.

The ports along the coast saw a massive exodus as French shipping fled the ports, heading to Britain, or to America and Canada, trying to escape the Russians. The Russians came in the wake of the fleeing refugees, carefully taking control of the areas that interested them, leaving pockets of resistance to die on the vine. In some places, they faced determined opposition, but in others, they were able to go where they wanted, or were even greeted as liberators. They represented law and order; for those who had hidden from the insurgencies, the Russians were even more welcome than French soldiers. The Russians had a stout attitude to Islamic terrorism, some of them whispered, and besides, the Russians were the winning side. Would it not be better to work with them until the wind changed? Besides, the Russians would show *les salarabes* who was boss…

A week passed as the Russians advanced into the south. French soldiers who met them found themselves arrested and sent to detention centres; French civil servants, policemen, and local government workers found themselves meeting the same fate. The Russians surrounded the hotbeds of insurgency and waited, patiently, for them to run out of food. The message was loud and clear; the insurgents could come out, naked, or they could starve. Civilians fled, chased by fire from their more radical fellows; the radicals rapidly discovered that the Russians were prepared to fire heavy weapons at snipers and that their supposed allies didn't like them much. Only a small percentage of France's Muslim population had known about the insurgency in advance; many of the young, trapped in an endless cycle of poverty, had welcomed the chance to take it out on the native French. They had looted, raped and burned their way through the cities, now, facing death by starvation or heavy guns, they too voted with their feet. The Russians scooped up everyone who came out naked – those who came out dressed were shot down in case they were suicide bombers – and processed them; they were identified, segregated by sex, and then sent into detention camps. The remaining fanatics, those who were not shot in the back by their own people, were rapidly wiped out.

Even as they set up the detention camps, under heavy guard, the Russians were searching through Europe's prisons. Many of the prisoners had escaped, but over half had remained in their cells; the Russians added the prison guards to their detention camps and carefully inspected each prison's records. The mild criminals, the white-collar criminals, were sent to camps where they would be added to the workforce. The terrorist suspects met two different fates; those wanted by American authorities were sent to a camp near a port, where they would be transported to America. Those who the Americans didn't want were quickly disposed of; the same went for the dangerous criminals. Murderers, traitors, child molesters…all met a final terrifying end.

They were merely the first to feel the weight of Russian power.

Chapter Forty-One

Covenants without Swords, Take One

Covenants without swords are, but words
Thomas Hobbes

Warsaw, Poland

"Caroline Morgan, come forth."

The voice stirred Caroline to her feet as she looked around the vast prison camp. The Russians hadn't been violent, or brutal; they'd merely frogmarched them into a captured Polish truck and driven them towards Warsaw, towards what had once been a football stadium. With armed guards surrounding it, it had become a prison camp for captured EUROFOR and Polish personnel...and people who had been caught in the middle of the fighting.

Caroline had tried to keep herself together, even as the weeks slipped by with little chance of reparation or even being freed from the camp. She was lucky; as a civilian, she had full run of the camp, such as it was. The prisoners from the different military forces were shackled permanently to seats designed to survive the worst efforts of football yobs. Their condition was far more desperate than hers; from time to time, the Russians triggered the auto-washing system and used it to clean up the mess. For them, their lives had descended into hell.

Others had joined them. Two women, Zyta Konstancja and Melania Kazimiera, had also been shoved into the camp, along with two young children, both Melania's daughters. Caroline had talked to them – the Russians didn't seem to care what they did, provided they didn't try to escape – and all they had done was been unlucky enough to be caught talking to a known resistance fighter. The fighter, from what Zyta had said, had been over sixty years old; the Russians had beaten him to death in front of her. They'd seen enough about Russian rule to know what was happening in Warsaw; the Russians were digging in for the long haul.

They'd talked in hushed whispers about registration, ration cards, and the promise of work. Many young men of Warsaw, those who were not connected to the military or the police, had gone to work for the Russians; it was the only way to feed their families. Caroline wanted to scream abuse at the handful of young men they saw every day, heading to dig graves or worse for the Russians, but she understood; the young men had had no choice, but to collaborate with the Russians. If most of Poland was in the same boat, resistance would be futile.

Marya had held out hope, for a while, that Captain Jacob Anastazy had survived; she had told Caroline that he was probably leading a resistance army by now, somewhere in the countryside. That dream had died the day the Russians had told her, without gloating, without even a leer, that Captain Jacob Anastazy was dead, killed in a gunfight along a motorway. It had been the fact that the Russians hadn't even tried to convince her that had convinced her, finally, that they were telling the truth; Marya had cried herself to sleep that night and had been broken afterwards.

As the weeks passed, the camp changed its composition. Caroline, as a long-staying resident, had found herself appointed camp supervisor by the Russians. She had refused, citing her media neutrality, but the Russians had pointed out that if someone didn't supervise the camp, everyone would rapidly grow sick and die in their own filth. Caroline had done what she could, but the Russians had very quickly removed anyone useful, such as the handful of prisoners who had medical training. She was improvising and knew it; people were dying, in some cases of avoidable problems, in other cases of nothing more than despair.

A month after they had become prisoners, Caroline, like all the other unshackled prisoners, was ordered into a side compound, where they were locked in and left to wait while burly Russian soldiers moved in on the military prisoners. Some struggled – one of them hit a Russian officer in the groin, sending the civilian prisoners into giggles – but it was futile; they were released, shackled together, and marched off out of the camp. A week later, they hadn't returned; the handful of guards who talked to the Poles either didn't know what had happened to them, or were unwilling to discuss it. The

Polish women, some of whom had become quite fond of the men, screamed and ranted, but the Russians just ignored it. Caroline found it a worrying sign; she had studied history privately, not in a British school, and she knew that the Russians had once massacred thousands of Polish prisoners to prevent them serving as the nucleus of resistance.

In their place, other prisoners had arrived; the young men and women of Warsaw. Their tales were grim; they had been arrested for one fault or another, mainly breaking curfew, and the Russians had arrested them, beaten them and in one case raped an offending girl. That girl had only the small benefit of seeing her rapist marched off into a penal unit; she told Caroline that the Russians had taken over the brothels in Poland and were using them for their soldiers under military control. The whores were the best fed women in Poland. Some of the young had had idealist dreams about fasting until they were freed, but Caroline had dissuaded them as best as she could; the Russians hadn't cared about anyone else who had died in the camps, so why should they care about young Poles? They had nothing, but their bodies; some of the young men were taken out, a day later, and sent to a labour gang.

She stumbled over to the gate. It was heavily guarded; the Russians insisted on watching the prisoners as if they were She-Hulk, or Supergirl. She wished that she was; the dream of crashing through the camp's guards and running back to safety kept running through her head whenever she was dozing. She knew what would happen if she didn't present herself; it had happened before, to other prisoners. The Russians had come into the camp, found them, and shot them in front of the others, a reminder that their lives were in Russian hands.

"Your food," the Russian soldier said, in halting English. He was one of the good ones, a soldier who had been disabled enough to warrant his departure from an infantry unit, but determined to serve the Russian President in whatever way he could. Caroline had tried to befriend him and a handful of the other guards, but that was becoming harder; more and more faces were vanishing, to be replaced by cold pale men whose gaze refused to even fall to her half-exposed breasts. "You will be summoned again later."

Caroline felt her blood run cold. Any change in routine was a danger, she had been told; she was normally summoned once every day, and then they were left alone. One of the kinder Russian guards had dropped in cards and several board games; the prisoners either spent their time playing, or discussing their fate in low voices. It hadn't escaped her notice that nearly half of the camp's population was composed of reporters and various other media workers; some of them had even come from as far west as Dresden. When the city had fallen, one of them had told her, the Russians had rounded up reporters along with the policemen and soldiers; they'd been dumped into trucks and shipped west to the camp near Warsaw. She had tried to view that as a positive sign, but it was impossible; they might have had a good reason to secure her, but not reporters they'd snatched off the streets.

"Thank you," she said, carefully. Her Russian was almost non-existent. "Do you know why?"

The guard raised his shoulders and shrugged in the universal gesture for 'don't know.' Caroline gave him a kiss on the cheek anyway and took the trolley of supplies, pushing it back into the camp, calling for the prisoners as she moved. One prisoner had tried to hide in the trolley; the Russians had seen a foot sticking out, burst out laughing, and dragged him out before shooting him. The meals changed only slightly; the Russians had captured thousands of EUROFOR MRE – Meals Ready to Eat – packs and distributed them to the prisoners. It was cruel and unusual punishment, as far as Caroline could determine; the prisoners who could cook had even offered to cook for the guards as well, if they were given some supplies. The guards had refused; their paranoia was such that they would count each and every plastic fork and beat people if they tried to keep them.

Caroline ate her food slowly, worrying; she was much thinner than she had been the day she had boarded the aircraft to Poland. She had never been as vain as some people in the media business, but she knew that her looks had their uses when it came to convincing people to talk to her; if they had seen her now, her boyfriends would have been shocked. She looked like one of those rape victims, carefully made up to seem pathetic, who were paraded in front of a jury. Her hair was dull and listless; her bones were starting to show through her chest. She wasn't sure how much longer she could go on…

There was an escape committee, of course; seven Poles who had been imprisoned and wanted out, or at least to see their families again. Caroline was supposed to report any escape attempts to the guards, but she hadn't bothered; escape seemed completely impossible. Under the torn-up turf, the stadium bottom was hard concrete, while the guards had been careful never to allow a weapon to fall into the hands of the prisoners; Caroline suspected that such a mistake would lead to the responsible guards, assuming that they survived the experience, joining the prisoners in the pen. More than one prisoner had been strangled by another, often for the smallest things; the guards wouldn't have cared if they had all killed each other. Only the steady flow of MRE packs convinced her that the Russians didn't just want to kill them all.

"They want to see me afterwards," she whispered to Marya. The Polish woman sat there, arms and legs akimbo; Caroline knew that she was almost completely broken. She would have spared Marya her torment if she could have done so; Marya was an innocent who deserved none of the horrors that had swept up and consumed her life. "They may hurt me..."

Some prisoners had been taken for interrogation, mainly policemen and a handful of reporters. They had returned, some of them; beaten and broken. It was obvious that they had been tortured to extract information, but all of it had been trivial; the policemen had been asked about a handful of criminals, while the reporters had been asked about politicians. It was brutal, pointless...and banal. Caroline's world had shrunk to the four corners of the prison camp; it was growing increasingly hard to remember London, or the politicians who had helped create the mess for Europe. She wanted to forget...

"No," Marya said. She clung to Caroline as if Caroline was her mother. "You can't go, please..."

"I have no choice," Caroline said. They'd become like sisters in the camp; Caroline, Marya and the other Polish women, who had worried about the two young girls. The Russians had reluctantly agreed to provide food for them and to look for other accommodation, but Caroline suspected that they would have either forgotten, or hadn't found anyone. The Polish sisters had been related to soldiers, after all; their relatives might have all been disappeared. Promise me you'll take care of yourself...?"

"Yes," Marya said. "Just come back, please..."

"Caroline Morgan, come forth," a harsh voice bellowed. "Caroline Morgan, come forth!"

Caroline stood up and walked over to the gate. The Russian guards raised their weapons as she approached; she almost laughed, aware that there was nothing she could do to them. She would have given anything for a shot of some superpower that would have had her breaking the guards with ease, but she was tired and wearing rags. What sort of threat did they think a malnourished half-dressed girl presented?

"Hands," a Russian growled. Caroline knew the procedure as well as anyone else in the camp; she turned slightly and put her hands behind her back, allowing the Russians to slip on a pair of handcuffs. That was a good sign; the prisoners had watched carefully and people who were handcuffed were normally returned to the camp, while those who were secured with plastic ties never returned. "Move!"

The darkness of the internal corridors, now serving as the barracks for the guards, left her half-blinded long enough to lose track of her position in an endless maze of facilities below the ground. Marya had told her that the stadium, constructed in 2020, had been the largest ever constructed in Poland; it could hold thousands of people, and even had other facilities, below the ground. The only sign of sporting equipment now was a handful of footballs on the ground; everything else had been removed, making way for Russian soldiers and their equipment. There were enough guns in the various storage areas to restart the war…assuming that they could ever get to them. The escape committee hadn't been able to think of a way past the guards after weeks of desperate scheming.

The guards finally led her into a brightly-lit room. She flinched back from the light, long enough for them to secure her against a wall, and leave her. Moments later, before she could realise what was happening, another Russian entered and studied her thoughtfully. Caroline felt like a trapped animal under his gaze; it didn't help that she was firmly secured to what felt like a shower pipe. The Russian was remarkably pale, with very dark hair; his eyes were soulless, almost lifeless. He was a nightmare made flesh.

"I am the commanding officer of the 4th FSB Security Battalion, Warsaw," the Russian said finally. "You will identify yourself."

Caroline couldn't believe that he didn't know her name already. The Russians had not only collected ID tags, but they had asked her, more than once, about her name, building up a picture of who they had in the camp, and why. She had cooperated as little as she could, but the Russians had been skilful at actually making their prisoners work for them, doing as much of the heavy lifting as they could without resorting to torture to 'encourage' them to talk.

"I am Caroline Morgan, reporter," she said, and briefly outlined what had happened to her. She knew that holding anything back was a bad idea; the Russians were prepared to use torture if they felt that they had no choice. Caroline wasn't a soldier, she was a civilian; she couldn't have held out for long against pain, even if they had paid her. "What are you going to do to me?"

The Russian looked up at her. "The question has been discussed at the highest levels," he said. Caroline, oddly enough, believed him. "We have faced a constant barrage of propaganda from Europe, condemning us for thousands of crimes and offences, some of them only theoretically possible. The European media has persistently taken the side of the enemies of Russia, along with the other enemies of the civilised world everywhere. I dare say that if French reporters had still been at work during the insurgencies, they would have claimed that the insurgents were actually somehow in the right, just because they were getting the short end of the stick."

"I am a non-political reporter," Caroline said. "I am not..."

He slapped her, hard, across her face. "You are a political reporter, all of you are," he said. "You repeated the lies told by refugees and Chechens who had an axe to grind; you'd think that you would have learned something from Iraq, but no, you chose to repeat their propaganda. The media played a role in the European refusal to grant us the support we needed when we needed it; now, we need no support and we have our enemies at our mercy."

Caroline could taste blood in her mouth. She looked for words to say, clever arguments that would win her freedom, but there were none. There was only force, and the threat of force...and Europe had acted as if both of those factors didn't exist. She could have argued, she could have pointed out that the citizens of Poland and Germany...and perhaps even further west...hadn't deserved occupation, but in the end, the Russians wouldn't listen to her. Her own helplessness buzzed through her mind; the Russian could do anything to her, and she could do nothing about it. What hope was left for her?

"I see you have nothing to say," the Russian said. His voice was icy cold, without a hint of gloating or pleasure. "A decision has been made about you, Morgan, and all of your kind. You have no place in the new world order."

He drew his pistol and chambered a round. "Do you have any last words?"

Caroline felt oddly calm. "Go fuck yourself," she hissed. She tried to kick the Russian, but it was impossible from her position; he just stepped back and watched her struggle to keep her balance. "One day, we're going to kill all of you."

"I don't think that that will happen," the Russian said, as he put the gun to her head. "The price of your socialist paradise was destroying the fighting spirit of the European Armies…and you gained your paradise at the cost of your freedom."

He pulled the trigger.

Afterwards, they took her body, dumped it in one of the mass graves, and buried it unmarked under the Polish soil. No one in Britain would ever know for certain what had happened to Caroline Morgan. Like so many others, she had just vanished in the nightmare that had consumed Europe.

Chapter Forty-Two

Covenants without Swords, Take Two

The problem with socialists, to use a general term, is that of the dog who had one bone. Carrying it in his mouth, the dog looked into the river, saw a second bone, and made a bite for it…with the predictable result that the first bone fell into the river and was swept away…leaving the poor dog with no bone. Humans do not have the excuse of being unintelligent animals.
Christopher Nuttall

Hanover, Germany

She was called Gudrun, a name that meant 'battle-maiden' to some ears; an irony that a handful of boyfriends had pointed out when they came face to face with her politics. Gudrun Krumnow was nineteen years old; blonde, tall and shapely, and deeply devoted to the needy of the world. Like so many others in her position, she believed deeply and truly in the need to 'Do Something' to tackle the many issues of the world; she had marched in protests, sung songs in support of the Needy of the Week, and had generally made herself as helpful as she could. Her education had been limited; at nineteen, she had only a few years of university to go, years that she had already committed to the Causes.

She was unprepared for the real world; German industries, already staggering under the weight of European regulations on this and that, had no time to take on more uneducated people that they could never get rid of, or lose. The best of them had the motivation to use the – unofficial – opportunities to train to an acceptable level; few of them truly had the motivation. Years of being told that they were due vast rewards if they were patient had taken their toll on the youth of Germany; no government could challenge the issue of vast unemployment without losing power. In a very real sense, Germany – and the remainder of the EU – was being red-taped and taxed to death.

Gudrun and her family had cowered in their house as the first chaos began in Hanover, terrified of what would happen to them when the looters and insurgents found them hiding; Gudrun might have believed that they were the poor, and the underdogs must always be in the right, but sheer terror was overcoming her political beliefs. The sounds had been terrifying; she had always disliked the police – and had led a boycott of girls who dated police officers – but she had prayed then that the police would save her and her family. When Lord Mayor Paul Steiner - a class enemy, of course, despite him being Green – had used the army to end the disturbances, or at least confine them to a handful of districts within the city, Gudrun had been relieved.

And then she hated herself, feeling like a traitor; she had silently accepted the treatment of the rioters and the looters, treatment that rumour said had been brutal beyond belief. It had led to her first serious argument with her father, ending with her flouncing off to her room and hiding; her father had threatened to lift his hand to her for the first time in her life if she even thought about going out and joining the protests against Paul Steiner. Her father, a civil engineer, had known what Gudrun had refused to allow herself to believe; the streets were no longer safe for protesters, or indeed for young girls. As the Russian armies had advanced, he had even considered abandoning the city, but where could they have gone? Gudrun had three sisters, each as pretty as she was, and her mother had held her good looks; how could one man protect them all against the evils of society's breakdown? They had remained in the city, hiding; keeping their heads down and hoping that they would not be noticed.

For Gudrun, a free spirit, it had been torture. "I am not one of those women whose menfolk keep them covered all day," she had shouted at her father, desperately trying to ignore the contradiction of her support for minority rights and practices such as the *Burka* and worse. "I am a grown woman and safe on the streets!"

Her father had given her the worst look she had ever faced. "Yes, you're a grown woman in body, if not in mind," he had snapped. "If you go out there, you may be raped and murdered and you are not going out there! Until you leave the house permanently, young lady, you are under my authority. Understand?"

Gudrun had subsided, muttering, as the noise of the advancing Russian Army had echoed out over the city. Her father had gone into the streets and brought back what he could in the way of food, quelling Gudrun's objections to the meat – she was a devoted vegetarian – with a sharp remark about beggars not being choosers. The Krumnow had never been poor; their area of town had been remarkably unscathed by the fighting. Gudrun believed that it would never touch her…and the decision of the Mayor to surrender the city had seemed to confirm her belief. The Russians had behaved themselves and accepted the surrender; they couldn't do anything to the citizens, could they?

Her father had been less convinced. His family remembered the advance of the Russians during the Great Evil War, the war where Germany had set out to exterminate the Jews and other ethnic groups, the same Jews who had crushed Palestine and sent thousands of refugees to Europe. The Russians had looted and raped their way across East Germany; he had had relatives, old now, who had been forced to endure Russian attention. To Gudrun, it was a different world; such things just didn't happen in her world.

For the first week, events had been surprisingly peaceful; she had watched from behind her curtains as the Russians marched into the city, pale-faced soldiers who seemed tired, but happy. Rumour had it that the policemen had been rounded up, along with the soldiers, and sent out to the detention camps, but nobody knew anything for certain. They were more concerned with stability and survival; the Russians promised stability, although it was very much the velvet glove masking the steel fist. They had insisted that everyone remain constantly tuned in to the emergency frequency and used it to issue orders; their first order had been a curfew on all Germans between sunset and sunrise. Other orders had followed; Gudrun had watched as young Arabic men were forced to work clearing rubble from the streets, before being escorted out of the city to the laminations of their women. Her heart almost burst.

In the second week, the Russians had caught up with her father; a Russian officer and seven armed soldiers appeared, bearing ration packs in one hand and weapons in the other. The offer had been simple; her father was a civil engineer who had worked for the city's infrastructure, and he was being offered the chance to take up his post again, at Russian wages. The Russian had been brutally clear; they would be rationing food, and her father had the choice between working for them, or not receiving any rations. Only the elderly or the very young would get rations, the Russians said, without working for them; in time, everyone would work or starve.

Gudrun had protested; surely everyone had a right to eat! The Russian soldiers hadn't understood her nearly-hysterical German, the Russian commander had rolled his eyes and made a comment to the Russian soldiers, who had laughed. Her father had interrupted, his face very pale, and sent her out of the room; Russian laughter had followed her all the way to her bedroom. That night, her father had admitted to them that he had seen no choice, but to accept the Russian offer; it was that, or the family would starve. Gudrun had said nothing.

The day afterwards, she met up with a few of her friends, male and female alike, including her current boyfriend. The Russians had closed the schools and universities for the duration of the hostilities, and they had banned large gatherings, but they couldn't be everywhere at once. The students compared notes, feeling strangely excited as they shared their stories; there couldn't be more than a thousand Russian soldiers assigned to the garrison, and most of the soldiers were clearly overworked. Some of the male students complained about how the Russians had taken over the brothels, but their female comrades had little sympathy; at least the Russians would be able to pay the whores for their services. European banks were still closed and European money was worthless.

The students compared plans; many of them had graduated with honours in courses on people power and civil disobedience. They knew the theory and even some of the practice; they had studied, not without a little delight, the experience of the British, the French and even the Russians when it came to facing People Power. The Russians, in 1991, had crumbled before the people of Eastern Europe; many of the students knew people who had been alive during the collapse of the Berlin Wall and the end of Communism in Germany. Without really noticing, they had gone from a group of young students to the beginnings of a resistance moment, devoted to peaceful protest. The handful of students who warned that the Russians would be unlikely to fold were laughed at; everyone knew that they were the ones who had volunteered to do their community service in the army. Gudrun had been *smart*; she had done hers in a university, soaking up knowledge and learning.

Three days later, the final straw came.

"Citizens of Hanover, this is an important announcement," the radio said. The Russians had told everyone that there would be an important announcement to make sure that everyone was listening at 9pm, the time that they had

set aside for such messages from their occupation authorities. "*Please listen carefully and comply with the instructions in this message.*

> *"In order that the inhabitants of Hanover be integrated properly into the new economic system, it is vitally important that all citizens be registered with the provisional government of the city, in order that formerly employed citizens can be aided to return to work, and unemployed citizens will be found work, payable in good Russian currency. Please report to the nearest government centre within a week, bringing with you your passports, European driving licences, employment details and other forms of identification. If you have a Prisoner's Card, or an Ethnic Entitlements Card, bring those along with you as well. An ID card will be produced for you at the government centre, which must be carried at all times and produced upon demand; failure to either register or produce an ID card after the week will result in arrest and detention. This message will be repeated every hour on the hour."*

Gudrun had hated the thought, every time successive European governments had brought it up; *ID cards*! The French and Spanish had had them and pressure from Progressive factions had forced them to abandon them; Italy's milder version had also been washed away under a tidal wave of public mistrust of the government. Sure, there were cards for prisoners, or Ethnic Entitlement Cards for those who had suffered because of their ethnicity, but they were all wrong; she hated the thought of being nothing more than a number on a card. She knew that others would be feeling the same way…

They massed in the suburbs and began a long march to the remains of the New Town Hall, now the centre of the Russian occupation authorities. The Lord Mayor made the occasional broadcast, but everyone knew that the Russians were pulling his strings; everyone suspected that the Russians might have even had him as a willing ally from before the war. It was easy to look for people to blame; was it the government, the skinheads, the Arabs, the…? There was no way to know for certain, although Gudrun's father had certainly had an opinion; Gudrun considered him, at least in part, a class enemy.

She had sneaked out of the house after her father had left for his seemingly endless task of rebuilding the city's infrastructure. The Russians had rounded up a few hundred trained workers, but they'd been massively over-stretched by the scale of the disaster; the city had tilted on the brink before they had finally managed to save it from drought and starvation. Her father hadn't known about the march; he would only have forbidden her going. The throng welcomed her, as they welcomed everyone willing to join them; they advanced towards the New Town Hall, shouting their defiance at the Russians. Gudrun, now part of the pack, shouted too; *no identification cards, Russians go home…*

The marchers thronged the streets, only vaguely aware of the Russian helicopters that passed over them briefly, taking careful notes. Their shadows sent gloom wherever they touched, but Gudrun was unimpressed and the gloom faded when they vanished again, perhaps having attempted to terrify the students into dispersing. They had failed.

"They can't scare us," a male voice shouted, and the crowd rapidly took up the chant. "Russians out, Russians out, Russians out…"

They had protested before; they had even played a role in the downfall of one German government. The crowd was almost a living thing; Gudrun could feel it as they focused their energy on the Russian guards at the end of the road, a line of Russians deploying themselves to face the crowd; they were useless, the crowd laughed at them and kept going. The wave of energy suffused them; they were unstoppable, the Russians would run, the Russians would hide from the power of the people united…

The Russians opened fire.

The noise of the heavy machine guns tore through the air, shocking the crowd; those hit by the bullets added their own noise to the racket, blood and gore splashing everywhere as the Russians fired directly into the crowd. For many, it was their first sight of blood; they fainted, or screamed, trying to run as the Russian troops waded forwards, weapons raised. Clubs came lashing down on skulls; anyone who tried to fight was gunned down mercilessly. The crowd, stung by a thousand red hot bullets, disintegrated; students and protesters tried to run, only to be herded back by more Russian soldiers, wielding clubs and shouting orders in German.

Gudrun had been one of the lucky ones; she had been knocked to the ground as soon as the shooting started, unhurt apart from bruised knees and bloody scratches on her legs. She tried to crawl away, only to be caught, secured, and thrown towards a group of her fellow female protesters, all forced to sit on the ground with their hands brutally tied behind their backs. The male protesters were rounded up as well; she caught sight of her boyfriend's broken face as the Russians escorted the male protesters into trucks driven by German drivers, all handcuffed to the wheel. She met his eyes, one final time; they were torn with horror and despair.

She didn't want to look at the bodies, or the blood; there were hundreds of bodies waiting for disposal as the Russian soldiers moved through them, inspecting them all, unconcerned about the blood. A handful of mortally wounded protesters were quickly shot in the head, their cries fading away as they were sent into merciful oblivion; a handful of protesters who had been playing dead were found and tossed in with the other trapped protesters. The Russians finally completed their grizzly task and barked orders; Gudrun, despite herself, wasn't blind to the implications of separating the men from the women. Somehow, she didn't think that their fate would be pleasant.

For the next hour, their hands were freed and their legs were shackled together, before they were given their orders; clear up the mess. Some of the girls became hysterical at the sight before them and refused; the Russians simply shot them in the head, leaving only a few hundred girls to clear up the dead bodies. Gudrun forced herself to work, picking up the remains of her friends and fellows; she forced herself not to look as the remains were dumped in the back of several garbage trucks and carted out of the city. Gudrun wasn't religious, but she didn't like the thought of the remains of her friends being dumped in a mass grave; she didn't dare protest. The slightest hint of defiance was met with death. Broken, sobbing, Gudrun worked until the Russians finally pulled them out of the hellish scene, loaded them onto trucks, and sent them out of the city.

She exchanged glances with the other girls. What was going to happen to them? They wondered; were they going to ever see their homes again? Some of them had small injuries, others had nasty-looking wounds; some of them weren't even properly dressed any longer. All of them were covered in blood, staining everything; she felt dirty, disgusting...helpless. Unable almost to breathe, because of the smell, Gudrun was forced out of the van by the Russians, still shackled to the others, and forced into a shower. The cold water was a shock, but it was a relief; the girls tried as best as they could to clean themselves before the Russians escorted them into the next room, and stopped.

"No," Gudrun said, or thought; it hardly mattered now. Their fate had become all too clear; she wondered, suddenly, if the same had happened to the boys, or if they had merely been dumped into a work gang. "No..."

They were facing a horde of Russian soldiers, looking at the girls with expressions that could not be described with mere words. Some of the girls tried to protest, knowing that it would get them killed...but they weren't killed, as the Russians started to undo their trousers and consider the helpless girls. They advanced towards the young girls...

And then the screaming really started.

Interlude Five

Nightmare

It was happening all over Europe.

The Russians had known, of course, about the depth of leftist sentiment in Europe, the feeling that protesters had the right to protest about whatever they liked, without any thought as to the consequences of their actions, or even possible punishment in the future. They had counted on it, flattered it, encouraged it…and ensured that many of the leaders of the 'left' were either brought under their control or disappeared before they could organise pacifist resistance. Many of them were realists and accepted the new world order; many more believed what they said, and had to be removed before they could cause trouble.

The Russians also knew the key to a successful campaign of civil disobedience.

It could be summed up as 'choose your opponent carefully;' the theorists of the left had never grasped that point. Looking for overall examples of people power – India, Mexico, even the Moscow Coup Attempt of 1991 – they had missed the specifics; the people had moved against opponents who had consciences. The British had not mown down the Great Salt March, nor had the Russian soldiers in Moscow fired on Yeltsin and his people; they had cared about their people, or about public opinion. The Russians did not care about either, particularly people who were useless; the students and young adults who thronged the streets of Europe were useless to them.

The wave of violence started and ended quickly. In Warsaw, a sit-down protest ended with the tanks ignoring the bodies in their path and driving over them; seventy died and twelve more were injured and died soon afterwards. In Berlin, students who tried to retake the remains of the centre of government found themselves fired upon, clubbed, and hauled off to detention camps. In France, protesters who had found their way to one of the Arab detention camps and protested the detention found themselves shoved into the camp; for the young women, they had been tossed into hell. Resistance was futile…

As the weeks passed, the Russians worked hard to bring Europe back to a state of normality, offering incentives to civil servants and engineers to return to work. Aided by vast numbers of Russians, the civil servants found themselves serving as Russian agents, registering each and every member of the European population from Ukraine to the Spanish border, excepting only the neutral Swiss. Trained workers found themselves working on rebuilding the shattered transportation infrastructure; farmers found themselves ordered to forget EU regulations and produce as much as they could, paid in Russian money. The Eurobank had been seized; Russian money had become the only legitimate form of tender and only the Russians used it, paying those who worked for them, who in turn used it to pay their own people.

Other factories were reopened and offered contracts with Russian firms. Europe had a high-tech infrastructure second only to America's…and on a fair level of equality with Japan, and a vast amount of technical workers. They found themselves working for the Russians, paid well to improve the Russian technical base and rearm the Russians for a future war. As more and more factories came back online, stripped of the red tape and European regulations, business even began to pick up; the Russians only had small taxes on business. All over Europe, workers were asking the same question; was it really so bad under the Russians?

The unfortunates in the various detention camps might have given them an answer. The Russians had put nearly two million people in the camps, from soldiers and policemen to insurgents and protesters. They now worked through them again, ensuring that they had the prisoners registered, before organising their final disposition. The protesters were informed that for their crimes against the new authority, they would be sentenced to a year of hard labour, helping to clear up the wreckage from the fighting. With new ID cards and uniforms, they found themselves attached to labour gangs and forced to work for a living in their home cities. They were the lucky ones; the remains of the male insurgents, beaten and cowed, were shackled and put to work clearing up the damage they had caused, including burying bodies and removing explosives; the death rate rose rapidly. The female insurgents were sent to Russian brothels; their fate would be worse than that of their menfolk. As a final slap in the face, their food rations included pork; many starved, others broke Islamic Law and ate it to survive.

But they were not the most unfortunate. The soldiers and policemen, those who had survived, had remained shackled in their camps under heavy guard. Day after day, the helpless captives would see new faces as the soldiers who had returned to their families instead of fighting were rounded up and added to the camps; night after night, bursts of gunfire split the air as escape attempts were foiled with deadly force. Fed only gruel and water, the prisoners lost their strength rapidly; they wondered if the Russians intended to simply kill them all without shooting them. One day, however, everything changed; bound and secured, the prisoners found themselves loaded onboard trains that headed east, directly to Siberia. As the weather grew colder, they wondered if they would ever see their homelands again...

Time passed. In the west, Russian forces gathered and a massive logistical effort began, focusing on the final stage in Operation Stalin. Europeans living nearby were removed from their homes and sent elsewhere, clearing the ports for Russian use alone; forced labour was used to clear the damage from the fighting, preparing the ports to support the largest amphibious invasion in the 21st Century...

The Invasion of Britain...

Chapter Forty-Three

Mr Luong Goes to Washington

I have ever deemed it fundamental for the United States never to take active part in the quarrels of Europe. Their political interests are entirely distinct from ours...They are nations of eternal war.
Thomas Jefferson

Washington DC, USA

The paranoia of the Secret Service had only increased a thousand-fold, Ambassador Andrew Luong realised, as he entered the Security Zone around Washington DC. These days, there were only a few regular air flights to Washington directly; only the highest ranking military officers and congressmen were permitted to enter the airspace surrounding the centre of America. Twenty-three years of seemingly endless conflict against a determined and multi-faceted enemy had left the American people all-too-aware of their own vulnerability; while Europe soul-searched over the creation of a European Identity Card, Americans not only had cards, but other tricks as well; no one could be allowed near the world's number one terrorist target without their identity being checked and rechecked. Luong, once one of America's most important Ambassadors, was no exception; they treated him like a suspect right from the start.

Some elements of the paranoia seemed ridiculous, Luong knew, but there was a reason for everything. They checked his blood, the implants hidden under his neck, and his eye-patterns, before escorting him into a secure room and ordering him to undress, inspecting each and every body cavity before presenting him with a White House issue suit – ill-fitting and very uncomfortable – and escorting him through a line of heavy weapons into the heart of the American Government. One enterprising terrorist had literally managed to make a vest that exploded when it reached a certain temperature; the attack had come far too close to success and it would never be allowed to happen again. The White House, the Senate, and the Pentagon were all secured; the workers either lived in them, or they went through the security precautions every time they entered or left the compound.

He smiled as they reached the White House; it was no surprise that the vast majority of Americans chose to telecommute these days, assuming that they weren't one of the unlucky ones drafted into the army. America had full conscription for the war, but not all of the males could be taken for the army; a third of the male population served in one of the armed services, volunteers first, then those who would benefit from a term in the services. It had had an effect; public health was up and crime figures were down. The problem was that America was vastly overstretched and, as he had said to Langford, not well disposed towards Europe.

CNN, which had become more right-wing than Fox following the horrific murder of several of its journalists, had reported on some of the demonstrations. Spanish, Irish and German Americans had demonstrated for helping their countries, but there had been counter-marches of Americans who remembered two long wars to save Europe from itself, only to be rewarded with scorn, disdain, and droll comments about empires. Luong knew that America had made mistakes, including allying itself with Saudi Arabia, but they had meant well; wasn't that enough?

It wasn't. European media had looked for the worst and found it; even some American media had followed the same path of endlessly nitpicking and ignoring all the good that had been done. He was sure that the Shias in Saudi Arabia had welcomed the Americans who had protected them from the mobs that had set out to kill them all, but no, the media had focused on protests at the American presence, because the Shias didn't trust the Americans. Luong didn't blame them, but he blamed the media; the Shias had thought they were going to be abandoned like so many other allies of America. And then Iran, and then Mike Collins, and then…

"The President will see you now," the President's personal assistant said. She was young, Japanese-American, and pretty enough to send heads turning everywhere. If it had been any other President, there would have been suspicions that she did more than just type, but they couldn't say that about President Kirkpatrick. "Please will you come with me?"

The White House had been refurbished after a terrorist missile had destroyed the original Oval Office. The new one was a strange mixture of comfortable, authoritarian, and high-tech, all concentrated in the figure of the slight woman who rose from behind her desk to greet Luong. Her presence was almost overwhelming; it was easy to see why she had a seventy percent approval rating, few would dare vote against her. Luong himself had voted for her.

President Joan Kirkpatrick was slight, but carried herself with immense dignity and *gravitas*; her long red hair was curled up neatly into a teacher's bun and perched on her head, her eyes were both smiling and thoughtful at the same time. She looked like everyone's favourite teacher; she was around forty years old, and looked around fifty. It had been six months since Luong had seen her in the flesh and the change worried him; she had grown older, with grey hairs appearing in her bun.

"Welcome back to the United States," the President said, without further ado. She was a Republican, but that meant less these days; she had expected to sail comfortably into her second term in office before the Russians had launched their war. "I'm very relieved to see that you made it out safely when so many others didn't have a chance."

"Thank you, Madam President," Luong said. The President had been married and then widowed; her husband had died on the *Kennedy* when it had gone down near Iran. There was no questioning her determination to fight the war to the bitter end. "I'm glad to be here."

The President briefly introduced the other men in the room, and then motioned for Luong to begin his story, which he did as quickly as he could. He outlined the warnings, such as they were, the chaos that had enveloped London, and the news that the Russians had invaded Poland and then Denmark. He explained what had happened to Colonel Seth Fanaroff, who was being debriefed at the Pentagon, and how badly EUROFOR had been hurt by the Russians.

"I don't understand how they're moving so quickly," General McDowell said. The President's Chief of Staff was a former tank driver himself. "We had problems in Iraq and Iran because we ran out of fuel."

"They captured stocks, apparently, and pressed drivers into service," Luong said. "There will be places that have hardly felt the touch of the Russian boot yet, but…it's amazing how far you can move if no one is trying to slow you down."

McDowell scowled. "What I want to know is how the hell they – and we – missed it?" He snapped. "They had a massive build up and no one even fucking – begging your pardon, madam – noticed!"

CIA looked uncomfortable. "We did notice," he admitted. "We didn't realise that the Russians had their eye on all of Europe; we thought, from the information that we were getting from Russia, that they were posturing to ensure that they had a favourable deal from Ukraine when the country finally managed to solve its problems. They did it before, at least three other times; the Poles just ended up being treated as the nation of boys who called wolf."

McDowell looked unconvinced. "And our spy satellites?"

"The Russians don't have satellites as good as ours, but they do have a very good idea of what works and what doesn't," CIA said. "They hid the sheer scale of the build up from us; by the time we had a handle on it, it was too late. Our human intelligence sources were either lied to or have been turned; there is no other explanation."

"Morons," McDowell muttered. "You couldn't anticipate my fist if it was right in front of your face."

Luong shook his head slowly. They both had good points; Intelligence was often about guessing from incomplete information, rather than knowing every last detail before it was too late. Dictator-led regimes were very good at security; it was quite possible that the spies had been sending information they believed to be true, rather than simply being Russian double-agents. There was no way to know; heads would be rolling back at Langley for that failure.

"These points can be addressed later," the President said, tapping the table for quiet. It fell very quickly. "The important question is simple; what do we do about it?"

Luong took a long breath. "The British have formally asked for our help, along with the Irish," he said. He spoke rapidly and well, covering all of the issues; the British needed help now. "They're short on everything," he said, finally. "If they don't get help soon, they will almost certainly fall when the Russians come over the Channel."

"I wouldn't bet on that," McDowell said. "We looked at the problem back during the bad old days of the Cold War. It's not like crossing a river."

"The British are certain that the Russians have the capability," Luong said sharply. "In a week, or however long it takes the Russians to get organised, they will launch the Second Battle of Britain; the difference being that they will almost certainly succeed in forcing the RAF to expend its remaining aircraft and units, while grinding away at the Royal Navy with bombers and missiles. There will be nowhere for the British to hide; they don't have the SHORAD assets needed to cover all of their bases, or indeed their cities. It will take time, but time is on the side of the Russians...

"Once they have air cover, they will move in using the transports we have tracked moving down the coast," he continued. "Unless the British get very lucky, they will gain a foothold on British soil and expand their foothold towards London. Once that happens, it's just a matter of time before Britain falls."

There was a long pause.

The President broke it. "Opinions?"

"I have never pretended to be a politician," McDowell said. "I understand that civilian control of the military is supposed to be absolute. However, it is my duty to bring certain points to the President's attention."

"Go on," the President said.

"At the moment, we are heavily committed in Korea; in fact we have two additional divisions heading there to reinforce III Corps after the losses they took in the battle for Seoul," McDowell said. "If we can hold on, we can break the North Korean Army once and for all, and this time, we won't have to worry about Chinese intervention in the north. Kang may go nuts and try to use his nukes, but with the FIELD GREEN system in place, that is no longer the threat it once was... I must stress, however, that the forces in Korea have been in a war zone for a month and they are faltering; they need reinforcements, not the removal of more of their units.

"At the same time, we have a number of units heavily committed across the Middle East, fighting a low-intensity war against various rag-headed factions," McDowell continued. The President scowled; as a woman, she was regarded with scorn and outright hatred by the more lunatic of the factions, some of whom had pronounced her a transvestite because they couldn't understand how she wielded the power of a man. "The game-play is basically simple; where we are strong, there is peace, where we are weak…

"Oh, we're making progress," he admitted, "we're helping our allies build up their own forces and in around ten years, we might even win the war in the Middle East. The sad thing is that the Russians may have done us a favour; their invasion and how they treat known terrorists means that they have done what the European Union refused to do, cut off the funding for the terror factions. The end of the war is finally in sight…"

"At the cost of thousands of European lives," Luong said softly. "Democratic states; democracy, the political movement that we are trying to encourage… lost forever in Europe under the Russians."

McDowell held up a hand. "If I may finish?" Luong scowled, but nodded grimly, privately promising himself that he would fight tooth and nail. "The main rapid reaction force here in the States was the Airborne unit, which we dispatched post-haste to Iceland at their request. We have a handful of National Guard units that are assisting the border patrols and units in Cuba that are holding the island down while the Cuban exiles make good little Americans of them. The long and short of the matter, Madam President, is that the most we can spare is a handful of units, none of which can be moved over to Britain in time to be useful."

He sighed. "We had plans drawn up for a rapid reinforcing of American soldiers in Europe during the Cold War," he concluded. "They included supplies that were pre-positioned in Britain and Germany; these days, we don't have anything in Britain that can be used beyond a handful of isolated airfields that the British kept in mothballs and have reactivated for their current predicament. It would take weeks to move a serious force into Britain, months, if not years, if you want to reverse the conquest of Europe. It can't be done."

The President looked up at him. "There's nothing that we can do?"

"We can send the British some of our supplies – I understand that Canada is doing that already; problem is that they don't have a serious army or serious stockpiles – and we can take in refugees if the British want to try to evacuate some of their population," McDowell said. "We have the *Clinton* sailing near Peru; we can move her down to the Falklands and cover the islands, ensuring that the British don't get knifed in the back by Argentina, therefore allowing the British to withdraw their task force quicker. We can continue to supply them with intelligence and perhaps even transfer a handful of aircraft to them, but...I think that that would be scraping the barrel."

The President glanced at her assistant. "Stephanie, I want to see the Argentinean Ambassador and read him the riot act," she said. "Right after this meeting, if possible; tell him that it's urgent. Are there any other considerations...?"

"Only that an intervention in Europe, even for Ireland, would be politically disastrous," Ambassador Eugene Lockwood said. He had been the Ambassador to France and had been lucky enough to be in America before the war had begun, sending insurgents to attack the embassy and butcher all the staff. Luong didn't like him much; Lockwood had ambitions of becoming President himself one day. "The heat on the Hill makes that clear; senators and congressmen are hearing things like thousands upon thousands of Americans died in two world wars...to make the world safe for the French to take cheap shots at us. They go into their cafes, eat Freedom Fries, and remember how the French and the European Union ensured that American blood would be shed in the Middle East."

He glared around the room. "The trade wars, the economic conflicts, the loss of Britain as a dependable ally...all was caused by the European Union," he snapped. "The General claims that the Russians may have cut off the terrorists; their very public offer to hand over whoever we wanted from Europe has been cheered on the streets. The average Joe and Jane Public would like nothing more than to see Brussels reminded of just how bad the world can be; a few years sucking Russian cock will do that for them. Why waste American lives on helping them when the Russians will collapse in a few years anyway?"

Luong stared at him. "Because they might end up as a threat to us?"

"How can they?" Lockwood asked. "They are going to have to spend years bringing Europe into their empire, and there will be resistance; hell, we can even encourage it for them. After the Europeans start resisting, it won't be long before the Russian Federation – the New Russian Empire – collapses under its own weight."

"I have made a decision," the President said. Luong saw her taut face and knew that the news was not going to be good. "General, I want you to see to sending the British as much in the way of supplies as we can, and accepting refugees as well. Have the NRO continue to send them intelligence, including the latest communications intercepts; they have to know everything."

CIA opened his mouth; the President glared at him, and he closed it again. "We will do as much as we can for them," she said. "Once we end the war in the Middle East, perhaps then there will be a chance to settle scores with Russia, and repay our debt to the British. Andrew..."

"I understand," Luong said. It was real-politic at its shameless worst. "I just wish there was a better way."

Chapter Forty-Four

Waiting

"My mother said violence never solves anything." "So?" Mr. Dubois looked at her bleakly. "I'm sure the city fathers of Carthage would be glad to know that."
Robert A. Heinlein

Near Dover, United Kingdom

It was the waiting that was the worst part.

Two weeks had passed since the Russians had chased the remains of EUROFOR off the continent and into Britain, two long hard nervous weeks. Colonel – he had been promoted for some reason - Stuart Robinson watched as the men under his command prepared part of the defence line, and scowled; the work wasn't going quickly. He had heard, during a brief promotion ceremony, that the remains of the high command had also been worried; if the Russians had managed to force a landing on British soil right after Ostend fell, the,y might well have defeated the British in a single campaign. Robinson might almost have welcomed the battle; the brief interlude with Hazel had only reminded him of how much danger the entire country was facing… and how weak the defences were. The noise of jet fighters, almost every day, reminded those who tried to forget; the Russians were upping the pressure every day.

Dover itself had been completely evacuated – including one very irate landlady who had complained incessantly about stains on the bed – and the city-port was carefully being turned into a strongpoint. The planning had been limited, there just hadn't been the time or equipment; there were accidents, some of them fatal, almost every day. Soldiers were everywhere, seeming to swarm across the land in infinite numbers, but Robinson knew better; there were barely five thousand soldiers committed to defending Dover and the surrounding area, while the remaining infantry, tanks and artillery were held in reserve. It had worried him; Russian satellites had doubtless probed all of the British defences from orbit, and they might try to land somewhere else, perhaps along the south coast, or even north towards Ipswich. Dover seemed the logical target, but the Russians might well know that too; all they had to do was land elsewhere and they would have valuable time to get established before the British forces could react.

"We have submarines in those waters," Major-General Langford had said, when he had seen the General and broached the issue with him. "I know the Russian commander; he'll try to keep the variables down to the lowest possible level, and landing elsewhere will mean exposing his forces for longer."

Robinson had accepted the argument, reluctantly; he still needed more supplies. Several of the soldiers had taken to burning photographs of Princess Diana in effigy; they needed landmines and they had almost none. The Americans had shipped over a few hundred mines and they had been carefully emplaced on some of the possible landing zones, but there were nowhere near enough. If there had been a stockpile maintained by the British…but no, the campaigns to ban the weapons had resulted in only a handful of mines being kept, all of which had been lost in the opening days of the war. They needed weapons, they needed SAM missile launchers; only the fact that they would have never have managed to save one of the CADS from Germany had saved him from facing a court martial over losing it. Intelligence suggested that *Generalmajor* Günter Mühlenkampf had met the death he craved…and failed to slow the Russians down for more than a few moments.

"There are more deserters from the Citizen Force, lad," Sergeant Ronald Inglehart said, interrupting his thoughts. Robinson would never be a Colonel to Inglehart; they had shared too much together. The Citizen Force, conscripted from the young unemployed, were nervous about their chances when the shooting started; they were neither armed nor trained to use weapons. They'd broken out a store of the dreaded and loathed SA80 automatic rifles… but even those old weapons weren't enough to arm every trained soldier who needed arming, let alone louts taken off the streets. The Russians might well regard them as illegal combatants…and so many of them deserted. "Shall I round up some redcaps to find them?"

Robinson nodded. They had had the unarmed soldiers preparing trenches and earthworks; given enough time, they could have made the entire area impenetrable. He didn't think that they would have the time; even with the weapons that the Americans had supplied, the Russians still raided the ground forces as well, causing soldiers to scatter as Russian bombers and fighters shot up irreplaceable equipment before the RAF could beat them off. He wasn't blind to the implications; if the Russians were hammering his force, and their forces were resting and ready to move, they would have yet another advantage.

"Get them back to work," he said, knowing that they would be lucky if they found half of the deserters. Some of them would have vanished into London's teeming suburbs, or Maidstone, or any of a hundred smaller towns and villages in the countryside. They could lose themselves there until close of play, whatever happened; some civilians might even help them. Not everyone thought that the survival of Britain was worth conscription. "Don't take too long over it, however; we don't have time to waste."

He stared into the distance, his mind's eye filling in details; hidden weapon emplacements, hidden bunkers and trenches, the telephone system right out of the Second World War that bound it all together without radiating a single betraying emission. The entire system had been linked into Britain's Internet system; they could download information from the AWACS and use it to plan the defence. The AWACS themselves orbited to the north, out of range of the Russians; the American-supplied tankers floated, waiting for pilots who needed to refuel.

The Russians had learned once that attacking the tankers was an easy way to degrade and diminish the RAF. They would press the attack again until they brought down the other aircraft as well, and then they would land with full control of the skies. Military history explained in quite some detail what happened to units in such conditions; they got pounded into scrap before they even reached the battle. It just didn't seem fair...

And the waiting was the hardest part.

There was a body in Flying Officer Cindy Jackson's bed. The gentle pressure of his presence brought her back to awareness, even as the aches and pains in her body refused to recede. The RAF hadn't flown flight schedules like it was doing now since 1940; even during the days of the Iraq War, there had been more pilots and more planes to handle a limited number of missions. Now, now the RAF was desperately exhausted, desperately overstretched, and seriously outnumbered. Every day, Russian aircraft would fly overhead, challenging the RAF to come out and fight, or watch bombs being dropped with cold precision on the defence lines. The soldiers on the ground were soaking up more Russian ordnance – a bloodless term for dead bodies and blood and gore everywhere – than any British soldier had had to face since the Falklands, and that had been nothing compared to the Second Battle of Britain.

The RAF pilots – and the naval pilots who had been pressed into service – were tired; they were making mistakes. The *Prince of Wales* had flown its JSF fighters to Britain as soon as it could, with some help from American tankers; they'd been added to the defence force, which had reached a high point of seventy aircraft, most of them older than Russian designs. A flight of RAF Tornados had launched a low-level raid on a Russian-occupied airfield in Belgium, the role that had been planned for them during the Cold War and proved suicidal during the Gulf War; all but one of the Tornados had been shot out of the sky. It had been the last attempt to take the war to the Russian bases in France.

She rolled over and contemplated the young French officer in her bed. He had been the bravest of the brave, risking life and limb to fly to Britain with his aircraft, and then to fight on alongside British forces to try to hold the UKADR. Lieutenant Jacques Montebourg might be the senior surviving officer of the French Air Force; only a handful more had made it out in the ships that had fled France as the Russians advanced. A few hundred French soldiers, thousands of helpless and destitute French civilians…she wondered just how long it would be before the Russians launched their invasion of Britain. No one in the RAF doubted that there would be an invasion; the Russians were bound to push their advantage as far as it would go. The Americans weren't going to get involved, but that might well change; if the Russians took Britain, American intervention would become much harder.

She knew that she should sleep, but she couldn't; she was literally too tired to go to sleep. She wanted sleep, but she also wanted to get fucked; Montebourg had proven himself good at giving her what she wanted, but he was sleeping, a design fault in the human male. She remembered the old joke about Adam trading the ability to piss standing up for multiple orgasms; the female body was much better in that respect. She didn't want to be deferred to, or treated as the bitch empress of Godforsakenstan; she just wanted a man who was her equal, who wouldn't bow down to her, and wouldn't take any shit from her.

She sighed, wondering if she should wake him up; duty asserted itself and she left him to sleep. It was odd, mulling on the possible futures she might face; the government had made no attempt to hide from the military personnel what was happening to their counterparts across the Channel. The SAS had small groups on French and German soil, reporting back through American satellites; their reports made grim reading. Mass round-ups of military officers, forced labour from unemployed and Arabs alike, and the compulsory registration of all citizens; she knew what it all meant. As anyone who had lived under the welfare state could testify, a grey man in a grey office with command over the files could dictate who lived and who died, without ever meeting his victims…

Her future…seemed bleak. She had wondered, the year before the war, what would happen to her; sooner or later, the RAF would either promote her for good behaviour, or fire her for bad behaviour. It would have been ironic for them to have promoted her, but…she would have had enough time in grade to be promoted, perhaps even to the point of commanding a Squadron…from the ground. Hell, in other words; she wouldn't even be allowed to fly. Outside the RAF, what career did she have? Her ideal would be to become a private jet pilot, but even that was less rewarding these days…and as for a family…? The men she'd met could either be dominated by her, or tried to dominate her…and she never gave up under pressure. She wanted a partner before she could have children; she had faced, a long time ago, the prospect of being the only surviving member of her family…and the last of her line.

Her hand reached out idly and touched Montebourg's penis; a slow motion and it grew hard in her hand, rising with all the vigour of youth. She climbed on top of him in one movement, gently kissing him as her urges drove her on, before pushing down on him and pulling him inside her, riding him into the light of the morning. It wouldn't be long before they both had to fly again…and so all they could do was make use of what time was left to them.

"I could love you," she whispered to his sleeping form. The pressure of war had brought them together; it wasn't as if they were squadron mates. "I could…and perhaps I will, one day…"

There wouldn't be much time before they both had to fly again.

An unbiased observer, assuming that that mythical entity actually existed, who saw the safe house would have wondered if its owner had known that there was a war coming. That unbiased observer would have been entirely correct; Zachary Lynn had bought the house a few years ago through several different shell companies – records said that the owner was still in residence – and even he had been surprised when he had examined the house in person.

The original owner had been paranoid enough to be Russian, he had decided, after his first visit. He had actually been a South African with a lot to hide. The house was not only set well away from any other human habitation, but had a bomb shelter, a private power generator and military-grade water filter, and a stockpile of food. None of those details appeared on the official records; some private checks had confirmed that no one in authority was aware of the building. He had wondered if he had accidentally stumbled upon a MOD building of some kind, but no, the owner was legitimate. He just hadn't bothered to tell the government what he was building.

Lynn sipped a gin and tonic and waited in the house. The satellite communications network in the house was normal to all, but a very careful inspection; in fact, it linked directly into an FSB satellite that was pretending to be a weather satellite. He had issued orders the week before the fighting had begun; his individual units knew that they would have no orders issued from him unless something went very badly wrong. Many of them would have hidden themselves; what Zachary Lynn didn't know, he couldn't be made to tell. The British would be quite likely to torture him, or indeed any of his agents, but they had only seen 'Control;' how could they connect him with Lynn?

The surprise had been that Daphne Hammond had been arrested. Truthfully, Lynn wasn't all that surprised; she had been trying to raise civilian protests against both conscription and the military government. If there hadn't been a clear and present danger, and indeed real benefits to military orders, lovely Daphne might have even managed to do real damage, but instead she had been threatened with lynching, and then the Police had rescued her. Personally, Lynn would have left her to die, even though she had been useful… and would be useful in the future. The danger, however, was that she knew 'Zachary Lynn' and could tell her interrogators everything about him, or at least enough to set them on the right track.

It hardly mattered now, from the point of view of the overall war; Lynn had carried out his mission and had done it well, well enough to distract the British long enough for his people to carry through and defeat the Europeans. They would invade soon, he had been told, or if not he could leave the house one night and be extracted by a Russian submarine. He was sure that other commandos had been landed on British soil; the British ships had been badly damaged and the Royal Navy was straining the limits trying to block Russian submarines from moving into position. His work, again…

But there was his failure. He had failed to find the location of the new government headquarters. There had been something missed, something that would have sent the British into the same kind of anarchy as the French and Spanish had it been destroyed; the British had a secret command post somewhere. Where? He had devoted a great deal of effort to finding it before Daphne had been arrested and drawn a blank; he didn't even have a rough location. If he could find it, he could end the war…but he had no idea where to start looking, and he was trapped in the house. He had studied maps, wondering; logically, it was somewhere near London, but where?

He sat back and smiled. Whatever else happened, he had done his duty, played the role of serpent in the garden to the best of his ability…and helped his country win the war. All he had to do was survive; his people would reward him for what he had done.

"More possible contacts, Captain," the sensor operator reported, as the *Winston Churchill* moved through the dark waters. "I think…I'm sure there was a Russian submarine out there, just for a moment."

"Go active," Ward ordered. "See if you can locate the bastard!"

The odds were that the Royal Navy had expended several dozen torpedoes on large fish and perhaps wrecks under the sea, but every contact had to be investigated. Only yesterday, a Type-45 destroyer had been sunk by a Russian submarine; the Russians were forcing them out of the English Channel. The *Winston Churchill's* luck had run out after they had escaped the chaos surrounding Gibraltar; they had been bombed several times and damaged, only dumb luck had kept them alive.

"Got him," the sensor officer crowed. The exultation in his voice made up for a lot of dangerous fighting. "One Russian attack submarine, trying to sneak out again when we pinged him the first time."

"Target designated," the weapons officer said. He grinned savagely. "Captain?"

"Fire at will," Ward ordered. A torpedo lanced away from the *Winston Churchill*. "I want this bastard sunk and disposed of..."

A burst of water appeared on the screens from an underwater detonation. "We hit the bastard," the weapons officer said. Their third kill. "I think they're gone completely."

"Captain," the exec said, very quietly. "Look."

Ward followed his gaze and cursed; the screen that was permanently pointed at the carrier was blinking up red light. HMS *Ark Royal*, a tiny joke of a carrier and their only source of air cover, was burning. Someone else had just scored a kill.

And the war went on.

Chapter Forty-Five

The Final Countdown

If I always appear prepared, it is because before entering an undertaking, I have meditated long and have foreseen what might occur. It is not genius where reveals to me suddenly and secretly what I should do in circumstances unexpected by others; it is thought and preparation.
Napoleon Bonaparte

Near Brussels, Belgium

"I cannot say that I am happy about it," General Aleksandr Borisovich Shalenko said, very calmly. "How many have died in the brief confrontations with the steel of our power?"

"How many of them were worth anything?" FSB General Vasiliy Alekseyevich Rybak countered. He had been placed in overall command of the occupation of Europe, leaving Shalenko in command of the forces massing along the west coast for the final stage of the campaign. "How many of them were actually inclined to help us, or at least to obey? Dissent is one thing; outright disobedience is another."

Shalenko said nothing. "We have to establish ourselves as The Boss and make sure that all of Europe knows it," Rybak said, looking up at the third man in the room. "You may have taken the girls out of the camps we established for the Arabs, but overall, you know that there was no choice; order had to be maintained."

"And others will be driven to try to fight us," Shalenko said, irritated. "The supply lines are still quite flimsy; a capable insurgency in Germany would force us to postpone the campaign for several months, perhaps long enough for the British to convince the Americans to interfere, or..."

"There was little choice," President Aleksandr Sergeyevich Nekrasov. The Russian President leaned forward, his face steeped with gravity; both men had protested loudly at his decision to visit Brussels. If the British found out about it in time, they might decide that the target was worth expending their remaining cruise missiles on an assassination attempt. The President was the one man Russia could not afford to lose. Without him, the new world order might totter…it might even fall. "We could not allow our supply lines to be limited even for a moment."

Shalenko nodded grimly. In many ways, Russian control over France and parts of Germany had been an illusion, in the early days. The supply lines had been far too long, and even if most of the fight had gone out of the French, and their Arab enemies, the Russians had been running a serious risk. The plan hadn't worked perfectly, but in the end…it had worked well enough. It was Spain that might prove a later problem; the multi-sided war raging there was sending thousands of refugees into France, all of whom had to be registered and put to work. Even a month after the Battle of Lorraine, the Russian grip on some parts of France was weaker than he would like, and there were entire armies lost somewhere within the mountains of Scandinavia. They dared not have their supply line disrupted…and they dared not create an insurgency in their rear; for the first time, Shalenko understood the problems that had faced European politicians since the first wave of immigration to Europe.

"There are even signs that large parts of the population are happier under us for the moment," Rybak pressed, taking his advantage and running with it. "They have law and order on their streets, the Muslims make scapegoats for all their ills…and they're stripped of red tape, taxes and nonsense that the European Union created to limit productivity. Many of the older ones were even sick of the protesters and their protests…"

"Those who haven't lost people to your…men," Shalenko injected.

"And they're quite happy to help us," Rybak continued. "The teams examining the European technical base and working on using it for our own advantage are working fairly quickly and developing other possibilities from it for later use. The Americans snatched the ESA launching base in South America – wisely, as we had hoped that one of our allies there would pick up on it – but the remainder survived fairly intact. Large wages, perks and rewards…they should be back to full productivity soon."

He paused; the President invited him to continue with a raised eyebrow. "Italy took the worst damage and the worst bloodshed; bloodshed by native Italians, as opposed to immigrants and Arab soldiers," Rybak said. Shalenko smiled thinly; the Algerians and Libyans had probably worked out that they had been screwed by now, but what were they going to do about it? Complain to the Americans? The United Nations? "By the time we got there, the Pope was thinking about committing suicide to avoid falling into the hands of one faction or another; our paratroopers saved his life and made him our prisoner. His support was invaluable, but Italy will be the poorest of the new territories for a long time. In time, however, they will be back to full productivity as well."

"Good," Nekrasov said shortly. He shared a thin smile with Shalenko; both men knew that the President's judgement about the Americans and the United Nations had been correct. The Americans had furiously denounced the invasion, but they had limited themselves to seizing Iceland and trying to send some supplies to the British, both expected. Rumour had it that the Canadians were sending some of the Eurofighters they had purchased from Europe to the British, but Shalenko doubted that that would get very far; the Canadians had their own worries about Russia. "That brings us to the final issue; Operation *Morskoi Lev*."

Shalenko smiled. He had chosen the name himself. He felt that it suited.

"We have continued air raids against the British bases and naval facilities since we drove them into the sea at Ostend," he said. They had also put thousands of Arabic men to work as forced labour, clearing up the damage caused by heavy fighting across the region, as well as moving the population out. Most of the citizens now had identity cards; unsurprisingly, the process had slowed slightly as the Russians had found themselves working on other problems. The one attempt by the Arabs to resist had been treated with deadly force; the survivors learned the lesson and worked. Besides, they had been promised access to their womenfolk if they worked hard. "The results have been quite promising."

He tapped the display in the bunker, hoping again that the British had no idea where it was; it was a tempting target even without Nekrasov's presence. "The largest force the British have deployed against us was twelve aircraft at a time; their numbers have been falling sharply to the point that several of our probes and raids were completely unopposed. We focused our efforts on the bases they were using to resupply their aircraft and forced them to fight; they must be running out of energy by now. They're definitely conserving advanced weapons; only a handful of missiles were fired over the last week."

"Perhaps they've run out," Rybak said. "They can hardly have an unlimited supply, even with American help…and the Americans can't have an unlimited supply either."

Shalenko scowled. One thing they hadn't anticipated had been the Americans taking over security duties for the Falklands; they had hoped that the British would either be challenged by the Argentines, forcing them into a desperate and futile struggle against superior forces, or pull out their task force and allow the Argentines to take over the Falklands without a fight. The Americans had told the Argentines flatly that the Falklands were under their protection and any attempt to alter the balance of power would be severely punished. The presence of a large American carrier nearby added teeth to the threat; the Argentines had reluctantly backed off, for the time being.

"Wishful thinking," he said, dismissing the hope. "If they know what we're planning, they will save everything for the most dangerous part of any landing operation, the moment when the troops are being unloaded. Once they are certain that we are not bluffing, they will throw everything they have into the battle, where it will be destroyed, terminating the RAF once and for all. Our air supremacy will ensure that the landing zones remain secure, and then we will probe up towards London. At some point, we will meet the remainder of the British Army…and crush it."

He had given serious thought to landing elsewhere; Rybak put his thoughts into words. "Should we not attempt to avoid a major battle until we have a large force on the ground?"

"I thought about that," Shalenko admitted. The plan had been hashed over, time and time again, stripping out as many of the variables as possible. There would be surprises – no campaign was ever fought without surprises – but he hoped that most of them would be limited. "The problem is that we have to crush the British Army; the British will have had time to burn records and destroy bases and generally make it impossible for us to be sure who has military experience, or not. If we can kill them all, or at least catch them quickly, then we won't have to worry about an insurgency later."

Rybak smiled coldly. The different Russian services had watched the American struggles in Iraq and later Iran with the greatest of interest, learning different lessons for different services. The army had learned about tanks that could be used for fighting insurgents, the navy had learned about cruise missiles, the air force had learned about heavy bombing…and the FSB had learned how much trouble former soldiers could cause. The remaining soldiers in Europe, surrendered or captured, would be sent to Siberia; let them work there or die.

Shalenko followed his thoughts. Europe was being quietly purged of elements the Russians disliked, or openly loathed, a long list ranging from former right-wing and left-wing leaders, to media reporters. Some were being given offers they couldn't refuse – work for the Russians or go to Siberia, or a work gang, or meet a bullet in the back of their heads – or were simply eliminated to terminate whatever problems they might have posed. The population at large was unaware of the tectonic shifts occurring under their feet; the absence of most media channels – replaced with a bland diet of soaps and television shows – hid much from their eyes… even the news from America was mainly sensationalist. Europeans saw the talking heads on CNN and FOX and GNN and knew that America had abandoned them; many would seek ways to please the Russians, rather than opposing them.

And the streets were safe. The Russians had made it clear what had happened to the prisoners who had fallen into their hands, including the death sentence for the dangerous criminals. Many who had been allowed to roam free discovered that the Russians were watching for them; they had the records from Interpol and Europol and used them mercilessly, arresting and executing known serious criminals. Crime was lower than it had ever been… and that too was popular. As long as serious incidents could be kept down…

"Operation *Morskoi Lev*," Nekrasov said, drawing his attention back to the matter at hand. His brief moment of distraction made Rybak smile; the FSB officer understood nothing of the true art of war. "General; how are the preparations for the invasion?"

The use of his rank was a quiet warning; Nekrasov wanted to talk to the General, not to the friend. "The preparations proceed apace," Shalenko said, calmly. "We have twelve divisions prepared for the crossing, using mainly captured European shipping and some of our own ships that we used in Denmark, all based at the cleared ports here. The British have launched several attempts to disrupt the process, but we have enough radars and missile launchers around the ports to make such attempts costly. All, but one, of the aircraft involved in the final attack were wiped out."

His hand traced the map. "Colonel Aliyev and his men will be landed first, here," he said, tapping a location on the map near Dover. "We don't anticipate that the British will leave the port in a useable condition, hence the pre-prepared jetties that we copied from the D-Day invasion years ago; they will be moved over to secured beaches once we have cleared them of mines and other surprises, and then the heavy units will be landed."

He spoke quickly as he outlined the other elements of the plan. "We have over five hundred bombers in position, one hundred of them under the command of Admiral Daniel Sulkin and tasked to destroy the remainder of the Royal Navy's fleet, should it attempt to engage our forces on the surface. Admiral Wilkinson is still ten days away from Britain and in any case flew off his aircraft a week ago; we do not feel that he will attempt to interfere…and if he does, we have the capability to destroy his fleet. The main British naval threat will come from submarines; to counter we have brought along our own submarines and ASW craft, and mines. It may be costly, as they will do what the Taiwanese did, years ago, and concentrate on the transports, but we will land a large force.

"The remaining bombers have their own targets," he concluded. "We have been chipping away at the British transport network; commandos inserted on the ground will be tasked with directing some of the bombers onto British reinforcements and other targets of opportunity, while others will blast British targets we have left alone to lull them into a false sense of security. Once we have total air superiority, we will be able to expand our control and advance towards London for the final battle."

"There is a British civilian population in Dover," Rybak said, needling him. There was a mischievous tone in his voice, quietly taking a verbal sally at Shalenko; the FSB and the Russian Army would never be friends. The secret to controlling Russia was to ensure that the FSB and the Army were used to keep the other in check permanently; President Nekrasov was a master of the art. "How do you intend to handle it?"

"The intelligence reports claim that the British have evacuated most of their citizens from the area," Shalenko answered. "They are not going to be a problem, although we may have to burn Dover rather than take the time to lay siege or accept the death toll involved in storming the city. Once we take London, your forces can fan out and secure the remainder of the country; some of my planners believe that the British will keep evacuating people to Ireland as long as they can, and then get them to America. They have some additional shipping, although less each trip; we're putting pressure on some of the shipping lines to close their operations with Britain."

Nekrasov nodded curtly; the Russians had made it clear that the seas around Europe were a war zone and any shipping that went in without permission did so at serious risk of being sunk without warning. The United Nations had tried to challenge it, but the Americans weren't willing to interfere, and the Turks had led a chorus of African nations that felt Europe deserved everything that was coming to it. In the long term, the Turks would start wondering what the Russians might have in mind for them, but for a few more years, they would be neutral in Russia's favour. The Japanese had protested the Russian declaration of a free-fire war zone, but they were in no position to press the issue; like the Americans, they were wrapped up in Korea and had their interests in China. A very quiet agreement had been proposed; the Russians would say nothing about Japanese plans to guarantee safe zones in China – occupation in all, but name – if the Japanese didn't press the issue of the sea-lanes.

"Which brings us to the final conclusion," Nekrasov said. He smiled tiredly down at his two generals. Shalenko knew what he was about to ask before he asked the question; they had tried hard to answer it. "Can the operation succeed?"

Shalenko weighed all of the factors in his mind a final time. "The operation can succeed," he said, and meant it. The entire plan had been wargamed several times, looking for every possible variable and unknown factor, giving the British far more firepower than they could possibly have, just to be sure that nothing was overlooked. The only real danger was tactical nuclear weapons, and the Russians had made that issue clear to the British Ambassador in Washington; the use of tactical nukes would be responded to with strategic weapons against British cities. It was the only communication that they had had with the British; they had refused to be 'reasonable' about the future. "The losses may be higher than we predict, but the operation can succeed."

Nekrasov nodded once. It dawned on Shalenko that the President was concerned about the final step in the campaign, the final stage of the conquest of Europe. A failure could dispel the newfound impression of Russian soldiers as invincible; it could lead to resistance rising up right across Europe and being brutally crushed...if it could be crushed. The Poles had a long history of rebellions against occupying powers...and while the European Union had helpfully managed to restrict the number of guns in civilian hands, there were still Polish soldiers out there, with Polish criminals armed with illegal weapons. A failure could be disastrous.

Operation *Morskoi Lev* would not fail.

Nekrasov steepled his fingers. "General Shalenko – Alex – I hereby grant you permission to proceed with Operation *Morskoi Lev* at the earliest possible moment," he said. Shalenko understood; when Nekrasov delegated, he delegated all the way. Shalenko was the man on the spot, the one with the understanding of what was happening that no one, even Nekrasov, could grasp back in Moscow. "Launch the invasion of Great Britain."

Chapter Forty-Six

Operation *Morskoi Lev*, Take One

The hour has come; kill the Hun.
Winston Churchill (planned speech if Germany invaded Britain, 1940)

Battlezone, English Channel

"I think that this is it," the coordinator said. Langford peered over her shoulder as the radar screen began to fill with detailed information; there were over a thousand aircraft rising into the air over Europe, many of them staggering under the weight of heavy bomb loads. The two AWACS that the Americans had loaned, added to the two that the British had deployed on their own, were picking apart the Russian formation. "That's an order of magnitude larger than any previous raid."

Langford nodded grimly. The Russians had worked the RAF over pretty hard; unlike Hitler, they had known beforehand that the key to actually winning was air supremacy, if not complete air dominance. They had been able to rotate their pilots through the war zone; Langford and his people hadn't had anything like the same luxury. Their pilots were exhausted; over the last week, they had lost several planes a day, including some of their most modern aircraft.

The American supplies had helped, but they hadn't been enough; the air bridge between Britain and America had been thin and the Russians had broken it more than once. The Americans had been careful to avoid something that would directly threaten the Russians; Langford would have given anything for the 8th Air Force or another American formation just to give the RAF a breather, but that was impossible. The Russians had ground down the RAF...and now they would be coming to finish the job.

"Send the alert down the chain," he ordered. The officers on the ground could pull downloads from the AWACS, but they would need to have the formal warning, just to put all of the emergency plans into operation. "Tell them that I am declaring a formal Cromwell Alert status and that they are to respond and report their positions."

"Yes, sir," the operator said. She paused. "Major Yuppie is calling you on the secure line."

Langford took the handset. "Major," he said. "I take it that you are seeing what we're seeing?"

"Of course," Erica said. There was a hint of relief in her voice; the waiting, at least, was over. "Sir, I know that we have discussed this before, but..."

Langford shook his head. "No," he said. She couldn't see him, of course; there hadn't been the time to create a proper video link for the field headquarters. "One way or the other, I have to make the stand with the army."

Erica snorted, but she didn't press the issue any further. She had wanted him to remain in the CJHQ, exercising command from well behind the lines, so that he could escape with the evacuation ships if it was necessary. Langford had put his foot down; the government-in-exile would be far better operated by a politician, if it came to that. The Ambassador and Foreign Secretary would take the oath as Prime Minister in front of the King; the Royal Family themselves were in Canada. Langford hated the thought of them running out on the country, but again...they couldn't be allowed to fall into Russian hands. The Pope had fallen into Russian hands and he now broadcast from the remains of the Vatican, praising the Russians in one breath and demanding a new crusade against the Muslims in a second. He hated to think what could happen if he fell into enemy hands; he had already determined that whatever happened, he would never allow himself to be taken alive.

"Yes, sir," she said, finally. Langford was watching the display; the force of Russian fighters was starting to advance, zooming ahead of the bombers and heavy transports that had to be carrying parachutists and other surprises. The British had learned that the Russians loved paratrooper assaults; every airport in the entire south-east of England, and most of the other airports in the country, had been rigged with unpleasant surprises. They were short on men, materials, and many other things, but they weren't out of tricks yet. "The Royal Navy is preparing to move in and reach engagement range."

Langford scowled. He hadn't liked that part of the plan; it would cost them, heavily, even if it worked. The Americans hadn't been able to supply many cruise missiles to replace the ones that had been fired during the early days of the war; the remaining fifteen surface combatants of the Royal Navy in home waters would be seriously disadvantaged, the more so because he could spare them no air cover. They would be operating at the limits of their range...and as for the ships from the Falklands, it would still be a week before they were in range. He wasn't convinced that they could do anything, anyway; the Russian control of the air would be absolute by that time.

"Good," he said finally. The submarines had been tasked with interdicting the Russian transports, something that would be difficult with the Royal Navy so badly overstretched and down to eight nuclear submarines. There were two more with Admiral Wilkinson, but they couldn't reach Britain in time to help. The Royal Navy, he suspected, was about to fight its last battle. "And the RAF?"

"Fighters are scrambling now," Erica said. "Operation Mousetrap has been activated and the American weapons are in place. If we can use it, we might just have a chance to limit the number of bombs and commandos dropped on our soil."

Langford tried hard to feel optimistic. They'd caught and captured several dozen Russians as they had attempted to launch more terrorist attacks, or killed others who refused to surrender, but there had been brutal fire-fights breaking out all along the defence line as Russian commandos had been slipped onto the shore and sent to wreak havoc and force the soldiers to become nervous in their trenches. No one knew how many Russians might have successfully made it into Britain undetected; a handful had escaped one of the refugee camps, having managed to sneak onboard a refugee ship.

"Good," he said again. What else could he have said? The pattern on the display was becoming more and more ominous all the time; the Russian fighters were streaking forward, hoping to force the RAF into a decisive battle. "And the evacuation?"

It had seemed as if everyone in Britain had wanted to flee the Russians; after CNN had broadcast some of the reports from occupied Europe, it was hard to blame them. The ports had been crammed with people wanting to flee, to get away somewhere, anywhere; there had even been more rioting as the fate of European Muslims under the Russians became clear. Langford had had to quell some of the riots with extreme force and ignore others; the only priority was to fight the final battle. If they could smash the Russian Army when it landed…

"The personnel marked for evacuation have been dispatched to the ports," Erica assured him. They had given priority to the relatives of serving soldiers and policemen; the police, in particular, had done wonderful work. There was something of the old determination and ethos left in them after all; Langford only wished that it hadn't taken a war and a threatened invasion to bring it to the fore. A handful of technical experts had been dispatched as well; the Americans had been insistent, once they had realised that the Russians were starting the long process of renovating the European technical base and using it for their own benefit. "Everything will be handled smoothly."

"I hope you're right," Langford said. The American satellite data was buzzing up new warnings; the Russian transport fleet had set out to sea and Russian missiles were being launched towards targets on the ground. "I'll see you again soon."

"God willing," Erica said. They had become friends in the terrible two months; he wished that he had known her before the war had begun. "For what it's worth, sir, it was a honour to serve with you."

Clutching their weapons, they waited all along the line; some confident, some nervous, some anticipating the moment when they would come to grips with the enemy. For some of them, it was their first shot at real combat; many of them had escaped being sent to Sudan. For others, it was the chance to avenge fallen comrades and even the score a little before there could be peace. They took their positions with care and forethought, hiding from the bombers they knew would soon be high overhead; it wouldn't be long before they discovered if they were brave soldiers, or cowards. No one knew until they came face to face with the elephant. Some said their final prayers as they braced themselves; Christian, Muslim, Jew, Hindu…united at last in defiance against the common foe. Others only waited for it all to begin. History was moving around them…

In Dover, Folkestone and a dozen smaller towns and villages, smaller detachments lurked. They had prepared the docks to surprise the Russians as best as they could; now they waited for the Russians to come within range of their weapons. They had prepared the towns and buildings for house-to-house fighting; the Russians would be forced to dig them out one by one if they wanted the towns. Many of them had sworn terrible oaths; the Russians would have to kill them all at their posts before they took the places they were defending.

Further back, mobile artillery and other systems waited, holding fire only until they had targets to service. The crews checked their vehicles carefully; they had seen all of the data from the handful of heavy battles the Russians had fought in Europe, and the Battle of Lorraine had made it clear; the Russians would hammer them into the ground as soon as they detected their fire and localised their position. They had prepared to move as soon as the Russians found them; they were determined that they would make the Russians pay a price for invading their country. Direct feeds to a hundred hidden soldiers, lurking near possible landing zones, lit up; all they needed now was targeting data, targets to destroy. It wouldn't be long now.

All along the line, they waited.

"I have a direct lock on seven heavy enemy transports," the weapons officer snapped, as the *Winston Churchill* evaded a missile from a Russian aircraft with ease. The Russians had concentrated most of their efforts on suppressing the land defences over the past few weeks and it showed; the Royal Navy had had enough time to muster its final stand. "Captain; request permission to open fire."

Captain Ward nodded slowly. The fighting was taking its toll… because they didn't dare head any closer to the Russian-held coastline. The *Winston Churchill* had grown up in a world where missiles and guided-bombs presented a serious threat to ships…and no ship in existence, with the exception of the really big carriers, could survive a single hit with a heavy warhead. Her class might have been designed as the closest thing the European Union had to a battleship, but her armour was puny compared to that of the battleships that had last contested the Channel, back in 1940.

"Engage the enemy," he said, as the first of the sea-skimming cruise missiles started to launch. The *Churchill* normally carried twenty-four; the battles had drained their stocks down to nine, and seven of them had just been launched against moving enemy transports. He understood the logic – without the transports, the Russians would be unable to land their army – but they had a *lot* of transports. Had they commandeered every last civilian ship in Europe? There had been hundreds of ships, many of them registered under different flags; had all of them been brought to land soldiers on British soil? "Air defence?"

"Four enemy bombers, heading towards the fleet's location," the air defence officer reported. Ward cursed; they had fired off most of their SAM missiles, and all they had left apart from that was the CIWS units, which were known to run out of bullets quickly. Replenishing them hadn't been a problem – something that had been a relief, as they were around the only items that could be replaced quickly – but there would be no time to re-supply in the middle of a battle. "Requesting permission to engage."

"Coordinate fire with the other ships and engage at will," Ward snapped. "Weapons?"

"Three direct hits; they went up like firecrackers, Captain," the weapons officer said. "Russian CIWS killed the other missiles and saved the transports!"

Ward cursed under his breath. "Bring us around and regain firing solutions," he ordered. "I want..."

"Captain, the Russian aircraft are launching missiles," the sensor officer said. "I have at least nine missiles homing in on our location!"

"Evasive action," Ward ordered, sharply. The Russians were trying to smother them; they were making up for problems in some of their targeting systems by overloading the British point-defence network. "You are cleared to engage the missiles with CIWS!"

The yammering of the guns could even be heard on the bridge...and then they stopped. "Weapons jam, weapons jam," the weapons officer snapped. "Three incoming missiles..."

HMS *Winston Churchill*, the last of her class, took three hits along the superstructure. The Russian warheads punched though the thin hull and detonated inside the ship, destroying the entire vessel in a shattering cataclysm. There were no survivors.

"I have fourteen Russian fighters advancing towards you, nineteen more holding in reserve," Lieutenant Jacques Montebourg snapped, over the command network. "They're trying to draw the RAF out to play..."

"I love you too, Jacques," Flying Officer Cindy Jackson said, as she banked the Eurofighter Tempest out over the south-east of England, waiting for the Russians to come calling. The Russians looked as if they had expected the RAF to come engage them right in the heart of their formation, and before the Americans had made their unexpected delivery, the RAF had planned to do just that. "We'll hold position and wait."

There were thirty fast-jet fighters left in the RAF, mainly Typhoons and Joint Strike Fighters from the Royal Navy; Cindy knew that it was their last shot. She'd had it made brutally clear to her; if the RAF could knock out the Russian transports, it might just save Britain from Russian occupation. The Russians themselves were coming forward towards the British fighters; a handful more were remaining with the transports, probably cursing their luck at being stuck shepherding the slower aircraft. Fighter jocks were all the same; the Russians had a three-to-one advantage, just in the battlezone alone, and they weren't going to waste it. They were coming towards her aircraft at supersonic speed and...

Someone down on the ground flicked a switch. A dozen CADS and several light American launchers that had been prepared for auto-fire opened fire, mingled in with old Rapier and Javelin systems, sending nearly a hundred SAM missiles into the air. The Russians, caught by surprise, scattered; many of them had already become victims as the American-made missiles locked onto their aircraft and entered their terminal runs. Some Russian pilots punched out of their aircraft, choosing to risk capture rather than die in fire; others tried to evade until the very last moment.

"Go," Cindy snapped. The RAF fighters hit their afterburners and streaked south-east at supersonic speed, their weapons systems already receiving the download from the AWACS as they passed over the hidden weapons and headed into the teeth of the enemy transports. A handful of Russian fighters, the surprised escorts, were desperately trying to come into position to take a shot at her, but it was too late; they were too late. The RAF fired a hail of missiles towards the Russian transports and bombers, ignoring the fighters; twenty-three Russian aircraft exploded midair as the RAF blew through them and kept firing, engaging every last target they saw. Russian fighters were trying to chase them out again, but the Russian formation was falling out of shape; their fighter controllers had to be going mental just trying to keep up with the rapidly changing situation. She laughed aloud, jamming her hand down on the trigger for her cannons; a Russian transport aircraft and its parachute soldiers died under her fire.

Her threat receiver screamed an alarm, moments before a tail gunner put a handful of rounds into the Tempest, which screamed in pain. She heard noises she had only heard in simulations as the aircraft started to disintegrate around her, but she couldn't eject, not in the middle of the battle. That would almost certainly be guaranteed suicide; the Russians had fired on ejecting RAF pilots before, another trick to weaken the RAF still further. She still had weapons and options; she still had some possible tricks she could pull...

And there was one weapon left. Pointing the remains of her aircraft towards another aircraft, she reached for the ejection lever...too late. Her Tempest crashed into a Russian transport and both aircraft vanished from the sky in a tearing fireball. No one ever found a trace of Flying Officer Cindy Jackson, or her aircraft.

General Shalenko gritted his teeth as the losses came in. They had expected losses, and they had almost wiped out the Royal Navy in exchange for losing several transports and ASW craft, but the losses in fighter craft were appalling. It hardly mattered; they had crippled the RAF and slaughtered the Royal

Navy. They still had most of the transports intact and the soldiers were waiting for a chance to come to grips directly with the enemy. He wouldn't let them down; Russians knew that victory was worth the price.

He turned to his aide. "Give the order," he said, addressing her directly. "Deploy the landing force."

CHAPTER FORTY-SEVEN

OPERATION *MORSKOI LEV*, TAKE TWO

Not one step back! Such should now be our main slogan.... Henceforth the solid law of discipline for each commander, Red Army soldier, and commissar should be the requirement—not a single step back without order from higher command
Stalin

BATTLEZONE, ENGLISH CHANNEL

The transport nearest his aircraft blew up in a massive explosion, tossing Colonel Boris Akhmedovich Aliyev's aircraft across the sky, sending a ripple of muttered curses up from the parachutists as they braced themselves for their coming mission. They had prepared for it as best as they could, but Aliyev knew – they all knew – that it would be their most dangerous yet. Nearly the entire paratrooper force had been committed to the mission, under a GRU General; failure was not an option.

"That was a RAF aircraft ramming a transport," Captain Boris Lapotev called back. Lapotev had been delighted to be at the controls of a genuine military transport again; the modified civilian aircraft would have been sitting ducks in the raging air battle, and the British would have known that they were hostile. All British civilian aircraft had been sent to the west of England, or to Scotland, where they laboured to evacuate as much of the population as possible. Aliyev knew enough about logistics to doubt that they had a serious chance of evacuating the entire population; it was far more likely that they wouldn't be able to get more than a few hundred thousand out at most, assuming that the Americans and Canadians were willing to keep taking them in. "Poor, brave, stupid bastard."

Aliyev shrugged. He had spent time fighting the Poles when they had rallied, only a few hours too late, to attempt to retake the airport. They had been brave as well, and determined; the few prisoners had all been heavily injured before the Russians had captured them. The civilians caught in the war zone had suffered badly; they would be repatriated to their home countries as soon as possible. Aliyev had promised them that and...well, he wasn't an FSB butcher. He wouldn't have hesitated to drive over them if they had been blocking his route, as the FSB had done in Warsaw, but he wouldn't slaughter for no tactical purpose.

"Five minutes to jump point," Lapotev said. Aliyev found himself tensing; he would be first out of the aircraft, as happened most of the time. Once they landed, they could expect to be attacked almost at once; if they were unlucky, the British might even shoot at them as they were falling out of the sky. It was early morning, but by now the British would be on the alert and gunning for the Russians with everything they had. "The air force is moving in first."

"Air farce," someone muttered, in the semi-darkness of the plane. Aliyev ignored it; the soldiers could bitch and moan as much as they liked, provided they obeyed. The policy of openness had transformed Russian life and it would not be failed in his unit. "They'll probably have left so that we get roasted as well."

"Two minutes," Lapotev said. "Prepare for jump."

Aliyev shuffled towards the hatch as it yawned open, revealing the English Channel being replaced by beaches and patchwork fields, heading over a large motorway and back into the countryside. The sky was lit up by explosions and glowing missile trails; the British had their backs to the wall and knew it. It was possible, more than possible, that they would fire a missile at his aircraft; he would have no time to pitch himself out of the aircraft and survive the fiery death of his comrades.

The Russian air force had been intended to assault their landing zone with bombs and napalm; the British could not be allowed a moment to realise that they had suddenly been dropped right into the front lines. Russian Intelligence had gone through all of the satellite images and other photographs taken by reconnaissance aircraft and had concluded that the British had prepared defences along the A20, between Dover and Folkestone; it made sense, from a tactical point of view. The British had to know that they would be assaulted from the sea and there weren't that many places to land, short of a suicidal dash into a port. Denmark had been taken by the Trojan Horse trick, but the British would never let anything land in a port without inspecting it carefully. Once bitten…twice very shy; it would be a long time before anyone relaxed their guard.

"One minute," Lapotev snapped. His voice was becoming more excited as an explosion rocked the aircraft. "The bombers have gone in!"

Aliyev counted down the moments as the paratroopers lined up behind him. The aircraft had been built purposefully for the deployment of paratroopers and it showed; they would be tossed out of the aircraft, along with some boxes of equipment, very quickly, and then the pilot would return to France and pick up more paratroopers. Aliyev wouldn't be allowed to remain without reinforcements; the mission was too important for them to be allowed to fail. They would take the British in the rear, and then they would allow the naval infantry to assault the beach and allow the soldiers to land. Failure was not an option.

A shrill whistle blew; seconds later, he was falling through the air, the wind blowing at him as he plummeted towards the ground. The thrill of it reached through to him, just for a moment, as the English countryside grew in front of him; the war didn't exist as he screamed in exultation…

Professionalism reasserted itself and he pulled the chute, sending it billowing out above him, catching the wind and slowing his fall to the bare minimum. The old Soviet Union had used dangerously slow descents; the newer Spetsnaz parachutes barely slowed the soldiers enough to prevent them from breaking their legs as they fell. Bursts of smoke were rising from the ground; he could smell the sickly-sweet roast pork smell of burning human flesh. He had smelled it before, but it never failed to make him sick; there were few fates worse than being burnt alive.

He could see a handful of British soldiers trying to fire at the parachutes as they came down, but it was too late now; even the bullet that cracked through his parachute and tore a steadily-expanding hole was too late to prevent him landing and bringing his weapon into firing position. Others from his unit had done the same; the British were mown down in a brief exchange of fire. Four of his own men had fallen.

"Rally," he shouted. The British would have seen them coming down and were doubtless preparing to react in any number of interesting and painful ways. There were plenty of ways to wipe out infantry and the British knew most of them; his soldiers formed up and advanced quickly before anything could happen. The motorway lay ahead; behind it, facing the sea, there were British trenches and even a handful of British armoured units. "All units; attack!"

The paratroopers had not passed unnoticed; British soldiers were already turning to attack them. A deadly series of fire-fights began, up and down the trench; both sides were calling in requests from their support units. Aliyev called a bomber into position to drop napalm and smoke grenades on the British; the British answered with long-range fire from hidden guns further into Britain. Aliyev dispatched a handful of his men to find the guns and assault them; those were light weapons that would otherwise be pouring fire into the transports and smaller ships convoying soldiers from France to Britain. He glanced down at his watch; ten minutes. Had it really been that long? It felt as if the fighting had gone on forever...

"Tank," someone shouted, as four light British tanks appeared, heading towards the Russian soldiers as they scattered under its fire. The commandos couldn't move; it was vitally important that they kept the British focused on them, rather than on the seas. It wouldn't be long before the first ships arrived and began to unload soldiers and equipment to assault and hopefully take the British ports nearby. The smaller commercial jetties and piers would probably have been mined, but the engineers had had lots of practice at disarming IEDs from Chechnya. "Tank..."

"Take them out," Aliyev snapped, into his short-range radio. Several anti-tank rockets were fired, designed to kill early Abrams and Challenger tanks, perhaps even Eurotanks if they were lucky; they made short work of the Scimitar tanks. The British kept up the pressure; it felt as if they would never be forced out or defeat the British. The entire campaign had boiled down to one long endless fight...and there seemed to be no end in sight.

Anton Mihailovich Sviridov, stripped of all rank and status, swam ashore through warm water, praying to a God he had abandoned long ago that he would make it safely through the British defences and onto the shores, and then perhaps to his old rank. *Sergeant* Sviridov had been having some fun with a German girl – the FSB had been given German girls to have fun with, but the common soldiers had been left with the prostitutes, and besides, Sviridov had fought his way through Germany and needed some fun – when the military police had caught him. The girl – naturally – hadn't realised that as a victor, her body belonged to him; she had claimed that he had taken her against her will.

So what? He had argued, when he had faced his commanding officer; the girl was a slut. All German and European girls were sluts; the Russians had seen more legs and breasts in their march across Europe than they had seen in anywhere else they had visited, from Moscow's own Red Light district, to places in Central Asia where the women remained covered and well out of sight of Russian patrols. She had teased him, and taunted him, and played hard to get, but he had known what she had wanted from the moment she smiled at him. She had wanted it rough, she had wanted the illusion of submission…and Sviridov had been happy to oblige.

The argument had cut no ice with his commanding officer. Looting, rape and unnecessary property damage were officially forbidden, and that meant a spell in the penal units for Sviridov. His rank and campaign medal had been stripped from him and he had been forced to wear the bright pink uniform of a penal soldier; pink in the hopes that the enemy would take a pot-shot at the obvious target rather than the more sanely dressed combat soldiers. After a short spell clearing up debris alongside imprisoned Arabs and the male survivors of various protest groups – he had taken some delight in telling them what had happened to the girls who had survived the protest – he had been sent along with his unit, like prisoners, to a base in Belgium.

"If you survive this, you will be freed in advance," the military policeman had informed them. Sviridov had three weeks left of his sentence, during which all he could expect was hard and dangerous work; he had gratefully accepted the offer as a way of regaining his old rank. His seniority would be permanently stripped from him, but he would have his rank back and in the future he would stick to the brothels; there was a constant stream of young women looking to earn money and rations lying on their backs. "If you survive…"

Sviridov had known how to swim, of course – it was a required skill in the Russian Army – but he had never swum in a sea before. He had heard that some officers had intended the penal soldiers to literally swim the entire

Channel, but sanity had prevailed before the Russian officers could take the chance to free themselves of a liability and send the penal soldiers on a suicide mission. Their current mission wasn't much of an improvement; if they faltered, or if they were slowed, the FSB marksmen in the boats would shoot them down on the spot. The water covered his head, a foul-tasting brine, and he was almost sick as he crawled up the beach, almost gasping in horror as he saw a crab for the first time. He didn't take chances; he brought his foot down on the animal hard and then started the advance up the beach.

The mission brief had been simple; the British would have mined the beach and prepared booby-traps. Sviridov and his unit had to clear all of the traps, a mission that would win them their freedom...or kill them all if they failed. The beach was strewn with wire and seaweed; the soldiers started to pull at the wire, wincing as British soldiers fired at them from time to time, the fire answered by the heavy guns on the naval infantry transports as they grew closer. A shell landed close to him and the shockwave picked him up, tossing him head over heels towards the water; he had a chance to see the approaching wave of naval infantry as they stormed towards the shore.

He forced himself back to work. Penal soldiers were held in contempt by all other soldiers; many of them wouldn't pause to piss on one if he were dying of thirst. The wire was reaching up a stairway heading towards the British lines; Sviridov pulled at it carefully, wondering what the British had been doing with it. The wires wouldn't snarl up a tank's engines; they would be lucky if they slowed down armed infantry. For a moment, the sound of firing seemed to die away as he crawled onwards, not daring to stop for fear of being shot in the back...and then he heard an audible *click*.

Oh shit, he thought, as he realised in a split-second that he had triggered a mine. Moments later, his body was blown to bits by an improvised explosive device...and the Russian naval infantry stormed onwards, heading towards the British lines, now caught between two fires. The might of the Russian Navy was about to be displayed on land for the first time since Denmark.

It was confirmed; the Russian's main landing site had been identified. Orders were sent out rapidly to the units caught in the firing line; they were ordered to break contact and pull back to the second defence lines as quickly as they could. For many of them, it was an impossible task; the Russian paratroopers might have been melting away, but the Russian naval infantry were hard on their heels, searching for targets. They knew that they were vulnerable; the cold knowledge made them deadlier than ever.

Further back in the British lines, expertly camouflaged, the remaining MLRS trucks in the British Army opened fire, sending a shower of deadly rockets down onto the Russian positions. The rockets had been supplied by the Americans, an improved version of the original rounds; they homed in on tanks and ships, often mixing kinetic speed with explosive force to knock out and destroy Russian tanks and landing ships. Others came in closer; a captured German liner was driven aground and Russian naval infantry stormed out of her, heading up the beach towards their rally points, and then being dispatched to link up with the paratroopers and expand their zone of control. Other naval infantry had to swim, or use smaller boats, but they made it to the shore; officers rapidly sorted out the chaos into slightly more organised chaos and directed them to their pre-planned points. The invasion would continue.

Far out to sea, Russian Mainstay AWACS tracked the location of the MLRS and directed bombers onto them as priority targets, along with the located positions of British soldiers. The British had come up with a handful of tricks, including American-supplied missiles and cannibalised CIWS taken from ships that had been damaged beyond repair, hacking bombers out of the sky as long as the missiles held out. The supplies had always been low; a handful of the MLRS trucks were caught on the ground and destroyed by the bombers, two more were hunted down by Russian helicopters as they started to enter the battle. The motorway had been secured rapidly and penal units were dispatched to clear the mines as far as the defences of Dover and Folkestone; the entire shore would have to be cleared to allow the plan to proceed. The Russian planners were pleased; they had taken heavier losses than they had expected, but they had secured a lodgement.

All they had to do was make it permanent.

The Spetsnaz commandos almost opened fire before they recognised the uniforms of the naval infantry; they had been completely focused on the fighting before the order had come to disengage. Aliyev checked around with his people as the naval infantry moved forwards; they could handle the fighting long enough for him to tend to his own men. Several hundred had been killed in the brutal fighting, including the General; Aliyev had suspected as much from the sudden end of barked orders. That gave him other responsibilities; he was now in command of the remaining four hundred men who were almost uninjured.

He grinned to the west. The British were falling back; all the Russians had to do was breach a major defence line and then they would have the lodgement they needed to build up the forces to advance into the two port cities. Even without the ports, it wouldn't slow the landing process much…and then they would advance on London. His men might even get another combat jump out of it before major combat operations came to an end; they could certainly act as shock infantry if they were denied any other role.

Once London fell…

Once London fell, it would be all over.

Chapter Forty-Eight

Operation *Morskoi Lev*, Take Three

For it's Tommy this, an' Tommy that, an' "Chuck him out, the brute!"
But it's "Saviour of 'is country" when the guns begin to shoot.
Rudyard Kipling

Battlezone, English Channel

Colonel Stuart Robinson peered through his binoculars along the road. The Russians would have to come along it to hit his defence line, such as it was; he didn't have the heavy weapons to make a proper stand. A handful of soldiers had been dug into Hawkinge, trying to slow the Russians; from the flames in the distance, it seemed as if the Russians had simply burned down the town and killed most of the defenders.

The line of survivors had passed through Robinson's lines minutes ago; there were no more active units registering on his terminal, no more little signals from the American microburst equipment reporting that a unit was still intact, if trapped. The forces in Dover and Folkestone had dug in to the buildings, but now the Russians had gained control of the countryside, the cities could be left alone until they were ready to deal with them. Robinson wished, desperately, for an air strike, or perhaps even a tactical nuke, but the former had been lost to the British when most of the RAF had gone down in the Battle of Dover.

"The next people who come along that road," he ordered, looking down at his veterans and the newcomers alike, "I want you to kill."

The very horizon seemed to be on fire. He could only be glad that Hazel was well out of the way in Edinburgh; if she had stayed in London, as she had wanted to do to be near him, she might have been caught in the chaos. The radio reports said that the entire city was panicking and demanding evacuation; there was no way that Britain's overstressed transport network could move even a small fraction of the city's population out in time. The noise of guns – Russian guns – and aircraft – Russian aircraft – was a constant crescendo; the Russians had more of everything and it showed. The British forces were operating right at the edge of their capabilities; it wouldn't be long, one way or the other, before they had to fall back to the line at Dorking. The Russians would probably try to surround the city before actually trying to enter it; Dorking was one of the strong points along the line surrounding London.

"My god," Sergeant Ronald Inglehart breathed, as they watched the flames growing in the distance. The noise of fighting never faltered; the isolated remnants of British units, trapped and turning like trapped rats to take a last bite out of the enemy before being overcome. The Russians would know that they had been in a fight, not like the Germans or the Poles, where only isolated resistance had been mounted across most of the country. Robinson had been offered a chance to leave the country and had rejected it; like so many others, he would make his stand with his men. "What are they doing in there?"

Robinson had no answer. The Russian jamming was affecting some of their datalinks with higher command, but they had enough information to know that the Russians had secured most of their sea-lanes to Britain and were pouring supplies through the gap; the little left of the Royal Navy was powerless to prevent them. They might not have a port, but they didn't need one to land some supplies, and given time, they would be able to jury-rig a temporary pier for unloading the heavier supplies. They needed interdiction of some kind, but the Company's EW officer had reported on the air-search radars and missile launchers that were being set up around the Russian landing zone; an air attack would be suicide with the handful of aircraft that the RAF had left. A suicidal strike mission that wouldn't even get close enough to make the loss of the aircraft reliable; only the RAF at full strength would have had a prayer of success... and that would have cost them dearly.

The noise of a CADS broke the sound of Russian weapons; he saw the flares of its rockets as they lanced into the sky, tracking an unknown target, perhaps a Russian drone hunting for British forces. The majority of the surviving forces were either trapped in the cities, part of his line, or falling back to the final defence line around London. The Russians had probably done a headcount...

"There," Inglehart muttered. Robinson blinked, confused, and then he saw the Russian attack helicopter drifting into the air, floating over a force of seven green tanks that was advancing into the English countryside. The force of Russian infantry were moving out in front – it took Robinson a moment to realise that he was looking at a penal unit, not a regular unit – and marching back and forwards ahead of the tanks. "Mine clearing, sir; I bet you..."

Robinson felt sick. The British Army had a great deal of experience in clearing mines, but it seemed that the Russian solution to the problem was to march their naughty soldiers in front of their tanks, down a road that might have been mined. Intelligence wasn't clear on what a soldier had to do to get into a penal unit; for all he knew, the men who were moving slowly along the road had objected to the thought of invading Europe. It was wishful thinking, he had to remind himself; there was no way that a few of the penal soldiers wouldn't be killed in the firing. Only a politician could believe it was possible to accomplish any such stupid ideal.

He lifted his field telephone. "Fire on my command; firing plan zeta," he muttered. They'd had the time to plan the action carefully. The war had been unpredictable, but the Russians had to answer to the same basic laws of military logistics as everyone else. The British Army had stripped the area of everything that might be useful; if they could give the Russians a bloody nose or two, they would win themselves time...

A little voice whispered at the back of his mind. *For what...?*

The Russians advanced closer. He would have been delighted to mine the road, but it had been impossible to produce or obtain enough mines for everywhere that needed mining; it had been hard enough to mine some of the most likely beaches that the Russians had used for landing zones. He could hear them now as they came nearer to his position; his people knew the area far better than any Russians could hope to know it without a few years living in the region. He refused to think about the possibility that the Russians might have someone with them who had spent a year studying the possibilities...

They couldn't have thought that far ahead, could they?

The lead Russian helicopter danced closer. He'd seen the formation before, in the training movies that had covered Afghanistan and some of the African missions the British Army had taken on and won. The real danger to the helicopter was ground-fire; the pilot was remaining over the ground forces to make it much harder for a single British soldier with a Stinger or a different antiaircraft missile to fire on him. Russian infantry, armed this time, were advancing as well…right into the teeth of his trap.

"Fire," he ordered.

A soldier carrying a Stinger missile fired; the other guns opened up at the same time. The Russian infantry threw themselves to the ground and returned fire, as three of their tanks and the helicopter were struck and destroyed by British fire. A fourth tank rumbled around the first tank, main gun already tracking on where it thought the attack had come from; the shell it fired missed the British and struck a barn some distance away, sending it up in flames. Robinson could only hope that there was no one hiding in that barn; certainly, no one had had the chance to get out.

The Russian infantry were brave; even the penal soldiers were showing bravery, though British Intelligence reported that the penal soldiers had been warned that they would be shot in the back if they retreated or slowed down. It was a mad way to run an army, but the Russians seemed to use it constantly; they had used the same tactics back in 1945, when they had crushed the SS and moved into Germany. The British soldiers, carefully positioned in their trenches, picked them off until a Russian blew a whistle and the Russians fell back, waiting.

Robinson knew better than to wait to find out what. He muttered an order into his radio and the trenches were quickly abandoned, a handful of weapons left behind on auto-target, scanning constantly from side to side for the first sight of anything moving. Robot guns were rare, because the slightest movement could trigger them, but Robinson was far too sure that there were no longer any friendly soldiers in the direction of Dover. He joined Inglehart in being the last to leave the trench, knowing that most of his soldiers would reach the second set of defence lines, fighting tiny battles constantly to slow up the invasion forces and force them to deploy to fight, all the while buying time…

The voice was back at the back of his head. *For what…?*

Two black shapes appeared at the corner of his eye, swooping down on their location; there was no mistaking the shape of the Devil's Cross aircraft as they opened fire with heavy machine guns and small rockets. They wanted to kill every soldier in the trench, he realised, as he threw himself into a ditch; they had brought along enough firepower to wipe out an armoured division. The explosions finally stopped and they crawled further away, refusing to be dismayed any more than they already were; they would reach the second set of trenches or die trying.

They didn't look back.

The skies were supposed to be clear of British aircraft now, but Captain Anatoliy Maksimovich Veselchakov was nervous anyway; his bomber was an older craft and carried very little in the way of ECM. It also carried no defensive weapons; given the nature of the craft's mission, it had probably been felt that Veselchakov didn't need any weapons to shoot back at British aircraft. It might have annoyed them.

Veselchakov had been orbiting in his flight pattern, well out to sea, for nearly an hour before finally being given the call to action. He had spent most of the day admiring the apparently chaotic scenes on the sea and in the air, and admiring the talents of the flight controllers who kept the Russian Air Force under some kind of control. Veselchakov had never intended to join the air force; he had signed up to fly for one of the Russian commercial lines before being drafted for certain missions for the military. His attempts to protest had been futile; there were hundreds of thousands of Russians soldiers fighting in the war and a civilian like Veselchakov could not be expected to shirk his duty. Besides, as a semi-civilian, he had some rights that none of the fighter jocks or the bomber crews had, including the right to make comments about the food.

Still, he had been dreading the missions ever since he had been told what he would be doing, and had tried to look for a way out. The only way he had found to get out – apart from suicide – ran through Siberia; the labour camps could always use people who shirked their duty to the state and the glory of the Russian Federation. Veselchakov was old enough, and travelled enough, to know that the propaganda wasn't all it seemed, but in the end, it was true that Europe had treated Russia like an ill-mannered bumpkin. Russia's culture had been dismissed as barbaric, Russia's legitimate concerns dismissed as relics of the old Soviet Union, and Russia's Army had been dismissed as a corrupt rusting war machine. The smile had been wiped off their faces now; Veselchakov knew enough about the FSB to know that certain politicians who had made political capital taking shots at Russia had probably been sent to Siberia by now.

"I am moving in now," he said, as the aircraft tilted around him. It was another reason for using a civilian pilot; Veselchakov's loss would not hurt the Russia Air Force one iota, although it might annoy them as one of them would have to take a second aircraft and try the same stunt themselves. He had done a few seasons of crop dusting, back when Russia had been experimenting with new ideas; the experience would serve him in good stead, even if the corn hadn't fired back. "Clear the airspace..."

Smoke was rising all over the English mainland; he could see the shore as he came in lower and slower, catching up with Dover. The British harbour was supposed to be captured intact, but the British had dug into the city...and his mission was to attempt to burn some of them out. The Russians on the ground had called upon the defenders to surrender; the only reply had been an instruction to do something biologically impossible. Veselchakov had never claimed to be a military expert, but he remembered the death toll from Groznyy and several other places in Central Asia; thousands of soldiers had been wounded, and hundreds had died. The planners wouldn't want to do that again if they could avoid it.

He had been promised no ground fire; the British had fired all of their missiles at the Russian Air Force, apparently getting in more than a few good hits as well. Veselchakov was as patriotic as the next man, but he found the thought of the Russian Air Force getting a bloody nose amusing; the fighter jocks had been so confident of their prowess and their success with the women of France. Their prowess had lasted as long as it had taken to come up against a prepared enemy...and Veselchakov knew that the 'women of France' were whores, paid for sleeping with the Russians. It was possible that there were some women who had slept with the Russians without financial inducements, but Veselchakov wouldn't have bet on it; the fighter jocks ran out of charm very quickly...

And then the penal units had a new slave for a month.

The English city was already burning in places as he came in for his attack run. The location of most of the defenders was already known and he angled the aircraft for maximum exposure. It was the work of a few seconds to prepare the bomb bay...and then the spray of deadly flaming jelly began, raining down on the British below. The Americans had taken the original idea of napalm and improved on it; the Russians had copied the American idea and added a few refinements of their own. Anyone trying to breathe near the flames would be lucky to survive.

Veselchakov winced as a handful of bullets cracked through the aircraft, but breathed a sigh of relief as he escaped safely, heading back out to sea and safety in France. The fighter jocks would be up there for hours yet; once he landed, unless they wanted him to repeat his stunt again, there were always the French prostitutes.

Behind him, Dover burned...

Langford hadn't expected to actually hold the Russians, not once the attempt to seal the Russians off and destroy them had failed; all that mattered now was pulling as many units back as possible, and then digging in to the final defence line. The remaining units in Kent had to be pulled back before they were caught and destroyed; the Russians would have problems expanding out of Kent for at least a week. The British had gone over the entire country and destroyed as many bridges, blocked as many roads, and generally worked hard to give the Russians serious problems.

The burning of Dover hadn't surprised him, but the sense that a city was steadily being literally burned off the face of the Earth worried him; the Russians might do the same to London, or Edinburgh, or any other city that had refused to surrender. They had used napalm before, in Europe, but...

Bad things were meant to happen elsewhere, he thought, laughing bitterly at himself. *They weren't meant to happen in Europe...*

He dismissed the thought. "Order a general pullback," he ordered. Special Forces would do what they could to delay and harass the Russians – landing a good punch, then getting out before the Russians could react – but the regular military would be needed elsewhere. He couldn't help, but thank God that the entire area had been evacuated; how many would have died if Dover had been left with its civilian population? "Tell all units to pull back to the secondary defence line."

He wanted to go on the offensive, but he knew that that was impossible; he lacked both the mobile firepower and the air cover to mount any offensive. There was one chance, just one...and if he didn't play his few cards exactly right, Britain would be lost along with the rest of Europe. It would have to work; he would do everything he could to make it work...

...Because the alternative was unthinkable. They had planned for a total defeat, but deep inside, he had never believed that it would be necessary, not until now. When had Britain come so close to defeat before? 1940? The humiliation of Suez had galvanised a stricken country, but that had been a political defeat, not a military one...and hardly fatal. The Falklands had been fought on a shoestring, but victory had come; defeat had seemed impossible. No nation had been able or willing to threaten Britain...

Until now...

Chapter Forty-Nine

Consolidation

Many people who would otherwise object to torture would permit it in the so-called "Ticking Bomb Scenario." This is, though few seem to realize it, an admission that, given a means of immediate feedback, torture works.
Tom Kratman

Near Dover, United Kingdom

Dover was burning.

General Aleksandr Borisovich Shalenko stood near the city and watched as the handful of British prisoners were rapidly searched, secured, and inspected by the FSB security detachments. Dover itself had been seriously damaged by the fighting, but the combat engineers were certain that they could repair the damage in a few weeks with enough labour, assuming that it could be found. There were thousands of dockworkers back in Europe who had taken money from the Russians; they could be shipped over as soon as a ship could be spared. For the moment, however, they had recovered enough of Folkestone to use it as a harbour and expand their control rapidly.

Another aircraft flew overhead, carrying supplies for the invasion force, as Shalenko turned to face the FSB commander, FSB Colonel Maliuta Vladimirovich Stepanov. His parents had been extreme Russian nationalists – both of them had worked for the KGB before it had converted itself into the FSB – and it showed in his name; Maliuta was a very rare name in Russia. His position within the FSB had been almost hereditary; he handled matters that were only spoken of in whispers, even by other FSB detachments.

Shalenko spoke first, unwilling to even suggest that they were equals. "Who is the senior surviving British officer?"

Stepanov bowed his head slightly. The FSB might be convinced that it was superior to the Russian Army, but a bad report from General Shalenko would have his career being rapidly reduced to a filing clerk somewhere in the Kremlin, if not being stripped of rank and sent in disgrace to Siberia. Some people had to run the labour camps, after all, and while there were plenty of brutes around, the hard work of administration needed talented – and disgraced – officers.

"That would be a Colonel Harris," he said, inspecting the terminal he carried in his hand. "We did recover a living General officer, but he died of his wounds soon afterwards; Colonel Harris is the only reasonably intact senior officer."

"Take me to him," Shalenko ordered shortly. "What condition is he in?"

He would find out if the General had died of his wounds, or if he had been helped; he had given orders that no prisoners were to be killed unless there was no hope at all that they would survive. The intelligence network within Britain had been severely damaged by the war and then the invasion; even the most blind of the useful fools might see that there was something not quite right going on. The active spies and agents wouldn't have the type of access they needed to know what the British intended.

"Battered, but unbowed," Stepanov said. There was a dispassionate note to his voice that chilled even Shalenko, even though he understood the requirement; he would almost have preferred a brute. A lot of brutes ended up in the FSB; a supply of victims and permission to do whatever they liked to them worked wonders for loyalty. "He was unlucky; we managed to knock him out in a bombing run and snatched him up before he recovered."

Colonel Harris was a massive black man; he was so black that Shalenko had trouble looking him in the face, his face scarred by the force of the impact that had knocked him out. Stepanov's men had already gone to work; he sat naked in a chair, various instruments of torture attached to different places on his body, although they hadn't started serious work yet. There was the hope that he would be reasonable; an American-designed lie detector electrode had been attached to the side of his shaven skull. He would have been a terror as a Drill Sergeant, Shalenko realised; it was a pity that he was on the wrong side.

He looked up as they entered. "Who...the hell are you?"

"I am General Shalenko, Commanding Officer of this Invasion Force," Shalenko said, without bothering with preamble, or justifications. They were both soldiers; only politicians would bother coming up with justifications for whatever they wanted to do anyway. "I require some information from you."

He made a mental bet as to what Harris would say first and won it. "This treatment is illegal under the Geneva Convention," he said, through gasps. There had to be some damage somewhere, even if Stepanov had thought he was unharmed; he looked as if he was going to be stubborn. "I am a legal combatant and...

"Well, perhaps," Shalenko said. "But you and I...we are both soldiers. We both know that sometimes you have to do things that you don't want to do, or that you will face the opinion of international talkers, or...things that your political leaders will disown you for, if they find it convenient to do so. Neither of us chose this war" – a half-truth at best – "and we do not want to fight it, but we have no choice. Having no choice...I will do whatever I can to ensure that my soldiers come through the fighting safe."

He paused. "Will you answer my questions?"

"Fuck you," Harris said. "I know the drill; it's only name, rank and serial..."

One of the FSB goons punched him in the chest. "We have to remain confined to reality," Shalenko said shortly, as Harris gasped for breath. "The blunt truth is that your countrymen are in no position to avenge whatever happens to you...and institutions like the International Criminal Court have been shut down permanently now that we have occupied Brussels. There is no power on Earth that will punish us for carrying out our duty."

Harris glared up at him, sweat forming on his black face. "Don't blame me when Russian soldiers start turning up with their balls cut off and stuffed in their mouths," he sneered. "Bring on your hired goons and let's see how far they can go."

Shalenko had to smile. "Do you know," he asked, "who these men are? Some of them are people who learned suffering from the Chechens, or others from Central Asia; some of them are actually Kazakhs who were more than willing to lend their services to the FSB. I think they were sick of western hypocrisy, myself; some of them even brushed into British forces in Afghanistan. Now, you can be as stubborn, and *heroic*, and *storoic* and many more words ending in *oic* that I can't be bothered to think of right now, but...eventually you will break and tell me everything you know."

He leaned closer. "Talk now and I promise you that I will spare you and your men," he said. "I have the authority to let them live, and even to spare them Siberia; all you have to do is talk now and spare yourself some pain."

"You'll have to get it out of me," Harris hissed. "Bring it on."

Shalenko stepped out of the tent as Stepanov's men started their grizzly work, some of them enjoying it, some of them as dispassionate as Stepanov himself about their task. He would have preferred to have dumped them all into a penal unit and sent them clearing minefields until they died, but that wasn't an option; they were unfortunate, but necessary. Torture worked, given enough time; it had saved too many lives to allow it to be thrown away.

"General," Anna said. Shalenko lit the cigarette she offered him and watched the smoke gusting away into the night air. They were in enemy territory, the one country in Europe that had had the time to get into position to give them a fight, and the loss rate showed that; thousands of Russians had died in a day of hard fighting. "I have the final figures."

Shalenko listened as she went through them, detailing deaths, units lost, some of them lost on transports before they had ever had the chance to get into battle, others scattered along the shoreline and slaughtered by British soldiers before they had a chance to collect themselves. The Russian Air Force had been hurt badly; over a hundred fighters had been lost, along with seventy bombers and transports. Civilian airliners would have to be pressed into service to speed the process of consolidation; they had to build up again before the British gathered themselves and counterattacked.

He held up a hand at one point. "Colonel Aliyev ordered his men to serve as light infantry?"

"Yes, General," Anna said. "They did good work, too, in rooting out a British nest. They're going to slow us up for at least a week, sir; they're using the German tactic of jeeps and antitank rockets, or sometimes a machine gun. The scouts have pressed forward as far as Hastings to Tunbridge Wells; intelligence believes that we will begin to encounter major enemy civilian populations once we reach Brighton."

Shalenko scowled. "Have we found any civilians here?"

"A handful, mainly a handful of looters," Anna said. "We interrogated them all; they were ordered to head for refugee camps in the south-west, decided that there would be good pickings in the abandoned houses, and ran into us instead."

"Good," Shalenko said. "And the enemy military?"

"The Air Force believes that it has wiped out the RAF, although seeing that they have said that several times before, I think we should be careful about accepting it on trust," Anna said. "The enemy has been digging in to small towns surrounding London, with a large force gathered up near Dorking, and smaller units gathering in London's suburbs."

Shalenko asked for a map and examined it. "Interesting," he said finally. "I wonder why Dorking; what do they have there?"

"Intelligence believes that they are massing there for a counter-attack," Anna said. "Our standard tactic is to surround cities before going into one and attacking London directly would be a nightmare; they may even be hoping that we would do so, which would allow their remaining forces to hit our flanks and pocket us. There are smaller British formations near Portsmouth, including Royal Marines; they may intend to keep building defences and inviting us to attack them."

"Then we have to move on Dorking," Shalenko said. It wasn't a hard choice at all; modern warfare was all about destroying the enemy's army…particularly if you didn't care about the civilians caught up in the meat-grinder. Inform the planners that I want operational plans within the hour, and we move as soon as possible; the air force can have a slight rest and prepare itself for the final battle. Once the British Army is destroyed, London is finished."

Stepanov appeared silently behind him; Shalenko sensed his presence and turned to face him. "Well?"

"He broke, finally," Stepanov informed him. A broken and bloody was being dragged out of the tent; Harris would be lucky to survive for another hour. "As far as he knew, all mobile units and ones that could get out of our clutches were to retire on Dorking and the other places along the London Defence Line; past that, he has no idea what the British command is planning."

"Tactical nukes, perhaps," Shalenko said. It was a wild card; they didn't know if the British military government had the nukes, or if they would use them in their own country. The President had warned the British that if nukes were used, they would start destroying British cities; Shalenko knew that the President wasn't bluffing. Did the British know that? Did they have any nukes to use? "See to it that he gets whatever medical care he needs; his men can be secured for transport back to the continent."

He paused. "And in a few days," he said, "we move on Dorking."

"And then we win," Anna said.

Two days passed as both sides worked desperately to prepare for the final battle. Russian forces probed north-west into England, slowly clearing out traps, dug-in infantry and TA soldiers, fighting to the last to preserve their country. In some places, morale collapsed completely and soldiers deserted, heading back to their homes, or deserting to the enemy; they were rapidly secured, interrogated, and dumped in massive prison compounds to await their fate. In other places, furious fighting broke out as British soldiers fought tooth and nail to hold a town or village, but the Russians had vast superiority in weapons and total ruthlessness; resistance was swiftly crushed by overwhelming force.

Russian soldiers brushed up against the main defence line, exchanged shots, and fell back, expanding their area of control around London. Both sides knew that it was only a matter of time before the fighting flared up again in earnest, and prepared hard for that day. As the air lanes over London were closed by Russian aircraft, the citizens began to panic; some of them demanding peace at any price. The overworked police, volunteers all to a man or woman, did what they could to keep the lid on; they knew what would happen if the Russians won.

The remainder of the country waited nervously to see who would win the coming battle. Planners on both sides calculated and recalculated the odds, comparing details like air control to precise knowledge of the terrain; everyone knew that what happened when the armies finally met in open battle would be decisive. The army that the British had raised would be the last; if it lost, the war would be over, bar the shouting. All over the country, some civilians remained where they were, watching events on CNN and a dozen other American media programs, cursing the limited details. The White House had invoked PATRIOT III, causing a storm of controversy; the legal wrangling over the question of how much of the British preparations they could show wouldn't end until after the battle was decided, one way or the other. Wearing British uniforms that fooled no one, a handful of Americans joined the British armed forces; their planes, technically non-combatants, would be a vital part of the RAF's last throw of the dice.

All around the country, people waited; rumours spread rapidly. Prince Harry had returned to his unit in its hour of need, some said; others remembered how the Prince had never been permitted to serve in Iraq and dismissed the rumour, adding others. The Royal Family had fled, rats leaving a sinking ship; the remains of Britain's noble families had joined them. The Russians were going to slaughter all the Muslims; the Russians were going to slaughter all the Jews; the Russians were going to rape every man, woman and child they encountered...

Escape seemed an impossible dream; there was nothing left to do, but wait...

And listen to rumours.

Major-General Charles Langford saluted as the group of soldiers paraded in front of them, before they marched off to the front line. They were young, many of them barely out of their teens; a handful in the strange grey-area of age where technically they should never have been recruited into the Army, but the Army had been so desperate for new recruits that they had been accepted...and for many of them it had been the making of them. They wore their uniforms with pride, some of them wearing unit insignia that had been lost long ago, under one government or another. The politicians hadn't understood; when they amalgamated regiments such as the Highlanders, or the Black Watch, they were killing something important. Men might think of fighting for their country, but instead...the factor that would keep them in the front lines was loyalty to their fellows, or a reluctance to run in front of them. They were the finest that Britain could produce...

He had lied to them, of course, and he had hated himself for it. He had told them that they had a chance, and that many of them would survive the coming battle; the latter, at least, was a lie. The SAS and other intelligence agencies had worked hard to slip operatives into Occupied Europe, where they had reported on the registrations, the employment, the rations, the brutal crushing of protests, peaceful or otherwise…there was very little hope for them. The warning had been simple; if you are a soldier, or a policeman… you have to hide and remain hidden, or you vanished. The Americans had sent images of the camps in Occupied Europe, and the work camps in the depths of Russia; that was the fate that awaited them all if they lost and were captured. There was no hope…

They'd consulted with the Americans, at length, looking for another solution. There wasn't one; even if the Americans could spare the forces to help Britain, there was no way that those forces could arrive in time. Even if they did, the fighting would devastate Britain from end to end…with no guarantee of victory. The Battle of the Mediterranean had warned the Americans of the dangers of relying on their own fleet defences; it was just possible that an American carrier battle group would suffer the same fate as Admiral Bellemare Vadenboncoeur. They would be looking at a war that would make the Second World War look like a child's spat, fought against the one thing America hadn't faced since 1945 – a fairly equal opponent. There was no political support for the war; President Kirkpatrick might have cost herself the chance at winning a second term, just for supporting Britain as much as she had…

And how had it all happened? In hindsight, it had been perfectly clear; they had known much about what the Russians could do, and what their capabilities actually were…they just hadn't put everything together. The Russians had boosted their military forces before and there had been panic, but every time, they had merely been shaking their fist, until the day they came rolling over the border. Europe had believed that they had moved past the days when conflicts were settled by armed force; they had been deluding themselves. They had had the choice between the American security umbrella, at its political price, or building EUROFOR into a respectable force…and they had chosen, instead, to stick their heads in the sand. The cost…

Langford stared down at his hands. They all would pay the cost of neglecting the defences. One way or another, matters would be settled soon…

It wouldn't be long now.

CHAPTER FIFTY

THE SECOND BATTLE OF DORKING, TAKE ONE

I can hardly look a young man in the face when I think I am one of those in whose youth happened this degradation of Old England. One of those who betrayed the trust handed down to us unstained by our forefathers.
George Chesney

NEAR DORKING, UNITED KINGDOM

"They're coming," the aide said. Major-General Charles Langford nodded; a week of waiting and preparing for the Russian offensive had come to an end. "The SAS are reporting heavy Russian forces moving towards Dorking from their bases."

Langford took a long breath. He would be running the battle from a carefully-prepared command tent, one with direct links to both the CJHQ and the different units of the surviving British army; the telephone system was impossible for the Russians to detect in operation. As the Russians tightened their control over the air, anything transmitting a signal had been targeted and destroyed, a sharp lesson in what happens when SHORAD was neglected. The handful of American units did what they could, but they weren't enough to make a difference; Langford wasn't sure if anything would make a difference.

The Russians had slowly secured their grip over Kent and the south-east of England, expanding their control and making it much harder for Special Forces to operate, even through the SAS was working wonders in delaying tactics. Their bases had expanded and as they had brought a port back into service, so had their forces; there was no way that their supply lines could be interdicted any longer. The handful of surviving Royal Navy units had been pulled back to take part in the final evacuation, but the Russians were still pressing at them; Langford knew that more ships would be lost before it was over.

He could have gone on one of the ships, he supposed; the thought had been tempting, even though it would have been the coward's way out. He could make it to one of the ships even if the battle was lost, but he had made up his mind; whatever happened, he would face it in the country he had become leader of, so unexpectedly. He had made his plans; all that remained was to carry them out and remain strong.

It wouldn't be long now.

"Send the general signal to all men," he said. "Tell them...to fight like mad bastards and give them hell."

The Russian tankers peered nervously at the English countryside as they advanced, watching for ambushes, mines, or other surprises that the British might have left in their path. They had learned to be careful in Chechnya, but the British had a few surprises of their own, including a handful of mines that looked harmless, or devices that somehow burned incredibly hot and burned through heavy armour as if it was nothing more than plastic. The Americans had supplied it, some of the tankers whispered, as they drove towards the British lines. One day, perhaps there would be a chance to settle scores with them as well.

High overhead, the first flight of Russian bombers headed west, their targets already preset and designated for attention. Their bomb bays had been loaded with heavy bombs; they now broke into attack runs and headed towards the British positions. Russian spotters and penal soldiers, volunteers trying to work weeks off their sentences, had penetrated the British positions and reported back; many of them were caught and killed, but others survived long enough to warn the Russian pilots of new targets. The bombs began to fall...

Further back, Russian artillery was already beginning to fire, targeting the British lines and the dug-in infantry in towns and villages. Flames spread rapidly as the soldiers dove for cover, the work of centuries being shattered by Russian guns as the Russians advanced; they braced themselves and crawled forward to the newer trenches they had dug to await the Russian ground forces. The British prepared themselves as best as they could for the final battle, carefully concealed tanks and guns becoming active and waiting for targets. Everything depended upon holding the line.

"We don't fall back," Colonel Stuart Robinson said, as the Company dug in and prepared to face the Russian attack. This time, they knew that they would be attacked; this time, it would be different from any number of skirmishes right across the continent. "Whatever happens, we don't fall back."

"Understood," Sergeant Ronald Inglehart said. He barked orders to the men holding the trench system; hundreds of man-hours had gone into preparing it as a deadly and well-hidden surprise for the Russians. The noise of Russian guns was getting louder; the handful of British guns would remain in reserve until they had targets right where they wanted them. The Russians would have difficulty assaulting their position with tanks; they would have to come face to face with the British soldiers as they fought. "We will hold."

Robinson touched the medal he wore on his chest. The Army had done the best it could for the wounded soldiers, including shipping many of them to heavily-defended Iceland under American care, but he knew that escape was probably impossible. He had asked Hazel to take the opportunity of a shot on an evacuation ship, but she had refused; how could she leave him? She was safe, for the moment, but it still worried him; what would the Russians do to her if they caught her? Reports said that the Russians cracked down hard on unsanctioned atrocities, and they had certainly captured more than a few penal soldiers who had been arrested for rape, but Hazel had thrown a spanner into their plans. The Russians carried grudges; the very war itself was proof of that.

"Yes," he agreed. "We will not break."

He peered through the camouflage down towards where the Russians would have to appear when they attacked. Everyone was certain that the Russians would come to confront the remains of the mobile British Army, the remaining force left on Britain itself; the bombers that had passed overhead and attacked Dorking were proof enough that the planners had called that one correctly. They could see the fires raging in the distance; he didn't want to think about what could happen if the Russians turned those firebombs on civilians. If the line broke, the British civilian population would be at the mercy of the Russians.

The sound of high explosives was getting closer as the first of the Russians appeared, moving carefully forward and looking for traps. By now, they all knew how to spot a penal soldier from the slumped shoulders, the absence of weapons or rank insignia, and the suicidal actions, even after their pink uniforms had been stripped from them. The Russian was crawling forward, completely unarmed; Robinson felt a moment of sympathy before hardening his heart and muttering a command for the sniper to take the Russian down. The Russian twitched once and lay still; the heat of the air seemed to suppress any noise he might have made, or perhaps it was the noise of the battle in the far distance that was concealing his cries. Other Russians appeared, crawling forwards; they were armed and fired as they slipped from cover to cover, hunting for the British sniper who had killed their former colleague.

They don't know we're all here, Robinson realised. The Russians clearly thought that they were dealing with a lone SAS sniper, like the one who had killed a Russian General two nights ago when the idiot had gone driving through barely-secured territory; their tactics were designed to beat the sniper out of hiding, not assault a dug-in infantry force. He muttered commands to Inglehart, who passed them along the line; hold your fire and wait.

The Russians came closer and closer, their bullets cracking through the air well above the heads of his men, the universe shrinking to the point where it held only the Russian company and the British company, men who were about to kill and be killed. Robinson felt deadly calm as he took aim, considering his targets carefully; a green-clad Russian officer, waving his men on with one hand, seemed the best possible choice. He used hand signals himself, issuing orders to the mortar crews; those weapons, at least, had plenty of rounds to fire at the Russians. Time ticked by…

"Fire," he shouted, and fired down at the Russian. He had no business in the line of fire himself, but he was damned if he was abandoning his men now, and it was a chance to hit back for all Hazel had suffered since he had gone off to war. It seemed a dream now; the universe replaced by endless war as Russians were caught in the stream of bullets, or threw themselves to the ground as British firepower poured onto their locations. The dull thumping of mortars could be heard as the soldiers fired antipersonnel rounds into the

Russian positions, slaughtering hundreds of Russians; the remainder scattered and returned fire as best as they could. The British mowed them down mercilessly.

Robinson threw his head back. "Plaza-toro," he shouted, words that would hopefully mean nothing to the Russians. "Plaza-toro!"

All along the line, most of the soldiers scooped up their weapons and hauled them away, heading towards the second set of trenches. A handful remained, brave volunteers; Robinson would have liked nothing better than to stay with them, but he knew his duty. He ran from the trenches as something changed in the air pressure…and then a mighty series of explosions blew him to his knees. The Russians had fired heavy guns, aiming them directly onto their positions; shrapnel and cluster bombs, even small mines, flew everywhere. Robinson kept his head down and watched his feet carefully; here and there, a soldier screamed as a tiny mine detonated, blowing off their legs and crippling them for life. It was easy to see why people had wanted such weapons to be banned, but in the end…the Russians had cared nothing for the ban.

A British MLRS rapid-fired a stream of rockets in reply, arcing over his head as the soldiers stumbled and crawled to the second set of trenches. It seemed like a nightmare, or something out of the First World War; the looming presence of a Russian tank, trying to flank them, underlined the strange nature of war in the new world. Inglehart blasted it with a Knife before the Russian tank could do more than fire a long burst of machine gun bullets at the fleeing soldiers; the Russian tank exploded into fire and died rapidly. Russian gunners were trying to target the MLRS; Robinson prayed that the crew had managed to move their vehicle before it was too late. The sound of shouts in Russian could only mean one thing; the Russians were in hot pursuit.

"Get into position, you worthless bastards," Inglehart was shouting, as the soldiers scrambled to obey. A handful of wounded were being carted away by medics, trying to get them to one of the evacuation ships before the Russians caught them; several more were refusing to leave and were preparing to join the final stand. "I want you to kill every god-damned Russian who pokes his dick over that crest, got that?"

The sky seemed to be lit up with rockets and aircraft, hunting for targets. Robinson looked for signs that someone else was mounting a defence, fighting the Russians in the air, but there was no sign of any British aircraft. The noise was strange; he could hear sonic booms and the thunder of bombs, and then there would be moments when it was almost quiet and peaceful. The shape of a Russian tank lumbered into view and they braced themselves as an infantryman took arm with an RPG, striking the Russian tank and destroying its treads. A second shot sent tankers boiling out of it; the British mowed them down before the flames consumed the tank and detonated its ammunition.

"There," Inglehart muttered. Robinson saw them briefly; a line of Russian infantrymen, preparing themselves to move forward. "I think that's our cue..."

The Russian shells landed.

"Hit," someone was shouting, as explosions raged through the British trench lines. Colonel Boris Akhmedovich Aliyev wasn't so sure; the shells had actually fallen short, digging themselves into the mud and probably alarming the British, but not killing many of them. "We killed them all!"

"Onwards," Aliyev shouted, as he hefted his own assault rifle. "Advance against the British!"

The British would be stunned, but that wouldn't last long; the British had held out stubbornly, long enough to convince him that it would be the greatest fight of his career. He was almost relieved to be a mere infantryman again; no choices, no serious responsibility...just the urge to kill the enemy until they were all dead. It had been his reward; a soldier who accomplished much in the Russian Army would be forgiven much...and no one would complain about him wanting to enter the fight. The paratroops had been badly mauled by the fighting near Dover; Aliyev would have one last major battle before he was sent back to Russia to start the long hard task of rebuilding the paratroopers into a new force.

The remainder of his paratroops moved forward with blinding speed, running up towards the British positions and preparing for the final lunge. The shells had disrupted the British; only a handful fired back as the paratroopers assaulted the position, moving from covering positions to wild desperate charges as they threw grenades and faced the British in close-quarter combat for the final time. The entire scene was beautifully chaotic; he loved it as the position disintegrated into a hundred tiny battles, even hand-to-hand combat between soldiers. He couldn't have been happier…

A British officer slammed into him and they went down, fighting a desperate struggle to kill each other before it was too late; Aliyev went for the neck and felt his tormenter's struggles die before he pulled himself out from under the body…and saw a rifle pointed at him from very near range. His hand lanced down to the fragmentation grenades at his belt; he just managed to pull the pin before the British soldier fired once, sending Aliyev howling into a nightmare of fire and death.

Robinson saw the Captain, a young studious officer who had handled his unit well, if without inspiration, go down on top of a Russian officer and screamed in outrage. The Russian broke the Captain's neck with a single quick moment and slipped out; Robinson knew that he was too dangerous a fighter to risk a hand-to-hand fight, no matter how much he wanted one; he lifted his assault rifle and fired in one quick motion.

"Oh, you son of a bitch," he said, as he saw what the Russian had done. Instincts took over and he threw himself backwards as the grenades detonated; screaming red hot pain cascaded through him as the fragments of shrapnel burned through his legs and chest. He couldn't feel his legs; the pain was too great to allow him even to think; the sense that someone was talking to him, someone very close, was confusing his mind. He couldn't even focus enough to rally and kill Russians…

"Hazel," he said, or thought he said, and blacked out.

Inglehart saw Robinson fall and cursed the Russians as he wounded one with a gut-shot, blowing the Russian's head off with a second shot. He had liked Robinson; had known him since he was a nervous common soldier, to becoming a commissioned officer, to becoming a competent Captain…and then the man who had saved all of their lives. He threw a grenade at a nearby group of Russians and knelt by his Captain – he could never think of him as a

Colonel – examining the wounds; they were bad. The ruined legs alone would cripple him for the rest of his life...

The choice wasn't hard to make. The Russians had fallen back; Inglehart knew what that meant, a bombardment. He shouted orders to two of the medics, ordering them to carry the Captain out of the battlezone, and turned back to face the advancing Russians. He owed Robinson his life; he could have fled, but in the end...he had accepted the price of duty a long time ago, when he had first taken service in the army, a long time before Robinson had joined himself.

Inglehart was proud of Robinson; he was proud to be a Sergeant in the greatest army in the world. It had been a long career, watching the army rise and fall, seeing newer officers prove themselves or fail under the supreme test of combat. It had been a good life, all in all; wine – or rather beer – women and song, all spent with the finest bunch of bastards on the face of the planet. He wouldn't have changed a thing.

Inglehart kept fighting until they overwhelmed him. He died surrounded by the bodies of his foes.

"They're punching through the main defence line," the aide reported. Langford could hear a hint of panic in her voice; they were on the verge of being trapped in the HQ if the Russian advance was not checked. "They're moving to outflank Dorking itself."

Langford scowled. The Russians had managed the penetration quicker than he had expected; he had anticipated the bombardment of Dorking, but not the almost suicidal tactics the Russians had used to break through. Time was on their side; was there some reason why they had forced the issue as much as they had, apart from sheer bloody-mindedness?

It didn't matter. "Contact Major Ryan," he ordered. The time had come to play the last card in his hand, the only card he had held back for the final battle. There had been no other choice, not until now; the last card had to be played, or abandoned along with the war. "The tanks will advance and engage the enemy."

Chapter Fifty-One

The Second Battle of Dorking, Take Two

Yet we had plenty of warnings, if we had only made use of them. The danger did not come on us unawares. It burst on us suddenly, 'tis true; but it's coming was foreshadowed plainly enough to open our eyes, if we had not been wilfully blind. We English have only ourselves to blame for the humiliation which has been brought on the land.
George Chesney

Near Dorking, United Kingdom

"Advance!"

Major John Patrick David Ryan settled himself firmly in his command tank as the Eurotank – perhaps the last Eurotank in existence – began to move forward. The command Eurotank had been designed as a larger version of the original, with space for the officer in command of the regiment to direct his tanks as he saw fit; the British Challengers that moved forward were older and slower, although tougher. The design was more than thirty years old – some of the tanks were older still – but they could still hold their own.

He held his breath as the final tank lunged forward. Hiding the tanks had been a nightmare; it had been hard enough moving them around without the heavy vehicles smashing up roads and motorways, although that, at least, was a positive bonus when slowing the enemy down was part of the mission objectives. The tanks had normally been moved around the country on trains and tank transporters, but there had been fewer exercises for coordinating such activity before the war began, and now it was almost too late. Had they been kept in Scotland, he wasn't sure that they would have managed to get them down to England in time to fight; the devastation the Russians had caused to the British infrastructure had been serious. They had been competing with various companies and government-run commissions, always hard men to beat, but the Russians had aimed to destroy, rather than milk a crumbling edifice of every last pound before it was too late.

It wouldn't be long before the Russians saw them and responded; it was all-too-possible that the Russians had seen them hiding the tanks, despite their best precautions. He had kept his men away from the vehicles right until the final moment, just in case the Russians caught sight of them, but it seemed as if the American data had proven itself and the Russians were completely unaware that they still existed. The Russians had destroyed enough tank parks and storage silos; he hoped that, perhaps, they were starting to wonder if they had destroyed all of Britain's tanks. They had certainly given it the old college try.

The Americans had supplied them with microburst communications equipment and they used them exclusively; the Yanks were pretty certain that the Russians would be unable to track them through their microburst emissions. He would have preferred more tanks, even outdated early-model Abrams tanks, but it had been impossible to have those shipped over for the war. – A handful of American EW gear had also been sent over; the Russians would be finding all manner of problems with some of their systems, problems that would make them wonder if they were having glitches, or if something was definitely out there, hunting them. The sensor ghosts would make tracking the second part of the plan difficult; a lot of men were about to die. Ryan could only hope that their deaths would be worth something.

The Russians had been forcing armoured columns up the British roads, springing ambushes and bringing up vast firepower to confront the British defenders, before trying to crush the entire British Army. The line had broken up ahead and, as Russian doctrine ordered, the Russians had thrown the better part of one of their armoured units into the gap, trying to push it open wider. They had to distrust the strange mixture of patchwork fields and houses on the outskirts of Dorking; scouts reported that the Russians had blasted a number of houses with heavy tank shells for no apparent reason.

The latest microburst update flickered onto his screen; the Russians had launched their main push into the region, breaking into a vacuum. His force was ambling onwards, picking up speed; they would be in a perfect position to ambush the Russians in moments. All they had to do was remain quiet…and hope that the Russians neither saw them, nor heard the rumble of the tank's diesel engines. It wouldn't be long now.

Colonel Bogdan Aleksandrovich Onishenko glared around him as the T-100 rumbled past yet another perfect ambush site, one hand on the holster he wore at his hip. He didn't like Britain; it went from strange countryside to patchwork fields to quite large habitations, all within the space of a few miles. Onishenko had been in tanks since he passed through basic training; he knew enough to know that the British were sneaky and very good at improvising. So far, there had been no real resistance once the main defence line had been breached, but the British would be scrambling to establish a second line as soon as possible, perhaps even before his unit could really put the boot in.

He muttered a curse under his breath, directed equally at the British and his superiors. They had insisted on limiting the amount of damage the Russian forces did – a tall order under any circumstances, and rather at odds with the ruin that Russian forces had reduced Dover to, before the fighting there had mercifully come to a halt. Several of his tankers had fired on buildings which had looked suspicious; he found it hard to reprimand them, although he had no choice, but to tell them off. They wouldn't face the penal units for such actions, but it wouldn't be good for winning hearts and minds…not that there were any civilians around to impress with Russian restraint.

Come to think of it, he mused, the only British civilians he had seen had been a gang of looters, who had been forced to face the jeers of the Russian soldiers before being set to work moving equipment for the Russians as part of a long sentence for looting. Their protests hadn't bothered the Russians; it was better than being dumped into a penal unit, assuming that the FSB didn't just shoot them on sight. One of them had refused, unable to believe what was happening to them; he had been shot down like a dog. Onishenko hadn't cared; discipline had to be maintained, whatever the price…

"Colonel, we may have aircraft in your general area," a controller called, from one of the Mainstays orbiting far behind the lines. Onishenko cursed again; the Mainstays had been having problems all day with sensor ghosts, sending out air raid warnings at the drop of several hats and ordering armed fighters to intercept phantom targets. It would be much easier if a handful of fighters were on permanent CAP, but some bureaucrat in the Russian Air Force had insisted on fighters maintaining distance to avoid them being shot down by ground-fire; the losses in the first day of the invasion had stunned them. "Please be alert for air traffic..."

Onishenko cursed again. The Russians had hundreds of bombers, criss-crossing the sky and waiting for targets; his men, spooked, would be likely to fire on them or call for fighter support for cover against their own people, let alone the dangers of Russian aircraft seeing what they thought were hostile units and opening fire at 'danger close.' All he had to do was cut through the British lines and sow panic in their rear; at the moment, he was wondering if they even *had* a rear. They could have been halfway to London by now if the higher-ups hadn't insisted on playing it carefully...

He heard the noise of an aircraft, then several aircraft, and then plenty of aircraft. He turned his head to the north, wondering why the noise sounded funny, and saw them making their way towards him. The sight made his mouth drop open for a long moment; he had expected to see combat jets and assault helicopters, not...he wasn't sure what they were, but he was sure that they were British. Many of them looked older than anything he'd seen in the Russian Army, others looked as if they could barely fly; he wondered if somehow they had blundered into an air show...

And then they started to drop bombs...

There were over three hundred older aircraft in Britain, some of them lovingly protected at various museums and air shows, others pushed into service by pilots who had volunteered for their dangerous mission, many of them without any means of hurting the enemy. Other aircraft belonged to display teams; the entire Red Arrow reserve squadron – the main pilots had been recalled to the RAF during the Second Battle of Britain – had volunteered to a man to fly their Hawks in one final glorious mission. A Spitfire, a Lightning, dozens of civilian aircraft...all flew towards a Russian force that could not believe its eyes. The American EW tech had provided just enough of a break; for a moment, the Russians couldn't hope to react in time...

Even as ZSU units swung around to fire missiles and CIWS shells at the incredible force, the Hawks of the Red Arrows swooped in low, just above the ground. They flew in formation every week of every year; they performed the craziest of manoeuvres, just for the benefit of gawking spectators. Now, they dropped makeshift bombs on the Russian forces, catching them before they could reprioritise their targeting and separate the dangerous aircraft out from the diversion. It would be bare minutes before Russian fighters emerged to challenge them and knock them from the sky; in that time, a single pass could do a lot of damage…

Onishenko found his voice as the first Hawk screamed overhead, dropping precision bombs on the Russian tanks, homing in on their turrets. "Open fire," he screamed, shouting for the ZSU units and the tanks armed with antiaircraft weapons to put them to use. A hail of fire, not all of it coordinated or radar-guided, shot into the sky; priceless aircraft fell out of the sky, or in some cases were guided by their pilots down onto Russian tanks and vehicles just before they crashed. "Take them down!"

It was impossible! He ducked as a biplane, a vehicle he could have outrun in his tank on open ground, passed overhead, low enough for his hair to feel its presence. A Hawk made a second pass, only to be blown out of the air and crash onto the road; the British houses nearby started to burn as more aircraft crashed into them, or started to make their escape. The sonic booms from Russian fighters echoed across the land…and then one of his tanks blew up. Onishenko whirled, to see a sight he had never expected to see; a British tank was moving directly towards his position.

He opened his mouth to shout orders and the British tank slammed an armour-penetrating shell into his tank, blowing it apart before he could react.

The aircraft had worked better than Major Ryan had dared hope; the Russians had been caught in a state of almost-complete shock. His force advanced carefully, moving as quickly as they dared and firing at every half-intact Russian tank they saw; there was no time to work out which were dangerous, and which could be safely ignored. There would be Russian aircraft overhead within moments if the news got out; the American jamming equipment might be better than the Russian equipment, but it could hardly fail to alert the Russians that *something* was going on…

A Russian BMP was moving slightly, turning as if it intended to escape; he barked orders and one of his tanks hit it with a high-explosive shell, sending it up in a shower of sparks…which rapidly became a huge explosion. Russian infantry scattered, some of them firing desperately at the Challengers with their rifles, others engaged in the more practical act of running away from their tormentors. Just for a moment, Ryan could allow himself to hope that they would have a chance, before the Russians counter-attacked. More tanks appeared and a brief exchange of fire left tanks on both sides flaming wrecks…

"Fall back," he ordered, as the American data revealed that there were no more Russian tanks close enough to be used as cover. He had soldiers with handheld SAM missiles scattered around, but he knew better than to think that they could provide the perfect air cover he needed; the Russians would be on them soon with heavy bombers, perhaps even MLRS launchers if they had any brought up in time. "We don't want them hitting us while there are no Russians left to use for cover…"

It had been an Iraqi trick, then an Iranian one, and finally the Palestinians had adopted it, although after the disaster that Israel had suffered, the Israelis had given up caring about such things as global public opinion. They had been close enough to the Russian positions to make any attempt to bomb the crap out of them an exercise in fratricide; the Russians were unlikely to condone any attempts to kill their own people when it was so much more sporting to let the British do it. Now, the Russians were gone; it was possible that the Russians would strike them as hard as they could.

The tanks moved back desperately, leaving three of their number burning in the streets, and a fourth disabled beyond the point where it could move. The crew of the damaged tank refused to leave; given one chance, they could still hurt the others. Ryan saluted them as the tanks pulled back; he knew he would never see them again.

"They're attacking with *what?*"

"Tanks," Anna said, precisely. "At least nine tanks, attacking our forces under cover of the crazy air force."

General Shalenko ground his teeth. Victory was close; he could feel it. He wouldn't let a handful of tanks stand in the way. "Orders to the MLRS commander," he said. He couldn't remember the man's name; the British had killed the first three officers to hold that role through accurate counter-battery fire. "He is to sweep that entire area."

"Yes, sir," Anna said. "Intelligence believes that it has located the enemy HQ."

Shalenko glanced down at the image from the orbiting satellite. Some of the satellites hadn't been responding quite right; he wasn't sure if that was because of overuse, or because the Americans were trying to disrupt their operations somehow. The Americans had shared some tricks with their British cousins; all they had had to do to make life much harder had been to send supplies. They had…and also opened a whole new can of worms.

"Order Colonel Aliyev to seize that place at once," he ordered. It was vulnerable; if they could take the British commander alive, it would be the end of the fighting. "I want…"

"Colonel Aliyev is dead, sir," Anna said. Shalenko winced; yet another good man, left behind to die in the British countryside, so close to London and the end of the war. "I can send a fresh unit…"

"Do so," Shalenko ordered. Victory was growing closer. The rumble of guns and rockets grew louder. I want this over before we all go mad."

The Russians had carefully pre-positioned thirteen MLRS launchers in a region near Reigate, a British town that had been reduced to rubble by a brief hand-to-hand fight and then a bombardment by napalm-armed planes. On command, they opened fire, spilling thousands of tank-killing rockets over the general area they knew the British tanks to be operating in. Guided by tiny sensors, the rockets homed in on their targets; no one ever found a trace of Major Ryan, or the remains of his unit.

"You and the others are to leave," Langford said, as the Russians closed in on their final location. The defeat of the tanks had ended whatever hopes he had had of winning the war; he had thrown his last dice and lost. "For what it's worth, you all performed brilliantly in the final battle, and one day I hope that you will return to Britain."

He sat back and watched as the small staff ran from the HQ, heading towards the jeep that had been placed there for a hasty retreat, hoping that they would make it to the ships before the Russians reached Liverpool or one of the other coastal ports in the west. Civilian resistance would be almost non-existent, but the Russians themselves had damaged the transport network; it would be weeks before some parts of the country saw a Russian, or were fully reconciled to Russian occupation.

Not all of the remaining soldiers would leave, of course. Some would choose to remain with their families, hiding as civilians, others had determined that they would carry on the war underground, forming a resistance movement that would violently oppose the Russians. There had been some seeds planted, some preparations made, but in the end, supplies had been too limited to arm a proper resistance movement. In the years to come, Langford was certain that there would be victories, but he knew that few of them would matter; the Russians were too strong.

They would grow lax, of course; they would even be influenced by British and European culture. It always happened; the barbarians at the gate would invade, thousands of people would get hurt, but in the long run, civilisation would spread further than it had before. Who knew what would happen in the future? Langford only knew his own future…and that had grown short indeed. He had planned for everything…

There were voices outside, speaking in harsh Russian; the tent flap was pushed aside and three armed Russians stepped into the tent, weapons pointing everywhere; they homed in on Langford as if he were wearing a tracer. He smiled at them.

"Hands high," one of them barked, as more Russians filtered into the tent. "You will come with us."

"No," Langford said flatly, and pushed the detonator in his hand. "Goodbye."

The explosion vaporised the tent and everyone in it.

Chapter Fifty-Two

The Fall of Night

For it was the same story everywhere. After the first stand in line, and when once they had got us on the march, the enemy laughed at us. Our handful of regular troops was sacrificed almost to a man in a vain conflict with numbers; our volunteers and militia, with officers who did not know their work, without ammunition or equipment, or staff to superintend, starving in the midst of plenty, we had soon become a helpless mob, fighting desperately here and there, but with whom, as a manoeuvring army, the disciplined invaders did just what they pleased. Happy those whose bones whitened the fields of Surrey; they at least were spared the disgrace we lived to endure.
George Chesney

United Kingdom

The Russian Army entered London two days after the Battle of Dorking.

Inspector David Briggs, created Lord Mayor of London – the previous Lord Mayor having vanished somewhere on the first terrible day – by Langford, waited for them outside Buckingham Palace. He hadn't been able to decide if Langford had appointed him Mayor as a perverted joke, an attempt to give him the authority clawed back by several Lord Mayors since Ken Livingstone had won the role in clear defiance of the then Prime Minister, or if it had been an attempt to give him some form of protection. The Russians were arresting and detaining police officers all over Europe, but some politicians were being left in place; it was just possible that they would leave him alone, or at least in Britain. Maybe…

He wasn't sure why he had stayed. The once-proud Metropolitan Police force had been reduced sharply to just over a thousand men in the last fortnight, as officers strove to vanish into the teeming mass of the civilian population, or attempted to get on one of the evacuation ships as the remains of the British Army embarked for Canada and the British dominions in the

Caribbean. They were terrified of their fate under Russian rule; Briggs himself could have fled with them, but he had stayed. He had written a final letter to his wife, if he didn't return home within the week; he wished, now, that he had spent more time with her before the war. It all seemed like a dream now...

The city had been on the verge of panic as the remains of the military pulled out. Briggs – as Langford and he had already discussed – had declared London an open city, in the hopes that it would preserve what remained of the city from a house-to-house fight to rival Stalingrad. The Russians, oddly enough, had honoured the declaration; it had been two days before their forces had finally begun to probe into London, a city that hadn't been attacked for hundreds of years. Londoners had had to relearn much their grandfathers had forgotten; they had faced air raids, terrorist attacks...and now a Russian occupation. They had tried hard to calm the city, but Briggs feared for the future; who knew what would happen once the Russians had the entire city in their power?

They appeared as they marched towards the city, hundreds – no, thousands – of infantry, marching in an eerie silence. Briggs was only delighted to see that they hadn't brought shackled prisoners as part of the march, as they had done in Berlin and Paris; it would only have inflamed passion on both sides. The irony was killing him; he had spent time enforcing ever-harsher bans on guns, and the net result was that now the Army had been destroyed, or at least soundly beaten, there would be no one to resist the Russians. There were still plenty of criminal guns on the streets, some of which had been used in the riots, but what good would they do against an organised army? The Russians had played it smart; before they had indulged in the victory parade, they had secured everywhere of vital importance, from power plants to the water supplies. They could cause the entire population to die of thirst if they felt like it; what could anyone do to stop them?

The Russians halted, just outside the gates; cameras were flashing, recording the historic moment, as a Russian stepped forward. He was tall and very pale, with jet-black hair; his cold blue eyes seemed to flicker power and responsibility. Briggs understood, finally, why some people couldn't face a soldier; here was a man who had killed others, many of whom had been trying to kill him. The Russian stood in front of him, looked the Lord Mayor's outfit up and down, and saluted.

"I am General Aleksandr Borisovich Shalenko," he said. His English was perfect, without the hint of an accent, or even a tinge of Russian words.

"I understand that I have the honour of addressing Lord Mayor Inspector David Briggs?"

Briggs winced inwardly. "I resigned my position in the police when I accepted the role of Lord Mayor," he said, wondering who the Russian spy had been. They knew who he was, and about his role; they had to have had someone on the inside, somewhere. "I am the Lord Mayor of London."

"Good," Shalenko said, very slowly. "I must formally ask for the submission of London to my control."

Briggs wanted to defy him, he wanted to spit in his face, but there was no choice. There were millions of civilians still caught within the city; a fight would be disastrous. They would all be killed when London burned like Dover had burned; the citizens had all seen the signs of battle from the hills. They knew what could happen…

"I surrender the city," Briggs said finally. He saw a flicker of respect in Shalenko's eyes as the Russians formally took possession of Buckingham Palace. "What now?"

"I need you to answer a question," Shalenko said. "Where is the command post?"

Briggs shook his head. "I have no idea," he said, honestly. Langford had never shared that information with him. "I was never told."

Shalenko looked down at him sadly. "That's not good enough," he said. He nodded to two burly-looking Russians, who seized Briggs, handcuffed him, and marched him off towards a large truck. "It would be much easier on all concerned if you just told us what you know."

"I don't fucking know," Briggs protested. The two Russians could have given the worst policeman lessons in brutality. The pain in his arms was utterly beyond comprehension. "They didn't tell me…"

"Take him to Maliuta Vladimirovich," Shalenko ordered tiredly. He still spoke in English. "Tell him to get what he can out of him."

They marched Briggs away to an unknown fate.

In the end, it took nearly a fortnight to locate it, despite the British command post being right under their nose. Shalenko hadn't wasted the time;

occupation authorities had reached as far north as Newcastle and would reach the lowlands of Scotland before too long, while Wales and Cornwall had felt the touch of Russian power. There had been an entire series of skirmishes with the remainder of British forces, but most of the surviving soldiers had either been captured, or had gone underground to await the chance to either escape, or launch a war against the Russians. Other elements of the Russian program had been launched almost at once; prisoners had been divided up as they had been in Europe, and the entire male Muslim population of southeast England had been conscripted to help repair the damage caused by the invasion.

There had been a brief, very brutal fight, before the Classified Joint Headquarters had been penetrated, a last ditch attempt to trigger a self-destruct system thwarted in the very nick of time. Shalenko entered the complex and examined it, pausing in passing to salute the body of a short blonde woman who had commanded the defence, her resistance finally ended by four bullet wounds to the chest. Others lay strewn around the complex, including a young Indian girl who had been shot down by a nervous commander, and a helicopter pilot who had used the helicopter's guns to mow down soldiers before he had been killed. A few more moments, Shalenko reflected, and he might have made it out and escaped.

"Impressive," he said finally. The CJHQ had only been discovered by chance. There might well be others out there somewhere in the English countryside, or somewhere far to the north in Scotland; time alone would tell. The Russians had put all of the civil servants, those who had survived, back to work; they had been interrogated, repeatedly, to see what they knew. None of them had known about the CJHQ; without that little bit of foresight, how long would it have been before the British pulled themselves back together. "I think we can make use of this compound, Anna."

He sat back as the helicopter headed back to Buckingham Palace. The President had been delighted with his work and his success, even though there were still many urgent requirements to handle before Britain could be termed truly pacified, but then…who knew what would happen in the future? Perhaps he would have the honour of the invasion of Spain, once the conflicts there had burned out, or…

For General Shalenko, the future looked bright and full of promise.

For Khadijah, the future had become a nightmare, one that was reaching out to embrace them all in its claws. She had never been superstitious, as opposed to religious, and she knew that parts of Islam's holy writings were parables, rather than direct orders – a point that many extremists missed – but she had the sense that something unpleasant was about to happen. She could feel it, right at the back of her head, even while she had been kept in Manchester General Hospital; something was going to happen.

She had been treated for smoke inhalation once the ambulance had finally arrived, her survival more a matter of luck – or Allah's blessing – than judgement. Khadijah had become an ideal patient at the hospital, helping out as best as she could with the thousands of other wounded, but finally it was time for her to be discharged. The nurse had told her, in whispers, what had happened to London...and implored the young Muslim girl to hide and sneak west to hopefully find a ship to Ireland or somewhere else that was free. Bad Things were happening to Muslims...

Khadijah had had no choice, but to go home. As a hospital patient, she had had no choice, but to be left out of the first wave of registration, but as soon as she was on her feet, she had to go register. Manchester looked, in places, as if it had been turned into a war zone; the Russian authorities had very strong ideas on what should happen to people who revolted against their rule. She saw, hanging from a lamppost, a young English boy...one of her tormentors from the burning mosque. He hadn't died well...

The Russians had taken her details, cross-checked them with other details in their vast database, and then asked her dozens of questions. Still terrified because of the body, she answered as many of them as she could, before the Russians gave her an ID card and told her the rules. Stay in your homes after curfew, unless there is a medical emergency; ideally, stay in your homes unless you have work. Report for duty if summoned; do not attempt to leave the city without written permission.

Khadijah cried, afterwards; her world had shrunk, once again, to the four corners of her room...

...And bad things were coming.

Hazel had held out hope that she would hear something for weeks, but as the Russians entered Edinburgh and tightened their grip on the city, she started to wonder if she should fear the worst. She was four months pregnant and her chest was starting to swell, but there was no word from her husband. The Russians had posted lists of prisoners who had been executed – including the infamous Edinburgh child molester, who had raped twelve children and had been remanded in custody for a mere twenty years – but her Stuart's name wasn't on the lists anywhere. She had searched them all, time and time again, wondering if she dared ask the Russians directly…but fear held her back.

Her father had taken her in; she had registered under her maiden name, rather than as Hazel Robinson, in terror of Russian spies and terrorists. She cursed that decision, afterwards; if they had found a body, who would they have known to tell? The penalties for lying to the Russians were grim; a shopkeeper who had lied about something had been assigned to one of the work crews, fading further and further every day through his month-long sentence of hard labour. Others had not been so lucky; Princes' Street Gardens had been full of bodies hanging from poles, people who had tried to resist the force of Russian might.

Like everyone else, she had grown to dread the knock on the door. When it came, she almost lost control completely before walking towards the door, noticing a single man standing there, and opening the door in hope…only to come face to face with Rashid Ustinov. The Russian looked taller, somehow, than he had when he had held her prisoner; there was a new scar on his cheek.

"You!"

"Me," Ustinov said mildly. Her father appeared and stared at him. "May I come in?"

"I don't think that we can stop you," Hazel observed bitterly, as he followed them into the lounge. She had thought that she was free of the two Russians forever. "What do you want?"

"They wanted to arrest you for interfering with an FSB operation," Ustinov said shortly. "I talked them out of it."

There was a pause. "Why?" It was her father who had spoken. "Why…?"

"Because in Russia, rank, power, responsibility and authority don't always go together," Ustinov said. "We have Captains who give orders to Generals under certain circumstances. There are Admirals whose only job is to look good, while their staffs do all the work; I once had two colonels and a lieutenant-general reporting to me. I am one of the FSB's heroes following" – he made a sweeping hand gesture – "and they will give me a great deal of latitude, within reason."

Hazel had only one thought in her mind. "And what about Stuart?" She asked, almost pleading. Tears were falling down her face; her father gently placed a hand around her shoulders. "What happened to him?"

"I don't know what happened to him," Ustinov said. There was a grim tone in his voice. "There's no record of finding his body, nor was he captured, but there were a lot of bodies that even DNA checks would have been hard-pressed to identify. I checked; the bodies of several men known to have served under him were recovered, but there was no sign of him personally."

He paused. "One possibility, the people involved with tracing the remaining soldiers thought, was that he was with you," he said. "Of course…they wanted to arrest you, but I blocked them…"

Hazel shrugged off her father's hand and leaned forward. "Why?"

Ustinov looked down. "Because…because you reminded me a lot of my mother," he said. "Because…you handled yourself well back when…well, that's in the past now. Because…you were kind to us when you thought we needed help. Because…you have suffered enough and…there was never anything personal, you know; none of us who went into Britain hated you, even Sergey. Hurting you would be spite."

He reached inside his pocket and brought out two passes. "There are some flights leaving Edinburgh airport over the next two months, convoying Americans and other foreigners who were caught in Britain when the war started," he said. "These two passes will get you out of the country; the Americans and Canadians are taking in refugees, so I expect that you two will find refuge there." He dropped a third pass into her hand. "If he should happen to turn up…"

"Thank you," Hazel said. She gave him a kiss on the cheek. "You could come…"

Ustinov laughed. "I don't think that that would be a good idea," he said. "Goodbye, Hazel."

He left, not looking back.

They were at the very edge of the range of Russian aircraft.

Admiral Geoffrey Bradford Wilkinson watched as the final helicopter came in to land, the fleet turning slowly and heading towards America. They would meet up with elements of the American Navy – HMCS *Lethbridge* from Canada had already joined the force – soon enough, but he had wanted to remain as close to Britain as possible, if only for a few more days. The ships they were escorting carried thousands of refugees; they had to be protected, even if the Russians seemed to be ignoring them. One way or the other, they would be leaving soon; the Russians had already begun to take over bases on Ireland and Britain itself. The loss of the CJHQ meant that there would be no centre of organised resistance left on British soil.

There was no time left at all.

He gave the order.

The remains of the Royal Navy – and a handful of surviving European ships - turned and sailed away from Britain. Few words were spoken as the fleet headed towards America, the crews lost in their own thoughts; what would happen to them in the future. Historical precedent was not good; French ships that had escaped the fall of France in 1940 had had friends and allies, they had…few friends and no allies if they were to fight to regain their homeland. A few hundred sailors had demanded to be put ashore as the fleet neared Britain, too late to be useful; they had been granted their wish. Wilkinson could only hope that they would have time to see their families before the Russians rounded them all up; the Russians had already placed a motion before the United Nations to declare the remaining ships pirates.

He turned his back on the distant hills of his homeland.

He wondered if he would ever see them again.

Epilogue

He came back to awareness in a burst of pain, memories flickering at the back of his mind; a Russian, an attack; grenades...the pain ebbed and flowed away as a soothing balm flowed over his body. Darkness rose and fell over the coming weeks as his body was slowly repaired by the latest in American medical science. The doctors had warned him that he would be crippled for a very long time, perhaps permanently disabled, but he would otherwise make a full recovery.

It was a month before they told him what had happened. He had raged then, screaming at them, demanding to know why he had lived when others were spared. They tried to tell him about the medics who had pulled out most of the wounded from England, convoying them to Iceland and then onwards to America, but he hadn't listened; he was the last survivor of his unit and he was miles from his wife. Eventually, they filled him in on some of the details, but the true horror had to wait until he was well enough to escape from the hospital bed and manoeuvre a wheelchair to a computer terminal. They found him there, crying, as he took in the news about the fall of night across the whole of Europe, the new Iron Curtain descending remorselessly around the continent. His wife...

They looked, of course; there was no mention of a woman fitting the name and description he gave in the registered refugees. Thousands had escaped the fall of night, some of them heading to Canada or Australia instead of America; she might have escaped the country, but as the Russians clamped down, it seemed less and less likely that she had escaped. The news was grim; it always was these days. Greece had signed a pact with the Russians to avoid a Turkish invasion, while a holy war was raging over Corsica, Sardinia and Sicily as the natives resisted the invaders with everything at their disposal. Spain was transformed into a nightmare of civil war, but the remainder of the continent seemed to be surprisingly peaceful; resistance seemed almost non-existent.

He had cursed them too as he raged.

The staff hadn't quite known what to do with him. One of them, a scholar and expert in sociology, tried to explain to him; most people only wanted a quiet life. The Russians weren't hammering them directly, so they cooperated and remained low, avoiding the Russians as much as possible. Some would resist, but the Russians were getting better and better at ferreting out resistance networks…and not all Europeans liked the thought of getting rid of the Russians. People who had been terminally unemployed, suddenly finding themselves with honestly earned money in their pockets, *liked* the Russians, others just liked the camps that been set up for Muslims, criminals and socialists…and politicians. Russian television had even broadcast views of Germans and Frenchmen jeering the detained politicians before they were whisked off east for an uncertain fate.

The staff had wondered what would happen to him; he didn't seem the type to just settle down in America, and even if he did offer his services to the government-in-exile, he was in no fit state to be inserted back into Britain, or to join the American Army. He himself had just given up; what was his life without her?

Two months later, she arrived.

She knew him at once, even though he was still wounded and hadn't been taking care of his appearance; she flung herself into his arms despite being heavily pregnant. The staff had smiled to themselves as they had watched the touching scene; the man might have been a problem patient, but they were used to those. He had deserved to escape; he had deserved to be reunited with his wife…

Stuart Robinson, no longer a Colonel or a Captain, held his wife tightly and felt her tears trickling down her cheeks. They had been the lucky ones; they had escaped the nightmare and found a new home in America.

For countless others, the nightmare was only just beginning…

Nikolai Lvovich Serdiukov – who had been known as Zachary Lynn, or Control, in another life – walked calmly down the corridors of the detention centre that had been established near Dorking, first for British soldiers who had been captured, and then for policemen and political prisoners. The serious criminals had been treated in the standard Russian manner; a handful, however, had been spared and told that they had a choice between working for the FSB, or death. Serdiukov smiled; few had refused the offer...

The President had made it clear at their meeting, when he had pinned the medal on his chest personally; Britain was going to be the hardest European country to rule. The British had had time to develop all manner of resistance cells and the records in the country's computers had all been wiped...well, mostly. Serdiukov was confident that Russian computer experts would eventually piece together a complete list of who had been in the army, or the police force, but for a few years everything would be chaotic. The Russians had to be ahead of the game.

There were two guards on the door ahead of him; they saluted him and opened the door, allowing him entry into the single cell. She sat there, hands handcuffed behind her back and secured to the chair, her legs shackled to the floor. It was overkill, restraints that would have been overkill for anyone, but a trained commando, but Serdiukov had wanted to make a point. She was completely helpless; she was completely at his mercy. Unlike so many others of her kind, she had a brain; Serdiukov knew that if she could be broken, she could be used.

"Good morning, Daphne," he said. He spoke in English, making his voice bright and cheerful. "How are you today?"

Daphne Hammond looked up. Her eyes widened. "Zack?"

"FSB Colonel Nikolai Lvovich Serdiukov," Serdiukov said. "I suppose you could say that I was one of those infiltration and destabilisation agents that you spent so much time accusing the Americans of creating and sending into" – he allowed his voice to become sardonic – "poor helpless counties who have never done anything wrong..."

Daphne glared at him. "Let me go," she snapped. "What do you want with me?"

"Well, we owe you," Serdiukov said. "Without you...perhaps it would have been harder to complete the conquest of Europe...but then, your sources will have told you what happened in Hanover and a dozen other places in Germany. The new world order has no place for your kind."

He paused, enjoying the moment, before continuing. "You have a choice," he said. "You can continue to work for us as a...legitimate politician trying to steer the ship of state through some troubling times...or you can die. No one knows what happened to you since your government grew a pair and dumped you in one of their detention camps; your supporters, most of whom believe that you believe the kind of stuff you come out with, will believe that it was the British Government that had you killed."

He saw fear flicker into her eyes. It was good to be able, finally, to laugh in her face. She was no innocent; she had taken people who had wanted to build a better world and used them to create power for herself, power that might have pushed her beyond the level where she needed the innocents who had believed in her...and then she would have betrayed them. She had no principles, no redeeming features; she wanted power and power alone.

She wilted. "Daphne," Serdiukov said, "I can have you thrown to the soldiers for their own amusement, or I can make you powerful if you work for us. Choose."

There was a long pause. Her body was shaking. "All right," she said finally. "What do you want me to do?"

Several thoughts came into Serdiukov's head; he dismissed them. "Oh, you're going to run Britain for us," he said. "Your assistance will be invaluable."

Daphne thought about it. He could almost see the wheels turning in her head. It was power and power was what she wanted. She would do anything for it; he would have considered a whore more honest in her work. "You would make me the power behind the throne?"

Serdiukov smiled. "I think that Prime Minister Daphne Hammond has quite a nice ring to it, don't you?

But every story has its end,
The tale has its final bend,
And set to wings of stone,
Must gently fly away,
The piper plays his saddest air,
The day is done, the shadows fall...
The lonely night comes to the land,
And darkness takes us all...

-Ian McCalman

The End

Afterword

The Fall of Night holds the record for my fastest-written book. I wrote at the staggering rate of 5 chapters per day (roughly 15,000 words per day) because the story just seemed to *want* to come out. Then or since, I have not matched that speed. Maybe, even then, the story was important – or, more likely, the idea just soaked into my mind and I ran with it.

Staying in the tradition of the better pieces of 'invasion literature,' I deliberately wrote the story with a downer ending. (See *The Battle of Dorking*, available online, for a sample of pre-WW1 invasion writings.) Such books were not attempts to write military thrillers, *per se*, but attempts to warn of the dangers of poorly-considered decisions that, in the minds of the authors if nowhere else, were likely to lead to a serious risk of military defeat. They rarely included a happy ending.

I wrote *The Fall of Night* in 2009. Now, if anything, it has become even more relevant.

The tactics I had the Russians use are ones they *planned* to use during the Cold War, merely modified to some extent. They intended to use commandoes, they intended to incite radical factions to war, they intended to use terror tactics...and they intended to put down all resistance swiftly and effectively. And how would such tactics work if aimed at a society as open as our own?

The world is a dangerous place. If anything, the end of the Cold War – while removing the threat of mutual nuclear annihilation – has made the world far more dangerous, while the spread of modern transport technology has lowered the distance from one side of the world to the other. A problem that would once have remained localised – the Iraqi Invasion of Kuwait, for example – now takes on global implications. A band of terrorists hiding in caves in Afghanistan can hijack aircraft and slam them into towers in a city on the other side of the world. And a bunch of pathetic cartoons (and some astute political manipulation) can trigger riots all over the world.

Nor is it lawful. Law is effective only as long as it can be enforced – and so-called international law has rarely been enforced. Dictators such as Saddam mocked international standards of decency simply by existing; states such as Saudi Arabia, Iran and North Korea spit in the face of any concept of international human rights. International law could only be made workable if there was a force with both the capability and will to uphold the law. There is no such force. Nor is one likely to exist. The Western faith in international law is, at best, naive. The response from a dictator to demands that he comply with the law is going to boil down to '*oh, yeah? Make me.*'

And yet, successive British governments seem unwilling to face up to the simple fact that the world is dangerous.

It is absurd beyond belief, despite the assertions of several politicians, that we can stay out of the War on Terror. Even if we hadn't joined the American invasion of Afghanistan (and later Iraq) we would still be targeted by terrorists. We would be targeted because we are a liberal free country with freedom of religion, freedom of the press, sexual freedom…all freedoms that are anthemia to our enemies. Indeed, we would be targeted because we represent a better way to live than a return to doctrines that were little more than attempts to impose a standard of behaviour on an entire population. The terrorists hate our freedoms because we might well seduce their potential recruits away from them.

Nor are terrorists the only threat facing Britain's security. We have dependencies in various global locations that are threatened, constantly, by nearby states. Despite losing the last war – despite the oft-expressed wishes of the population – the Falkland Islands are still claimed by Argentina. Gibraltar, too, has been claimed by Spain. Indeed, in both cases, the wishes of the local population have not been taken into account by the hostile power. The belief that they *would* be taken into account is, like the faith in international law, the refuge of fools.

Yet we persist in making heavy cuts to our military capabilities. Right now, Britain does not have a single aircraft carrier. Furthermore, we have made serious cuts in our infantry, navy and other deployable forces. Indeed, if we were forced to refight the Falklands War, we might well find ourselves incapable of doing anything more than blockading Argentina with submarines. Maybe it would work, but I wouldn't care to bet on it.

Worse, perhaps, we have created a colossal military bureaucracy that has dampened our ability to fight and signed international treaties that cripple our ability to wage war. Despite having (at least at present) the fourth-largest defence budget in the world, our forces have been badly weakened and our ability to take part in campaigns (like the war in Libya) severely hampered.

Worst of all, the military convent has been shattered. Soldiers returning home from the wars, having taken ghastly wounds in the fighting, have had to endure endless torment from government bureaucracies just to get treatment. Some of the unwounded soldiers are getting out, fearing the care (or lack thereof) that they would receive if they are wounded. If that wasn't enough of a problem, the cuts (which are aimed at the soldiers rather than the excessive number of senior officers) leave them in fear of losing their jobs. Morale is badly damaged and civilian leadership seems unaware of the problem.

This is potentially disastrous.

The problem with almost any kind of modern military capability is that it takes time (often years) to build up from scratch. Even something as basic as training the modern infantryman can take months; producing tanks, jet aircraft and naval ships can take years. (The largest aircraft carriers in the world, the American *Nimitz*-class ships, can take over seven years to construct.) In certain situations, the producer would actually need to produce the production plants from scratch, adding more delays. This is not an unprecedented problem; in mid-2001, the USN was having real problems keeping its aircraft carriers operational, while the US had to buy bullets from Israel and South Korea to fight the wars in Iraq.

What this means, in realistic terms, is that we might find our ability to respond to a military emergency hampered by sheer shortage of supplies.

Ah, the critics will say, but we're part of NATO, aren't we? NATO will help.

That too, I'm afraid, is wishful thinking.

The blunt truth is that we *cannot* trust any other country to uphold British interests in anything, particularly not when they may find it politically inconvenient. Despite clear aggression against Britain (and an innocent civilian population) in the Falklands War, no other member of NATO offered to send military forces to assist – and this was when NATO needed to remain a creditable force. (Thatcher being Thatcher, they might not have been accepted if they were.) Now, we are more likely to be sneered at by the rest of the world rather than helped. If this seems unlikely, please consider Hilary Clinton's dismissal of the whole affair as a 'colonial' matter, with the obvious implication that *Britain* is the bad guy in the matter.

Does this seem absurd? Saddam was one of the most evil men to walk the planet. His regime murdered millions of people, committed genocide, wiped out entire cultures, used gas against civilian targets and launched two separate wars of aggression against its neighbours. Yet how many people believed that the US was the bad guy for moving to depose him? How many nations slipped away from even verbal support for the war? How far have we fallen that we are prepared to support an evil dictator over a country that may be a clumsy giant at times, but has a good heart?

But, even if we could trust another power to handle our defence, we would compromise our independence if we did so. We would be completely reliant on that country. And, if that country changed its mind, we would be abandoned to the winds.

This is why we need to maintain a formidable military force, including nuclear weapons. Quite simply, we cannot trust anyone else to look after us. We have to do it for ourselves.

Having an army is an insurance policy. If you don't need it, it's expensive; if you do need it, you'll *really* need it.

Readers may doubt that Russia can do all I suggested in the novel. It seems to us that the end of the Cold War and the collapse of the Red Army put an end to the Russian threat once and for all. But that is far from the truth. Yeltsin's failures to prevent a colossal economic crash (the inevitable result of poor communist management) ensured that Russia would turn to a strongman to reassert itself. Putin may not be Stalin, but he has been quite successful in turning the Russian economy around and restoring Russia's power in the world. Indeed, as the recent clash over Syria has shown, Putin recently scored a number of points against President Obama.

Nor is this his only success. Russia's brief war with Georgia in 2008 demonstrated, quite nicely, that Russia could act as it wished along its borders and outside powers (specifically the United States) couldn't act to prevent it. In addition, Putin has built economic ties with European powers (mainly Germany) that create economic incentives to support Russia and abandon Eastern Europe. Indeed, despite constant civil unrest, it is unlikely that Ukraine and Belorussia (the latter run by a dictator) will manage to slip out of the Russian shadow, while NATO membership does not protect the Baltic States from Russian interference.

In fact, Russian influence has reached quite alarming levels. Russian agents have been caught spying in America and Europe, Russian operatives murdered a former Russian officer in London - Alexander Litvinenko – and may well have been involved in the death of Anna Politkovskaya. European and American businessmen who invest in Russia have often found themselves economically raped by Russian bureaucrats (the government is often a large part of the problem) and anti-Russian parties outside Russia have been harassed by Russian spies.

And, in Russia itself, those who oppose Putin find themselves in deep trouble. This is often petty – witness the treatment of Pussy Riot, a punk rock band – but has a numbing effect on free discourse. The shadows of oppression are falling over Russia once again.

In short, we are faced with a Russia that is growing more and more assertive…and confronted with an increasingly weak and divided Europe, one that is growing apart from America. Will there come a time, I might ask, when the military balance will fall towards the Russian side to the point where Russia's leaders will consider a military invasion of Europe?

But invasions are so *passé* nowadays, aren't they?

The world can change. It can, in fact, change at terrifying speed. And when it does, we have to be ready.

Christopher Nuttall

Manchester, 2014

Made in the USA
Middletown, DE
02 November 2016